T0247701

Story of a Stammer

THE HUNGARIAN LIST

GÁBOR VIDA

Story of a Stammer

TRANSLATED BY
JOZEFINA KOMPORALY

LONDON NEW YORK CALCUTTA

The Hungarian List
SERIES EDITOR: Ottile Mulzet

Seagull Books, 2022

First published in Hungarian as *Egy dadogás története* by Magvető
© Gábor Vida, 2017

English translation rights arranged through Magvető, Budapest.

First published in English translation by Seagull Books, 2022

English translation © Jozefina Komporaly, 2022

ISBN   978 0 85742 985 8

British Library Cataloguing-in-Publication Data

A catalogue record for this book is available from the British Library.

Typeset by Seagull Books, Calcutta, India
Printed and bound in the USA by Integrated Books International

CONTENTS

Scenes from a Life

BUT is not a word we tend to start sentences with, my father urged, and I immediately snapped back: but we do. This is a recurring scene whenever my father happens to leaf through some or the other text I had published—he puts it down with a bored look on his face, remembering that at some point in the fifties, Dénes Ficzay, the well-known teacher and self-appointed custodian of the Hungarian language, had taught this rule to him during his high-school years at Arad, together with a number of other infallible rules of grammar and correct usage. We don't start sentences with conjunctions—that's the rule of thumb. I don't know where those who champion this precept got it from, who devised it and for what reason. Perhaps they were waging a war against filler words, in the wake of which no one bothered to ask: why wouldn't it be acceptable to start a sentence with just about any word of one's choice? I have even found several sentences starting with 'but' in our great epic poem *Toldi*. In fact there are many examples in Arany's usage that the guardians of the language would deem inadmissible or wrong. Homer sometimes nods too, one might add. I wouldn't actually point out to my father that he had just begun a sentence with 'but', we aren't that close to allow myself to challenge him by scrutinising his sentences and claims. With a shrug and a hum, he somewhat concedes the point about *Toldi*—he grants it as it were, but well, just saying. He doesn't claim that Ficzay was right as opposed to János Arany, it's just something that had come to his mind prompted by one of my published pieces. I wasn't taught by Ficzay, though I attended the same school thirty years later. At the time of writing that sentence picked up by my father, I was a reasonably well-known author of fiction, a Hungarian writer from Transylvania, a sort of Hungarian teacher who had slipped through the system, as it were, although I never had any dealings with kids studying composition at school.

I'm certain my father hadn't read my story from beginning to end, or any book of mine for that matter, and I have no idea how he had come across that incriminating sentence which exposed me in my true colours, betraying how little I knew—how in vain did I expect major international recognition. It's pointless arguing with him over matters of linguistics or philosophy because he would never put forward his own opinion but rather refer to some authority figure, it doesn't even occur to him that in this case I might actually have some expertise myself. Meanwhile, I'm fully aware of what he really wanted to convey—at that particular literary event, two minutes of which were shown on TV, I should have worn a tie, and this meant, more or less, that I should have shaved my beard off for the occasion of my stint on TV. He didn't put this quite in these terms, but he had often indicated as much before, seeing that for him my facial appearance and sartorial grooming were in direct correlation with my intellectual worth, or, rather, with success.

My mother was obsessed with the state of my nails and the cleanliness of my hands when I was a child—I always had to wash hands, with or without a reason, before and after, almost irrespective of anything, at times just because she thought it was time for a hand wash. Whenever she got the chance, she'd cut my fingernails so short that I could barely hold a pencil—don't worry, it will grow back, she said. My ears received constant cleaning too, with matches or hairpins wrapped in cotton wool, at times it tickled, at times it hurt, and once we had almost perforated my eardrum for I simply wouldn't sit still. Later my father had issues with my hair and beard, as if time had stood still, and what could we possibly talk about if I wasn't even prepared to look like a human being anyway? I couldn't make him understand that this was an issue only when he was young. Those were the days of the Beatles and the Rolling Stones, *Hair* was basically meant for him, but he was unaware of these bands even at the time or doesn't remember them any longer, and, if I wanted to be niggling about details, I should point out that he has other preferences. The football players of my childhood wore their hair long, like girls, my father would say talking about Mario Kempes or Dominique Rocheteau, and they did score against us, but this was a long time ago, in 1978. No player would sport a beard in those days, with the exception of Paul Breitner a few years later, and we could occasionally see long-haired and bearded rock musicians on TV, as he'd say, looking like monkeys. But since I had once pledged that if Ceaușescu's dictatorship ever fell, I'd grow a beard, I cannot shave it off now—I wouldn't even do that for a woman, let alone for the sake of my father, in the year twothousandandsomething. It's pointless to keep explaining this to him, he had spent most of his life under a dictatorship yet never wanted a beard. As for women, we have never even approached that topic, just as we steered clear of so many others.

What I do remember with certainty is that my father wouldn't have spoken up for me, even if he had happened to be there with me in front of the railway station in Arad, when at midday one

Saturday a policeman sent me to get a shave, knowing that he was able to get away with impunity. He wouldn't have challenged a policeman, he wouldn't have brought up human rights, privacy issues or the constitution—those days in Romania, it wasn't the done thing to refer to such-like. I really couldn't expect this from him, and he wasn't the one for heroic gestures either, at least not in matters concerning me anyway. He wouldn't have said, Comrade Officer, this is my son, and I'll take him to the barber, or will give him a shave myself. This might have implied that he was compensating for the gaps in my education, after all, that was what this was ultimately about—this child is badly brought up, it is manifest, on his face. We are not about to attract the attention of the authorities for an unkempt teenager, and anyway, in this case it is the authorities who are right, having regulation hair is a top priority. One shouldn't conclude though that I took my father for a coward then, nor is he a coward now, although he was given regular lessons in fear when he was young. He could have of course later added at least as much as 'fucking hell!' or 'Goddammit!' He should have known the meaning of these terms—he was once a student of Calvinist theology, so he had reasons to loathe the regime despite never being ordained, and perhaps not even believing in God. Yet he should have realized that the policeman's actions were an abuse of his powers, and he could have at least mentioned it to me in confidence that he was aware of this, even if this had to remain strictly between the two of us. But no, neither did he say anything later, to me or in my favour. So I didn't tell him that the policeman made me miss my train, and that this wasn't a one-off event, and only told him my reasons for growing a beard much later, together with why I kept it. There was no point in discussing this, after all it was me who in 1984 staged a provocation against the defender of the Romanian state and all people with well-groomed faces.

That was how we communicated most of the time. I can't claim that we had conversations with each other—he didn't converse with anyone, or certainly not in my presence. I'm not a great conversationalist either, I tend to just say my own lines, and have been doing that ever since I learnt to speak fluently. Yet this wasn't easy. I have no idea what he thought of the other sentences in my short story, I'm not really sure if I expected him to have an opinion of his own, be it literary or paternal. It would've been nice, of course, perhaps. But I may have actually been pleased with no opinion, or at least I accepted that, because my father never seemed to have his own views on anything, just facts that were more or less accurate, and you get used to that. When he did have an opinion, he wouldn't let us know what that was, only remind us, later, that he had known that this was so all along, but didn't specify what was so and when. On the whole, his verdicts were generally quite damning . . .

As for my beard, he agreed with the policeman at the railway station, who has since retired, but my father's views won't ever be retired or repudiated. I'm sharing a stage with writer turned politician Béla Markó, and all my father can see on TV is the tie of Romania's deputy prime minister and points out how befitting the occasion it is. That's how much of me is visible to him, and that's all he chooses to tell me that he saw. I must have been around forty at the time, if not more. He hadn't read any of Markó's poems, he might have perhaps heard him speak on TV, yet he can't see his beard, only his tie, and that he is the modern-day Prince of the realm, seeing that we now must live here, and he had to move for my sake close to Marosvásárhely in Transylvania, because I couldn't afford to buy a place of my own and make a living. Yet what other ambition should a man have than buy a house, if he doesn't already own one, and add an extension to it, if he has, and support his family. In actual fact, it was only my mother who wanted to move to Transylvania at any price, once we had no relatives left in Kisjenő, where they'd lived until then, and it also became clear to them that I'd never return since I must have put some roots down where I was, right here. My mother had also decided that after all those years, coming up to thirty or thereabouts, she wanted her only son back at all costs, even if this meant relocating or starting all over again. The situation was somewhat complicated by the fact that my father was heavily Hungarian—it's beyond his comprehension that one can be of any other ethnicity, what would that actually mean anyway? At least he does somewhat understand Romanians, Germans and Gipsies, but not Transylvanians, and when it comes to Székelys he dismisses them with a wave of the hand. As far as he's concerned they are just a matter of history or a misunderstanding. My father has issues with things that are hard to pin down, he'd prefer a single system for every one of us, and to live happily ever after according to its rules.

He has lived in Romania all his life, yet never considered himself a Transylvanian despite studying in its capital Kolozsvár, and cannot fathom why the Hungarians in Gyula, in Hungary proper, would label him a Transylvanian, after all he's from the village of Ágya or from Kisjenő—or perhaps from Arad, to make concessions for the geographically challenged. He speaks the same dialect as the Hungarians over the border, and although his pronunciation has been polished at school and university, his Romanian sounds just like the one spoken by the Romanians in Gyula. This was what he picked up as a child, it being the dominant variant spoken at the time. In other words, he can grasp the situation, he knows why things are the way they are, how they've turned out so, but he finds it deeply offensive and so humiliating that it's not even worth mentioning it. For him Transylvania is as disappointing a world as it is for most Hungarian tourists—after stardust falls off from their rose-tinted glasses and reality reveals itself. Needless to say, my mother is Transylvanian and, what's more, a proper Székely.

Whenever he feels like expressing his views on the state of the world, my father tends to read out loud a few sentences from the daily paper he happens to be reading. He gets really worked up if he can't find anything that fits in with what's on his mind, this disarray infuriates him. My mother tends to put everything away, my father never does, so whenever he's looking for something he scolds her: where have you put it this time? In case he wants to talk about viniculture or about how grapes should be tended or wine stored, back copies of the vinicultural magazine *Kertészet és Szőlészet* would do just fine, even if they are ten or twenty years old. In the late eighties this was one of the few Hungarian periodicals permitted in by the Romanian authorities—by the end of the decade even this was forbidden, but the back copies tied together with a string managed to fill an entire chest under the bed, and he always has a few bundles to hand. He takes his time searching for the right article—grape varieties, grafts, equipment, chemicals. Wine has a soul though it is doubtful whether people have one too, on the other hand, alcohol is the devil incarnate, my mother would claim. My father is a passionate winemaker, on occasion, he even managed to make some really fine white wine, and another time, some outstanding vinegar. We'd also drink all the other stuff, of course, except that no one remembers those. In our garden in Kisjenő we can grow everything that's needed for the kitchen—carrots, red

onions, celeriac, parsley, tomatoes and peppers. We also have rasp-
berries, redcurrants, apples, peaches, jostaberries, plums, apricots,
and even a Székely pine tree reaching for the sky of the Great
Hungarian Plain. Yet the area is barely suitable for the cultivation
of grapes, and the soil in our garden certainly isn't. My father
chooses to ignore all this—the soil and the climate are none of his
doing—and it was my mother who had dealt with purchasing the
site in the first place. It was also her idea to build a house, despite
always wanting to live in a town, up on the umpteenth floor, so
she didn't have so much housework to do, as she puts it—towns-
people just go home from their day job and switch on the TV. My
father prefers reading to gardening, winemaking or farm work, he
drinks rarely and very little, and far from enough to believe in his
dreams or to dream of things beyond belief. In this respect, we are
poles apart. He is able to calculate the cost of a glass of wine down
to the last penny, and it's cheaper than the shop-bought stuff, plus
for many years one could barely find any decent wine in Romanian
shops, we have high standards after all, not to mention that he
prefers white wine while I like red, obviously. According to his theory, making and drinking our own wine helps us save money. I no
longer remember whether he was trying to boast or apologize for
the plonk, which it undoubtedly was, but there you are. We'd save
at least this much if not more money without cultivating grapes
or drinking wine, I point out, because I feel like challenging him.
In my mother's eyes, wine isn't worth a single scoop of the shovel,
she's a hardliner in this respect—in the corner of Székely Land
where she's from, grapes are only known from books, though this
is a malicious exaggeration. More to the point, she's a teetotal and
constantly wants to protect me from the deadly drink, as we've
later seen, not without good reason, but she had really started

worrying too soon, and I simply couldn't follow what the fuss was all about.

The question on DIY work around the house—whether it was actually profitable or simply a matter of not making a loss—would lead to blazing rows, year in, year out. In vain did I point out that in case we were after a profit, we should offer to construct the neighbour's footway and make them pay for it, or sell our wine for instance, though that's something only my mother would like us to do, or at least we shouldn't monetize any surplus. My father calls me a Marxist, coming from him that's a swearword, yet I wasn't arguing for being paid for my labour but for him to admit that what we gained as our profit was the footpath and not the stonemason's wage, and that we are the beneficiaries of our wine and not its retail price. He thinks that a son is obliged to work for his father, it is this that will lead to surplus, and we work for ourselves for free. I have everything I could possibly need anyway, but I can't grasp why we should work for free for ourselves, particularly if we already have everything. Do I owe anything to anyone, or is this simply the custom around here? And come to think of it, who *are* we anyway? I get the bit about work—it has to be done as and when it's needed—but unlike my mother, I don't actually enjoy working. I don't have to occupy myself at all times, I'd rather just get it over and done with, like my father, but I can't follow this business with it being for free—how is that relevant here? My father gets it but wouldn't delve into an explanation because that would lead to an argument, he'd have to set out his case. I must be a Marxist, I loathe it when they make me work, particularly when the term 'for free' is involved. These exchanges drive my mother up the wall, for her peace and quiet are of utmost importance—that's her attitude, and she avoids any conflict, so if we argue and she doesn't succeed to calm us down, she just walks away, feeling offended and claiming that she has some other business to attend to.

In his spare time my father often engages in a bit of DIY with me, and our first attempt, whatever it may be, generally falls flat or turns into a botched job. These are usually things instigated by my mother that my father took on but didn't manage to finish, so I tried to have a go or we wrestled with them together. Woodshed, chicken coop, footpath, fence, whatever might be needed around the house, without which one cannot survive. I enjoy handling wood, taking measurements, designing things, and am a dab hand at several tasks, I went to technical college and worked in a factory, but I can only tackle these jobs up to a point, and loathe it when I'm being bossed about. My father can't even hammer a nail into a wall, and for a proper man that, and putting in a screw askew, is as humiliating as an apron for a goalie. He's held down an office job all his life, was originally left-handed but they retrained him to use his right, and thus messed up his coordination. He is very demanding and nothing is ever good enough for him. I'm quite slapdash by comparison, nothing I do will be up to scratch, even if I push myself to the limit. He is thrifty verging on stinginess, the materials we use generally go to waste, iron, nails, screws, cement all cost money, are expensive or hard to lay hands on, our tools are rudimentary, bought cheap-and-cheerful, and if we happen to have two, you can bet we use the one that's in a worse nick. In actual fact, my father isn't stingy or someone with two left hands, he's just insecure, anything he's ever done has been proven to be bad, invalid or can go dead in the water at any point. Our entire life is one long DIY session—a succession of moments when I realize that I sawed into the plank at the wrong place, but it's too late, and everything will be adjusted to this ill-measured beginning. We always realize what's happened just a little too late, it can't be helped, now that we cut it off, we can't throw it away, we'll patch things up, make it good, tie things together as best we can, wire, foil, superglue, we'll *make do and mend*. Do it yourself, sir, if you have no servant who could do it for you! Everything, always unfinished, imperfect, improvised. There stands my father, folding rule or saw or spirit level in his hand, twiddling with his glasses and thinking. He tends to look like an intellectual released from some re-education camp, he always has to weigh things up—what can be done, what must be done or what's not allowed. He's mostly preoccupied with the whys, why he must, beret on head, come up with something he has no clue about, that is doomed to be a flop, make him agitated, and will break, rip, bend, tear or collapse. Having the time to do this is not an issue, weekends, statutory holidays, national holidays, at most we get fed up that time passes so slowly, but soon there'll be some footy match or a handball or ice hockey match, or some athletics or ski jumping, so we have to push on after all and get on with the job. Lunch will be ready in no time—this is of utmost importance, that's what it's all about—so we can have lunch, that's my mother's take on this. Hers is the only work worthy of the name, anything else is just a hobby, a pastime, but provided we don't hinder her, then it's fine, though it would be best if we helped her out. Measure twice and cut once, the saying goes, but in our household we take measurements three times, once prior to cutting, and twice after, to make sure that we've really screwed up yet again. At least we have no machinery, though my father is actually planning to get a circular saw in due course, but that scares me to no end, as it could be a real danger to life and limb.

No wonder my mother was thrilled whenever she was able to bring round a skilled colleague from the workshop or a neighbour, regardless of the cost, we wouldn't engage in any DIY and risk life and limb. No materials would be wasted or tools damaged, we wouldn't argue over the whys and hows, besides everything would look as if my mother had handled it all by herself, as though she'd done it on her own. The expert was generally available when my father wasn't at home, he'd work quickly and smoothly, whether expensive or cheap is irrelevant now. My father should have been pleased that yet another job had been done properly, but he wasn't, he immediately found some flaw—the fence, the paving, the colour was no good, in fact just about everything was rubbish, and even years later he was able to point out an entire cluster of blemishes. As for the views of the women in the neighbourhood, we never thought they'd carry weight. We knew exactly what was what. Later it turned out that it didn't matter that we knew the truth, that everybody knew that moonlighters were up for doing any odd job during their official working hours, and that we knew gossip was gossip, easy for those not being in regular employment. Gossip is king though. Another tradesman turns up at our house, and yet again it's before midday.

My mother considered herself head of the family, although she had never put it in this way, everything had to be the way she wanted. This came to her naturally, and indeed everything revolved around her, yet she believed that she was doing everything for us and she was sacrificing herself for our sake. If things don't happen her way, she just points it out forcefully, then says it again, and if we don't obey her she simply starts doing it, pushing, pulling, lashing out: my mother holding a shovel, spade, axe, pliers, socket wrench is an everyday sight; fence post, footpath, tree stump, gas cylinder, my mother is indestructible. Then *she'd be feeling unwell any minute*, it's always her gallbladder in the end, at times she'd be preparing for this for weeks, because she couldn't get her way every time, not even if we had also sacrificed ourselves, body and soul, to this cause. By far the worst, however, is when she is against something, in such cases she is even capable of transcending illness, or feeling sick, in between two bouts of throwing up, she has to oversee things, so she gets out of bed, takes action so nothing she opposes could happen. She never feigns, she lives everything to the full.

My mother has a schedule for her life, some sort of work around the house that she must do. She was tasked with this by God, like everyone else, and life is all about fulfilling these tasks even at the cost of our lives: sacrifices have to be made. The snag is that I happen to be my mother's main mission, the obligation she fulfils, as a rule against my will. What a cross to bear you two are, she often sighs, her other mission being my father, obviously. She's not above putting up a fight if there's no other way. She'd also like to be in charge of the wine, but that leads to verbal wrangling, for my mother, alcohol is pure poison, while for my father it's actually a healthy drink. So he starts to list its positive biological effects—vitamins, amino acids, antioxidants, several hundred specific compounds, all mentioned by name—I accept all this, my father is an authority in this field, alcohol is a universal solvent in which the heavenly chemist dissolves all useful ingredients. At this point we often take a break, my father would ideally consult a reference book or a specialist journal, then he'd pour a glass of wine to verify the information that he'd just obtained. According to my mother the only healthy activity is round-the-clock labour, because the cost of living is going up, money's worth less and less, because it has no gold standard behind it, therefore one has to keep active and be thrifty, and save wherever possible for a rainy day. One should first use the leftovers up, finish off the dry bread, open the jam bottled two years ago, there should always be some lunch left for the next day, and if possible for the day after, too, there should always be something to eat, as she puts it, no matter what. At home, we are dressed in our shabbiest clothes, we throw nothing away, everything will serve some purpose or other, at times she even retrieves items I have thrown in the bin, or at least checks them out. She is focused, indiscrete and overbearing. I'm a born drover, she says of herself, and no one knows that this droverhood doesn't refer to the activity of driving oxen, camels or mules but to the comrades in charge of forced collectivization, this was the term used in Székely Land in the fifties. By the time I'd get started on the task allocated to me she had already done it, so she just shoots a reproachful look at me. What she'd really like is for us to do it together, so she could direct me and dictate the pace, in the end she'd thank me for helping, even if it was me who had actually done the job by myself. In our household everything happens because and by way of her saying so—she doesn't take to signs of independence too kindly, she has to meddle with everything even if she has no clue whatsoever about the matter in question. She'd outdo my father as well if she possibly could, no matter whether it be digging, chopping wood, shopping or the acquisition of firewood or building materials, and her organizational skills are unrivalled. She invariably gets up earlier, on her feet sooner, is the first to suss out what needs doing, and my father lets her—if this is what matters to her, let her get on with it. My mother likes men's work, she'd rather haul sacks all day, she says, because she doesn't like to cook, nothing remains to show for that. She doesn't enjoy eating, she's always suffering from digestive complaints, eating is another mission, and so is feeding others, what she likes is doing the dishes and the laundry, ironing and cleaning the house, because there's something to show for these, albeit for a short while. I was a poor eater as a child, causing her a lot of hassle, and after a bout of heavy flu she lost her sense of taste and smell, so she couldn't appreciate herbs and spices such as rosemary, thyme, marjoram, nutmeg, although she could still distinguish soap, petrol and varnish.

My father tends to break out of this system every now and then. My mother is also aware that my father ought to be head of the family, but he's struggling with that role—winemaking is such an attempt at breaking out, and at times so is DIY and farm work, but mostly it's the illness into which he withdraws. There wouldn't actually be any problems with my mother being in charge, because she is meticulous, determined and energetic, but she's always complaining that she has too much to deal with and organize, and how hard, dreadful and hopeless that is, she's always left to her own devices, and anything that doesn't work out is down to her. Because we always work for ourselves for free, that is for nothing, and I can't help adding under my breath that we also tend to work against ourselves. My father points out that all this looks as if it had been entirely my mother's doing. He tells this only to me, never to my mother, and he doesn't really say it out loud but whispers it rather into my ear and with a dismissive gesture. As far as he's concerned, I'm also like something *sorted out* by my mother, he had always known that this wouldn't lead to anything, but he'd just let it be regardless. What would have been the point? My mother tends to complain only to me about how hard life is and how unhappy she is, her relatives live far away, these people here are strangers to her. Whenever I fail to behave the way she thinks I should, I'm labelled one of *these* Vidas, too. Otherwise, she's pleased that she had ensured I had everything, and she'd been instrumental in my turning out well.

In return for these sacrifices I owe her obedience, I'm up to my ears in her debt, my mother hastens to remind me, so I should do as I'm told, and this is forever and for always and applies to everything. It's not just that she can have a say in my life, since after all she wants what's best for me and knows exactly what that is, but some sort of tacit agreement had also been entered into at my birth whereby I'd live the way I should, the way in which I was brought up. I also have a mission allocated to me by God and mediated by my mother—it is up to her to keep an eye on me and hold me to account. Yet I'm obstinate, *headstrong*, this is my nature, she says. I'm sat without wearing a tie and sporting a beard at some literary event next to Béla Markó, he's the big man, I'm the little one, he's rich, I'm poor, he's the Prince, and I'm just a writer, this is all my parents gather from TV on the topic of contemporary Hungarian literature in Transylvania. Still, it's good that they get to see me in the company of the great and the good, my father even wants to know whether this Péter Esterházy happens to be related to the ex-footballer with the same surname?

II

Literature

I've never been able to explain to my father what being a writer actually means. What's more, it wasn't easy to persuade myself that I was a writer—although I've been heading in this direction ever since I was a child, I haven't figured out since what makes me want to do this, and yet, I have various theories, which are acceptable up to a point. When in the Spring of 1985, I decided that I wouldn't become a geologist, but apply to study Hungarian literature at university, I had already filled two entire notebooks with my handwritten texts. Over the last two years, I haven't done much else but pen my *memoirs* instead of studying, following which—since I've used up all my personal memories—I got started on a novel. At that stage, I'm not yet thinking that this should be published, it doesn't even occur to me that one day I might write, or that I could write, books. I don't remember how it all started, what prompted me, it seems as if I'd always been scribbling something into a half-filled notebook. I don't want to show this to anyone, and as it happens, no one's interested anyway, people simply don't take any notice.

In this novel, I elegantly got rid of my teenage hero's parents, like György Dragomán in *The Bone Fire*, because, in my view, if parents were to be part of the story, they wouldn't allow any pets, such as horses, dogs or cats, for instance. We weren't allowed to retrieve Grandfather's gun, left behind from the war, from under the creaking floorboards. My sister and I weren't allowed to swim over to the island during river floods, because my parents kept saying that there was no such thing as an island there, thirty years later a military map confirmed that in actual fact there was an island, which in the past wasn't visible only during floods. We aren't allowed to shoot the first and last roe buck of our lives, which by the way would have to be roasted on a spit, and anyway, according to my parents, one could get sick if eating roast meat without some bread on the side. What's more, one must stop all this pointless daydreaming, there are jobs that need doing, and one has to study and learn to live in the real world, my mother keeps stressing. Novelists tend to eliminate such scenarios with the technique of introducing a car accident, but we've never owned a car, and I don't have a sister, I'm an only child, I'm Hungarian, there's no gun, we don't swim across rivers and I haven't had roast deer to this day.

The novel is about entirely different things, because it isn't me writing it, it's actually writing itself, it isn't following my carefully drafted outline, but back then I don't quite understand why prose behaves like a river running wild, I don't yet know that language is in fact an enormous living being, although I can feel it. I don't really consider my relationship with my parents precarious, after all they are doing everything they can for me, they have brought me up, had me educated, saw to it that I had everything I needed. My father had never hit me, and my mother only as long as I allowed her, but for some reason I don't enjoy being in their company for too long, and for this, I feel guilty. Unawares to me, I'm a teenager, in our family adolescence hasn't yet been invented, only over there (in Hungary), and on TV. In our household, there's only a well-behaved child that's docile, or a wilful one that's unruly and good-for-nothing. I would loathe it if that novel suddenly cropped up and someone would just dip into it, although back then I was very proud of filling the pages of that notebook. I was upset by impossible situations, this isn't right, I said to myself, my imagination had made me feel restless, because my heroes and the narrator were only engaging with a single issue: escape.

I discarded the text of the memoir started earlier, though it would be really handy to have it now, I'm actually continuing it at the moment, because after going round in circles for ages, I realized that I'm always writing about myself. It seems as if I had sensed this quite clearly at first, despite at times managing to pleasantly distance myself from my own self, and then it turned out that this wasn't the case. As it happens, I've settled for an overwhelming proximity, foregrounding tiresome and manic similarities and repetitions, because my own self always protrudes in, the very self I loathe to spend time with. There are so many tiny details I can't recall, and I've told so many stories and tall tales, adding or removing bits, that I ended up seriously doubting myself.

So now it's time to write about myself, I said in March 2015 when I put aside the first few chapters of a novel and felt the relief of someone who had stepped out of a particularly awkward role. I visited the ruins of Szentháromság Castle (the Bereczky mansion), where my grandfather in the novel was about to move. I relocated the castle near Nyárádszereda, into a delightful valley, so it isn't far from built-up areas, yet I don't have to illustrate the world of village life, because I wanted to write a novel and not a monograph, though this latter task wouldn't be an entirely thankless one either. Nyárádszereda is a onetime market town, in many ways reminiscent of Kisjenő where I grew up. After the decline of the local industry, it turned into the kind of village it had never been, the more mobile strata of its population moved away, taking anything that had to do with culture and memory with them. Those who stay put are cultivating the land that was eventually returned to them, and are wrangling over the grievances of the past, the future being uncertain as always, they belittle Romania, berate gipsies and Europe, everyone would like to live in Hungary, or at least by way of the Hungarian language. Human relationships are conducted in a rural manner, whoever isn't a relative or a neighbour is a stranger. An entire life wouldn't be sufficient for me to understand the complex connections between people, partly because I'm not related to anyone, and partly because I find it hard to bond with others—this is the way I am, I was brought up like this, or perhaps I'm just too preoccupied with myself.

My grandfather in the novel is a quick-witted and well-travelled Székely, who'll move into an abandoned mansion on an available estate that he chooses to call a castle. He had worked in Galac and Bucharest, and returned to Transylvania with a pot of money in 1933, a year that will turn out to be highly symbolic. He ends up in the Nyárád region by chance, as he's passing through he falls in love with the area and the abandoned estate conjures up a secretly harboured dream that he could become his own man. He really likes the region, but is intimidated by the situation, the house and estate are far too grand. Like many of his contemporaries, he is confronted with the problem that a piece of land that's too large is hard to cultivate, whereas one that's too small doesn't allow for making a proper living. He's reluctant to hire day labourers, since these people won't really put in the effort, so he'll just get his family to work till they drop. The only arrangement he's prepared to consider is an independent peasant-style small holding, ignoring any form of joint or cooperative venture, seeing that his favourite neighbour is the forest. He neither wants to be a landlord, nor an entrepreneur or speculator, he's simple village folk who has seen a lot of hardship in his time, so all he's after is a secure livelihood. Even if he did make it to a financially secure level, he wouldn't join the landowning class, or even the group of large-scale farmers. He'd always prefer to eat with a penknife, though it's an ironic exaggeration to suggest that he'd use this for scooping up his soup too. He'd wear boots or walk around barefoot in summer, as shoes tend to hurt his feet and don't support his ankles properly. For him, living the good life entails grilled meat for breakfast, lunch and dinner, and better life means having all this twice over. Yet his favourite is polenta with milk and cottage cheese or with anything else really, and he always opts for some *dish that can be eaten with a spoon*, ideally involving cabbage, potatoes, beans, meat and, better still, some roast bacon.

He'd feel averse to the castle, just like I would be averse to the role he was cast in, as there is something artificial and constrained therein. My real grandfather would send me to hell if I wanted to move him into this castle, he'd happily live in a barn or a stable, he might even piece together a hut by the woods, or he'd find shelter in the servants' quarters for the winter. I also write about his aversion—he'd find himself thrown out of the estate, first in 1940 by the Hungarians gloriously marching in, then by the more glorious Soviets, and finally by the inglorious communists, though the latter have managed to settle this matter for good. I don't want to offend my Székely grandfather, after all, he would have appeared in a typical Transylvanian story, even if with slight modifications, and I wanted to move him upwards in the social hierarchy because our family always aspired upwards, having the necessary enthusiasm, mindset and will, whilst patience and consideration were clearly in short supply.

The trouble was that I wrote neither about my real or even an imaginary grandfather, nor about a potential grandfather who could have come to life in the novel, but always about myself. And meanwhile, I also acted as my grandmother, and this had surpassed all my writerly abilities, I'm rather alarmed when I realize that she hadn't actually said anything about herself because she wasn't used to talking about herself, to me or to anyone else. So I tried to imagine them as people my novel would have benefitted from as characters, but I failed. They lived a life of their own, and then escaped from this world I had built and left me alone behind the scenes. My grandmother wouldn't be wary of the mansion except for the fact that it was at the end of the world, albeit in a picturesque, calm and relatively safe area. She came from a family of industrialists, her father learned his trade as a bootmaker in Brassó, he wasn't any old cobbler, they had a small patch of land but they didn't cultivate it themselves. The men in the family tend to become tradesmen if they are lucky, if not, they work in factories, constructions or mining, but they aren't peasants, this is an important facet of their consciousness, that's not the way they lead their lives, not even if they are poor. In case they aren't married off in time and to the right man, his sisters enter service as maids in Brassó, Budapest or Bucharest, their education allows for them to switch from being a maid to the role of the lady of the house should they get lucky or clever enough. Only my grandmother marries a peasant, and posterity can't figure out what made her do that. Love, is the convenient explanation. There was no one else, so they got to love one another, this is the fact of the matter, but we don't have to necessarily situate these two poles in opposition. We were related to the Daniel barons before they had obtained their title, my grandmother observes in another novel, and I put this question to her in real life too. She wouldn't find it difficult to handle such a Transylvanian country house, run the household and manage the staff, this is what she was brought up to do, but I can't get a sense of this, no matter how much I read about the topic, I simply can't make it my own. Working the land is troublesome for her, although during the war she takes to ploughing with the help of the buffaloes and of the older children, just like other women do in the village, later she does wonders in the kitchen garden and also gives birth to a bunch of kids. She knows that there is such a thing as bone china, but can't afford it, so earthenware dishes and wired or tin pots will have to make do. She is aware of silver polishing, though we only own alpaca metal items, silver only appears on the handle of the cake slicing knife—I later find out that it's actually made of nickel. All the same, it's not the handle but the blade that matters. She prefers English tea, and later Russian, with lots of sugar for taste. She cooks following Mrs Zathureczky aka Manci Zelch's cookery book from 1934. Whenever possible she enjoys a hearty meal, although she's suffering from gallbladder and our larder is often empty, but she's as precise when having to cut something into nine equal sections as if she were cutting it into four. She is the proud owner of a damask table cloth, a silk camisole and an incredible thirties hat, like the one Greta Garbo wears in one of her films, for years I had no idea what this Greek helmet lookalike made of felt was actually used for.

This would have been a colourful family saga focusing on the clash between an ambitious peasant and a lower middle-class world, but meanwhile the war broke out, followed by a Hungarian regime, the Holocaust, then the communist terror and the Hungarian Autonomous Region, so no rest for the wicked. The role of the castle, as it had been and what was left of it, alongside all sorts of local history data—I put together an extensive documentation—was to serve as a rather botched set design to help me imagine what it would have been like had I been the one there at that time. I could immerse myself into the spirit of this situation, I could construct a story line, but the more I was scribbling away, the more I found myself distanced from all this. I've given myself boring homework, I'm a Transylvanian writer after all, my entire life's work to date can easily fit on a bookshelf, though as my father had once put it, it's an unfinished body of work as yet. His comments make me smile, were I to pass away right now, this would be it, with nothing more to follow.

I still can't write *The Great Transylvanian Novel* because deep inside I'm preoccupied with something else. Anyway, Transylvania has shrunk into a novella, people are fed up, have had enough, and find it tiresome, it's like a chewed-off bone, and whilst we are dwelling on the future built on the past and on tradition, everyone's actually on their way out. Despite appearances, there hasn't been a Hungarian future in Transylvania for a hundred years, perhaps for longer, we don't even have to acknowledge this, we are past that stage, although I'm now actually writing about the fact that I don't want to get over this matter just like that. This notion of a *purely Hungarian* Transylvania has always been fake, reading a hundred years' worth of Transylvanian literature wouldn't reveal that in this area there have also lived and continue to live Romanians, Germans, Jews, Armenians, as well as Gipsies. We only tend to react whenever someone forgets about the Hungarians or says something that doesn't fit with our expectations. One can write novels about any topic, by the way, but the point isn't that I should also produce one and then perhaps another, though it would be great to have a go at a proper novel. We should let the professionals deal with this, they know what it is that readers want, because readers also know that if the forthcoming pages don't serve up the plotlines they are after, they'll put the book down, though lo and behold, suddenly something else is happening, something actually much more exciting that they haven't anticipated. I'm an amateur really, only having a go at a sort of DIY job, this is my method and concept, but I'm neither diligent nor humble enough, meanwhile I envy, without realizing it, those who are more successful than me. I'm a minor writer, I say in my defence. I tend to reread the fruit of my extortion on an almost daily basis, and I increasingly like it less and less, meaning that I only like those bits that have emerged from deep down, be it an acquired role that I've identified with, be it the dark reality that I've experienced.

To arrive at an abandoned and derelict castle a decade after the end of the First World War, wander around and try to imagine how people lived there and what could have happened so they no longer carried on, or what would one need to do so they could revert to that lifestyle again. The last lord of the castle was beaten to death by peasants from the nearby village in the Autumn of 1918, all the furniture and other belongings were looted, the land was expropriated by the Romanian state, at present someone is renting it from someone else who's also renting, and it's barely cultivated. The place isn't really a castle, only my grandfather sees it as such, it's more like a mansion, but for Transylvanian standards that will do. Romanians hadn't yet started to settle here in large numbers back then, but whoever came from elsewhere was met with suspicion. Those of Romanian origin had just realized what an advantage this could be, so they were branded as traitors by everyone, though we were also a little envious of their ability to change sides so smoothly and so successfully. This will lead to a lot of trouble, causing ethnic and conscience-related chaos alike. I found the task of imagining this castle beyond me, in vain did I look at the detailed restoration plans, nothing had become of it, and frankly I couldn't see a future for this lifestyle anyway. Over the years, the castle had housed a power plant, purchased in 1925 by the village from Ganz and Co. for nearly a thousand dollars, threshing machines, a brandy distillery, water and steam mills, a narrow-gauge railway, a county court, a choral society, high society and Székely casinos, industry associations and hunting societies, a library and a bowling alley, as well as a weekly market, and in case the country fair fell on a Saturday (August the first), they moved it to another day to accommodate the Jewish merchants, the latter even taking place with the approval of the Romanian minister of commerce. In these villages, remnants of a traditional folk culture were still visible at the time, albeit not considered noteworthy by ethnographic studies. Béla Bartók had also visited these surroundings, and whatever he jotted down is all that remained of folk music, because people were already into Schrammelmusik, and they hadn't reverted to folk music since as they found it too rustic. The village looks more urban than many towns of that era, despite the fact that there are hardly any paved footpaths or roads. It's impossible to make good wine, but everyone is toiling away in their vineyard, be it as it may. Wheat is an equally inefficient crop, but bread is in great demand, especially white bread, and real men produce their own flour to make their own bread. Whoever is poor, is really poor, but even the rich only get richer in modest terms. The 1921 Romanian land reform is a fiasco, just like all other earlier and later reforms, the largest Transylvanian estates suffer the most, though no one really benefits from these anyway, genuinely large estates haven't existed around here by the way, and land ownership will not change much until collectivization kicks in.

We could easily get lost in the details of this world, as they are colourful, interesting and heart-warming, whilst reality can be rather stark. In the thirties, Romania is in the turmoils of a latent civil war, there are hundreds of political murders, amid total chaos. Sometimes, there is a king in place, other times, there isn't. Sometimes, there's such a thing as democracy, other times, there isn't, there's the occasional state of siege that leads on to dictatorship, king, Conducător, party, and those in charge vary. Economic policies are liberal, hair-raising corruption ensnares everyday life which makes us Hungarians dislike all this at first, but we soon get used to it, as it has clear advantages. Freedom of the press and censorship are operating side by side, there's no need for publishing licence, though Attila József's book entitled *With a Pure Heart* cannot be distributed in Romania either, I wonder whether the Romanian authorities consult their Hungarian counterparts in such matters. One government crisis follows in the wake of another, and we Hungarians have no idea which side to back. We have no clue what's going on, except that we are going to die out soon, this is what it's all about, because as long as Hungarians continue to live and breathe in Transylvania, the foundation of the Romanian state cannot be fully completed. Politics are conducted *down there* in Bucharest, according to our mental map that is abroad, for us only oppression can come from there despite the relative economic prosperity. We are looking forward to a border revision, if not possible by other means than by way of war, and we mainly write in the press about the fuss around schools because that is the only truly public affair linking Hungarians from Temesvár to Máramaros, and Szatmár to Brassó. Those who want to study and live in Transylvania in a Hungarian way have to deal with more unfairness that they can possibly handle, and the list of grievances has only grown since, nothing has been resolved, although some of the issues have since become obsolete. The statue of István Bocskai has to be removed every so often from its location in front of the church, and then it can be reinstated again, as if it were the utmost indicator of the political climate at a given time. The dream world emerging from the nostalgic fantasy of the Austro-Hungarian Monarchy and the ethos of survival turns into a beautifully sweet yet ultimately artificial and fragmented gloss which is mandatory for each and every Hungarian staying put, whilst the wealthy elite secretly repatriates because the homeland is promoted as being in Budapest. We tend to *go up there*, a place that increasingly turns into a sort of foreign land not only geographically but also emotionally, though the 'Székely Anthem' was penned there—where else could it have possibly been written? What's visible to my grandfather from all this, and what I make him see is entirely up to me, I can be imaginative when I'm entirely objective and professional, and could get away with generalizations sprinkled with the odd matter of special interest. I'd have my work cut out for me big time if I ever wanted to find out what Transylvania might actually be about, it's certainly not what I have had in mind so far. I'm torn between desperation and the joy of discovery in equal measure, one day I get the impression that I've got it, the next, I become aware of the enormity of the problem.

I could probably come up with my own views on the world, all four corners of it, relatively easily, but I'm struggling with having any clear thoughts about myself. My life isn't about settling down but about migration, it is a quest without aiming for foundation, I can't settle down long term any more, everything is conditional. I own no land or other forms of property, my knowledge is worth increasingly less, and I often feel that I'm just stranded here and have no idea in what direction I was initially heading. My grandfather's experience was that he returned from Bucharest, the war, captivity and other dramatic experiences to the exact same place he'd left behind, whereas I did realize that while I was hanging out somewhere else, everything had changed. This includes the woman who should have been waiting for me to get back home, and who moved on despite being the actual centre of my world. I'm always returning from some battlefield, be it actual or symbolic, and whilst I was away there was a battlefield here, too, and just in case there wasn't, I brought one with me. Property, land, forests no longer signify permanence, people, human bonds and relationships transform too, at a pace that's much too fast for us to follow, but this is down to the nature of these times. There's no way we can adjust to this and modernise ourselves accordingly.

I might actually manage if I spent the winter in one of the rooms, lighting a fire in the old tumbledown tiled stove, grilling some bacon, and dipping into an old book before rolling up in a few of blankets for the night. My grandfather would do the same, he'd manage to get a small holding set up for sheer survival back on its feet, and then they'd either tolerate him or chase him away. He'd join the agricultural cooperative in no time, because his own patch of land wouldn't be sufficient for him to secure a living, or perhaps he wouldn't own any land at all. He wouldn't join the communist party though, not because he'd be reluctant to set his hopes on a just division of property, but because he'd find atheistic propaganda scandalous. Being a deeply religious man, he'd believe that Jesus Christ could appear around the corner any minute, the four years he'd spent in primary school were all that separated him from mythical times, and the fact that he'd always count his eternally diminishing money. Perhaps he'd even have a go at poaching, a forgivable sin in dire straits, though game was at a premium in Transylvania, and provided they owned a gun, everyone would keep shooting at just about anything that happened to take their fancy. There was no Romanian legislation to regulate hunting until 1935, so it was a matter of personal decision whether to observe the Hungarian law.

The Jewish shopkeeper, for whom my grandmother used to work, was taken to Auschwitz—his name had only survived in census records, his shop was looted by the locals, and the synagogue demolished without a trace. My grandmother did everything in her power to save at least one of the boys, but didn't manage, or perhaps she didn't actually do anything because those were such times. She should have, of course. Or shall I just accept that it wasn't possible? Can I possibly expect from my grandparents that they should have had themselves shot to death rather than assist the frightful operation of history? Would anything be different had I been there? They should sort this out without being shot to death, yet with dignity and without arriving at a compromise, after all this would make a really great novel! We didn't get rich but held on to our dignity, or perhaps not even that, there was nothing for us to hold on to and there were no set rules. We can't ascertain what exactly happened when in 1944 my grandmother retreats into a cellar, because the frontline is in transit. The splinter that had pierced the table top is now gone but we can easily make out its shape. The Russian soldier decides to throw the babe in arms in the redcurrant bushes, so it needs to be nursed back to life. According to family legend, a pendant representing the Virgin Mary disappears from grandmother's gold chain, a confirmation present, it must have been nicked by some adulterous wench romping with the Russian soldiers, but at least my grandmother didn't come to any harm, she got away with it . . .

The treasure must have been hidden under the old pear tree behind the castle, Transylvania is teeming with hidden treasures. In case we find anything, we'll share it out in a brotherly fashion, and then denounce one another. On autumn nights, bears descend from the woods to feast on the pears, there are plenty of bears around here, but we aren't afraid of them, or just in case we are, we wouldn't admit to it. The wilderness lies just a few paces away from our house, perhaps because of our lifestyle, but perhaps this is simply all that we managed to come by. There should be a gun somewhere in our home, if not, we piece one together, this is also a sort of DIY, though it belongs to the story of my other grandfather. I could easily continue this storyline, there are plenty of details, a sea of stories I heard from others or made up myself. After a short dilemma, or rather a terrible agony, I decided that I'd like to be the grandson of my actual grandfather and the son of my actual father, even though I'm also a writer, or I pretend to be a writer, not that being a son and grandson is that easy, just as being a father and grandfather isn't easy either. Being a mother is the hardest of all though. This is no place for irony, it's hard to be a woman in this world: it's often cold, both in our climate and in our soul. It makes no difference that I jot everything down exactly as it happened, or as I think it happened, to the best of my knowledge, because it will instantly turn into fiction and fabrication that attracts further flights of the imagination. I always opt for speakability as I'm unfolding a story, and what I write may well be the truth but who could possibly vouch for that?

In the spring of 1985, my father can't possibly know any of this, neither can I. There's a World Cup qualifier, I don't recall whether it's on TV or only on the radio. My father finds it strange that I don't want to go to my room, despite the Hungarian team's fate being a matter of life and death, Mexico's coming up, and we are still hopeful, for the very last time. I've just abandoned the Hungarian team, so we lose to the Dutch, but this is just a temporary faltering at that point. I write a short piece for the Hungarian daily in Arad, the *Vörös Lobogó*—appropriately named as *The Red Standard*—this is my third article to date if I'm not mistaken, back then there's a lot at stake when it comes to counting and writing. I have no idea why this matters so much to me, I'm practising self-censorship, I want to be a journalist or simply to prove it to myself that I'm capable of finishing a text by the evening. It's going slowly, so my father asks how I will manage to make a living if this is so damn hard. Well, I won't. Or rather, just fine, because I've been devoting myself to my whims and vagaries ever since, not in the sense of making a living from what I write, but insofar that there's still such a thing as literature. I could also tell him that I have no idea how exactly I'll be making a living, yet again I've botched a novel. I haven't built a house or secured my livelihood, everything's hanging in the air around me, despite my parents giving their all so I turn out well, but I won't, and this is no longer just a fleeting vision but a state of affairs. I was in a similar situation thirty years ago, back then half of my life's work wasn't yet out in the public domain but there was Hungarian football, I was struggling with writing, it was difficult to trudge along in a forced way so it was high time I confronted my own self a little, together with the world.

Confronting myself was fairly easy back then, I had a serious speech defect, I was stammering, and this had made my life pretty dreadful, not only as far as women were concerned, I barely had any dealings with them, but also as I realized that I knew next to nothing from what was required at the university entrance exam. I had no chance in hell to get in to study Hungarian and French at Kolozsvár. In Transylvania one gets in to university, in Hungary one enrols on a course, minor linguistic details to denote a major problem. After an unsuccessful entrance exam, they enlist me, or rather I join the army, then work in a cannery, Steinbeck also started off in this way, and whoever hadn't been in the army would never become a proper man, this was the commonly held view around here. I won't get a place at university for years, I can't get in but I keep trying, I can be really headstrong when it comes to my whims and vagaries. The fact of the matter is that it wasn't me wanting to go to university, my mother had made me do it, she had rammed it into me, apparently this was what she had wished at my birth, because it was customary to wish for something, such as to be good at school and not to drink. So I think I'm continuing my mother's schedule for her life, warts and all. In that era, aiming to go to university is a goal akin to preparing to climb the Everest, or at least the Mont Blanc, it seems just as hard, distant and hopeless a task, so we adopt a suitable attitude.

The world is a rather straightforward place at the time: Ceauşescu's dictatorship is just about to liquidate everything that has survived from Hungarian culture in Transylvania, not only the faculty of arts and literature but entire parts of towns, villages, dramatically transforming the lives of millions. The programme for the destruction of villages hasn't yet been officially announced but it's already underway, the towns and cities have already been dealt with, in all significant cities the ethnic balance has finally been settled in favour of Romanians. Hungarians, Germans and Jews are emigrating on a large scale, their place being taken over by peoples of different cultures and customs, Romanians and Gipsies, entire areas being eroded with an impact lasting to this day, lifestyles, traditions and worlds disappearing for good. It isn't easy to separate socialist modernization that transforms the whole of Romania from nationalist politics, even if we are aware that in the fifties and sixties, communist party secretaries and Securitate agents were actually of Hungarian ethnicity in Székely Land—they were more eager and often more cruel, not to mention more consistent than their Romanian counterparts. As it happens, we Hungarians in Transylvania have never been and still aren't too bothered about what else this system managed to destroy in addition to Hungarian culture, that's up to the Romanians, let them fuck this shit, this is how we tend to put this if we are really honest. We don't like to address the fact that in Romania the victims of socialism included mainly Romanians, it does them good, after all they were the main beneficiaries of the system, although we did envy them for the latter, seeing that this simply was neither just nor fair.

In twentieth-century Transylvania it's a given that all evils are the work of Romanians. No Hungarian person argues against this, Hungarians either joined the resistance or had to put up with the status quo. Yet they participated, that is, they put up with it, by the sheer fact of moving over to a free, happy or at least Hungarian world. This was the main principle, the fact that they also had a dictatorship didn't seem to matter to anyone, people couldn't really be aware of this anyway, because back then, the Romanian press cried shame upon Hungary at all times but no one had actually mentioned that there was a dictatorship in Hungary too. In 1985 everyone's preparing for the imminent fall of socialism, although we do know that it could take forever, and the real issue is whether we'll actually survive it. It's still not clear whether we've survived it, according to some we shouldn't have, and to others, we couldn't have died in the process even if we had really wanted to. This is an exaggeration, many people died in the process, countless and nameless, no one knows how many to this very day. I have no idea whether there existed in Europe a country bleaker than Romania at the time. I also wonder whether there existed a career with less prospects than being a teacher of Hungarian language and literature in Romania back then, or aiming to become one. Not that I had actually prepared for it, hardly anyone wanted to be a teacher at the time, even though teachers weren't quite as low on the social hierarchy as they are now. I still don't understand why there were ten candidates for a place. Looking back though, it comes across as the only intelligent form of resistance, a defiance and exasperation of sorts, anything goes, so why not? There was a kind of communal solidarity, or at least a need for it, so that all of us applying to study Hungarian huddle together as a large group despite being contenders, precisely to form an alliance against those who forced us to participate in this humiliating competition.

How will you handle the oral exam, my father asks, as do most of my close friends because I keep stammering in a hopelessly hideous and disappointing manner. No one seems to dwell on whether I might have exam fright, or whether it is the continuous fright that makes me stammer. I hope I'll manage to overcome it. It should be quite obvious that, since face-to-face communication had often made me confront an insurmountable task, I opted for the solution offered by writing, yet this wasn't the case. I don't have to go out of my way to see that stammering isn't a mere question of articulation or breathing for me, but a state of mind, a personality crisis and a cognitive problem that I learned to bridge or conceal to a point, but not to solve. I stammer even in writing, every so often I run out of breath or have a lapse in formulating thoughts or sentences. Yet I won't fall silent, I say what I can say, and it's no longer me who's talking or who falls silent, I don't know who I am, why I talk if I should be silent, or why I don't say something when I should be talking, why this hindsight, what's this endless talk beside the point, it's always a matter of the wrong pace and of bad timing although I can actually write rhythmic structures if I feel that the time is right.

I'm a writer, and during my authorial crisis lasting over thirty years I generated about a thousand pages worth of pauses, and the times when I didn't stammer at all or only stammered in a manner unnoticeable to others, were sufficient for me to delay choosing a serious, civilian and grown-up profession to a point of no return. I like to engage in DIY and am not above hard work or menial jobs, but it has become rather complicated for me to make others believe that I'm actually able to hit a nail into a wall, turn a screw, dig up the garden, especially if the person in question is also after a surplus arising from my work. Not that writing isn't a proper profession or proper work, but unlike most professions, in this case the goal isn't achieved by way of safely repeating a sequence of operations, but the rethinking of the goal is achieved by way of a sequence of operations that are non-repeatable in a safe manner. This entails a reformulation of everything, testing the credibility of the short story or of the phrase in each and every sentence. So what kind of profession is this? People pretend that they have some expertise, but they can never actually ensure that the next sentence doesn't reveal the limits of their knowledge. And what if this doesn't even come to the fore, or only after several hundred pages, perhaps after the book is published? What happens if I realize that my book is bad, untrue, inauthentic? Or if I don't even realize this? What if I adopt a radical change in the process of writing? This is partly the aim, but there you are. What if I have changed so much that I can no longer identify with what I wrote earlier? Do I start anew, or a new work? After all, one always writes oneself, pulling things apart or braiding them together, it's not quite the same yet all the same in fact. In the process of writing, one senses that language is much more than one's self, one can freely immerse in this spatiality, relying on it to the full. Whoever had already experienced this sensation continues to desire it over and over again, as with love and wine, it's possible to live without them but not really worthwhile.

By the time I got to an age where I could read or talk about such things, my father had lost interest in literature and in most forms of written culture. He heard about Domokos Szilágyi, he killed himself, and he was a total alky. He doesn't recall anyone by the name of Ádám Bodor when he studied theology, or if so, is he related to Pál Bodor? Names don't mean much to him, except for the ones mentioned on Radio Free Europe. He had heard of András Sütő, he's positive that in 1958 Sütő had written a fulminant opinion piece against operetta, arguing that this genre should be banned. Star performer Hanna Honthy was touring with the Budapest Operetta Theatre, and *The Csárdás Princess* was performed in Kolozsvár. Like thousands of other potential spectators, my father failed to obtain a ticket, but he did read the article. He keeps reminding us of it when in the late eighties Sütő is put on a pedestal in Hungary, he has no interest in works such as *Egy*

lócsiszár virágvasárnapja [The Palm Sunday of a horse dealer] or
Anyám könnyű álmot igér [Mother assures me of gentle dreams].
He hates communist comrades turned lords and former writers
turned activists, he doesn't believe in those who resist or in resistance as such, and certainly not in the resistance of writers. They
should have carried on as comrades, or never joined the party.
Once he got a sparkle in his eye when hearing about Gyula Illyés,
because the latter decided to stop offering wine to someone who'd
finish their glass in one gulp. This is wasted on you, Illyés said.
Wow, my father reacted in an approving voice. He leafs through
Illyés' book *People of the Puszta*, then puts it down, yes, this is
exactly how we used to live, too. He says this with tired resignation,
he doesn't want to dissuade me from anything, and doesn't say that
I'd rather train to be an agronomist or a horticulturist. He'd prefer
it if I went to live in Germany or England, irrespective of what job
I would have to do there. He is convinced that nothing will
become of Romania or Hungary, there'll never be a normal economy, or a dignified life, he hadn't been dazzled for a single second
by the Kádár-era welfare, and the regime change occurred too late
for him. The oppressed want to become oppressors, he says, and I
immediately protest—not me. Well, then you'll be oppressed, he
says, putting an end to the argument. Aren't there any other
options, I'd like to ask, but I don't, and later I find out what he'd
respond, or not respond rather. He'd start searching for a newspaper article, and since he couldn't find it, we'd end up talking
about something else, such as Chinese cabbage because it had a
high Zinc content, or about the fact that even the Egyptians were
into garlic, as it was a great remedy against most illnesses, at least
according to the always handy *Kertészet és Szőlészet*.

Every now and then, I might say that my father and I would
share a glass of wine, and in essence this is how it should be. Yet

my mother wouldn't refrain from horning in at times, there, you're at it again. She's also concerned about my future, for her literature is a distant and beautiful thing, she enjoys reading, her favourites are moving novels and poems that are easy to understand and speak to one's heart, A. J. Cronin's *The Citadel* and Sándor Reményik. This is of course a simplification, but she had never got anywhere with modern poetry, she wasn't taught that sort of thing at school, and in her view novels should have a clear storyline, no corpses, riddles and swear words. In December 1989, when I stop shaving my face and Ceaușescu is shot in the head like a dog, my mother jubilates that now it's finally worthwhile to become a teacher of Hungarian in Transylvania. Nice touch, she's always the optimist, furthermore, she thinks I'm talented and good at composition. She doesn't realize that I can never be a teacher, I keep stammering despite being offered a place at university. For her, writing is a nice hobby, like macramé or crochet. I tell her that this is correct, however, writing requires a whole person, not just a table, paper and peace and quiet but mental space, so one doesn't have to think about anything else except for the stuff one is actually thinking about. When I'm reading one of Péter Nádas's books, she remarks that there was a photographer by this name in the sixties, she's glad that she knows him from somewhere. She points this out every time I'm reading Nádas, because we also had a subscription for the women's weekly *Nők Lapja* as long as the Romanian authorities allowed it in, and we had a chest chock-a-block with these, too. In 1985, my father knows with utmost certainty that we'll get into trouble with the Securitate if I study Hungarian, you'll only bring danger about, he says reproachfully. My mother's attitude is that those who don't do anything bad, won't get into harm's way, my father dismisses this with a wave of the hand, while I think that if a policeman can beat the living daylight out of just about anyone then nothing really matters. My father is afraid, because he knows the world we live in, my mother isn't, because she doesn't, and I don't want to be afraid, I want to conquer fear, and looking back, this is the phrase that sounds by far the best. By then, Éva Cs. Gyimesi had already written her letter to Ceaușescu, in which she let the big cheese know about the nightmare conditions Hungarian teachers were facing when being sent to compulsory teaching posts upon graduation, we also knew about *Ellenpontok* [Counterpoints] as Radio Free Europe reported on this topic several times. Cs-Gy told me that she was hoping I'd study Hungarian, but this may well have been in '86 when I had a bit of a starring role in a lesson as my school teacher was being assessed. Of course, I told Aunt Éva, as we affectionately called her, that this had already been decided, but I was flattered by the invitation all the same. In hindsight, I still feel that no one could have possibly been serious about me getting anywhere in this field, for those who knew about it, this must have looked like a distant and surreal goal, and for those who didn't, it was borderline impossible to even make sense of what I wanted. Everyone could get to grips with what reading and hiking meant, but it was I who refused point blank to understand the business about making a living. To say the least, I can't be a teacher on account of my stammering, this much was obvious. The rest will take shape somehow, I said to myself.

III

Family

We aren't that kind of family, my mother points out whenever there's talk of people who, in her view, are of a bad sort, yet somehow I'd happily swap with them, they have plenty of good qualities in my eyes. There's usually talk of our neighbours and acquaintances, who are something of a mixed bag, and we can clearly see, sense and grasp all their contradictions, and hence distance ourselves from them as much as possible, not in an overt fashion of course—only in the good old Hungarian style of keeping a distance just for our sake. We were poor and had to work through our holidays, she adds, we'd work on the fields, help our parents around the house yet still get good grades at school, respect others and ourselves, and spend Sundays at church where we prayed and sang songs all day. She tends to say this whenever we disagree over something, or I don't want to eat or would prefer something else, or I want to do my lessons at a different time or in a different way, or I hate my clothes. Perhaps she realizes that there are differences in opinion between us, I'm cheeky and I answer back—even destroyed the garden flowers during a football match with my friend, also managed to bend the metal bar in the fence because I used it for gymnastics—and generally think that things shouldn't be the way they are. She's most likely to go on about this when I want something she thinks I shouldn't have, for instance when I'm contemplating my long-term plan to go to Everest, or at least to the Fogaras Mountains, or when I'd fancy a record player or a bike. The record player is expensive and unnecessary, aside from the fact that when she was a child, a bike chain had caught the hem of her skirt and she received a beating for it. She also fell over while skating and broke her head—got another beating. As it happens, I've never asked for skates, yet I'm told that mountaineers only exist on TV, why then would I want to become one, at least not a footballer though, seeing that playing on a pitch is more or less like taking a hike to the fields . . .

There are plenty of other useless items that I'm desperate to possess, yet my mother thinks I don't need, or rather that such a need would lead to my certain ruin. She has practical, emotional and religious counter-arguments, but all this really is about her knowing exactly what I need—I should be grateful for what I do have, she didn't even have this much, and perhaps I won't in the future, either. You'll see when I'm not around anymore, I work all day for your sake and this is the gratitude I get! Gratitude is essential in our case, because we owe it to our parents, and indirectly to God, for everything we have. At times, I suspect that I'm given things only so I can be grateful, and in case I pass them on, I can enjoy other people's gratitude in return. Ingratitude is a capital sin. In case some kid in the neighbourhood lays hands on any of the items I have a burning need for, it transpires that all this happened to the detriment of much more important things, it couldn't have happened any other way. She doesn't forbid anything in particular, only makes me acknowledge that it isn't essential, considering that it's actually harmful, expensive and unnecessary. It's acceptable to ask for books though, we already have plenty of those anyway, and books are a forgivable sin, but we'd rather get a bookcase first because the one we have is overloaded. To be fair, aged thirteen I was given a Soviet telescope that had cost a fortune, no one understood why I had such a burning need for it and why my mother bought it for me. He's going to break it, my father said, as if I wasn't even present, but I didn't—still have it to this day.

As far as I understand, we lived in poverty during my childhood. This *we* comprises the entire family in time and space, and extends from 1904—when my grandfather was born—to our days. This explains everything—our house, our lifestyle, our flaws—and, of course, also offers an excuse: we couldn't possibly do other things or do things differently even if we were to break our backs. We don't work on the fields—we don't even own a field—I don't have to help out at all or hardly ever, perhaps at weekends, because my job is to be a good student, to do well in life, or at least better, everything serves this purpose. We have a home, food, shoes and clothes, we aren't in need, yet. I can't decide whether we are constantly disgruntled because we don't have everything we need or because we actually crave more. My father and mother take turns in telling me that nothing is quite right in fact, the house shouldn't have been built right here or in this way, the windows aren't in the right place, the pantry is too cold, the wind tends to blow snow into the attic, there are packs of dogs on the streets, my mother is afraid of them though only my father ends up being bitten, we live at the edge of the village, where there's at least peace and quiet, as long as the train isn't rattling over the small, and then the large, iron bridge, and the neighbours aren't actually screaming and shouting. Dissatisfaction is a bad thing, God punishes the ingrate, my mother reminds us, not to mention that we have everything we need, so we could just as well be contented with our lot, we must understand that there was no other way. This is it, so we'd better get on with it. So we keep quiet and carry on working.

Others steal, cheat and lie, but we don't. We can have a quiet sleep, our hands are not tarnished by anything dodgy, we make an honest living. We go to church on feast days when we have time, but the church is really far away. During the summer, my mother and I visit my grandparents in Barót, in Székely Land, we help them to harvest potatoes or take part in other important work, mainly cleaning, my mother has no time for anything else, we go to church while we are there too—they call it a chapel—after which she travels back home and I stay behind. We don't have a car, don't go on holidays or excursions or to the seaside, when it comes to this, my mother seems somewhat offended but also quite proud. Compared to others, we lead a simple life: her younger sister, for instance, has a car and goes to the seaside and even to Bucharest, but they live close by, both to the seaside and to Bucharest, and also to *home*, so that's convenient. Her older sister also has a car, but it's all down to her husband, and they also live close to home. Her older brother doesn't have a car, only a motorbike, yet they have also been to the seaside, but they live close by, while her younger brother has a motorbike and still lives at home, he spent two years at the seaside—in the army. According to my mother, everyone has it easy compared to us, everybody benefitted from some sort of a parental, family or state support that we didn't get, we should have been entitled to this as well or else—no one should get it at all.

I don't know what my father thinks about all this, he didn't say anything about duty and gratitude or that God would protect or punish in case of this, that and the other. My mother was the one who formulated the family ideology, including the bits on my father's place and duties, at times she might have even been a little surprised that this had been spelt out in the Bible, but clearly this was God's will. It looked as if he would have never wanted to go anywhere, and he never spoke of home or homeland. My mother had been to Budapest once, so had my father, but not together, there was no money for such things, later this wasn't even allowed and they didn't insist, if it's not allowed, it's not allowed, besides it would have cost an absolute fortune. They had also been to Bucharest, sent on some course by their company, again, not together, because they weren't employed by the same company, and it wasn't that sort of place anyway. We don't tend to eat out, and we don't visit anyone and aren't visited by anyone, except for the odd relative or neighbour who wants to watch a match in case their TV set is out of order. We don't quarrel, don't scream and don't swear. For us, it is work that prevails, together with family, study, peace, love and harmony. All this is a priority for us. We don't have anything in second place, let alone in last place. We don't do anything that could be in last place. I don't even know what that is, and when the neighbours are supposedly at it, we look away. We are a regular family, my mother points out whenever I conclude that certain things aren't actually in order, as there aren't in the case of any regular family, either. Nothing is in perfect order, only it seems to us, and we pretend that it is, others either believe this or are indifferent. Questions are unacceptable, and neither are doubts, dreams or desires. I know that if everything is in perfect order then we aren't a proper family, and in case we wanted to be one, we shouldn't find what happened to us and without us over the last century quite so much in order. In hindsight, of course, I only say this in hindsight and not back then. If this is order, then it's best to be without! If this is order, then I'll subvert it and leave things as they are, so time, gravity and oblivion can put them back in place, but perhaps all we'll do from now on is toss and turn sleeplessly, and perhaps get used to that, too. Let those with a clear conscience sleep, as they say. Come on, why would anyone have a clear conscience? Because we'd like to be innocent although we are nothing but innocuous? I sometimes marvel at my own passion as I'm noting down, and at times caricaturizing, my mother's monologues. I feel that I can't be accurate if I want to be precise, and if I want to be accurate, I'll end up distorting reality. What am I actually missing in this world?

I was about to write a family novel, sometimes I thought I would manage, other times I had my reservations, after all in the wake of *Harmonia Caelestis* [Celestial harmonies] and *Egy családregény vége* [The end of a family story] one can only be afraid of such a task. I doubt anyone is actually capable of keeping an elegant and moderate distance with regard to their family, and in case they are, then this distance should be interpreted as a form of understanding and sympathy, and moderation as an instance of poetics. As for me, I had read the most striking family novel in the Házsongárd cemetery, all it said on an enormous yet simple and masterfully carved marble block was Tata Mama Eu—Father Mother I. In other words: My father's and mother's message was I, and my message is that I don't have a message. I walked past that area many times, and would always wonder why was it necessary to use up tons of marble in order to come up with what, more or less, looks like a Brancusi-paraphrase? This is cemeterial ostentation, a joke no less. Who does this 'I' think he or she is?

But who do I think I am? I should substantiate the narrator, and the position I'm talking from. What kind of pedestal is this, what sense of superiority and what tangle of reflections, in which what I know and when this happened is entirely unreliable. At the age of almost fifty, I have to acknowledge that I don't have a clue about human relationships, in other words, I keep projecting my own models onto everything, and I only notice in hindsight that I might have slipped back into some sort of arrears relative to myself. I can't see myself from the outside, only those few images that I created and that I cherish, I'm the victor of my own life and the victim of others. There's always some excuse and some quibble, although there's no need for them really, one gets used to them, unnoticed as they say, just as one gets used to tobacco and alcohol. Come on, he knows exactly what's going on, but there you are.

So I'll pretend to tell everything as it was, as I can, as it's easier to tell, although this will only end up like any other construction: whatever we can't imagine, will have to imagine itself or, failing that, just hide in a blind mirror. I attach some imaginary geography and personal chronology to it, and we now find that everything had happened in a way that I can actually narrate. I could also write a novel, a work of fiction, more than one even, though I wouldn't want or hope to do that as far as this material is concerned, I'll just move on. I'm a writer, in the business of making a hash of novels.

IV

Tom and Will

My uncle Tom was buried on 4 March 1987, he was my mother's younger brother, a heavy drinker who hanged himself in a barn, with a chain used for calves, at the age of forty. This is the first tragic event that made me realize that the image my family had created and cultivated of itself didn't quite correspond to reality. I'm 19, born on the 4th of March, though it may well be that Tom was buried on the 5th. I wasn't actually there, this is the main problem, dates can be amended after all, but I don't think that this had anything to do with my birthday, and neither did the 1977 earthquake in Bucharest. I was completing my compulsory military service in the Romanian army somewhere beyond the Carpathians, and had just happened to arrive home on a short leave when someone knocked on our door on a Sunday morning saying that they had received a call at my parents' workplace, there being no phone lines on our street back then. We are no longer asleep, but the gate is still locked, there's no one in the front room, so they have to knock really hard for us to hear. My mother jumps up, she's the one always on standby, as if she knew that someone would look for her, and even if that's not the case, it's best if she opens the door. My first thought is that they've come for me, a soldier on leave isn't really on leave, I shouldn't even wear plain clothes for those five days. I think of my usually smelly broadcloth uniform, freshly laundered and still soaking wet at present, and all I want is that our socialist Romanian homeland holds out for a few days without me. My mother opens the window, it's cold outside and there's snow, as is usually the case on my birthday, and her colleague says with a sad but apathetic face that he's got some bad news, upon which my mother snaps back: *Tata, Mama, Fratele* (father, mother, brother)? Indeed, that's right. I sigh with relief, they haven't come for me, then I run through a sequence of images in my head, and after the last one I conclude—well, that's that.

I did like my uncle, who was Tom only to me, but at this point I wasn't in contact with him. He was a dominant figure in my childhood. All summer we used to stay in the same new-build, semi-furnished, bare and cold stone house. He'd always come home late at night, wake up at dawn, as tractorists tend to do. He has no wife or kids, my grandparents live at the back of the house but he's on bad terms with them, I'm initially unaware of this and later can't quite understand it, this is unimaginable, unspeakable, this can't possibly happen in our family. My uncle is a soft-spoken, quiet and modest man, and on the rare occasions he has time, he can talk endlessly about the world I only visit during my summer holidays. I spend my childhood summers in Barót, in this small mining town in Háromszék District, situated at the margins both in a geographical and social sense, in a close religious and family bubble, though I can't possibly be aware of this at that time. My uncle takes me for a tractor or harvester ride every now and then, and lets me have a go at driving whenever there's an opportunity. Other times, we take the motorbike and head to the iron blast furnace in Bodvaj, the Hatod Peak or Lake Saint Anna. We are free Székelys, despite not much talk of this topic, I can easily pick up the local dialect at the beginning of the summer, and know this world inside out, it's a second homeland to me. Back then, being

Székely is self-explanatory to us, there's no need to explain or jus-
tify this, and it's hardly advisable anyway. In those days, it was
unwise to show awareness of a separate Székely identity, so the fuel
for the ethnic conflicts raging in the contemporary period is building up nicely, for my grandparents religious allegiance is their top
priority, and as a child I'm under the impression that Székelys must
on the whole be Baptists. We tend not to put our Hungarian or
Székely identity on display, instead we get on with all our neighbours, avoiding conflict, we love our friends, and they love us
back—but this is more than enough family ideology for now.

My uncle wouldn't just tell stories about bears gazing at tractors while standing on their hind legs at the edge of the cornfield
before dashing off, but also about people who were *fouled* by bears,
and others who were befouled by policemen, suffering abuse at
their hands. Some of these people are criminals and thugs, and
they do deserve this treatment, but there are many innocent ones,
and we aren't meant to talk about them despite this being much
more exciting than talking about bears, and in case this did come
up in conversation, we quickly glance at the window to check
whether it's properly shut. Grown-ups are always quick to remind
me that I'm not allowed to talk to anyone about what had just
been said, because it could lead to trouble. I keep this secret heroi-
cally and loyally. At one point, someone mentions that Ceaușescu
has prostate cancer, I don't yet know what a prostate is, but cancer
is certain—the regime will soon collapse. I guard this secret until
I overhear people talking about this loudly on the bus, hooting
with laughter, and I find out what a prostate is, perhaps not quite
the exact details but something thereabouts. This lot keeps knocking back beer out of litre bottles, and in case they need a wee they
just make the bus stop, that was the norm back then, men get out

and, standing shoulder to shoulder, just water the field, while women head to the cornfields or bushes. On one such occasion, they find a new-born baby left behind. This happened because one of the women had to go far into the woods, and since she didn't come back in time, they went searching for her. They found her standing under a tree holding the baby turned blue from the cold, as if it was she who had given birth to it in secret. Now she'll have to convince the police that the child isn't hers.

We have plenty more secrets. We aren't allowed to say, for instance, that Father listens to Radio Free Europe at night, hopping between the Hungarian and the Romanian channels, or that in the bed made up in the living room there's a Hungarian flag my grandmother had sewn from some linen back in 1940 when the Hungarian Army marched into Transylvania. We've been cherishing it ever since, fearful though that we'd get into trouble in case they found it in the course of a house search. I have no idea why there would be a house search at our place, we aren't that kind of family. There's equally no talk of my uncle being an alcoholic, though I've never seen him drunk or even drinking, no one uses this word in relation to him, or terms such as boozer, drunkard or zonker for that matter. I'm already ten when I finally understand why he always comes home so late at night, once I decide to wait for him because I need to ask something, and then I can see him reeling about and sense the smell of alcohol punching through the stench of diesel oil, rubber, straw and sweat. That was the first time I got a whiff of this otherwise familiar scent, and to this day I can't grasp why I didn't pick up on it earlier. All of a sudden, I understand why my grandmother is so sad and why my grandfather is angry with my uncle: because he drinks every single day, and that is a sin, the second most serious sin after atheism that one can possibly commit in this environment. Everybody knows what's what, yet we aren't allowed to talk about this, and we aren't allowed to talk about a whole raft of other things, either. He mingles with the wrong crowd, this is the most serious verdict I hear about my uncle in the course of my entire childhood. Get yourself a wife, relatives tend to tease or chide him. You still don't want to get married? Everyone smiles enigmatically, Tom comes up with some funny Székely phrase and then vanishes, something urgent has just come up. Only rarely does he attend service at the chapel, he works even on Sundays, this is socialist agriculture, ongoing even at night, by moonlight or artificial light alike. My uncle is a spiritually lean and well-built bachelor, he doesn't give in easily and does what he pleases, he is his own lord and master but people are envious of this and want to have him tied up. It's great to be a bachelor, that's freedom itself, and it's bad to be married, because one is tied up, but those who don't fulfil their duties will be damned. As for me, I find duty rather straightforward in those days, bearing in mind that a Székely 'would rather break like a tree, than succumb with glee' or suchlike.

I understand virtually everything from the snippets of dialogue that reach me, all these people want to get Uncle Tom to commit an act of betrayal. At one time, as we are riding his motorbike, I even tell him that I think he's being maltreated without any reason, and urge him not to give in. I don't know whether he can actually hear what I'm saying, that I'm on his side, for me he's the most likeable character, and he'll teach me to drive a motorbike when I'm older. We are sliding down the Hargita Mountain, balancing as best we can, then come to a halt at a large puddle, we can't cross that on two wheels. There's peace and quiet in the woods, the petrol smoke disperses and the engine starts to cool down, letting out a crackling sound, and as we are having a rest seated on a tree trunk, my uncle tells me something I think he had never told anyone, and in case he had, that was in vain. This is the kind of confession a man can't make to a thirteen-year-old boy in that world, the problem of grown-ups doesn't concern children. He's had enough of this life, he can't carry on like this. His father, brothers and sisters, the Church, his work and the police, to say nothing of that dirty old whore of a bride who, inspired by the Holy Spirit and in full knowledge of the congregation, returned his engagement ring and went off to fuck someone else. This is the way he puts it, words are pouring out of him, I've never heard him speak this long and this coherent about anything, except for his soldier memories, but that's different. I'm unable to recall any of his words afterwards, and only manage to piece together this jigsaw puzzle in the fullness of time, the odd initially incomprehensible detail finds its place, but names and dates that aren't connected to any of my points of reference are lost forever. He dragged me into his dark shadow, which was scary and I felt utterly helpless. For a moment, my Székely wonderworld breaks into smithereens but it soon reconstitutes itself, another topic I won't be talking about to anyone, or at least not for a very long time. We take a rest, go round the puddle, get on our motorbikes and ride away as if nothing had happened.

I keep thinking about all this that Sunday morning when the news of my uncle's death breaks, and my mother is trying to stifle her tears. She was very fond of her younger brother, I'll never understand her commitment, I have no siblings and although I had the chance to witness what siblings can do with and to one another, I have never experienced the intensity of such a relationship. I'm equally unable to render the sense of total commitment that those who live far away from their families can feel towards their loved ones. Circumventing day-to-day routines, these people are able to retain their childhood innocence, and we are just as innocent as they are when we think about them or write letters to them, this entire relationship moves into an ethereally pure dimension that is constituted by words and sentences, the rhetoric of word-based routines and mundane correspondence. Following this, on the third day of our long-awaited annual or bi-annual meeting, we either travel back home or have an epic fight. This is also a matter of routine, it arguably works with ritual precision, suddenly someone starts talking about something that is off limits, and that's the end of the idyll, it emerges that things aren't and weren't quite like so to start with. When will you get married, they keep asking Tom in the days when one could still meet him. This question makes him lower his head, as if he'd rather say never, and you all know this, but since we don't, well, come on, it will work out somehow. The fact that they found morphine in his system only came to the fore twenty years later, someone blurted it out by accident. A morphine-addict Székely tractorist—now that's a catchy headline!

We can't talk about this back then, and it isn't really that important. My mother pulls herself together, she bakes, cooks, irons, occasionally dashes outside to sob, later I accompany her on a walk along the rail tracks, that's where I usually go when I want to think things through with a clear mind. I'm trying to raise her spirits, so we talk about practical things such as shoes, food, train tickets and money, not about problems. The next day she has to leave at dawn, I at night, a family tragedy awaits her, a funeral, and then the sharing out of possessions that will take years and will unleash a family conflict in which everyone messes up their rehearsed role, everyone will say the wrong thing at least once but, obviously, repeatedly. The barracks are waiting for me for about another year, my father will take us to the station one by one, clothes, luggage, look after yourself, I'll write. My father's place would also be at the funeral, I have an acceptable excuse, though if I really wanted to attend, I could have managed to make it to the wake, but I didn't even try. By this stage, my father has hardly any contact with the Székely relatives, especially as it isn't compulsory. He loathes the long uncomfortable winter journeys, he's a sick man and this is his main preoccupation. He doesn't go anywhere with my mother, except for the doctor or occasionally the church at religious holidays, he doesn't travel with me either, but I don't need him to accompany me anymore. That ominous night, I wake up as the train rattles over the iron bridge at Alsórákos before pulling into Ágostonfalva station. This was the train station of my childhood where we'd always get off, and I've been continuing to wake up when travelling through Ágostonfalva ever since.

It will take months until I'm allowed home again for a few days from the army. My mother will write about the funeral in her letters, she should be the family chronicler because she keeps track of everything and everybody, she makes a note and takes pictures of absolutely anything. I think at that time I'm uninterested in all this, simply disgusted by this story—there is something fundamentally bogus therein, as if it were engulfed in greenish mucus and acrid stench. I shall also write a brief version of my uncle's story one afternoon in the barracks, when the boys sneak into town for a few drinks, then there is a huge brawl the whole night through, and in the morning we are marched, wearing gas masks, to storm at the nothing on the freshly ploughed field. I'm sketching the family novel I'm imagining at that very moment, aiming to get down to it one day, really thoroughly, with fortitude, honesty and precision. I'm writing these few pages for a woman, my one-time unrequited love interest, with whom I'm involved in a life-saving correspondence, which actually has the ability to save my mind and soul, as she'd tell me later that back in the day, it was a patriotic duty for girls to correspond with lads in the army. I won't send her this draft, I soon admit that I'm ashamed of opening up to this extent, as if I wanted to drag her into the darkness my uncle had dragged me, and I realize that all she could say is precisely what I had to say at the time: don't give in! My current thoughts are that I don't send her this text because I'm still respectful of the family taboo, meaning that we don't talk about them to anyone, we don't expose such things, despite already being aware of the fact that we cannot get to the bottom of things unless we think through and articulate them by way of intelligent and coherent sentences.

Those few pages kept being tossed about in a French grammar book for years, I don't know where they vanished because I'd need them now. I recorded several details that I remember only vaguely or not at all, I feel that I was honest back then, I understood less and perhaps also knew less than now, but I was coming to all this fresh. My closing sentence read as follows: troubled waters are smoothed over, I have always attempted to turn my letters into short stories, or to give some sort of shape to what I was committing to paper. My mother kept complaining that what I wrote wouldn't shed light on anything, whereas my thoughts were, so much the better, partly because of censorship, and partly because this was an excruciating phase in my life, and it was better if there was no one to lament, seeing that they couldn't help anyway. There's no war, yet I can see death from a close up, the army is a dangerous enterprise. I hate it, even though, in retrospect, I'm also proud of the fact that I stuck it out, it's certainly neither a scout camp nor a house party. This is what I discuss with my father in the course of that afternoon after my mother had left and we had lunch together. I seem to recall that we had bacon omelette, as always whenever my mother wasn't at home. We had some wine, my father and I, this is the proper way to put it, finally there's no need to come up with various tricks to get to the cellar and back when the bottle is empty, this time my mother won't comment and stand in my way. A single bottle isn't enough for us, and if we get to drink a second one, my father gets animated and we are almost having a conversation, he carries his sentences through, rather than simply read them from the papers. He tells me what he thinks of the Székely relatives, after all we have to talk about the situation we are in. Those members of the family who aren't particularly religious are almost up to the mark, they are well-meaning primitives, but we live on the Great Hungarian Plain, in Kisjenő, we are Hungarian and we find everyone who's different from us rather shifty. Romanians are beasts, Germans penny-pinching, in those days the butt of ethnic jokes in the Bánát region are the Swabians, there are no more Jews left, and Armenians can only be found in Franz Werfel's *The Forty Days of Musa Dagh*, even though only my mother had read this novel at that point. My father's verdict on the religious branch of our relatives in Barót is damning, he has always found their primitive religiosity and aggressively hypocritical bigotry, championed by my patriarch-like Székely grandfather, stomach-churning. You had studied all this in theology, my grandfather apparently said to my father, who took a deep breath, well no, never, not in this way, but my grandfather took this as an act of modesty, and kept pointing out what my father had apparently learned. My father will never go back to that chapel in Barót, and they don't invite or nudge him anymore, I guess they must have figured out from his strong tobacco smell that he doesn't really belong there.

We rarely talk between the two of us, and we aren't in the habit of interpreting the behaviour of the family. My father is strict, precise and outspoken, who quickly shuts up after making a point, as if he'd regret it already. This business at the moment is really annoying, my mother has freaked out, I'm on military service, soon to board a train, what is he supposed to do in such a turmoil on his own? In his view, people who construct their lives following the wrong dogma should simply take the blame, moreover, this dogma should either be perfect or not demand total adhesion, otherwise we are talking fundamentalism. These religious sects imported from America, however, are just like potato beetles or communists, they are equally harmful and hypocritical. They are harmful because they depart from an indiscriminate interpretation of the Scripture—they don't follow a particular tradition but adjust their interpretation or even the very text itself to their momentary agenda. They are also hypocritical because they behave as if they had a recipe for salvation, some of them even seem to know what role they'd fulfil in heaven, and feel compelled to say at a glance about others that you, my friend, you won't partake in salvation, at least not with us. Even this wouldn't be so bad if they could only refrain from calling themselves Christian or followers of Christ, because if this isn't all the same then people are either insane or simply don't speak Hungarian. Being a graduate of theology, my father considers that God or Jesus can exist in multiple ways, except for the ways propagated by the theories he had studied. He is positive about that, as he understood these matters as a student, which is why he didn't become a pastor, though following the regime change he did end up a presbyter. On that afternoon in March he tells me something I keep hearing from many others too: the youngest son of a god-fearing family, exemplary to all in piety and hard work, shouldn't drink himself stupid and hang himself in a barn, especially since he had everything. Scandalous! Just look at the number of people who refrain from hanging themselves despite having nothing to their name.

I feel at the edge of reason just hearing this claim: he had everything. Clearly no one had ever asked him what it was that he didn't have, what he would like or want, what he lacked, or whether he actually wanted anything? These continue to be hypothetical questions, of course, I'm not sure whether one could have asked such questions there and then. Perhaps because time and place won't allow them, or because people just are as they are. There's no space in that world for such questions, this problem is not (to be) interpreted, and it isn't intelligible. People's duties have been dealt out once and for all, they have always been from the beginning of time, and in vain would I argue that the world hasn't always been and isn't now as it had been when right and wrong were dealt out for all eternity. As I'm writing this now, I have to admit that I know next to nothing about my uncle, I won't be able to write about his life, I will never understand the details of what happened to him and what was taking place in and around him. I have so few reliable personal memories that I must weigh up whether what I claim is actually true, and whether I understood those few things I was told or overheard correctly, perhaps people didn't really want to say these to each other, perhaps this wasn't even the truth, and anyway everything was always in hindsight. It is my uncle's death that puts an end to my childhood, not only by blasting the bubble that surrounded me in that Székely world but also by reconfiguring its memory and illusion, and covering it with the acrid smell of an unpleasant film that cannot be concealed, not even by an atticful of thyme and hay. It would be good to remember the last time I had seen him, but I'm unable to recall this, the summers spent at Barót blur into one another. For me, being there has always meant holiday, summer and happy abandon, into which sombre things tend to mingle for the sole purpose of making light shine even brighter on the aspects it wants to put in focus. I barely remember anything prior to the great flood of 1975, and even thereafter, my memories aren't grouped according to particular years or summers but mainly according to floods and events that can only gain meaning in a personal chronology of sorts. That memorable motorbike ride will persist as our last meeting, closely attached to it is my mother's facial expression showing concern over her brother, as if she was worried about us or about the vehicle slipping from underneath or about other misfortunes of this ilk. She tends to read my grandmother's and her sisters' letters twice, the second time on a Sunday afternoon when she's working on her response, this is a small ritual after lunch and dishwashing, she lays out a newspaper on the oilcloth, a cardboard sheet on the newspaper, and finally a piece of writing paper on top. *Dearest Mother*, she begins her letter, letting out a big sigh, her eyes filling with tears, so she has to take her glasses off and, for a second, there's such an abandoned look on her face that I'm afraid to even glance in her direction.

There are countless updates on the weather, the progress of gardening work, the situation of domestic animals, the mood and health of relatives and my uncle's exploits: the drink, the bad company and an evil female who's clinging on to him and from whom he can't get away, he came back totally plastered yet again, he's been shouting and screaming at his parents, he doesn't bring any cash home, his clothes were once more in tatters, his lips were bleeding, he must have been in a fight or, worse still, beaten up. One could carry on like this, his parents are still providing for him, they are paying for the damages he causes, he's being fired from all jobs, in short, he's on a direct way to hell. My mother is crying and wringing her hand, she's just as helpless as everyone else. Tom will get into trouble, she keeps saying, and I can hear this but this is all she tells me, I don't know what she tells my father, do they even talk about this, would my father express himself in full sentences or just shrug as usual. I now got to the conclusion that both the family, as a whole, and everybody one by one, reached a point where they gave up on Tom, when they accepted that he couldn't be helped, only a miracle perhaps or not even that. Nobody articulates this, there's no formal meeting of the family council or tribunal to decree that he was weak, spiritless, worthless, or substandard. We just suddenly know this for a fact, as I myself have given up on him long before the funeral, just as the long summer holidays first get shorter and shorter until they come to an end altogether. It is this easy to dispose of an uncle.

Of course, I also have a legendary uncle, his name is Will. He's the one who witnessed his younger brother's forensic autopsy, I don't know whether he had no choice or he simply had the opportunity, but most people find this act on par with particularly cruel murder. A few years later, he won't attend his own father's funeral, everybody knows that he hated him, such a thing tends to happen between fathers and sons, even in the Bible. Sure, but in our family? He's the scion of a family exemplary for their hard work and piousness, and according to the dominant point of view, he also had everything he could possibly want. They raised him, fed him, clad him, had him educated but he hates everyone, terrorizes his ageing parents, calls my aunts and mother whores and other names, makes use of all the swear words that we not only don't use but also close our ears should someone else utter them. He always has a few flowery words in store, and although practising Christians are unable to swear in a truly poetic fashion, his sudden bursts of rage generate a sense of near-death in those present. He jumps up from the table while chewing the tastiest bits of rabbit roast, spits it out and starts shouting, chasing the family invited for dinner away, an endless monologue gushes out of his throat, and he yells his way through a long list of grievances. Totally over-whelming. If I were to be ironic, I'd say that Barót is situated in a volcanic area and that one of the best mineral waters on earth springs from a spot that is within walking distance, perhaps these facts have something to do with this passion. Such sudden and unprovoked bursts of rage, on the verge of paroxysm at times, are characteristic for all of my grandfather's children, women included, and none of them can later reflect on these outbursts or even remember what they actually say.

We could easily carry on going through Uncle Will's sins, and he doesn't even need drink to commit them. He tends to burst forth such profound grievances that many people are afraid of him, he's strong like a buffalo and would charge at anyone in case he thinks he is right and this isn't adequately acknowledged. He doesn't bother to check whether the window is latched when he thinks aloud—may Ceaușescu rot in hell together with his damned party and Securitate agents, and all the bloody Romanians are a bunch of bandits. His father is an old fart who's always cuckooing like a grimy wall clock, his mother a wicked stepmother, his sisters spruced up damsels who only return home to show off their genteel cunts in front of the congregation before they quickly pack up some valuables from the family home, his brother got stuck into a filthy whore, while his own share in life was nothing but work and toil, his father cuckoos, his wife refuses to let him have some pussy, his sons eat his flesh and drink his blood, but in case he needed some help, everyone's busy. The litany's endless, my uncle was harmed by existence and no one is prepared to apologise to him for that, most people feel that existence is in the right, everyone else that is, it's not acceptable to talk in these terms, especially for a devout Christian in front of other believers. People are seriously afraid of him in the wake of such outbursts, let them be afraid, he muses. I also ride a motorbike with him in the Hargita Mountains, I'm not afraid, and this ride is the proper deal, once he even shows me the tree on which he wanted to hang himself in his youth, but decided against it, he's been trailing the woods whenever possible ever since, because the forest is the best psychiatrist there is. This sounds reasonable. Zsigmond Széchenyi puts this in more elaborate terms, Will can quote him verbatim, having memorised the entire text although he isn't into reading or reciting. I have shortened this here, but all I learned about the forest I owe to Will. We wander around the vast forests of the southern Hargita Mountains as if it was our backyard. I can claim that I have first seen a bear in the woods, and not in a zoo or on TV, all because of this, and it always feels like the first time. The same is true for deer, wild boar, roes, hares, weasels and foxes, we are delighted to see them all, and the forest in its entirety. It feels as if it was our first time and suddenly realized that life is beautiful. God is following us somewhere at the height of the green canopy. At times, my uncle breaks the silence, words keep pouring out of him, his father, mother, sisters, the church, his boss and the police, not to mention

his younger brother. He isn't furious, only sad and tired, like someone worn out by an unexpected spout of anger, he doesn't apologise for his behaviour, he doesn't say that he shouldn't have said all
this, yet he is embarrassed, as he has no explanation, excuse or
ideology.

I hang out in sombre woods with sombre people. In case bears
come too close to us, we just let them know to go away, or we keep
chatting to keep them at bay. Will has been chased several times
by upset bears, he didn't come to any harm but has been warned,
he knows a few people who haven't been this lucky, and he also
knows many other stories, not all about bears. In those days these
mountains aren't dangerous on the account of the wildlife, but of
the foresters whose job is to guard Ceauşescu's lot, although in the
meantime they also steal trees or shoot game off their own bat. In
the afternoon, we hide the motorbike and head into the tickets on
foot, we don't even take a penknife so they can't say we are going
hunting. At times, Uncle Will goes straight to work from here,
on a few occasions he can't find his motorbike for days, he has
received several death threats, has been denounced, had his house
searched—they confiscate the deer antlers he found in the woods—
and ends up in all sorts of troubles. These policemen are playing
dirtier and dirtier, he notes, but he isn't afraid of them, one time
he even gets embroiled in the presidential hunt, though he didn't
get to meet Ceauşescu, only Maurer. I'm unaware at the time, and
perhaps so is he, that according to current legislation any sort of
following, observing and photographing wildlife is a criminal
offence. Now I know that he doesn't have a healthy sense of fear,
perhaps because there was a time when he wished for bears to
gobble him up or for sly foresters to shoot him, and since none of
this happened and he became familiar with the woods, he realized

that there were more grounds for fearing a sprained ankle or knee, as this is the most underhand danger that threatens the lone forest walker. As a child, I think he's a giant, and I'm astonished to notice one day that I'm already two inches taller than him, but this doesn't change a thing, he remains a tough, dark-skinned and stout alpine dweller. I can't wait for him to ask: are you coming? Nothing pleases me more than this simple question.

When we make it to the edge of the forest we agree that we'll meet by the crab-apple tree at the end of the clearing, I'll walk round to the right, and he to the left, it is dark and the stars are sparkling that autumn night. If I tell him that I'm scared, he won't bring me with him again, so I choose not to be afraid, and soon I learn the ropes. I inch forward stealthily under the trees, trying to move very quietly, the deer rutting starts soon, and that's what we are after, but I have no idea where they are. All I can hear is the noise I myself make, I'm too loud and this drives me mad, I grope every single branch and step forward as softly as only Native Americans and fur hunters can do according to the books. I have just got used to the night, immersing myself into it and enjoying the sense of space that takes over from the initial fear and loneliness. Somewhere behind the brow of the hill, there's a full moon, its yellow light already visible on the treetops. In a few minutes, we'll be able to see the clearing, I can't wait, yet won't move forward as something must surely be awaiting us, right there in front of us. All of a sudden, a wolf howls nearby, and there's something utterly gruesome in its voice, I have heard this sound several times since, and it has stayed the same. In vain are we trying to stealthily make it to the nearby clearing where the sound supposedly came from, this is a cautious animal that is seldom sighted. It's looking for the others, Will whispers, and since it doesn't make any further sounds we move on, and try to spot deer elsewhere, as we have managed on so many occasions since. This is an initiation of sorts, I'm fourteen and almost alone in the vast forest, I'm not Abel but a bit like him, though I inhabit the dark and not the humorous side of the world. I learn that it is great to spend time in the forest, and this moment turns into a defining encounter that I have found impossible to explain or conjure up, except to people who have also shared this experience. So there won't be any description of scenery here, there's only complicity and exchange of significant glances in the subtext.

My uncle is an unpredictable beast. You belong to the woods, my mother often says in outrage when I later try to interpret his behaviour, I stir the family dead water that doesn't want to settle, he even calls the vicar a cunt in front of the congregation, and he can barely refrain from striking a blow at him. He often drinks, and a lot. It's hard to decide whether this is the reason for his endless shouting at his relatives or he's just simply an idiot. Our family mentality would go for the drink, that's the simplest cause of all evils, that is the weakness whereby all evil, filth, deviance, to say nothing of the devil, can creep in, and it wouldn't occur to anyone that alcohol is just another effect. By the time it becomes a cause, there is nothing that could be done.

One night, Will unexpectedly tells me that he didn't have a mother. For some reason we come to a halt on a meadow and he starts sobbing, for a moment it seems as if he was having an epileptic fit, he tries to hold back but can't. We are on our way home from our hike, we haven't seen anything but managed to make a bear flee and could hear it clomp in the brambles, our excitement is short-lived though, we've been here before. This sobbing comes to the fore so suddenly and unexpectedly as if we were inching forward under the menacing and tragic sky in some film, such nerve-racking music reminds me of the film *Emberek a havason* [People of the mountains]. I'm unsure what it is he's trying to say and where this ensues from and how, after all my grandmother is his mother, and this is how he calls her: *édesanya*. I'm around seventeen or eighteen, he's almost fifty. I always found this term irritating, perhaps because I addressed my parents in a formal way, even when most of my classmates were on a first name basis. My Romanian acquaintances have never used such formalities, there is something excessive and of course compulsory in this form of address, and there isn't anything suitably cordial and intimate in our relationship. A Székely mate even ridicules me in the army because of this form of address, you are such a country bumpkin, he says. My uncle was left behind by his mother in 1940, she put him out in the backyard, next to the well, this *édes* was my grandfather's first wife, in other words his current mother isn't his natural but his stepmother, and this is how Will tends to call her when he's on a rampage, except that I didn't understand this earlier. The woman he has to call 'édesanya', is in fact his stepmother, although she treats him, in conformity with family tradition, as the birth mother should have done, and the woman who is *édes* put Will out, because, we can't use this word, she was such a, you know what, I don't want to write it down.

We are witnessing a magical night on the Hargita, the deer are rutting somewhere in the distance but we won't make it there today, perhaps tomorrow or next time. I have just learned that nothing is quite the way I have heard or thought so far. I don't even know then that my grandmother was also married before, and had a child from this relationship, Aunt Thea, who also had a first marriage to an alcoholic husband and gave birth to a daughter.

This daughter, in turn, will have an alcoholic husband, just like my grandmother's first and Aunt Thea's second husband, despite them being in all respects at the periphery of the family, as if they represented another culture, which they in a sense do as they don't live in the same bubble as us. It is of course an exaggeration that I find out about all this on that same starry night when Uncle Will tells me about his life in a nutshell, but revelations make me realize that I don't actually understand anything. I hang around the woods with these two giants of my childhood, they burst into tears every now and then, as if I was the only person they could open up to, but I'm not. They actually tend to weep in front of many people, though no one understands them any better than I do, perhaps because they are unable to tell a coherent story, though at times I'm unsure about the existence of a coherent story in the first place. It is up to me to work on such a story, at least this is what I think of myself, being a writer after all. I could easily say, if we were only talking about the woods, that I walk round the woods in the company of weeping giants, but the woods are the least of our worries. The woods aren't good psychiatrists, as they neither ask awkward questions, nor expect precise answers. They don't press questions, only keep silent, and this makes people think that they are right, every word of theirs is true, including the unuttered ones, because they can't or won't articulate them.

When I take a first stab at discovering the truth, because it seems to be quite near and I'm on the right track, my mother nearly knocks me into the middle of next week. By then, she has stopped hitting me but this situation warrants it, her eyes are like fire and I might have had a drink or two. We are having some sort of an argument over other arguments running in the family that shouldn't have taken place, and in case they did, truth is not where the person vindicating the last word claims it is, and anyway, what my mother sanctions as being untrue is simply untrue. We are in a bad mood to start with, of course it's my fault that I kick off by asking about what my uncle told me in the woods, so what's actually happening? My mother instantly snubs me, this isn't so, partly because nothing is the way Uncle Will claims it to be. After all, someone who says about our 'édesanya' that she isn't a natural but a stepmother, yet calls his mother who left him 'édes', despite she being, let's not even say what kind of woman, so whoever denies their actual mother and father and slaps their sister in the face, in full view of everyone when not even drunk, isn't to be trusted. Besides, the latter have raised him, had him educated, built him a house to live in, he was handed everything on a plate and no one had ever reminded him of the fact that his mother had abandoned him by the well, without leaving as much as a farewell note, the 'édes'.

Whenever I try to talk about these events in the future, my mother is on the verge of tears, as if I was reading out some indictment. She usually tells me that I shouldn't say such things, despite the fact that all I want back then is to find out what's true, because I think that there is a silenced truth behind the official facade. We don't even know the question but she has already recited the whole family ideology, it goes so fluently that we both know that there's something dodgy therein. She cannot say anything different, and as for me, I'm not content and can't be content with this, especially since I've also turned into a weeping giant in the woods, albeit without suicidal tendencies as far as I know, though I can't make any firm promises to anyone. As soon as it occurred to me that the forest wasn't a good psychiatrist, and our problems weren't really taking place in the woods anyway, I went to see a psychologist who asked very uncomfortable questions, so I learned that I was telling only half a story, or in case it happened to be a whole one, it was only half true. Everybody goes through a seemingly endless dark hour at some point in their life, when they think through what will happen if they are no longer, and what would happen if they suddenly weren't. This is mainly a matter of vanity with which we keep the world and ourselves in check, but there have been some accidents too. In such moments, I tend to ponder on half of my life's work, fuck the other half, then I go to the woods and think about what I'll say when I'm back where I started from. I'll dip into it here and there, but usually won't, or not like that. Speaking of life-work, or half of it in my case, I tend to mull over ways of continuing the plot while I'm out walking in the woods, I'll definitely end up writing something else, and usually that will work, or will at least prevail.

V

The Other Side

I'd have plenty of material for a great Transylvanian novel even if my family comprised only of Székely relatives who thought that they were living their modest, quiet and pious life in peace and harmony, despite passionately hating one another and despite every question and comment revealing some hitherto silenced or untrue aspect of reality (in conditions when those inquiring into this would find themselves threatened by paternal slaps in the face or maternal curses on the mere basis of intention, hypothesis or speaking up); and even if I only had to take stock of what took place in Barót, Szárazajta, and in general in Székely Land between the marching in of Horthy's army and the Russian occupation, or the pillaging of Maniu's Guard members, the exploits of comrades in charge of collectivization or the contribution of socialism until Ceaușescu's fall, let alone its legacy. It would seem that I have always wanted to write something along these lines, this is what I've always been preparing for, this is why I'm researching my immediate and broader homeland, this is why I explore woods, villages, towns and archives, though I now know that I'm in fact only hiding from myself. The Székely relatives would be more than sufficient, and a particularly attractive material at that, since reality and our image of ourselves rarely coincide, and novelists can rejoice in this enchanted neurosis until the end of their days. The great novel is right in front of our eyes, all it needs is to be written down, neatly and carefully, and to be structured garrulously: stern father, abandoned child, religious fury, Trianon, Northern Transylvania, Ceaușescu, Hungarians, Székelys, Romanians, and splattered with lies wherever no truth can be found. I don't mean the multiple or branching-out variety but lies regarding the lives of men and women, a lot of suffering, little sex and loads of alcohol, or perhaps there should be loads of sex with loads of alcohol, incest is no longer fashionable these days or it isn't an issue, so let's throw in some paedophilia, that's in demand, it doesn't need to be legitimized but can be approached in some pseudo-dialect, together with a touch of Transylvanian gastronomy, pure nature, mineral water and bear shit. So what if my tractorist Uncle ended up in hell because he was gay, perhaps raped as a child, there is of course a more heroic narrative according to which he joined a Székely resistance movement, the wild Hargita bikers, who wanted to reclaim Lake Saint Anna from the Securitate agents and hung the Hungarian flag on Csala Tower. In the end, the Securitate agents got the upper hand, and it may well be that they had given Tom a large dose of morphine because he had resisted until the bitter end, even though we don't know what and whom he resisted. In any event, one could riff on this topic a lot further.

God will punish you if you write such things, my mother observed after she had read the first draft of this manuscript. She doesn't say that I'm lying or that this isn't so, except that in her view, such things are not meant to be articulated, neither to oneself nor others. At this point, she doesn't yet know that she's also a character in this story, but she can sense that I'm sarcastic and ironic despite not realizing that most of my material actually comes from her narratives, and I know all this from her. These are topics we don't talk about, we just blurt them out whenever we forget about the prohibition, and emotion makes us ignore the barriers of speech. Within my mother, there is a whole world in hiding and in denial, which occasionally gushes out with elemental force. Yet as soon as she becomes aware of what she's saying and that I'm listening, she brings this flow to an end with some practical observation. I only find out much later that she burns the majority of carefully guarded letters and notes, and that she screens family photos and makes all negatives disappear as she used to be the family photographer for ages. She acts like an uncompromising censor, and she's not the only one, since both her younger and older sister think the same way, they share the same ideology, though they often remember different things or details, which is entirely normal, but then they boo or lecture one another because this or that wasn't actually quite like so.

I'd have my work cut out for me even if this was all to take on board. It isn't. Because my father, in whose view *but* is not a word we tend to start sentences with, looks down on them, like people from the Great Hungarian Plain usually tend to do, and this comes naturally to him, it goes without saying, so it doesn't even occur to him that this isn't right. My mother is Székely, I'm half-Székely, and if he has issues with this, then he himself should be talked down to, or these other people with whom he has somewhat mingled, shouldn't be. As if he allegedly didn't even know who these people were or what all this could lead to, but in hindsight—we are always looking at things in hindsight—he insists that he isn't like them, he's different as he is Hungarian. There is some sort of pride and sense of superiority in this Hungarianness that can only be perceived in relation to other kinds of being Hungarian, to an extent because linguistic nuances are only apparent to other Hungarians. After all, a German, French or even Romanian person wouldn't be able to follow the gist of all this, despite differences and divisions existing within all national groups. Behind every egalitarian ambition, there is a strict hierarchy that isn't governed by reason, and one doesn't have to rely on a vivid imagination in order to admit that best is the way things are done in one's village, town or street, or at least that was the real deal as long as there was such a thing as one's own village, town and street, and in case these no longer exist, then all the more so. One can take this with a pinch of salt, or entirely in earnest: what sort of people live in a place where sausages are made without any paprika?

The first wave of Székely refugees emerges in inner Transylvania in the wake of the 1916 Romanian invasion, many of them making it as far as the Great Hungarian Plain. We are talking of a population of about hundred thousand, with carts, animals and bundles, poor, frightened and in utter despair, marching along the main road from where the army occasionally orders them off and makes them take to byroads, even though they wouldn't protect them from looters. This isn't the first wave of refugees in Hungarian history which the country can't handle, but unlike the Galicians, the Székelys are Hungarians, or at least this is the official version of history. There's hardly any talk of this event these days, yet it had left deep marks on the collective memory, every subsequent wave of migration is reminiscent of this, the authorities are helpless, the population suspicious and hostile, and it's protective of itself as it has enough to worry about as it is. The saga of migrating Székelys goes on for months, and the government earmarks large sums for their wintering and repatriation. The Székelys are in no rush to get back home, and as it usually turns out—not so much prior to this event, but frequently thereafter—these moneys don't even exist, or in case they do, they end up in the pockets of unscrupulous officials or speculators, and those who'd really need it see none of it yet everyone is blaming them and everything is allegedly their fault. Trianon is next, then the Second World War, and the wave of migration following the 1946 draught in Transylvania and Moldova firmly consolidates the view among Hungarians living on the Romanian segment of the Great Hungarian Plain that there's something deeply wrong with the Székelys. They might be Hungarian, but they speak, think and behave differently, there's always extreme poverty at the times when they come, are allowed to come, are sent here or are brought along. Hungarians couldn't be different from one another anyway, for, in that case, who are we. For Hungarians, especially the ones living on the Hungarian Plain, any form of difference is unacceptable and suspect. After all, even Székelys can be Hungarian but surely not people, just like Gipsies or Romanians aren't people either, though at least they aren't Hungarian, and therefore cannot and will not assimilate anyway. In some villages, they refuse to sell houses to Székelys to this day, or at least they make a point of saying no.

In other words, my father's immediate and extended family looks down on my mother as a matter of course, because she is *just* a Székely girl. Someone dismisses her with a wave of the hand when their intention to get married is announced, and of course this soon comes to my mother's knowledge. They wouldn't say it to her face, but she knows how this is meant. They could just as well call her Romanian, but that would be an actual error, which she could immediately protest against and clarify with some mild indignation, this way, however, there's nothing to be offended about. Neither does my father object to his bride being called a Székely girl, I don't know whether he can actually hear this hurtful 'just', or this is something only Székelys can sense, but for them this has been loud and clear, always and everywhere. They think of Trianon first and foremost, although this sense of inferiority doesn't start there, but it has been bubbling ever since, to near-pathological levels. The gesture with which people deny or question one's Hungarianness at the first regionalism or unusual accent is like a verbal mob law, one shouldn't take it seriously, even though Pannonia had amply demonstrated in the course of the twentieth century that this is a dead serious matter, after all anyone's Hungarianness can be withdrawn at random.

My mother has strong feelings of inferiority anyway, regardless of this. She comes from a poor family, and my grandfather's belonging to the Baptist religion seemed like a particularly unusual thing even in the allegedly tolerant and multi-faceted Transylvania. In the Romania of the fifties, the main enemy is not the Baptist congregation but the historical churches, however, openly belonging to a dogmatic sect is a dangerous matter. My mother is excluded from the Union of Working Youth because she went to a religious instead of a school event, not to a gathering of comrades but to worship god. So this exclusion is a public humiliation, like being put in the pillory, because her family and her father are what they are, back then it wasn't advisable to oppose those in power, people could end up in prison for a lot less. My mother doesn't even understand what's happening in fact, as if everything was taking place above her head, not to mention that she's actually Roman Catholic, following her mother's religion. This is another source of conflict in the family that I struggle to get to grips with, but no one is in a rush to explain it to me. My grandfather, also known as Uncle Gyurika, makes everyone go to the Baptist meeting house, whether they like it or not—he hasn't heard of religious tolerance or the Diet of Torda, the Bible doesn't say anything about that. Matters are more complicated than this in reality, because according to old Romanian legislation, in the case of parents of different denominations, the child's religion can be decided by the father, but my grandparents agree that boys should follow the religion of their fathers and girls that of their mothers, and this custom has persisted in Transylvania to this day. The Baptist church formally allows everyone ample time to get baptised, let them decide what they want, it's a liberal church after all, quite American in this sense, and it's pointless to dwell on what a teenage girl could possibly decide about freely, and how much all this might cost her in emotional terms. My mother is a good student, she's ambitious, hard-working and obedient, and of course she attends a Baptist meeting hall, though for some reason she isn't prepared to get baptised, she's the only child who opposes this, and even in hindsight she can't quite articulate why—just. Nevertheless, she finds herself humiliated on account of the Baptists. No one can be a servant of two masters at the same time, we all know that, but how about three?

And then my mother finds out in 1963 that for the Hungarians in Ágya she's just a Székely girl. She's one of six siblings, grandmother Zsüli notes with horror. Good god, this is worse than what's going on with the Gipsies, perhaps even they have fewer children. In those days, there are an average of two children per family in my father's village, and by the time we get to my generation, having an only child becomes the norm. My grandfather, Joszip Vida is a chronic alcoholic, and so was his father, also called Joszip. This is openly spoken about, we aren't trying to conceal this and nobody thinks that such a thing shouldn't happen in a god-fearing and hard-working family. They aren't afraid of god, nobody likes to work, there's always poverty, truly dreadful poverty, my grandfather went to America twice, yet in vain because he drank everything that's liquid. According to the family saga, he didn't perish on the Titanic because he didn't manage to secure a ticket, but this isn't true since he had left Fiume in 1912. This is the information I obtained from the Ellis Island Digital Archive, where his name is recorded among that of many other immigrants, together with details of the ship called *Ivernia* on which he arrived on 9 May.

Had I not spent the first five years of my life with them, and had I not felt for a long time, in fact forever, that Grandma Zsüli was in fact my mother and Grandpa Joszip my father, I probably wouldn't have to deal with my paternal grandparents at such length, seeing that they had led really simple lives. I have parents too, especially at weekends, they are always tired and rushing to work, they are in the process of building that nice big cube-shaped home in Kisjenő, in which I'll be entirely theirs during the greyest nine years of my life. At Ágya, we don't even live in a proper *house*, but in a summer kitchen directly linked to the stable. At night, one can hear the sheep ruminate on the other side of the mud wall, this is a calming humming sound in the dark, and should we enter, hurricane lamp in hand, their eyes are flashing a green light. There's no electricity in the house, it will only be connected to the grid in 1980 because by then my grandfather's portable radio, on which he could catch twenty-six different Hungarian language channels, had finally given up its ghost, and no battery-operated radio was available in the shops, only models that had to be plugged into the mains. When you die, I'll buy a TV, my grandmother threatens him, and this is indeed what will happen. We used to listen to the radio a lot, Radio Free Europe, Voice of America, Radio Subotica, back then Radio Istanbul had a Hungarian broadcast, too, and so did Radio Beijing.

Our favourite programme is the musical quiz *Játék és muzsika tíz percben* [Ten minutes of play and music]. My grandfather can't contain his amazement at these people who can recognize musical pieces that are incomprehensible to him, though he's actually quite fond of music himself, I must stay quiet while this programme is on. He's usually curled up on the sofa covered with a green blanket, I'm sitting on the small stool, it's twilight, my grandfather is smoking, the fire is burning in the stove and the radio's on, every so often he gets up and takes a swig of brandy or a has a glass of wine, then lies back. We sit together like this and listen to *Abel Alone*, but my grandfather can't make sense of all the words and phrases. As it happens, I can, so when a section is over I try to explain to him what these mountains and forests are actually like, after all I'm Székely myself, but I get irate when people call me 'góbé', I find that term offensive. I object to the fact that there's no talk of bears in *Abel*, I feel somewhat let down by this, because we have been to the places mentioned in the book and have seen bears there. I'll find out much later that there are hardly any bears on the Hargita at that time, and only the odd one here and there in the rest of Romania, however, there'll be many more of them as of the sixties, in order to please the communist comrades, annoy shepherds and farmers, and bring joy to us all.

Peter and the Wolf was another programme my grandfather and I listened to together. This is the first cultural experience of my life that continues to remind me of that endless dark fear, of loneliness and anxiety. It's summer, or at least the weather is warm because the doors are wide open, my grandfather is sitting at the table cutting tobacco, whenever he doesn't have money for cigarettes he just keeps smoothing and wetting the tobacco leaves he had himself collected and cuts them with a sharp knife. He is retelling one of his wartime memories, he served in the Romanian Army as a gendarme in Temesvár and the Bánát area. I recall him talking of a warehouse in flames, wherefrom a group of Russian soldiers are trying to steal some tobacco, even at the cost of their lives as many of them perish inside. There's still a piece of tanned leather in our larder, of the sort officers would have had coats made from, after all the leather factory had also been blown to smithereens or bombed and then looted. I can barely hear my grandfather's stories, all these war stories blur into one, there are many people like him in our village, every time they gather for a drink or a round of card games they talk of nothing else but the war, wondering when the Americans or Brits will finally arrive. Never, Grandma Zsüli says curtly, and the other elderly women agree. They are more or less like the women in Tiszazug, they share the same experiences and the same worldview, rancour and headscarves pulled over their eyes, representing the only form of opposition to this regiment of drunken old geezers, life had nothing good in store for them, and in case it had, they can't remember it any longer. As for my Rhédei grandmother, it hasn't even come up that we might have something to do with the family of earls with the same name, of course we haven't. My grandmother is an embittered and spiteful woman who was embroiled in a court case over some bits of land with her own mother, following which they didn't speak to each other for thirty years despite living at the same address. When my grandfather falls off the ladder leading to the attic and can't get up from the floor, *she just leaves, heading to the village*, get up by yourself, Vida, she says. Grandfather crawls into bed, straight from the mud, he isn't actually drunk at the time yet his heel bone will never heal again. I find out from Grandma Zsüli that my mother and Uncle Will aren't full siblings or blood siblings as she calls it, and my mother goes nuts at the mere mention of it. My grandmother, on the other hand, is the kind of woman who looks as if God had made her with the express aim of turning her into a mother-in-law, or a witch, she can see and understand everything, she's harsh, outspoken, ruthless, and doesn't follow norms or like anybody, me included.

I can't get away from Prokofiev, Grandfather somehow vanishes beyond the music, it's wartime, there's a grey horse on which he's galloping past a building in flames, they keep shooting at him in vain, he can't be found. Meanwhile, the wolf eats the duck, and I know that the twig fence around our garden is flimsy and wobbly. It surely won't be an obstacle in case a wolf wanted to come in, and I'm unable to climb the walnut tree, even its lowest branch is too high for me, I'm a bad climber anyway, skinny and weak. Wherever we end up, we always live at the edge of the village, in Ágya gardens are the size of football pitches, the street is fifty metres wide, apparently on Empress Maria Theresia's orders, so that fire couldn't spread from one row of straw or reed-covered roofs to the other. There's space to waste anyway, this is the Romanian section of the Great Hungarian Plain after all. Next to our garden is the field, it's a barely tended orchard known as the Kenderes garden, and beyond that it's just pastures and wasteland, complete with marshes, reed, clump, salt and fata morgana. Petőfi will be my favourite poet for many years to come, day after day I keep dipping into a volume published in 1878. I'm a great admirer of Mihály Zichy's etchings and my favourite poem is *Kutyakaparó*, until I swap it with *National Song*, that's the first poem I learn by heart out of my own initiative and spurred by patriotic enthusiasm, but somehow I keep replacing the fourth stanza with the fifth, no idea why. A stork is nesting on the roof of our house and I have to guard the newly born chicks because, unlike the children's rhyme, in vain do Hungarian children heal the wounded and blood-stained feet of storks, these birds aren't choosy and just grab the first chick. They aren't afraid of the hen, the rooster, or me for that matter, so this stork just swishes with its beak when I try to grab its neck, and simply flies away, up to the chimney where it starts clappering triumphantly. I have no chance at getting my revenge using my slingshot or bow and arrows, my grandmother insists on getting the hunter to shoot the stork, but I wouldn't like this to happen, so it doesn't. Storks are useful birds, they eat snakes, of which there are many in the area and I'm afraid of them, there are frogs too, and many other species, but I'm not afraid of those.

My third defining radio experience is about the Hungarian events in 1956, it's a terrible wartime radio play in which they depict the carnage brought about by counter-revolutionaries. I remember vividly the scene where an evil counter-revolutionary rips out the heart of a man hanging upside down, but this heroic heart manages to beat a few more times before landing on the ground, by which time the brave liberating Soviet army is already around the corner. I might later say that this took place at the Corvin köz in Budapest, but I can't make sense of this at the time, my grandfather is carefully listening to the script and then suddenly switches the radio off, saying in an angry voice: these bloody fucking communists! He swears for ages, like when he's cursing the smoking stove and the slaty coal, bringing everyone's mother as well as God into the mix. What happened in 1956, I ask with deep concern, and my grandfather explains that the *cececes* called in the Russians who once again blew Budapest to smithereens. The Russians and the *cececes* have been in charge ever since, because those motherfucking Americans didn't get involved, they didn't fucking drop their nuclear bomb on Moscow. I'm about eight, perhaps nine, and I've learned that the socialist regime we live in and have built is the best social arrangement in the world. I can come up with a whole raft of reasons, we've learnt this at school, and my mother goes on about this, too, in the old regime we didn't even have enough to eat, despite the fact, as grandfather points out, that she wasn't actually alive in the old regime, yes, but she learned this, I say to sometimes defend my mother.

My grandfather tells me on this occasion that in 1946 he sold two young bullocks because he wanted to buy a horse. He had always dreamt about a horse, but Alexander, his younger brother, persuaded him to buy a tractor instead, which was later taken away from them, and so was the land. Some people were beaten to death because they didn't want to hand their belongings over, others just went home, lied down and stopped living, died of the grief that the land and horse was no longer theirs. My grandmother just nods when she hears this, and then suddenly bursts out, you haven't even had any land, Vida, the land was mine, and yes, they've taken it away. They rarely agree on anything, having hated each other for a lifetime, for over fifty years of living together. The world turns into a scary place in the wake of this first lesson in politics, because I understand that nothing is the way my mother and my teachers say. How come we have everything if they took the tractor away from Grandfather, the tractor that should have in fact been a horse? The radio play carries on, it must be a series, one horrific detail after the other, but by then I know that this wasn't quite like that, in fact everything was the other way round.

My grandfather also tells me about a species of snake that he calls *büntős*, and he shows what that means with his hands. It takes time, perhaps years, for me to understand that he is talking about vipers. They used to live in the surrounding woods but have now died out, this snake tends to hold its tail in its mouth when fleeing or chasing an enemy, and it rolls like a bicycle wheel, being fairly thick with a whip-like pattern on its back. There's mention of snakes rolling about in hoops all over the Hungarian-speaking areas, from Székely Land to Lake Balaton, but having checked numerous dictionaries and asked linguists and ethnographers, the term '*büntős*' snake must be one of those words that only I'm familiar with, it may well crop up somewhere one day, in case it wasn't a plain misunderstanding. Many many years later, after my grandfather's death, I spot the tail of a smooth snake sliding under the dry leaves in the forest at Ágya. I poke at it, I'm no longer afraid of snakes, though I'd rather not touch them, and I'm quite right as this isn't an ordinary smooth snake but a common European viper. I instantly recognize its triangular head, and as it pulls its neck back and swishes at the stick in my hand, it turns out that it's a proper *büntős*.

The forest at Ágya is much more sinister than the one at Barót, when I'm there as a child I'm not afraid of bears, wolfs or packs of shepherd dogs, but of a historical event, seeing that prince László Habsburg–Lotharingen happened to die here in 1895 in a bizarre hunting accident. They even erected a chapel in his memory, in my childhood it used to stand abandoned and looted, none of the children had the courage to go there on their own, or even as a group, it was surrounded by marshland and giant oaks, looking every inch an abandoned and cursed place. When I finally go there with my surrogate uncle, it seems to me as if someone was watching us, we find the corpse of a roebuck hanging by the wrought iron fence in front of the altar. I'm somewhat disappointed that nothing happened, by then I have seen dead animals in the meadows and in the woods, I know that I shouldn't touch them, but there's not a single ghost in sight, of course it's pointless to scare me with made-up beings. Since we spend so much time in the dark, I've learned that darkness isn't scary in itself, it's empty at best. This emptiness is residing in us though, we are this emptiness, and we populate it with beings and images of beings, and I know full well that the giant snake can't possibly hide behind the chimney on which there's a stork's nest and where the stork took back the chick it had snatched. That summer, I end up spending time in the attic because it keeps raining for weeks, and to kill time I shell corn, it's a great pastime that hardens my fingers. There's all sorts of trash in the attic, one could tidy them away or try to guess what's what, a wired pot, a fistful of twenty millimetre cartridge cases, a spinning wheel, a loom, cog wheels, ploughshares and an entire pile of other junk that I don't even know the name of. The rain keeps falling or pouring rather, and my grandfather is always drunk, he's curled up in bed, his cigarette usually falling out of his hands. One time, my grandmother puts out the burning blanket, pouring an entire bucket of water on him, but all grandfather says in his sleep is 'this bloody rain', he turns over and carries on sleeping, the water seeping out of the pallet gathers into puddles under the bed, but the cob floor just drinks it in. He has just been to Kisjenő, being a voluntary blood donor, his blood is B Rh (–), for which he gets a tidy sum by the standards of those times, and while it lasts, he doesn't tend to sober up, I have the same blood type but this doesn't yet mean much to me. I keep fumbling in the attic for days on end, shelling corn, cracking walnuts, I set a trap for the sparrows preening in the attic door but I fail to catch any. Suddenly, I sense that a giant snake is lurking behind the chimney, it must be an anaconda, I have just read something along these lines, and although I immediately go there to check, I won't be able to see it because it will always hide on the other side of the chimney. After a while, I start carrying an axe as well, to have something to protect myself with in case it was to attack me. I also take some cigarettes, just to try them, but I find them really awful. The last thing I'd need is for the snake to tell on me, I'd swat it straightaway then, but being a clever beast it won't grass on me or attack me, yet one day it suddenly isn't there anymore, so I also stop heading to the attic for my daily dose of fear.

The reason why Grandfather isn't always drunk is that village people are always short of money, there's simply nothing to drink when he runs out of home-made wine and brandy, and has nothing left of his meagre pension. True, he also rummages for surgical spirit and pre-distilled brandy that Grandmother stores away in order to soak lily petals in them in case they need a remedy for wounds and boils. He also knows that Grandmother has the habit of hiding the odd bottle of brandy in her wardrobe, cupboard or other such places, you never know, it might come in handy for the doctor in case we are ill or need anything sorted out, brandy is hard currency around these parts. My grandfather objects in principle to the idea of hidden brandy, and like all alcoholics, he's very resourceful, one can find the hidden alcohol if one searches thoroughly, or in case I help, too, after all Grandmother can't always make sure that I'm not around to witness the misleading manoeuvres of concealment and redeployment. Once these extra bottles I find are also gone, and his drinking buddies run out of supplies, there's nothing left but a period of sobering up. This is when he tells stories, and my favourite time with him. He makes bows, carves guns and swords, takes me fishing and trailing the woods, we do all sorts of things together, we work, collect insects, fix the odd broken item, saw wood, carve beams, bend wooden forks, hammer scythes, and all this at a slow and leisurely pace. He doesn't educate me, he just demonstrates something, I try to copy him, he shows it again, we sit down, he lights up, we take a rest, go for walk, come back, time is endless. I'm always fully involved with whatever we happen to be doing, weaving fences out of twigs, picking plums or rolling watermelons, skinning sheep, stuffing and plucking geese, heating stoves or baking bread. The entire house, backyard and garden is mine, perhaps the only thing I'm not allowed to touch is the lye when we're making soap. I can put logs on the fire, I watch my grandfather grab some embers in between his fingers to light his cigarette, the skin on his hands is that crusty, but in case there's fuel in the lighter, I'm allowed to give him a light myself. He lets me cut tobacco on the threshold, he shows me how to tear out the veins from the leaves, how to roll them up and kneel on them, and then start slicing, thinly and evenly with the largest and sharpest breadknife we have. We gather tobacco in the fields, and then string it in garlands, as we tend to string the paprika as well, the best smell is to be found in paprika mills, perhaps with the exception of dried ham or Grandma's mutton stew, she also adds offal to it, that's a key ingredient. My favourite food is a sort of cheesy dough ball, called 'túrós gubó', when baking bread Grandma pops a few walnut-sized dough balls on a baking tray, when they are baked they have to be scalded and then served with cheese or sour cream, the other is 'lángos' baked on the wooden peel, that I like eating folded in four, with goose fat. The oven needs to be heated further for this, until its floor sparkles at the mere contact with the scraper, this is hard work, I have to keep gathering and throwing in dried stalks, then scrape the ash out, watching the flames all along. In case I come across suitable stalks, we fashion them into violins and I squeak on them, my grand-father teaches me the tune of Sándor Rózsa, just like he was once taught by his own father, 'his horse stumbled on the root of a tree, this is how they captured Sándor Rózsa for free'. In my imagin-ation, this must have happened somewhere by the chapel.

One evening we head over to Vilma's, who lives at the back of our garden, to collect our dues. We don't say that we are going to the Patkány family, despite that being their name, somehow the entire village is embarrassed to utter this as it means rat, so we just say Vilmathegipsy's. Their son Zólti will later be my classmate, we were born on the same day in the same hospital, initially my name was also meant to be Zoltán, but my mother was tipped off that in Ágya every single Gipsy boy is Zólti, so I ended up as Gábor. My mother gets really angry with me one day, and blurts out that I'm actually not her son but a Gipsy woman's, that we were swapped at birth in the hospital. I immediately think of Zólti Patkány, that I am he, I don't know why my mother chose to say this at that point, I guess she must have been taught to frighten children with such claims—dark man, bogey man, owl with the copper dick. Zólti is my brother for a while, then he pegs at me, so I grab him in front of our house. We grapple for a while, but the thing is that they live far away, in a different world, I'm not allowed to go there, so we tend to meet in the chest-high grass at the end of the garden, he's not afraid of snakes and shows me how to get hold of them, they are harmless, but I'm too scared. We aren't able to talk much to each other because I stammer and he barely says anything, we mainly sit around in the grass under the walnut tree, seeing that we can't yet climb it. Occasionally my grandmother comes to find me and orders me in, she then sends Zólti home, no one ever tries to get him.

As we are heading to this first meeting, Grandfather brings an axe with a long handle, and I carry a storm lamp. The light is on at Vilma's, but not yet at ours, it's dark and muddy in the village, there are no street lights around here, only packs of stray dogs, hence the axe, Vilma's family is harmless. Their house is larger than ours, and one can tell from the remaining furniture, windows, doorframes and tiles in the hall that it used to belong to a wealthy family, it certainly wasn't a peasant house back then. There are kids all over the kitchen floor, on rags and bits of straw, Zólti is there, too, but I don't yet know him then, he's one of the many kids, that's all. Vilma seems to be a little pissed, her beautiful hair is let down, she's about thirty but looks like a wrinkled old hag in her stripy man's shirt. With a cigarette butt in her mouth and sporting a bored look, she tells us that there's no fuel, no corn and no money, she can't return the amount she borrowed last week or last year, her man has yet again been at the police station and they've beaten him black and blue, I can't remember what else she says. Grandfather lowers the axe, I blow the storm lamp out, and we breathe in the stench for a while, then visit someone else, to borrow some fuel, money or corn. So that your grandmother stops cackling, Grandfather says in an angry voice. We are trudging the muddy streets but won't light the lamp, and head straight to the pub from where he brings me home clinging to his neck, he's drunk by then, every so often falling over in the mud.

To this day I'm unsure why we went to Vilma's, perhaps Grandma sent us to collect some debt, or Grandpa wanted to show me what poverty really was, it was a study trip of sorts, and perhaps an excuse to go to the pub. Aunt Vilma often works for us, she plasters the outside wall of our house, I always have to alert people when I see horse droppings on the streets because we collect the manure, it's used for the plastering. One day, I witness a tiny bug with a shiny carapace crawl out of the cracks of the freshly plastered wall, and fly away. So I keep staring at the crack for ages, in case other bugs come out, but they don't, and I can no longer tell whether there was indeed a bug in there or I was only imagining it. There were no children of my age in the neighbourhood except for Évike and her younger sister, but one summer the little one died of meningitis, Évike was taken by her parents to Arad, and I ended up entirely on my own. This is the fault of the old woman, my grandmother says, who hated all women in the neighbourhood. She had to go far for a little company, to Aunt Lidi or to her sister-in-law, who wasn't really her sister-in-law only Uncle Polyánki's wife, but we called her so regardless. Aunt Lidi was a tiny old woman with a stooped posture. I enjoyed spending time at theirs, it was a sort of time travel, they had no clocks, watches or wardrobes, they kept everything in a chest. They would grind corn for the chicken using a handmill, the millstone bearing the mark 1806, though I was unable to read these numbers back then. The hens would sleep on the mulberry tree, and the rammed earth wall of their house was even thicker than ours, so thick in fact that I could barely step over the threshold. On the only wall that had seen some decorating, there was a hand painted oil picture, showing twenty-six dogs being transported across a river in a boat. I could have looked at it forever, and don't understand to this day how this painting could possibly end up there, whose it was and where it came from, as it is dead certain that they didn't buy it themselves.

Sanyi Kappan was their son, he was the village idiot who talked all sorts of rubbish, giggling and cackling all along, he was also the main purveyor of gossip, and he knew something squalid about everyone. My grandmother was his godmother, so he came to see us quite often, and in case we didn't keep a watchful eye on him, he'd gobble up all the scones, cakes and apples. He'd have three helpings of soup, he was always hungry despite being offered some food everywhere he went. He even demolished a whole bucket of plums we had just picked in the garden. My grandfather had sent him to empty the bucket into the barrel in which they were collecting the mash, but he kept being delayed, and when he finally turned up, he told us, as he guffawed, that he had actually eaten all the plums. Grandfather was livid, you'll drop dead, you idiot, he said to him, but all Sanyi did was snigger and repeat this ditty, 'grandpa'n the plum orchard, fartin' away like no joke', finally running away in his oversized and tattered wellies. Needless to say, he came to no harm. He seemed to know that the reason for being such a loony was that he was frightened to death by Russian soldiers as a child. Yet the Russians didn't actually make it to Ágya, only the Romanians, who had even shot a boy in front of the church because he didn't stop when ordered to do so, I have seen his grave in the cemetery myself. The soldiers were followed by Romanian villagers from the neighbouring Nagyszintye, they came to ransack Ágya because the Hungarian soldiers had used this location to shoot at them with their canons. They spared our house because they recognized Grandma Zsüli, she came from their village and spoke decent Romanian, seeing that they were the settlers there.

Grandfather really enjoyed talking about his father, who had been to America and burned his leg with liquid iron in a foundry, almost all his money went on doctors and treatment, and he drank the rest, but at least he wasn't sent off to war, he came back limping, and continued to limp for the rest of his life. He had even brought an almanac back from his journey, it contained lots of interesting things, such as the sinking of the Titanic in colour print, and the launch of the Prinz Eugen battleship. Plenty of people had written their names on its pages in the process of reading it, we know nothing of them except for the fact that they must have laid hands on the almanac at some point, and later lost it while moving house. When we are not listening to the radio, I tend to read out loud passages from *Toldi* for him, that's his favourite, and I like it a lot too. I don't understand or enjoy *David Copperfield*, or *Švejk*, yet I often read them out loud. A woman in the neighbourhood gave these titles to us, she's from Slovakia, she was brought along by the war, or to be precise, by German soldiers, she's been smattering in Hungarian ever since, as for Romanian, she didn't even bother to learn it. There are other Slovaks around here too, but Aunt Bözsi always insists on setting herself apart: I'm a proper Slovak, these others are only 'tót'. Hašek is a great Slovak writer, she says, and your Petőfi is Slovak too, we don't argue over this, after all she's the one in the know. I like Aunt Bözsi, she's nice in a very different way from my grandmother or other women like her, perhaps it's her accent, or that she's a touch more joyful, she comes round often and says interesting things, mainly about the splendid High Tatra mountains and that she'll return there one day. Grandmother tends to dismiss this out of hand, she has never seen mountains of any description, only Romanians and Székelys come from the mountains, nobody ever returns there, and anyway, even bread is made out of stone and wood in those parts.

It's usually Aunt Bözsi who tells us what's happening in the village, everything tends to happen around the artesian well a kilometre or so away from here, and she goes to collect water with a three-litre pitcher several times a day. Her cunt must be itching to walk this far for three litres of water, Grandmother observes. We also get our drinking water from there, the water in our well isn't drinkable, there's allegedly a sword in it, left behind by a Hungarian officer who went into hiding. Despite looking for it with long slats, we can't find it, so one day I throw the lid of our enamel water pitcher into the well, so there's finally something in it apart from frogs, but Grandmother gives me a good hiding. I tend to pay no heed to her repeated calls, and anyway, there's a quince twig hanging on the coat rack, so it's always at hand in case it's needed. I don't think I received a lot of beating, but I do recall this punishment when Grandfather suddenly growls and curses out so wildly that my grandmother shows signs of fear, and I begin to pay attention even beyond my tears and pain. Only Aunt Zsófi tends to excel at such curses, usually when the men are playing cards and she's looking on, standing behind her husband, but he doesn't listen to her advice and ends up losing, so Aunt Zsófi lets out a 'may this bloody god stick his stinky and filthy cock up your arse', and carries on endlessly and irately. I don't yet understand that they are playing for money. Whenever Grandfather wins, and he wins quite often, we go to the pub.

I naturally have only few memories from the first five years of my life. The first one is that we are travelling through an amazing brightness, the sky and the landscape gleaming all around us, and there's a single row of poplars, marking the road ahead. In 1970, the river Fehér-Körös flooded the village, breaking the dam and surrounding the village with water. A new embankment is put up in great haste, this is called *dimony*. Women and children are rescued, there are no fatalities, but the Romanian part of the village known as the *Colonia* is entirely under water. The Romanians brought in as settlers don't know at the time that this area isn't suitable for building houses, the land here is situated a metre or two lower than the rest, and this difference is a matter of life or death on the Plain. I'm two, standing in the midst of random belongings on a tipper truck, and someone, obviously my grandmother, is holding on real tight to my hand. My grandfather refuses to leave the house, he knows that it's built high up so the water won't reach it, but the well and den will be filled with water, there are deep puddles in most gardens and this former waterland will continue to claim its dues for months to come. I try to imagine my grandfather standing in the doorway, staring at the tractor heading off on the sea-like mud-covered street, it stops everywhere to pick up women and children—I guess this must have happened with the Titanic, too—he then shuts the gate, the *street-door*, and only he knows what he's thinking about. There's water everywhere as far as the eye can see, our house is built of earth and the floor is a hand span lower than the threshold, but my grandfather knows that the water won't get in. He takes a seat on the threshold, lights a cigarette, pours himself a glass of brandy, and then another, he must know that this half a metre will make all the difference, or perhaps he doesn't, and what he actually thinks is—let the water pour in and just take whatever it likes.

There's another scene, when I'm really young, as if I couldn't yet speak or utter sounds, but I can see and hear, and perhaps even understand everything. My grandfather is drunk, he isn't tottering like he usually does, but he doesn't quite head in the direction he'd like to go or where he started off. He's chopping wood for some time, his hand movements are precise as he used to be a woodcutter for years, in winter they'd carve railway sleepers in the Réz Mountains or in the area where the Berettyó river springs, he'd never let go of his axe or hatchet, not even when he could barely walk for in that case he'd actually need them for support. Coal is piled up in huge blocks in the shed, of which he breaks off chunks with his axe, I like the smell of brown coal, it often has brownish-yellow veins, back then I don't yet know that coal originates in wood, for us it's just a kind of rock that burns. We fill the basket with wood and coal and go back to the house, it's cold and we have to light the stove. Grandfather grabs the basket and asks me to open the gate to the flower garden, but he can't quite find it, not even on the second attempt, the coal falls out of the basket, we pick them up, he then bumps into the doorpost, starts swearing, but then we finally make it inside. He's heading to the larder to drink some wine, but then remembers to light the fire, also he doesn't have the rubber tube needed to transfer wine from one container to another, for some reason that's in the summer kitchen. He sends me to fetch it, I rattle through the oak board lying across the courtyard, that's our footway, I like the way it's thumping and the mud is squelching underneath, I fetch the rubber tube and the bottle, once again thumping along the plank. I'm really keen, I don't know where Grandmother is, it's dusk already and my hand is stinging from the cold. Grandfather is kneeling by the stove, blowing on the embers, the stove is spilling smoke into the room. I like the smell of coal smoke, especially when pouring out onto the streets on winter nights. Right now it's bad news, he's always in a foul mood when this happens indoors, he's cursing those bloody fucking communists, may God the almighty finally plonk the heavens upon them, this roll carries on of course, but I don't want to hear it, I'm really scared.

This isn't the first time I'm devatting wine, I know exactly how to attach the rubber tube siphon to the fifty-litre demijohn and slowly blow air into it until it reaches the wine. When the wine starts to bubble, one needs to draw in a few times and swallow some air so that the tasty sourish juice appears in the wake of the bouquet, I'm allowed one sip but not more. One has to be quick at fitting the rubber tube over the end of the bottle, and to make sure to remove it on time, when the bottle is full to the rim, not a single drop should land on the floor, which would be embarrassing. I don't quite understand why brandy is now in the demijohn, it's beyond horrible, hurting my mouth, throat and stomach, this fright almost makes me burst into tears, I spit a large mouthful on the floor, this will lead to trouble, but I'm on my way, taking it to Grandpa and making it clear that this was brandy. He doesn't say a word, the stove is still smoking, he carries on cursing, come what may, where there's smoke, there's fire. Later, my grandfather heads out to the shed, tottering badly, he stops every now and then in his tracks, looks up to the sky and then wobbles along the barn, holding on to pillars on his way. To be fair, this isn't quite a barn but a straw roof mounted on pillars, underneath which they store the hay, the hens lay their eggs and the cat gives birth to its kittens. Grandfather is standing there, crumbling and panting, with a chain in his hand, he's trying to do something with it but I can't figure out what, I can see he's drunk, so I think I should help him. He's trying to throw one end of the chain over the cross-beam under the eaves, he succeeds after several attempts and is then holding on to it, but soon falls over and pulls the chain after him, so it ends up rattling in the mud. I don't know what it is that he's trying to do, so I go over to check close up, he's throwing the chain again and holding on to it for ages, like someone who wants to pull himself up, but I have no idea whereto. All of a sudden he looks at me, lets go of the chain which then starts swinging idly, we keep staring at each other for a while, then Grandmother appears from the blue, strikes like a black blizzard and drags me away. There's a particular phase in Grandfather's drunkenness when he always wants to hang himself, but in such moments he can no longer handle the rope or the chain, Grandmother is quite certain in this regard, or perhaps it's all the same to her by now. I often hear Grandfather pray to God: please take me away, my Lord, so I won't live to see another day!

Church was an interesting place, too, in the days when grandfather was the assistant bell-ringer and had a watch that he borrowed. It was impossible to read the exact time on the dirty brown face of the alarm clock lying about on the window sill, even though this watch also had a brown clock face, and it was hanging lose on his thin arm, fastened by a wide strap held together with a copper buckle. To be honest, I was expecting this watch to fall off his wrist, but Grandfather had giant hands, I was also afraid that he'd fall asleep and we'd miss ringing the bells, it would have been really embarrassing if at noon the bells of the nearby churches had rung earlier. Yet this never actually happened, Grandfather would always wake up on time and we'd head to the belfry as if we had the most important job in the whole wide world. While Grandfather was pulling the ropes, to ring the small bell because the large one was cracked, I was on cloud nine, delighted that we were in charge of bell-ringing, and overwhelmed with pride and joy at the sight of Szalonta Tower where János Arany used to live. I'm still not sure why I don't just say, whenever I have to explain myself, that every time I went up to the attic in my childhood, on a clear day I could see both Szalonta Tower and Világos Fortress. *Naturam furca expellas* . . .

VI

The Stammer

I don't, and probably couldn't recall when I actually started to stammer. I can only picture myself as someone who has always been stammering, but this isn't quite right, there's no such thing—no one is born with a stammer. Yet someone notices at some point, and there you are. At some point, someone brings it up. At some point, someone corrects you. Then they realize and diagnose—I stammer, falter, and have a speech defect. I don't understand what the problem is, but I have to repeat what I say, over and over again, and it's never right, it won't work even if they kill me: slower, say it again, pay attention, not good . . . I'm standing on a bed in a surgery room, with my feet on the rubber mat, it's soft and creaks when I drag my shoe soles over it. They make me recite a poem, there are three women in white uniforms enjoying this, and it's actually quite fun for me too, it's easy for some reason, although I hate the stench of disinfectant. I find it quite bizarre to recite poems at the doctor's, but everyone's very kind, only my mother is angry with me when we eventually leave, because I jumped off the bed, although I did ask whether I was allowed to do so and the lady doctor, her stethoscope around her neck, said yes. Despite that, my mother tried to grab my arm—what sort of behaviour is this, son?! She was already in a bad mood when we got there, but I was reciting really well, no idea what was wrong, I didn't fall over and hurt myself, did I? This is my first memory of something not quite being right. Years will pass without me having a clue, no idea how many.

The lady doctor in Arad is beautiful, she looks like Victoria Principal in *Dallas*—a composed, American face that doesn't belong to the world we live in, she has a flamboyant charm but doesn't understand anything and just wants to cure me, like all the others. She hands me a prescription for medication of all sorts, praises me for speaking so well, and I'm not blinking that often anymore, not when I'm looking into her eyes, not then, but if I'm looking at the dolls and soft toys in the glass cabinet, and fail to pay attention to what she says, then I still do. They don't say that I stammer but that I fumble for words. It's always the same scenario, we wait for our turn among drooling and jerking children, after hours of queuing and elbowing we finally make it to doctor Pamela, who recognizes us and is seemingly pleased to see us, finally a simple case to handle. She talks to me at length, and longer still to my mother. She writes a prescription, adding her doctor's stamp, we say our goodbyes and leave through the main exit, where the red stone balustrade used to feature an angel just about to unfold from a sheet, it had attractive legs and arms and a characterless face, but by now, only the pedestal has survived. When I'm a bit older it occurs to me that the face of doctor Pamela would fit this body, but it may well be that I'm making this connection only now. I enjoy going to the surgery, I recite, we talk and then we head to the banks of the river Maros, there's a playground with several swings, a boat bridge over the river, and the thirteen martyrs in the museum, or rather their relics, though I know that there were actually fourteen. In those days only the smaller items, such as coins, bullets and documents, are kept in glass display cases, the larger ones are mainly on free display, and the attendant even allows me to take a pistol and sword in hand. We are the only visitors at the museum, this being a weekday morning. My favourite general is Damjanich, and I keep thinking that the sword used to belong to him, it will take years until I accept that the sword was actually that of an officer in the First World War, it was a genuine artefact nevertheless. I could with ease be a museum guide myself, quite so clever that I am, but after a visit to doctor Pamela I come across the Dacians, Dacian relics and Daco-Roman artefacts that I find more petrifying. There are monstrous flags and drapes, in addition to bad lighting, the smell of glue and blue crepe paper everywhere, and above and beyond the menace of all this, there's Ceaușescu's portrait hovering about, the president sporting a polka-dotted tie, just like my father.

Suddenly, not even leaning as close as possible to the glass case will do it for me in order to examine the various tiles and tiny, faded Roman coins on display. My carefree museum-visiting days are over, and I still long for that, though perhaps not quite enough. I stick with the medication, the sundry restorative tonics, fortunately I can't recall the name of any, but you can probably picture these ministrations—these placebos I've been taking just to placate Mother, except for a few particularly bitter liquids I simply had to protest. Between seeing the child psychiatrist and heading to the station, I examine the objects that used to belong to the Arad martyrs, and on our way home, I tell my mother what I saw at the museum. I explain the difference between a musket, an airgun and a firearm, but the truth is that Hawkeye's gun is much better than any of these . . . We've been to see the doctor, I'm ill, my mother had to take a day off work, and I was off school. I stammer. My mother, despondent—nothing has come to light or been resolved, but for me, this day was another pleasant experience.

This is in hindsight, of course—I remember the end rather than the beginning—the bit when doctor Pamela tells me that I'll only do something about the stammer when it will bother me personally. Only then will I try to remedy it, will I carry out the prescribed pacing, articulation and breathing exercises, and pay attention and concentrate—all will be well, and she won't prescribe any more medication. I'm fourteen, have started school in Arad, and she adds that I can now come and see her on my own. You don't say! No one is willing or able to tell me in hindsight what my problem actually was, and soon there won't be anyone left who could have a clue. Only my mother keeps repeating the same old story: I'm careless, I'm trying to say things too quickly, I act in haste, I don't breathe properly, I don't think through what I want to say, my nerves are weak and I shouldn't drink any alcohol. It's my fault, this is all that stays with me. I distress my mother, like an unruly child, although there are none in our family, and in case there are, they have been re-educated, healed. There's something wrong with me—by my own errors, of course. They tell me not to do it, not like that, but I do it regardless, so it's my own doing, my own fault—after all they did warn me. They berate me to repeat what I've been uttering, to think it through again, to start from the beginning, to stop, breathe in and take a rest. I don't understand what they want, but can sense that, increasingly, I'm being embroiled in an invisible net of unspeakable and speakable words, a multitude of traps that I'm trying to avoid without avail, there's always a spot or a situation where I find myself stuck. He'll grow out of it, they say, but what must I grow out of? I don't know when it is that I finally hear my own voice as a problem, and recognize that I have an unbearable stammer. This is now dreadful from my point of view too, though most kids my age only laugh at it despite everyone initially being taken by surprise, horror and repulsion at my efforts, this is what I see on people's faces—indignation, pity and superiority, I shouldn't even say anything, they snigger. I suppose people must built this impression upon noticing my condition, and then were confronted with it repeatedly, until they understood that this isn't something aberrant or accidental but *this* is it. You should do something about it, this can't go on like this, they even tell me not to do such and such or not to say such and such in a certain way. But what is the cause, they keep asking for the umpteenth time, to which no one has yet found the answer to this very day.

He must have been scared by something, Grandmother says and takes me to her sister-in-law, Mrs Polyánki, coal water doesn't seem to help so she should cast some molten lead, as the shape of the hot metal sizzling in the water would show what it was that had scared me so much. We place this peculiarly shaped tin mould that looks like a lamb beneath my pillow—everything will be fine. As it happens, the day before I was indeed pushed against a wall by a lamb, and although this was in play, I was terrified until Grandfather eventually freed me. Another time, a turkey jumps on my back in the orchard, a giant *male*, it scratches my face so scathingly I'm lucky it didn't gouge my eyes out. I also see a mouse caught by its tail curling up and biting into Grandmother's finger, blood spurting out, the mouse disappears in the flour bin, and I keep tracing its tiny red footprints for ages. I can see all this in that dainty piece of metal we put under my pillow that night. Perhaps I should also see a donkey following my whooping cough, as they make the same sound, or my tonsils do, despite the fact that they weren't removed in the end, they were not the problem, or the snake lurking behind the chimney, but I don't mention that to anyone. So many causes and explanations for my stammer, they will accompany me until the age of thirty-five, when I finally accept and understand it, and reconcile with it. This will become one of my pastimes. Doctor Pamela was right, I'll do something about it when I myself think it pertinent, twenty years isn't a long time after all, though bad conscience can only beget bad conscience.

One barely puts a few paragraphs to paper and already pictures oneself in possession of a certain standing. One tends to think that everything one says is by default significant, valid and of relevance, usually being about oneself. I clamber on to my own sentences like a Native American holding on to the mane of his horse on a burning prairie, or my grandfather to the tobacco factory in Temesvár, when they are shooting at him but they miss, he is unaware whether this is the work of the Soviets or the Germans. There is some prowess in this desperate galloping, because, for a while, I'd always picture my paternal grandfather, the one from the Plains, on horseback, I did the same thing with myself, but this race didn't last long. I'm thirty-five when I first sit in a saddle and probe how far I can actually get with a horse: not far at all. I have just finished a novella in which a young man, suspiciously similar to myself, forms a close friendship with a horse, and it occurred to me that I should try this out, the text was published and well received, but there you are. I know everything about horses, everything that can be learned from books, that is. A real horse, however, can only snigger at this, and at me, because I'm unable to control it, I should clearly practice this, but in any case, how could one possibly control somebody else when losing control oneself? A much better story presents itself when I spot a dun horse in the fair at Székelyhodos, or rather the horse spots me, we look into each other's eyes, and after some hesitation the horse places its head on my shoulder, we stand there like that for an endless minute. Sir, this is your horse, you should buy it, the Gipsy horse dealer urges in an earnest voice, and I know he's right, the horse from the story that I had written has just come forward, it found me and recognized me, not as its owner but as its double. Neither of my grandfathers owned horses, despite Joszip Vida being a carter and a Romanian gendarme, he was given horses whenever he needed to sit on the coach box or in the saddle. My Székely grandfather, Uncle Gyurika, kept cows and buffaloes, and one could sit on the back of the latter. They were tame and slow, but riding them wasn't much fun except when they slowly kicked back into the mud, and one had to quickly take the yoke off so they wouldn't throw the whole cart over, cargo and all, in case they decided to have a little tumble as they happened to be hot or bitten by flies. We knew all too well that they wouldn't get up until they had their fill with this wallowing.

This will hardly turn into a chase. I can't help marvelling and rejoicing at the fact that my childhood is spent on the verge of archaic worlds, where I not only return time and time again for my summer holidays but where my grandparents actually live. It doesn't even occur to them that they could live elsewhere, and they don't merely talk about their childhood and the past but also make my childhood self a part of their present. There is a single irresolvable contradiction between them, namely that one is an alcoholic and the other a believer, one doesn't have an ideology, while the other does. The fact that the world inhabited by one was written about with utmost precision by Zsigmond Móricz, and that of the other by Áron Tamási isn't an issue. These peasant worlds blur into each other, and although it sounds like blasphemy, it is sadly true that alcoholism and religious obsession hail from the same place, as two sides of the same coin. The trouble is that all my childhood I was under the impression that my devout grandfather was a good man and I should follow in his footsteps, whereas my booze-gulping grandfather was bad, at least according to my mother. For a long time, I shared this view, just as I also thought that I was on good terms with her, but not with my father.

My parents do everything they possibly can to break away from the village that socialism had put an end to, because this regime had not only reconfigured people's relationship with the land, but, under the guise of modernization, systematically liquidated and deliberately destroyed the culture that had always preserved and perpetuated village life. Mentalities, however, cannot be rewritten or changed at the drop of a hat. My parents have remained village people all their lives, and I'm one too. My childhood reverted me to the place where they had started off and fled from, where it was no longer possible for them to remain. My rightful outsider status as a grandchild protects me from the brutality of authoritarian grandfathers, I don't have to take part in their fight for survival, I'm not being prepared for this lifestyle, yet I have an immediate experience of the vestiges of villages on the Hungarian Plain, and to a lesser extent, in Székely Land. I have seen the devastation whereby people no longer believe in the possibility of a meaningful life, they are merely toiling about, although my alcoholic grandfather decided to put an end to this toil, he would no longer do that, not even for himself, whereas my other grandfather didn't, as he thought he'd do it for the sake of others. I have no recollection of society, customs or habits, these were no longer tangible for me, but the forest has always been really close by and, in the absence of alternatives, it often seemed as if everything that had ever mattered had always emerged from and retreated there. I have seen the solitude, bleakness and deprivation that follows the waning of organic communities, and I have seen wretchedness and drink. This is far from a world that makes you feel at home, and yet this is the only home I've ever had.

I've just realized with horror that I wanted to move all these people into the castle, to make them cohabit—let them grind each other, as they are wont to do—in order to give all this a befitting backdrop, and to have an opportunity to weave history in, to find relevant parables for what had happened in Transylvania from the thirties onwards. This could perhaps explain what is taking place in the present, or simply illustrate that such things do happen, by stating the normality of the particular or the distinctiveness of the universal. Having said that, I might not have even been born had these people lived side by side, for they would have torn each other to pieces long before that. So I have to start somewhere, as if it were any old story, told by me, perhaps true, perhaps imagined, and my job is to tie loose ends together, undo the tangles, interpret and understand, and make up for what's missing. Not that I'm necessarily craving a sense of unity when only fragments are at disposal, but the mind tends to round things up regardless. My aim was to commit my homeland to paper, for my own sake, as if our homeland found an existence only when we, upon necessity, created it. Nobody can conjure up a homeland out of the blue, everyone is working from own material. Yet flowers bloom in each and every village.

VII

The Székely

For a very long time I was under the impression that all my ancestors were Hungarian, and even the grandparents of my grandparents would have considered themselves Hungarian through and
through. At times I was quite annoyed by my ordinariness—without a trace of Jewish, Armenian or Saxon ancestors. Lately it has
become fashionable in Transylvania to acknowledge this otherwise
natural ethnic multiplicity, we aren't quite so proud of Slavic or
Romanian ancestors but at the very least we tend to own up to
them, as opposed to the Gipsy ones. Other times I flaunted the
fact that I was utterly Hungarian—this is just fine, it will do for
me. One day, however, I stumbled upon the marriage certificate
of my maternal grandparents and saw that my grandfather's
religion was listed as *greco-catolic*, that is Greek Catholic, and this
wasn't recorded by the Romanian notary in Barót in 1939, but by
his Hungarian counterpart in Szárazajta in 1904. This is marginally
better than being Orthodox, but only a touch. Up until then I
thought that, prior to joining the Baptist congregation, he had
been a Calvinist, this is what my mother and practically everyone
else thought. Székely with an Eastern religion, as historian Orbán
Balázs classifies this, though my grandfather didn't read this monu-
mental work on the history of Székely Land and, in my view,
hadn't so much as heard about it. This sort of thing had no significance in his world, everyone would think of themselves as

Hungarian, and nobody would speak Romanian in Szárazajta, not even those who, for some reason or other, would later declare themselves as belonging to this ethnicity. I regret enormously that I wasn't suitably receptive at the time my grandfather would still have been able to tell me the story of his village. I feel that I should know something important that I don't, and now no one ever will. The pointed question is not how we are related to the Berszán (Bârsan) family that took part in the massacre of 26 September 1944—after all, my grandfather was a prisoner of war and was no longer living in that village. I'm concerned with why that massacre had to happen in the first place. I have a feeling that my grandfather knew about its causes, many others did too, but he never spoke of it to anyone, and with the passage of time, this increasingly turns into a story impossible to tell. The contention that the evil Romanians killed the innocent Hungarians simply doesn't cut the mustard.

My grandfather was orphaned at a young age. He's more or less the only survivor of the First World War in his family, his two elder brothers died on the front in Galicia and his mother of consumption, his father wouldn't survive the misery of the war either. I'm aware of no relatives in that village, it wasn't among my grandfather's favourite places, he has never mentioned it to me and I haven't been there either, despite having visited most other villages in the vicinity. All I'm left with is a story whereby the neighbour generously gifts them some bread stolen by the dog, adding that they should cut out the bits on which the dog drooled, in case it had rabies. Of course we didn't, Grandfather tells us, we ate every last crumb. A Baptist relative takes over as his guardian, and it is this person that initiates Grandfather into the religious life. I know nothing about my grandfather's conversion, and I know equally little about these years of his life or his first marriage. I can't even find out whether he was a soldier in the Romanian army. Quite likely he wasn't, he couldn't speak a word of Romanian, not to mention that he would have told us about it, as he talked in great detail about the coal mine in Köpec, the war and about being prisoner of war. He married at a very young age apparently, perhaps in order to evade conscription, given that he was thus considered a breadwinner. In the wake of the 1923 Romanian Constitution, foreign nationals living on the territory of Greater Romania were granted citizenship, this included Hungarians, Germans, Jews, Ukrainians, Rusyns, Turks, and even Gipsies, causing major outcries and riots among the majority population that was unable to handle the chaos following the war. I seem to remember that my grandfather actually told me about being sent back home from the enlistment because they already had enough recruits, or they had found him too short—he wouldn't even come up to my shoulders—whatever the real reason might have been.

For me, his religious universe is more important than the historical environment in which this manifests itself and operates, because in this religious consciousness there is something delirious, something beyond time and history, something of a deformed immaturity. He doesn't look like a theologian, more like an insider, who was once shown the order of things by some mysterious teacher or master, and who has been able to live according to God's commandments ever since, although he doesn't actually manage to stick with this at all times. In the early days, he simply dips into the tattered and mice-nibbled Károli Bible translation whenever uncertain, and reads it until he comes across the relevant instruction. Later, now familiar with the text, he knows where a particular passage is to be found, and even underlines the more important sections. Later still, he doesn't even have to leaf through the Bible anymore, he knows it by heart, and recites the relevant verse at the right time, with the right emphasis. It's God's will written down here, he doesn't dispute this, doesn't interpret or explain, and simply doesn't engage in arguments. He's keen to hear the opinion of others, but vehemently opposes anything he disagrees with, and in case this is uttered by someone with a higher rank, he only smiles, sporting a dreamy look, or perhaps nods. He sits through any ceremony with ease, enjoys singing, and generally has a good musical ear. As for religious tolerance, he shares the view of most Transylvanians, anyone is free to believe what they like, I know what I know and that's that. What could freedom be but the correspondence between faith, knowledge and truth?

Grandpa, known as Uncle Gyurika, is in possession of the truth once and for all, and does everything in his power for his family to live according to their principles, he spares no effort to chastize anyone for their sins: verbally, when that is sufficient, or by way of the whip, cane or fist, when that isn't. He is a Székely peasant, an ordinary paterfamilias who doesn't spend his time musing about why his instructions ought to be fulfilled, his words are commands to buffaloes, women and children, in this exact order. He hails from an archaic world in which the ongoing abuse of women and children is a daily occurrence, and it's accepted as such despite not being an imperative. Paternal authority is inviolable, but this doesn't need constant reassertion; subalterns don't need to be put to the test at all times, and most people don't even bother with this unless they are unsure about it because they themselves are struggling to believe it or, conversely, can't get enough of it. My grandfather is a frustrated man, probably abused as a child, and is now constantly on guard, harassing his own family:

whenever the cane is having a rest, children get out of hand. He is convinced that he wants only the best for us and is indeed educating us, but his restlessness causes an awful lot of trouble. According to the family, he gets up before the crack of dawn to earth up the sweetcorn or the potatoes, he is a very hard-working man, but we know that this is the fruit of no diligence but a sleep disorder. He thinks nothing of being the first to leave the table, and once he's gone, the meal is over. One could dedicate entire studies to the operation of sectarianism along social processes, and to how extreme religious doctrines depreciate people and life, and breed further division amidst already problematic communities.

We keep plodding away, all day, all week, in order to make a living, on Sundays we praise the Lord for being able to work, and beg Him to be able to toil further for His glory, after all this is what our life is all about. The Lord helps us if we are well-behaved, and punishes us if we aren't, we live in an alliance of sorts with God, but this is in fact just good business. If I wanted to be ironic, I could say that Uncle Gyurika simplified the Ten Commandments for the sake of his family: honour thy father! He is an authoritarian figure, who legitimizes his power with verses from the Old Testament, and is touched by the story of Jesus, like someone who experiences the death on the cross with all their being, for Jesus from Nazareth died for him, and whoever believes in him shall not perish but have eternal life . . . He names his first-born son Isaac, and I don't wish to speculate what he might have thought of himself, perhaps that he was some sort of a new-age Abraham at the very least. Ever since Protestants had set foot in Székely Land, and people had been able to read the Old Testament in Hungarian, Biblical names have become fairly common even among the lower social classes. Having said that, back in the thirties Isaac was a name reserved for Jewish peddlers alone. Like other Székelys, my grandfather can't follow the political situation either, he likes to speak in tongues, and so do I, and besides, there are several others christened Isaac at that time in the neighbourhood. The bond with the Old Testament is very strong for several neo-Protestant sects, because the patriarchal age helps to reposition mythology to the place where theological rationalism had previously banished it from. As far as his mentality and emotional make-up is concerned, Uncle Gyurika isn't far off the Székely Sabbatarians and the Jews in Bözödújfalu, all his leanings push him in this direction, besides, we've been shepherds too, *people in sheepskin*, as Balázs Orbán puts it. Grandfather is fascinated by the patriarchal age, he knows the Parables by heart, as well as the Psalms, but he can't quite make sense of historical books, and finds civilization fairly complicated. God strikes the enemy down, this is of utmost importance, and he enunciates this over and over again, like someone who's experiencing a sense of doubt. My grandfather's zeal goes well beyond that of the Sabbatarians or Székely Jews, and he is of a restless, violent and aggressive disposition. At times, I feel that this simplified or perhaps even outright misunderstood religious ideology and heightened enthusiasm imported from America at the end of the nineteenth century colonizes a rich mix of popular religiosity. In the name of the former, my grandfather violently oppresses and eliminates the imagination and multi-faceted tradition, remnants of which continue to mesmerise everyone who catches their glimpse. It was my grandfather who told me that prior to the Turkish invasion there had been vineyards, orchards and fields of wheat here, instead of evergreen forests. He also said that there had once been a sea in Transylvania and King Stephen gave orders for the creation of a pass in the Carpathians at Vöröstorony in order to drain this sea. So yes, he could tell a few tall tales. I didn't actually believe these, he must have stumbled across them by hearsay, and he stopped believing in these himself, I certainly don't think that he'd have read such stories in the books of local folktale teller Elek Benedek.

He'd tell Biblical stories with great gusto because these had always included a morale, and thus it became clear that we were on the right path, hand in hand with God, whereas our neighbours were not, despite having been large-scale farmers in the past. In any case, it was paramount to remember that 'it is easier for a camel to go through the eye of a needle than for a rich man to enter the kingdom of God.' He'd try to trace everything back to the Bible, aiming to create a unique tradition, of course he was unable to step over his own shadow, whatever cannot be integrated into his world, he'd simply ignore, labelling it superstition and idolatry. He is a man who wants to belong to God's chosen people, he knows that ever since Paul the Apostle this is simply a matter of decision and not of birth right, it's based on faith and faith comes from hearing, they even tell you what to believe in, so honour thy father! This is why we can eat pork, for instance, it isn't forbidden to us, we have always been eating some, this is why we don't consume animal blood, because the Bible says we shouldn't. We don't go to the cinema or to restaurants and pubs, we don't watch TV, don't listen to music, for all this is ostentation. King David had played music and sang, but only to glorify God, so one is allowed to play the guitar in the church hall, and at home too, as long as it's religious music. We don't eat fish because that's fit only for Gipsies, we haven't the time for fishing, and *trout* is only eaten by masters when on a hunt. We eat chanterelle and porcini mushrooms, and to be fair, these are gathered by Gipsies but they taste really good, and the Scripture doesn't actually forbid its consumption. We don't drink *redcurrant wine*, my grandmother sells that to pagans for money, so let them drink that. It's forbidden to smoke, and coffee isn't a sin but tea is cheaper. When they teach us at school that there is no God, one mustn't dispute the teacher, only make sure not to believe such claims, as for the homework, well that just has to be done regardless, even the history assignments that teach there is no God.

One could easily scan through Uncle Gyurika's selective interpretation of the Scripture, I found plenty of contradictions even as a child, for a while I'd raise these to him but we didn't get very far, he didn't like my reasoning, and whenever we came across a contradiction he just told me to shut up. I started to read my father's notes from his theological studies at a fairly young age, especially the introduction to the Old Testament, and even though I din't understand a great deal, I was able to display a sense of doubt with regard to Grandfather's religious teaching. He keeps educating me, goading me, wanting to convert me and, for ages, I'm afraid that I might end up in hell, together with the unsubmissive and the obtuse. Even when I don't yet know what my father said to him, I already harbour some resistance, I'm also quite ashamed of this because I'm hard-hearted, and insist on being even more so. When in the early sixties Grandfather's daughters, then in secondary school, start reading *Joseph and His Brothers*, he immediately rips out the pages that don't square with his religious stance, in other words, he's censoring Thomas Mann. Unfortunately, that copy of the book hasn't survived, so I can't reconstruct the pages that annoyed him, but one can perhaps picture this Székely man, sitting there in a quiet moment and tearing out the pages of this world-famous book.

One can equally deride my grandfather's attempts at settling into day-to-day life during the fascist and then the socialist era in Romania. He had experienced serious trauma as a member of a Neo-Protestant confession imported from America, striving to follow the principles of a pragmatic and puritan religion. He's unable to ask questions regarding his thoughts and teachings, in his culture there is no such thing as self-reflection. Not for a moment does the question arise whether the maxims presented as revelation are in accordance with the Scripture, and whether day-to-day activities are indeed conducted according to these rules and principles, or this is simply something that we just unquestioningly assume. Everything needs to be in unison, or else, nothing is. The Scripture is interpreted literally, they can't possibly know about the distance that separates the culture of Biblical times from ours, and the fact of the matter is that the language of Gáspár Károli is fairly close to everyday speech, to this day village elders find reading this first Hungarian translation of the Bible much easier than many contemporary theologians. Another aspect my grandfather is unable to perceive is that, whilst the Bible had once been the sum of all knowledge on the world for a particular mentality, by the mid-twentieth century it lost its status as the exclusive source of information. Adhering to its spirit and letter increasingly demands specific patterns of behaviour, especially if we insist on this adherence and if we do this with all our might, hoping that in return God will help us. But perhaps none of this would matter if his son Isaac didn't end up being run over in 1946 by the only lorry to be found in Barót, as it was driving out of the butter factory. It's impossible to reconstitute the details of this accident, we know practically nothing of Isaac, except that he was a well-behaved and obedient boy whom Uncle Gyurika brought along from his first marriage. The court decided from the outset that the boy should live with his father, unlike baby Will, who was abandoned by his mother and who later took the place of the firstborn; he was a devilishly ill-behaved child though, and the entire family would reach a rare consensus on this. Following the model of the Old Testament, it's possible to imagine what could have taken place in my grandfather's mind: the Lord didn't send me a ram, to replace Isaac. And one is welcome to figure out whether Isaac, who is accepted-or-taken-away, is or isn't a victim seeing that, following Thomas Mann, Isaac is the 'non-accepted sacrifice', what this actually means and what my grandfather thinks of all this, before and after reading the relevant passage.

It's relatively undemanding for the religious to accept God's will, but what does God actually tell us? I don't want to push the narrative in this direction, but it's fairly easy to see that my grandfather went from being Abraham to Job in an instant, and his fate was sealed at that blood-stained factory gate. Irrespective of what happened later, he could no longer abandon the path set out for him, and there was no test he wouldn't submit himself to, for he was God's chosen son for all eternity. The following year sees the birth of his youngest son, Tom, known in Hungarian as Tamás, another heavily charged name, and he is the son who will hang himself in the barn at a delirious daybreak, and I refuse to identify him as Benjamin, although that would be the most obvious parallel. No desperado or perverse novelist would dare to consciously opt for such a logic of naming, models from the Old Testament or mythology do indeed enmesh events in our lives but not to such an extent, this is an exaggeration and a simplification at once. I can detach myself from this model, I don't have to identify with it, but it's unlikely that my grandfather was able to do this, for him these are not only talking names, similes, metaphors and analogies but realities, and when, in the heat of the moment, he calls one of his daughters Potiphar's wife, he actually means 'whore'. The last thing to add is that Uncle Will is in fact Ishmael, Hagar's son, whom the Lord will indeed multiply to form a large community, he'll have three sons, and as a child I consider myself the fourth. This is only an alliance though, we'll be 'American Indians' and spend the most wonderful summers of our childhood in a reservation of sorts.

I can't hear Grandpa-Uncle Gyurika's inner monologue, although he's perpetually mumbling, muttering something, it seems as if instead of contemplation or mulling things over, he was walking or perhaps gardening to the rhythm of murmured psalms. I should add that the American brothers expertly adapted a variety of blues and jazz rhythms for religious use, this is certainly a more colourful musical universe than the organ music and singing of elderly ladies as practiced in Calvinist churches, or the psalms notated by Clément Marot, even when sung by a really competent choir. I can't hear Uncle Gyurika's inner monologue because such a thing doesn't actually exist, how could he possibly ask why, my lord, why?

At this point, I'd be more interested in my grandfather's first marriage than his godly cosmos, but the latter counts as a taboo in the family, and so does my grandmothers' first marriage. Grandfather's first wife was a wicked woman, despite being a Baptist; the man my grandmother first married was a drunkard as well as a Catholic. One can imagine what must have taken place in these marriages if they decided to opt for divorce in that tightly knit, religious Székely community, at a time when courts were run by Romanians and cost an absolute fortune. In addition, my grandmother gets rid of a man who isn't even a drunkard or debauched, but ends up excluded by the church community, to ease things, after their divorce, her husband goes to a fair in Debrecen and there's no mention of him thereafter. There isn't a single piece of documentary evidence on any of this in the family archive, no one remembers the exact dates despite endeavours to preserve all the paperwork. We have postcards from the First World War, two bits of scrap paper thrown out of the train by my grandfather in the Autumn of 1944, saying that he's being taken to Russia and letting his family know who he's travelling with; there are cattle passports issued in both Romanian and Hungarian, marriage certificates, land registry entries, rental contracts, photos of the old house needed for the demolition permit, myriads of exciting bits and pieces—we don't throw anything away, and nothing tends to get misplaced either. There is no divorce decree, it obviously had to be shown in order to be allowed to remarry, and then there was no further need for it, although it would be worth a fortune to me right now. The legal papers might have included important information on this forgotten and denied past, but they probably felt ashamed in front of each other, and perhaps even themselves, that such things could have taken place. Yet it's crystal clear that the other party was the guilty one, nobody can take this entirely seriously, as it takes two to make a quarrel. Back in 1940, my grandparents can only flee to the future, they love one another, own a bit of land and forest, have three children, they are young and thrilled with the excitement of a new beginning. Their first child together is born soon after the instauration of the Hungarian regime, in 1941: Heléna, she'll be my godmother and the first in the line that dies out with Tom.

No one knows back then that threats at knifepoint will break out among the children they had together and the ones they brought into the marriage. These fights aren't about possessions, those are insignificant, but for the right to be loved, as that is an entitlement too, and one has to fight for one's truth and for leadership, as that is a position wherefrom one can decree to others what their place is, what they are and aren't allowed to do, and what they should be talking about. They always lecture one another from above, high-handedly and without tolerating the slightest opposition, as if they were not battling for power but for truth, the biological children know exactly that they are the real deal, and the children brought into the marriage are palpably aware it's the biological ones who are in receipt of more parental love. Székely reality penetrates the egalitarianism of the Gospels. According to family ideology, everyone has an equal share of everything, since polenta, milk and sausages can be portioned into equal shares, but caring, love and tenderness cannot, these can't be rationed seeing that they are based on a unique and personal relationship.

According to the Biblical model, the first-born is the dearest, but as a matter of course, the youngest inherits the estate, and it is their duty to take care of the parents. Uncle Will ends up hating his younger brother all his life, for he will always remain a foreigner despite being the first-born. Will isn't the biological child his parents had together, Tom is, and hence the house should belong to him. He's unfit for life though, and the law dictates that all heirs should benefit equally, including the girls, who aren't even home because they went off to study and then got married, they don't take part in day-to-day chores or conflicts, they only assist with these on an as-and-when basis. Grandfather is no Solomon, to be able to do justice in this matter or to reconcile these three systems of thought, not to mention that no one has ever managed to disentangle the envies and jealousies of siblings.

1941: Heléna, 1942: Violetta, 1944: Anette, 1947: Tom. Whenever Uncle Gyurika is allowed home from the war, he quickly makes a baby. He and Grandmother live together for fifty years, they build houses for both sons, marry the daughters off, theirs is a good marriage as far as everyone is concerned, and even I have to put in some serious effort to find grounds for doubt. I don't want to hassle them in hindsight, but there should be reasons to ponder about why the two children brought into their marriage presented the world with six grandchildren, while the four biological ones with only two? What sort of change of paradigm is this? Aunt Heléna couldn't have children, Uncle Tom didn't produce any descendants, I'm an only child, and so is the daughter of Aunt Anette, to say nothing of the fact that both of us got divorced. This will be the branch that dies out. Rachel's sons and daughters, I could say, although we do know that she didn't have daughters. But where is, or rather who is, Joseph? I'd of course claim this role for myself, but well, there you are. There's a reason why we shouldn't insist on Biblical or mythological parallels: it could easily transpire that we aren't the chosen people, but a family that thinks of itself as different from the others, when in fact it isn't. I now have to confront the fact that I barely know anything about my maternal grandmother, despite being related to half the town on her account, my mother's sister once listed seventy-second cousins. People with such-and-such surnames are all our relatives, she says, but I don't know anyone from this lot. All I remember is that everyone seems to be accounted for through the female line, such as the brood of Klárika, Gizike, Aunt Marika, Annuska, Bözsike, as if alongside the strict paternal world there was a maternal dimension as well, which continues to count married women as our own ilk, and their daughters thereafter. My mother doesn't really keep in touch with anyone, except at random and sporadically, as if we only had close contact with those relatives who could also be our friends, but my hunch is that we've never really had any friends, seeing that human relations based on mutual sympathy were not allowed: whoever isn't a relative, is a stranger.

I have already forgotten the castle by now, although it would have come really handy, seeing that in the period between 1939 and 1948, even 1950, this extended family comprising Székelys and people from the Hungarian Plain could have been confined there together. The Székelys wouldn't have lived on Water street in Barót where the small house could easily fit into the large barn, and where, in heavy rainfalls, everyone had to keep an eye on the stream in order to be able to flee to the attic when the floods came. Neither poverty nor the sheer thought of it would have been such a burden and source of shame in front of the other poor, supposing that wealthy people actually existed at that time and in that community, when just about everything was taken away from ordinary folk. In this scenario, the branch of the family living on the Hungarian Plain would have been spared vegetating at the edge of the village whilst my grandfather was away for weeks and months on end, working on building sites or as a carter on some estate or other. This is the reason why my father was born at Világos, at that time they happened to be living there, in utter destitution both in a material and cultural sense, leading a cotters' life, as described by the great Hungarian realist author Zsigmond Móricz. Moreover, I wouldn't have to go to great pains trying to understand that in the Székely branch of the family the issue isn't poverty itself but the awareness of poverty, not to mention the marginal situation that my grandparents' religion and belonging to the Baptist Church entails. Like other sects, this congregation is willing to endow those who join them, and thus repent, with a brand new religious identity, into which they can then swiftly regiment them. Of course, this is a ghetto, a very sharp 'them versus us' situation, because we also hail from there, from among the sinners, after all, those who are late to the party always tend to be the most eager, keen to make up for lost time. We are the believers, and they are the faithless, the secular ones. We reject their habits, we are the people of God, and they are not. We are Christian, they are pagan. We live in Gospel poverty, they carouse in excess. We could easily riff on this further: they drink, smoke, live in debauchery and fornication, and we don't. And we shouldn't forget remorse either, because we used to be just like them, and are now repenting with the enthusiasm of neophytes. But why are children sinners, and why should they be penitent?

Once theological problems have been suitably solved, provided they've even come up in the first place, founders of new religions tend to move on to reforming people's way of life. Bona fide founders of religious traditions constitute theological matters in their own right but, thankfully, these cases are extremely rare. The Baptist congregation in Barót purchases the building of their future meeting house in 1954, from the Calvinist church. I have no idea what sort of sum Grandpa-Uncle Gyurika dedicates to this deal, there must be some mention of this somewhere, among the Securitate documents if nowhere else. One can certainly ponder over how much money someone might have managed to put aside for religious purposes in conditions of a collectivized economy, whilst having to feed, clothe and educate six children, this is happening right after the war, the land yields extremely little, and the climate is austere. Figures don't really amount to much, God's house is more important than our home, yet this is very difficult to explain to the lot of starving children. The little ones don't understand this at all, but the older ones do, and keep rebelling. Grandfather's harshness and brutality can barely reign them in. And whenever my mother, Violetta, tells us that they used to work on the fields over the holidays, because they were poor and they liked working, Uncle Will reminds us that he had always hated work, because they had never actually been this poor, except that their father chose to drive them as if they were slaves in Egypt. The latter would have made Moses blow his fuse time and time again, and this is exactly what happened to my uncle. I should add that in those days knowledge on slavery doesn't derive from the Bible but from Stalinist manuals, as I find out after lugging them down from the attic one rainy summer. My mother is also unable to tell the difference between religious and school education, there are commands to obey and that's that, this is the bottom line for her, and she tells us that as children Will used to play being the Pharaoh and his sister the Jewish slaves, there's always a whip to hand at home. There are a bunch of other horror stories, such as that Grandfather locks them into the cellar or the stable, where the older kids torment the younger ones to death, or that he keeps hitting his son until the neighbours hold him down and then the girls lock the youngest child into the house, lose the key and a locksmith has to be called. The whip is always to hand, everyone is screaming and bellowing, and when a doll is ripped apart, because everyone wants it as their own, Grandfather throws it on the fire so no one can have it—you are all Philistines and Edomites.

It's evident: despite all members of the family working day and night, there's no visible growth, they have no clothes or shoes, all eight of them live in misery crammed into a single bedroom, they don't drink or party, so something must be out of order. What can they possibly do with the money, what are they saving for? Gospel penury, Székely rule, puritan lifestyle—no one is actually happy, yet they should be, for there is a recipe for salvation to hand, but even in hindsight people can only talk of privation and austerity, with so many children there's no other way but sticking with a sense of order. Of course, there's something behind all this that nobody is willing to address or acknowledge, and this attitude is consistently shared by the whole family, even when they'd rather drown one another in a teaspoon of water, nobody is allowed to shake up taboos—whatever we leave unsaid doesn't exist. Only certain things can be discussed, and only in a clearly prescribed way, all else is forbidden. Most frightening to me is the way the operation of the Barót family is reminiscent of the fifties. Despite this decade being long over, it lingers on in our heads and souls—that the dictatorships of the past century have been kept up so successfully because oppression is in fact constituted in the very foundation of family structures is an ineluctable conclusion. Not that families have always been like this, and yet it seems to me that the agrarian societies of the late-nineteenth century have come up with this system of organization and passed it on to the next era. Our father treats us the way the police officer patrolling the local streets would, but to complicate things, he loves us. This is the era of the Stalin Autonomous Region, later known as the Magyar Autonomous Region, which has recently stirred a strong nostalgic wave because Hungarian nationalist feelings in Transylvania have never considered Soviet-style dictatorship to be the worst political arrangement in the world, that role befalls the Romanian state and government in power.

It's obvious to me today that my grandfather's devoutness would have operated in the exact same way had he been a member of the Nazi or Communist Party, and not the Baptist congregation. He's the kind of person who's prepared to sacrifice everything for an obsession, he's fanatical, determined, ruthless, principled, with the necessary faith and energy to boot. In his view, everyone would benefit from believing and doing exactly the same, with the same enthusiasm and willingness to make sacrifices, and if not, he's ready to beat the living daylight out of them. He has no capacity for self-reflection, yet he isn't stupid, but as far as I can tell he has never felt remorse. He gets to bury two sons, one of them repudiates him, his biological daughters marry men of other denominations, be it Unitarian, Calvinist or Orthodox Romanian, and he can't get to the bottom of this. Towards the end of his life, he ends up entirely on his own, and notes with a sigh that everyone has become so secular. In case I was writing a novel, I'd deal with the fact that there are serious issues with Grandpa-Uncle Gyurika's religiosity, he doesn't actually believe in anything, he can't forgive or be reconciled with anything. It looks as if he carried the burden of a mortal sin and did everything in his power to conceal this, despite not having a clue as to what this entailed. I shall never find out what my grandfather's real problem was, perhaps he never had one, and it's only my invention that everyone must have such a thing. I'll learn only decades later that he and my grandmother didn't have a religious wedding. My grandmother remains a Catholic, my grandfather a Baptist, which is why the congregation denies him the right to preach, as he's living with a concubine, so to speak. My aunt is formally excluded from the community for marrying an Orthodox man, but my other aunt, who marries a Unitarian, is not, after all they continued to stay Hungarian. Religious tolerance works and doesn't work in Transylvania, seeing that it's always dependant on who happens to be in charge at a given time.

VIII

The Great Hungarian Plain

There's nothing here! my godmother Heléna allegedly exclaims in the early sixties, when she and Violetta are walking along the embankment of the Fehér-Körös river, the construction of which had been initiated by István Széchenyi. They don't know this at the time, as they don't approach the landscape from the perspective of history, they merely take a look in the direction of Hungary. They are Székely girls looking like twins, their younger sister a spitting image of them too. The three sisters (although they haven't read Chekhov, despite the similarities) form a united front and a tight community of interest in all situations. Virtuous, sororal, they often help one another, especially against their half-siblings, although they are not likely to use this term. The older ones are very badly behaved and disobedient. The three sisters protect their parents and familial unity, and urge their brother Tom to be a good student, to abstain from drinking and get married. But there's no need for this just yet, everything seems to be fine. They are in the middle of contemplating the Great Hungarian Plain, discovering this landscape that is nothing to write home about, and realising that on the Plain there isn't anything one could actually call a scenery. It's sweltering, this is the main complaint of Székely people even at the seaside or at the Lake Balaton, despite everyone being Hungarian, or at least German. Only Romanians are worse than the heat, but in the early sixties, in fact, there aren't any major issues with them either—not as many as had been or would be—for the time being, then, the horizon is endless. The girls are talking about their lives, they want to get married. Heléna has just met the man of her life, but alas he is married with two children, but he'll soon divorce, it's a marriage made in hell, he'll bring with him both children for his wife is a dreadful, unbearable female. At this point a series of events should ensue, the role of which is to provide evidence for these claims, even though I shouldn't write these down in her view. I can't actually hear them anyway because I shall only be born years later, and only decades later will this segment of the past pique my interest, and besides, we aren't that kind of family anyway.

Violetta, who will be my mother, also wants to get married. With her first salary, she has already purchased some green kitchen furniture that was considered very modern at the time. She doesn't yet know that it will always be the centre of her world, everything that matters fits into it: the tea set that we never use, the twelve-person dining set that we use only on rare occasions, bread, spices, coffee, brandy, later my school equipment tools, our shoe cleaning kit, socks, handkerchiefs, the sewing kit, medication and a present from Heléna: the ceaselessly ticking Soviet alarm clock on the shelf. Life is hard, for despite graduating with top marks from an accounting course in Udvarhely, and despite having the option to stay on as accountant at the local school, Violetta asked to be sent as far away as possible, an indecipherable choice. She is sent to take up a job in Várad, but as it turns out, there's no job for her, so she ends up in Kisjenő, in the office of the agro-mechanical station, where she will eventually retire. She had to be remote as the community had already found her a groom, whom she didn't like, or at least this was her version of events. The reality is that it's essential for her to make it to a safe distance from her family and congregation. Uncle Will will also move to Brassó with his wife, but Uncle Gyurika goes after them and takes them back home, and builds a house for and with them, such are his powers. He'll build a house for his younger son too, but the latter won't really stay in it for long, not even my grandfather has the powers to make him do so. Decades later, Aunt Anette will move to Kolozsvár with her husband, following in the footsteps of their daughter, as my mother will also join me from the Great Hungarian Plain to live in the vicinity of Marosvásárhely. These daughters are carbon copies of my grandfather, they have the same build and eyes, behave just like him, ruling the roost. His youngest son takes after Grandmother, they are the oppressed ones, the eternal losers in life.

Every night, Violetta laments her pitiable fate, like girls who had to take up a maid's life in Budapest. She's haunted by the remorse that she had run away, and in addition, she's also had bad luck—she ended up in a predominantly Romanian area. She doesn't speak the language, and this place is more or less like Bucharest, not to mention that even Hungarians can't quite understand her, so she's mocked for both her Romanian and Székely accent. She doesn't mind the Romanian being scoffed at, but she's deeply offended by the Székely taunts, although this isn't *just* a Székely girl issue. She finds herself in a world the representatives of which are towering above peasants, tractorists and manual workers, this is the world of county officials, who are educated people to some degree and descendants of the petit bourgeoisie, keen to dissociate themselves from anyone who's different. Professionally, Violetta manages just fine, she's diligent, precise and direct, but she doesn't really understand the mentality of shopkeepers and office workers in Kisjenő. She's unable assimilate their habits and values, she isn't familiar with their music, she can't dance and is hesitant, awkward in her ways. She feels the locals are supercilious, since she's very beautiful, women see her as a rival, but she's no rival, and since she's beautiful, men want to bed her, but this is out of the question. The moral laxity is frightening, but she thinks of herself as ugly, she lacks even the most basic fashion items, I'm not going to dwell on whether they are forbidden to her or she simply doesn't have the means to buy them. The point is that she still gets a smack for a shorter skirt or curled hair, and this isn't entirely a matter of religious conviction—this is law and order. The first pop-music festival hasn't yet launched, but there's radio and Hungarian television, Hungary is in the immediate vicinity despite there being no border traffic, but one still knows a lot about what's happening *over there*, and this has a different relevance here than in Székely Land. Throughout the socialist period, this area is the epitome of welfare in Romania, there were no food shortages even in the darkest times, and one could always obtain everything, be it from the black market if from nowhere else. No wonder that, apart from a few half-hearted attempts, Violetta has never seriously considered returning to her beloved, lamented and mourned Székely Land, as haven't most other Székelys: we learn to speak Romanian, get used to the heat, and we don't swap a good life for paucity, homesickness doesn't cost a thing after all. Like many Székelys, she doesn't know how to interpret the emotional culture of Hungarians from the Plain, she doesn't know when they are happy or sad, what they like or dislike, when to look disinterested or enthusiastic. It seems to her that all this is out of kilter with her thinking, and most of the time she doesn't know what she should take at face value and when people are pulling her leg, the language of gestures and faces is different, people walk differently on the street, women in particular. She doesn't understand that not only did she end up in a different region but she's also encountering a different social stratum that she'd like to join but with which she can't identify, her religious education doesn't allow it, the very religiosity that she has fled from. These people have no soul, she often says, and doesn't realize that they do but carry it differently. She gets on better with Romanians, for her they appear warm and open, whereas Hungarians are selfish, rancorous and materialistic. This is the mutual image of Romanians and Hungarians of each other, with the proviso that Hungarians consider Romanians a dirty, uneducated and thieving bunch, and Romanians find Hungarians arrogant, uppity and envious. But, as Heléna says, there's nothing here. So one has to come up with something.

Violetta was warned in good time not to marry Vida. His father is an alcoholic and they are poor as church mice. Vida is a chain smoker, and the food Grandma Zsüli packs for him ends up mouldy, stored between two windowpanes. He's seriously courting someone else anyway, this is why he didn't become a pastor, the woman told him she won't marry him for then she couldn't become a teacher of Romanian. It will never become entirely clear to me why Vida didn't become a pastor, after all he could have taken up the position of curate in Máramarossziget. The hypothesis that perhaps he wasn't cut out for being a pastor isn't really tenable, since the Lord is likely to endow those who obtain office with the necessary wit, even though being a pastor wasn't exactly a promising career option in 1961. Come to think of it, I'm puzzled that he was actually able to graduate from the school of theology. He was even ordained! How could he get through all these pious texts when he didn't believe a single word remains a mystery to me. He wasn't an atheist, there was simply no religious sentiment in him, he didn't even experience doubt or opposition, he just didn't feel anything in the place where faith tends to scrabble about in one's chest. He only thought of confirmation just before the admissions exam, and in my view, even this idea didn't come from him. There is a certain insensitivity, claustrophobia and spiritual absence that can well result from rigidity and from being neglected, it's the stubbornness of rural folk who weren't informed of the birth of Jesus and didn't figure it out themselves. He's the sort of person who doesn't yet know what he should be when he grows up, and then, all of a sudden, he no longer knows. It's unclear how much time passes in between these stages, it can be anything from a few minutes to half a lifetime, after which it's utterly pointless to come up with anything, especially with stuff one should have raised earlier, let's call it a day and that's that. Vida, of course, is much more complicated than this, but since he doesn't tend to talk about himself, or talk at all for that matter, he's seen as a calm, quiet and placid individual who doesn't drink or engage in debauchery, who likes reading, he must be a devout Christian, after all he trained to be a pastor. All these are favourable points from Violetta's perspective, she singles him out and drifts along in the canteen, so they end up having lunch together, she denies this turn of events, but the likelihood of Vida initiating the courtship is entirely out of the question. This will lead to forty-two years of marriage, I won't call it happy because I had the chance to look into it from a close up. Some people expect happiness from a marriage, while others are realists. My parents were unhappy, yet no realists. Violetta wants to get married and Vida doesn't know whether he wants to marry or not, so events will follow what Violetta thinks, or perhaps doesn't even think through, but she gets started with the schedule for her life in any case. She already owns a kitchen cupboard, and they carry on by purchasing seventy volumes of Jókai's work, the 1907 edition by the Franklin Társulat, and a Stassfurt TV set, costing an absolute fortune, a gas cooker and a fridge. There's no prospect of obtaining a home, but since they are poor, they keep saving. They are renting, which isn't easy in such a small place, nobody likes newcomers, the memory of lodgers forced upon people is still vivid, and owning a TV set and books is positively scandalous, and as Grandma Zsüli will point out sarcastically and reproachfully, they don't even have anything decent to wear. I grant them three years of peace and quiet, this is how long love lasts according to my father, and I'm generous. I'm born after this, to mess everything up. This couldn't take place in the castle, the only suitable place for this is a mouldy summer kitchen, a village hospital to be precise, the walls of which are decorated with a memorial plaque to the glorious Soviet army, later exchanged for a Romanian one.

Following a near-fatal labour, my mother falls into depression, her milk dries up after a week, but she doesn't realize that I almost starve to death. This child won't survive, my grandmother declares, and travels back to Barót where another child is about to arrive. Everybody abandons my mother, a wicked landlady terrorises her from morning to night, and my father is temporarily relocated to a workplace at the opposite end of the county, he's barely home. I could carry on listing further horror stories, tenancy, washing house, lack of money, a raft of irresolvable problems. I can picture my helpless and desperate mother cradling and bathing me, the water either too hot or too cold, she doesn't know or understand what's wrong, I scream incessantly until she furiously immerses me into the water, and I suddenly stop, because being in the water is pleasing. She swears that she won't have any more of this, and at the earliest opportunity, she casts me off to the countryside to live with my grandparents, she literally doesn't know what to do with me, since nobody gave her any pointers or supported her during the most difficult times. When she has to choose between me and her work, with pathos she opts for the latter, like so many others in those times, we need the money, she keeps saying in her defence, as if I was blaming her for this choice. Sadly, her distress at not knowing what to do with me, that I'm not like the other normal kids, will stick with her to the end. I'll continue to remain the major problem of her life, there was no happiness and joy in her experience with me, and in lieu of feeling like a Madonna, she has to make do with anxiety and helplessness. What's more, she was expecting a girl, not a boy.

My paternal family would have also been organized according to a very straightforward pattern, had Uncle Joszip Joszipovics not started to envy that my father received an education and he didn't, had he subsequently not deprived my father of his inheritance and had his second wife not tapped him for this, and had all the family squabbles not covertly centred on this very topic ever since. I can't grasp how such a tiny estate can mean so much to these people for ages. Everything could have turned out differently, had the teacher visited the family not only for the sake of my father but also that of Joszip Joszipovics, but the biased and possibly frustrated teacher, with an inexplicable commitment, singled my father out as the clever one who should receive further education. The older brother was envious of this, just as later he'd be envious of his brother's son, because he'd feel that he was more deserving. Yet he counts as an important male figure in my early life, he also stands for engines, forests, tractors and brandy, everything my father doesn't, furthermore, he's the jovial kind, who tells me stories and plays with me, for he only has a daughter with whom he can't do any of this.

These days we can't really grasp what it meant in 1948 to move from a village environment to grammar school, yet my father got away with the fifties, the process of collectivization and the extreme poverty in rural areas that characterised this era, one of the most hopeless facets of the twentieth century. He attended secondary school in Arad and only went home during the holidays, although he had never really told us much about this period or his school. It was good, of course, a privilege of sorts, a clean student hall on Tchaikovsky Street, where his favourite dish was boiled beef in a rich sauce called 'hunter's stew' but nobody was ever able to prepare this quite the same way. There was a decent basketball team that played proper league matches, and he had many classmates who lived in town and who, in this nascent popular democracy, wouldn't call him a peasant or look down on him, but become his lifelong friends. He was also taught by a few young teachers who will only retire when I'm about to graduate from the same school. In short, this was a model school that sheltered its students from the dreadful reality of the fifties, because even the worst school is a protection of sorts. Or could it be that it didn't actually shelter them, only they were young? He had barely told me anything about this world, just as he kept silent about his years studying theology. As if he had something to hide, or he was ashamed of this, or he was of the opinion that he should have done something else in some other way. It is of course likely that everything was just fine, and he simply didn't want to ruin this later with some randomly patched-up sentences because he struggled with speech and writing, meaning that he was aware of his own linguistic inadequacy and of the tension between the existing and the speakable. He was perfectly aware of the distance between the linguistic culture he had started off from and the one he was heading towards, and of the fact that he wouldn't be able to bridge the gap between the two.

He's a gifted young man of peasant stock, whose aim in not to find validation or simply move away from his poor village, but, to use a fashionable term, to be integrated and become like the world in which education takes place and in which the latter has meaning and place. He'd like to become a civilized man, who dresses well, looks after himself and converses with intelligent people. He's not after power or a well-paying secure job, but basketball, which at the time, and compared to football, is seen as an elegant and sophisticated game, accessible to people with an average build and on a par with pentathlon, fencing in particular. There's no resentment in my father, he isn't angry with his village or his family, he doesn't want to break out, run away or refuse to look back, he doesn't think that he grew up on the Hungarian fallow lands, despite that being the case, with the additional added twist that it was actually in Romania. Following his graduation, he settles for an office job at the parish hall in his village. He only goes to study theology because of his friends, and in this way he won't be drafted into the army, later he'll return to another office job as he has no further ambitions. You should become a pastor, then you won't have to work, Grandfather Joszip Vida allegedly said, and he won't speak to my father for a year when he graduates from theology yet decides against being ordained. He also adds some ornate profanities about the money my father's education had cost him, but Grandmother quips, shut up, you've been drinking all along, it was I who paid for everything. Yet there's no grudge or excommunication, Grandfather carries on drinking and will later become a presbyter at the church in Ágya, as if he wanted to at least mend his relationship with God since he was unable to do the same with his son.

Kolozsvár in the fifties. Lots of people tend to write or talk about this period these days, but naturally my father isn't one of them. One of his most eloquent sentences is that in 1958 four students were taken away. Much later, following the regime change, he suddenly raised his head when an entrepreneur appeared on TV alongside the then bishop, László Tőkés, whom he hated from the bottom of his heart. This guy is the bishop, he said, dismissing him with a flick of the hand. That entrepreneur was the informer in our year, my father said, and we can indeed imagine the kind of person who transfers from Catholic to Protestant theology in the fifties, and then abandons his studies, only to re-emerge in the nineties as a large-scale entrepreneur in the entourage of László Tőkés. This is what the church is like, my father pointed out in 2000. There were probably very few people studying theology whom the secret police didn't try to recruit, I have no idea how my father fared on this front, and I won't take the initiative to obtain his secret files. By now, I have given up on the belief that there are people impossible to recruit. If the secret police need the services of someone, they make sure they get them, be it by force, blackmail or negotiation, but they don't need just anyone. Everybody can try to avoid ending up in their net, but if one tries too hard, one might actually find oneself recruited for this very reason.

The Protestant Theological Institute in Kolozsvár, as well as every other historical congregation, was an enemy of the socialist regime by definition, as they represented a worldview and a society that Stalin's followers wanted to eradicate. Joseph Vissarionovich also studied theology, so he knew exactly whom he was facing, lots of people who believed in the same thing, and he also knew that, from the point of view of power, it was irrelevant what this commonality actually consisted of, so he cunningly thought: let it be me. The Romanian party leaders would have liked to rid the nation of their church and god, not realizing that atheism is a sort of religion too, therefore the faithful didn't see it as an alternative but as a rival sect which didn't offer an experience of freedom, although this wasn't the aim anyway. Today we know that in Romania the Orthodox Church, together with any other congregation that preaches in Romanian, is the depositary of the concept of the nation, as Hungarian congregations are of the Hungarian nation. Internationalism was only embraced by the Jews and some Hungarians, certainly not by everybody, albeit they would have had good reason to do so, and even in these circles it was short-lived. It wasn't possible to cease the operation of all churches at the stroke of a pen, despite thousands of priests and monks ending up deported or sent to prison, since most communist comrades didn't seriously imagine that there was no God. They secretly had their children baptised, held church weddings in the woods or in hidden monasteries, and there were very few Romanian desperados who'd willingly give up on a religious ceremony at their funeral. So they involved the churches into the construction of socialism, and, despite being a strict atheist and an opponent of the clergy, Ceaușescu found them a particularly useful partner and made them instrumental to his nationalist policies.

The church is the only platform that has a coherent discourse on the final outcome, my father stated thirty of forty years after he decided not to become a practicing pastor, because God and

Jesus Christ can manifest themselves in many ways, but certainly not in the fashion this is being preached in the church. I don't know when he realized this, when he understood that there was nobody standing behind him, not even a coherent text or a believable story, except for the fact that he didn't really know or believe in anything, or in case he did, that wasn't in the way others experienced unfaltering belief and promise. My view is that my father didn't feel comfortable studying theology, because the sons of Transylvanian Calvinist dynasties, the offspring of pastors as it were, represented a gentrified world that wasn't appealing to him. In the liberal climate of the college at Arad, he could still entertain the hope that anyone has a chance for gentrification, but at the Theological Institute in Kolozsvár he had to learn the hard way that this wasn't the case. Too many people keep preaching Christ-like humility with supercilious arrogance.

It was around this time that he must have learned what fear was. I'm talking about an elemental and visceral pain, experienced by those who live under brutally oppressive regimes, societies or families where there is no sense of security or protection, and escape doesn't even come up within the realm of the possible because there's simply no way out. This is an intellectualized fear, as one is fully aware that power is not only stronger and smarter than one's self, but that there is nothing out there that is worthwhile to raise an objection for, or to run away from. This is recognition of the fact that everything in the name of which resistance occurs is just as much a matter of fiction, just as much a random act as its very cause, and there's no rising above, withdrawal or peaceful contemplation. At some stage or other, one will have to take sides, at which point one will finally have to answer the question: and how about you, comrade Vida? To be precise: *domnu'*

Vida. In hindsight, I find the latter the most suitable explanation. My father did everything in his power to avoid this situation, he tried to be as invisible and as quiet at his workplace and in the world as possible, he carried out everything he was tasked to do, avoided conflict, gave way to everyone, always had a clean shirt and an immaculate tie on, and never ever showed up unshaven. He didn't join the Communist Party, as he wasn't asked to do so, he spoke good Romanian and Hungarian, he was quite aloof, well-behaved and quiet, he was never late and didn't truant from pointless meetings, he neither took the floor nor objected to proceedings, and he didn't even pride himself of this. I have no idea whether this was the result of some meticulous conception or simply a well-oiled technique that suited his personality, it worked really well for a long time anyway, and he'd sense in good time if there was danger on the horizon or he was about to be pushed to cross boundaries.

Perhaps it was human dignity that he believed in, some sort of inner freedom insofar that when he'd sit down to read the papers, watch some football or work in the vineyard in the afternoon he was a free man, and nobody could take these moments away from him. Yet he must have seriously misunderstood this because my mother didn't consider any kind of inner freedom a reality, for her none of this existed, nobody pays money for such a thing and it can't be eaten either, she'd say. She'd always charge into my father's personal space reserved for peace and quiet, withdrawal and dignity with some excuse; she'd say something, start talking without pause, only to hear her own voice or to be spoken to, and to engage in conversation because that is just a nice thing to do, and, failing that, it's much better to quarrel than to keep quiet. Other times she'd delegate tasks, could we just stir the mayonnaise while watching a match, could we do the dusting while listening to the radio, though one could be engaged in any other activity really, and anyway, how could one just sit there and do nothing? One should at least shell beans, it's possible to practice reflection while being engaged in this task, but she is exasperated at the sight of others are just sitting there, idle, in contemplation, while she has to polish the floor. It's so easy for men, my mother says with a sigh a million times, because she would have liked to be man all her life. I don't know how all this went on before I was born, or when I didn't live with them. I obviously ended up being the third shift for my mother, and by the time she'd finish, it was midnight. The day would start at 5.00 a.m. with the weather forecast on Radio Bucharest. This is our country, my mother would point out, for her the weather in Konstanca, Toplica and Brassó was of crucial importance, for my father the one in Békéscsaba or Debrecen, but even Novi Sad was more relevant than Joseni (as Gyergyóalfalu is known in Romanian, that's where it's usually the coldest) which meant absolutely nothing to him. As soon as he gets up in the morning, the Hungarian Radio Kossuth comes on. For my mother, priorities include making fire, tea, breakfast, child, coffee and then work.

I have clear memories of my father coming home from work late in the afternoon, producing the leftover packed lunch he took with him and me being very pleased with it, then taking all sorts of paperwork and hefty files out of his bag and burying himself in work. I have to stay quiet, and even my mother doesn't bother him on such occasions, we are in the kitchen, my mother is cooking, doing the dishes or sewing, and I'm doing my homework. My mother tends to keep silent, occasionally checking how I'm getting on, but if I'm playing she's just chattering about. My father is working in the living room, he occasionally comes over to the kitchen for a drink of water and at seven o'clock, he listens to the Romanian broadcast of Radio Free Europe, after which he carries on working. He doesn't speak to us or make any comments, he goes outside for a smoke every so often, then it's time for the children's programme and the news, we go to bed early, although my mother is still in the kitchen as if she actually lived there. My father is pedalling so slowly on his bike that I'm really surprised he doesn't fall over, he's become a laughing stock to my classmates for this. As it happens, he actually does fall over at times, and as I can now tell, he's probably suffering from depression.

In hindsight, it's hard to ascertain whether Vida had this much office work to deal with or it was easier for him to hide behind a pile of documents whenever he didn't feel like taking part in the activities run by Violetta or in my education. I have no idea whether there was anything else he cared about at home or whether he even enjoyed being here, besides not being out on streets, where he'd have to meet people who might try to speak to him or might expect him to say something when he couldn't engage with them, and when the sheer fact of him coming up with feeble greetings was already a major achievement. The house was meant to have three rooms and a kitchen, but it never got completed. We only lived in half of it, the two interconnecting rooms facing the street had no heating or furniture for years, they acted as a sort of storeroom or boxroom, as if there had been neither the money nor the will to have them finished. I guess the one bedroom plus kitchen arrangement was just fine for us, and there's no boxroom we couldn't immediately fill up with items we no longer use. Even when there was finally some furniture and heating in the *living* room, we still didn't use it much. It was mainly under lock when

I was a child, I wasn't allowed in without permission, that was the tidy room where we kept money, documents, diplomas, our savings book, commemorative photos taken at school leaving, and everything in there had a particular scent. After my release from the army, this became my room even in the cold season, and money and important documents were moved into the *back* room, which was of similar size, its door still locked, but this time my mother didn't hide the key, she left it in the lock only turning it once.

The garden didn't give us much work in the early days, we were under the impression that we lived in town, and this small plot of land was too large for a hobby but too small to allow us to make a living. We had no animals, grapes and fruit belong to a later phase when it has become obvious that one can always find potatoes, they are the cheapest vegetable, so we'd be better off planting some vine and apricot trees instead. This is exactly what will happen, only that it takes time until these yield crops and, in the meantime, one expects to be in continuous need of the vegetables planted under the vine and fruit trees. My mother keeps complaining that nothing can grow in the shade, while my father is panting and mumbling on account of the carrots and onions, he can't even spray the vine with pesticide, there's no place for him to set his foot, and anyway, one can only expect some decent wine if everything else dies out because of the draught. As for me, I can't help wondering what has happened to this town where I was born, by the late eighties our neighbours end up keeping chicken, goats and geese in their gardens, they allow their cattle to graze in secret, and under the guise of the night they glean everything from the surrounding fields, literally stealing from the state. This panic for survival is a clear indication of where this world is heading, urbanization is clearly suspended for a while, rural customs taking over and coming to the fore like an underground stream. Following the 1989 somersault, I fell the last Székely fir tree in our garden, I mourn it suitably, we build a pig sty because my father is overwhelmed with a passion for farming, since he retired he realized that he had always wanted to be a farmer, a self-sufficient smallholder who can make a living on his own. This is indeed going swimmingly, provided the entire family is working for him for free and the weather and economic circumstances allow it, but mostly they don't.

IX

Kisjenő

The very name of this settlement is bound to cause problems, because in the wake of the Trianon Treaty, Romanians added the qualifier Criș to the existing Chișineu, obviously to distinguish it from Chișinău in the Republic of Moldova. This is the background to the emergence of Chișineu-Criș as the Romanian name for Kisjenő, which later ended up being translated into Hungarian as Köröskisjenő. This is rather confusing because there is already another place near Várad with this name, known in Romanian as Ineu, the latter also being the Romanian name of other villages such as Borosjenő, Csíkjenőfalva and Ünőkő in the Rodna Mountains. Just for the heck of it, I have to add that Google Earth lists Kisjenő as the Hungarian name of the Moldovan Chisinău (Кишинёв), our ancestors must have resided there too, in the course of their migration to the Carpathian basin. These complexities don't make it any easier to explain my birthplace in any language. Those who listen carefully, end up with ideas and usually get it wrong, or I start clarifying place names, and just in case things were obvious up to a point, they no longer are, not to mention that Romanians usually assume I'm from Moldova despite not having a typical accent. This sort of thing tends to happen when someone comes from an insignificant place, sooner or later, people will suspect that they aren't in fact from there, but there you are. To make life easier I tend to say I'm from Arad, which isn't true although I attended school there, I never got to like the city though as I went through difficult times and didn't feel at home. Now I realize that I probably would have felt like a stranger pretty much everywhere, for this feeling was inherent in me, besides, socialism had excelled in prising people out of any sense of potential well-being.

My sense of alienation can't be solely credited to the system, it's far more elaborate than that—home isn't a landscape, an actual place, society, family or environment, it isn't a succession of life-styles that follow one another seamlessly or by way of dramatic transitions, yet all this is part of home. The key thing is the way one thinks about one's given situation, how one relates to it, ident-ifies with it or, conversely, distances oneself from it, and whether one considers these given circumstances as a natural or as an eternal question and problem. As far as I can remember, my mother dis-liked living in Kisjenő, she didn't feel at ease and wasn't at home there because she couldn't find her emotional distance from her family in Barót, or in any case from what she felt and thought of as her family. She didn't realize this, so she considered that the town, its surroundings and life in general were insufferable due to the rigidity, indifference and soullessness of local people. At home, everything was always different, whilst she kept drumming into our heads that what we have is just enough and just right, we are a proper family, we have everything we could possibly need, so whoever heard this, couldn't help but get a little suspicious. The fact of the matter was that only about a quarter of the population in Kisjenő was Hungarian, and most of these Hungarians lived on the other end of town in a Calvinist village called Erdőhegy that administratively belonged to Kisjenő yet not for long enough to obliterate its distinct past and mentality. Even the dialect was different, and people were not inviting enough to make us want to live there despite the larger houses and gardens. The Hungarians in Kisjenő represent a heterogeneous diaspora, most of them Catholic and descendants of Hungarianized Slovaks or Germans. Those who are Calvinists have all come from somewhere else, like us, my mother keeps stressing, and whenever she says this, I feel like pointing out that I personally haven't. Back then, I don't realize that my mother is only a Calvinist because she is my father's wife, and she wants to be a Calvinist because everybody has to belong somewhere. Yet all this is far from being so simple. In short, we lived in a Romanian environment yet we didn't end up Romanian-ized, on the contrary, we did everything in our power to fight it, in fact we should be proud of our Hungarianness since we had to work on it—for us, it isn't just a mere state of being. Perhaps this situation contributed to the way we related to our neighbours, situ-ating ourselves self-consciously apart from them, yet with a sense of loss since we were so *apart*. There was no ill feeling between us, but, frankly, we didn't have much to do with anyone. The lack of social contact can become truly oppressive, and one starts craving to speak Hungarian. This absence, whereby the mother tongue sig-nals its existence, can be really horrible, as there is no such thing as a language or dialect spoken all by oneself, language is a com-munal creation.

My father's village was only seven kilometres away, and it would seem that this was an ideal distance or proximity for him. Yet it could have been any other mileage, since what he was miss-ing was a community of minds, people with whom he would have been able to communicate on his own level whenever he felt like it, hard that it was to imagine. For him, our neighbours were not unlike beasts, while the people he found acceptable were in the distant past, some of his teachers and classmates, there were a few intelligent people on the radio, fair enough, but not in real life. Since I didn't spend the first five years of my life in my hometown but in Ágya, at my grandparents, topped up with a few weeks at Barót that counted as the other side of the world, Kisjenő came across as a strange provisional place where we only happen to be in transit. We live here because our house is here, my parents work here, I attend school here, yet this is some sort of exile, some kind of magic, a Sleeping Beauty situation we should awake from and step out of, because this is anything but the real world. The temporary quality of this arrangement was also emphasised by us living at the edge of town on an estate developed in the seventies, where rows of identical houses were built on small plots of land, residents moving here from the nearby villages, mainly Romanians, but also Romani, Hungarians and Schwabians. As a rule, these houses would be semi-finished, almost everybody lived in one-bedroom-and-kitchen homes, people wearied by the protracted construction work, as the short-lived economic prosperity, when there was some chance for growth, albeit at the cost of significant personal efforts, came to an end. By the time these houses were finished, people became ill, senile, the young moved away, or simply everything was destroyed by the futureless misery of the eighties and the subsequent upheaval, when industry ceased to exist, and towns morphed into villages they had never been because agriculture was also about to collapse—neither a village, nor a town, a settlement known as a *Cartier*. Most men work in one of the local factories, several commuting to Arad, while women stay at home or work in the cannery to sort tomatoes, stick labels, fix crates, look after the children, work the tiny garden, tend to the pigs and chicken, wire, tin, tarpaulin, an entire bidonville among these semi-finished houses, soon to be surrounded by a fast-growing rubbish heap. There's no plumbing, gutters, gas, telephone, public footway or street lighting, we have to bring water from the artesian well, at times there is a queue, it takes time until the jugs are filled up, but this is also an agora of sorts. My parents were the only adults who worked in an office, so we were the elite, together with the family of the Romanian teacher who lived a couple of streets away, we'd always greet one another but had no other contact, they also had only one child, they were part of the elite too. This wasn't the same Romanian teacher for the sake of whom my father didn't become a pastor, though I thought she was. She was exceptionally stunning, stylish, kind to everyone, courteous, urbane, an outstanding figure—liked by the Hungarian children too. My mother and I visited them once, they had mountains of books, I had never before seen such a large library.

My first couple of days at the Romanian kindergarten were thrilling. Early morning half-light, only a few children in a large room, and my mother's voice getting to me from afar, saying that she'd collect me in the afternoon. I can see the chubby face of doamna Șerban, she's the teacher, looking like somebody one should already know from somewhere, she'll look after me, it goes without saying. I can vividly recall the toys, I had never seen so many of them before, because in Ágya I had nothing to play with apart from building blocks, a car and a train set displayed in the glass cabinet that Imike Papp had once broken with his head. He kept screaming that I'm dead, I'm dead, but he wasn't, he didn't even bleed, yet he just kept screaming, lying on the floor until someone poured a glass of water over him, as it was customary to cure such sudden bouts of madness. I remember a battery-operated car driven by someone looking like Elvis, with a female passenger in a white dress holding a camera. I know that the flash should be working, so I open the battery compartment and find it empty, it's always empty, so one day we dismantle the whole thing, and to our great disappointment there's nothing inside, someone had already removed the engine, yet we are punished for it, being made to stand in a corner and weep. On my first day, I play with the car all the time, nobody takes it away from me, I only put it down to have lunch and for my afternoon nap, I do understand that I'm not allowed to bring it with me into bed. I'll find it again tomorrow, but by then it's less interesting, so I let someone else play with it, there are stacks of other fabulous toys after all.

There were a great many children at the nursery, all wearing the same blue smock with a white collar like mine, but there must be something wrong with these children, they are so strange, I haven't seen anything like this. By the third day, I conclude that these kids must be mute, I can't hear anything they say, this is what I shout to my mother every morning, and that I don't want to be here anymore. In vain does doamna Şerban smile at me, I can't hear her either, in vain does she caress my face, in vain does she take me for a hand wash into the first bathroom I have ever set foot in, lukewarm water spouted from a giant copper boiler, and in vain is the car mine to play with all day. I still can't hear what the others are saying. I have no idea how long this carries on, but my memories of the nursery have been filtered through a water flow ever since, there's a warm yellow light, plenty of toys on a red carpet, and the whole house is wobbling. Mircea, Adi, Sebastian, Veronica and Alina have faded away, like watercolour, and doamna Şerban caresses my face with her soft and scented palm. The copper boiler makes an interesting sound when I tap it, and beyond the blue curtain, rain is pouring down, crows are huddled together on the branches of the old tree. In the afternoon, it's usually my father picking me up on his bike, and, as we are pedalling homeward through the puddles, he has to dismount because he can't push on any longer. We carry on in the middle of the road and I dangle my feet from the child seat fitted onto the top tube, and even then my shoes end up completely soaked. This is no flood, only the state of our street in the mid-seventies when the whole area is a building site. There are no trees, houses aren't yet plastered, chain-link fences, lime pits, water and mud everywhere, reeds at the end of the street, pheasants roaming freely in gardens, grass snakes in sheds, swamp turtles in the potato patch, and plenty of rain.

I never said at home or en route/on the move that I disliked nursery, my hysterical attacks would always emerge once we were already there, just about to step into the building, and I wouldn't stop crying until naptime, after which it usually got a little better. I understood, or rather accepted, that my mother and father had to work, and hence I had to attend a Romanian nursery, such as it was. There was a Hungarian one too, but very far from us, at the other end of town in Erdőhegy, and it wasn't a day nursery, there was nobody available to take me there in the morning and pick me up at noon, feed me and look after me, not to mention that I would have to learn Romanian anyway. The same old problem again, they don't know what to do with me, despite them working and building the house for me, the whole world is spinning around me yet I am, in fact, an obstacle to the functioning of this world. One day I spot Grandma Zsüli through the chain-link fence at nursery, she's on her way to the market to sell some eggs and chicken, but I think that she has come to pick me up. I wave and shout at her, but she can't see or hear me, there are at least fifty children squealing about, this is prior to the measles epidemic. I'm among the last to contract it, those who got it first have recovered already by the time I fall ill, at one point there's only three of us at nursery, everyone else is in bed at home. When my temperature soars, my grandmother moves in with us for a few days, I'm under the impression that she'll take me with her to Ágya, but no, she's just here to look after me. I'd quite like to be ill again, though I don't manage to catch any other illness despite running about barefoot outside.

At some point in the winter, I drop a slice of bread on the floor at home and burst out in perfect Romanian: *Bagă Dumnezeu pula-n tine*! May God stick his dick in you! It must be a Sunday, that's the only day we have lunch together. Back then, my mother still makes me pray at the table, before and after each meal, as if it were handwashing, I have to actually chant the prayer together with my mother, and even my father would put the spoon or salt cellar down at such moments. So one can imagine their shock, this utterance feels like a fireball that's literally just bout to strike the room. This is what the Romanian kids say at nursery if they drop their bread, I point out with confidence, and can't understand what's dreadful in this, my mother doesn't translate my words, my father smiles mysteriously which is a rarity even then. The Romanian children would come up with elaborate swearwords in most situations, and despite not realizing, they'd testify to the fact that religious life and sexuality were truly inseparable. If I look back on some of these gems, I can see that they were literal translations of Hungarian profanities, so it didn't take me too long or too much effort to learn Romanian.

The major problem with me, and my mother's main concern, was that since I didn't spend my early childhood with her, she ended up in a bizarre situation whereby she had a son who wasn't quite how he should have turned out. Until the age of five, I was a peasant boy from the Great Hungarian Plain, a sort of farmhand who was in possession of a knowledge for which my mother wouldn't have had any use in her mind or world, horses, bulls, geese, ducks, entering the house with muddy feet, there was no carpet or floor in these village homes, there was no difference between indoors and outdoors, and in case there was, that only applied in winter. There was always mud and dust everywhere, it was impossible to get rid of them, ash, smoke and soot are part of our world, we have clothes in order to wear them, not to look after them, and the destination of objects is different too, toothbrush, slippers, towel. There was no light switch, so naturally that would become the main attraction, though it was out of bounds because the bulb would burn out if I kept switching it on and off, one couldn't tire of this of course. I wasn't allowed to touch the TV or the radio either, in case I ruined them, and I was only allowed to open the fridge door under her supervision. My mother is always keen to point out what I'm not allowed to do, and she also explains why not. Somehow, a little girl got into a fridge and froze to death, the TV can give you an electric shock, as there's electricity inside, one mustn't swat flies on the TV screen, the whole appliance might blow up, and the gas container can also explode if we check it with a flame rather than lather, as regulations would require. Knives, forks, scissors, flames, these have no place in children's games. It's forbidden to drink vinegar or sprinkle lemon salt on toast. It would have never occurred to me to try any of these when someone wasn't looking, in fact no proper naughtiness would have occurred to me as such, it's my mother who tells me what I'm not allowed to do, what she and other kids used to carry out, and for what they had earned their well-deserved punishment.

My favourite occupation is to open the door of the wood-burning stove, I enjoy glaring at fire, just like we used to peer at it in Ágya every single evening, but I also love the flame of the oil lamp and cigarette embers too. They could barely recognize me when I returned from my five-year holiday, I was the spitting image of my father as a boy, sounding and looking just like him at my age. For him, then, this wasn't unusual and neither was the fact that I was on first-name terms with his parents, despite him addressing them in a formal way, as I also tended to do with my own parents. I was rude, reckless, unsubmissive, not in the habit of washing hands or praying before and after meals, and I couldn't make head or tail of what my mother could have possibly wanted from me. Only she could be serious about the fact that these rules could be learned on Saturday afternoons and Sunday mornings, perhaps that was feasible, but this should only apply to Saturdays and Sundays then, or to the times when she'd really insist. She keeps going on about this even after I eventually get used to the routine, after all, I need to be told, as does everyone else, about everything, at all times.

So I returned home from the sense of spatiality I enjoyed in Ágya, moving from öcsöd to öcsöd, and from village to town. My mother always wants something from me, but I don't get this, another child, who isn't me, does understand—perhaps Zólti, with whom they had swapped me. I scream and stomp my feet, I burst out in hysterical fits but apparently there's no need to pour water over me more than once, because if I start crying I can't stop for hours. I'm stubborn and if I want something I do it anyway, and what I don't want to do, well, that's a lost cause. I'm quite picky, if you don't finish your lunch you'll get it for dinner, but this punishment doesn't really work. At times, they try to please me, but I simply refuse to eat, and this goes on forever. There's a picture of me on a nursery holiday camp at the seaside, everyone's quite skinny but I'm the skinniest. My mother struggled really hard with me, and won in the end, I don't think she hit me much, though I can recall a few instances. Once I wanted to grab hold of our *large knife*, I needed it for some reason, I was magically attracted to it, I was allowed to do this at Ágya but not at home, in fact I was hardly allowed to do anything that meant the world to me. Your grandparents let you get away with murder, my mother tends to point out disapprovingly, and she doesn't realize that her normative pedagogy and all these prohibitions and restrictions are dated. One has to break the child's will, the wife of the preacher in Barót tells me much later, and indeed my mother is also breaking my will, this is her way of educating me. They are unable to wean me off swearing, I swear away like a trooper, like my grandfather, Aunt Zsófi, Tarsanyi and many others. After such a scene, and after I finish screaming, I have to say sorry and that this won't happen again, because God is watching us and he'll punish me if I'm ill-behaved, for example the angels won't bestow me with presents, meaning that the angel won't, who is in fact the baby Jesus. This is a proper theological tangle, in Ágya it was the baby Jesus who brought my pyjamas and socks at Christmas, this was the custom for all other children around there, but in Kisjenő, as well as in Barót, it's the angel visiting us, although I never went to Barót at Christmas time. I never understood this, my father could have probably explained it to me, but he couldn't be bothered. God sends this stuff, the angel brings it, and that's that, there's no contradiction. After a while, it strikes me as weird that my father and I have to go to the post office on Christmas Eve, in Barót the angel came earlier, after all it's more to the East, and the relatives send their presents in the post. By the time we get home, the angel has been to ours too, we enter the *small room*, that's where the Christmas tree is, my mother sings *Silent Night*, but I find all this rather strange, I'm unable to sing along with her and father has no musical voice. The next day, we move the tree to the *living room* so we have more space, and so it doesn't drop its needles too soon. At some point our Moldovan neighbours come round to wish us a happy new year, one of them is jumping around in a colourful goat costume as is the tradition in those parts where he comes from, all this is accompanied by song and dance and joyful well-wishing, but mortified, I will persistently dream of a goat with clapping jaws.

There's nothing in Kisjenő that fits with what my godmother saw, but she meant something else of course. I lived in a place without memory, where nobody knows anything because there is no shared past, and there is no one to ask about what's what, why are things in a certain way, whether anything actually happened around here or whether history ever made it here at all. There were words and place names that nobody knew anything about, and in case some people did, I haven't met them, most places didn't even have a name, so I named them for my own sake. The social layer that had or could have had a past and memory disappeared, or was assimilated or forced to take a back seat, and my parents and acquaintances didn't belong there. There was no dance group, theatre company, choir or reading group in Kisjenő, people didn't go to church, there were no balls or events, not even Romanian ones, any kind of community life was absent, so people just worked, ate and watched TV. One couldn't even hear people talk about the good old days, because for ages it looked like there was nothing going on in the past, the traces of self-organization being rather intangible. I found out that there was once a princely castle and estate here, a hunting society, an industrialist association, a printing press, a newspaper, a law court and a reading group, a lad's club, a choir and a Chevra Kadisha. The poet Lajos Olosz lived here, and he was visited by the entire collective of the Erdélyi Helikon [Transylvanian Helikon], not all of them at once of course, but Sándor Reményik came (if only my mother had found this out in time!), and Áprily and Károly Kós too, though I only read about these much later, once I was already in Kolozsvár. In our time, teachers, doctors and white-collar workers in general were not from Kisjenő, they were only dispatched to work here, and they tended to move away as soon as they possibly could. Those who stayed put were experiencing the same nothingness as my parents, pre-occupied with everyday concerns, and when in the seventies border traffic with Hungary was authorized, shopping trips became the main attraction for both ethnic Hungarians and Romanians alike. It's quite likely that this sensation of nothingness is unfounded, and it was only us who didn't go anywhere. Only we lived in that strange isolation that we ourselves have created and that fashioned our otherness into some kind of an excellence, only we were unprepared to participate in whatever happened to be taking place there, because it was easier for us to complain that there was nothing.

As a rule, Violetta blamed Vida's unsociable nature and surliness for our isolation, but now I'm aware that social contact was actually a problem for her, it was she who found it awkward when she had to make contact with people of a higher social standing, or as she put it, with the rich. It was she who saw herself as awkward, clueless, incongruous—it was more convenient for her to disappear into her daily routine from the eyes of the world, despite being tormented by claustrophobia, loneliness and a sense of absence. Her idea of life was going to work, coming home, having dinner, talking about one's day and spending one's free time with useful, and ideally peaceful, activities. It's okay to pop round to the neighbours to borrow something, ask about the homework or help out if necessary, but we aren't allowed to just take a break, start chatting and sit around like everyone else, we don't do such things, as we have better ways to spend our time, so we must get a move on. There was a time when my father and I would go to football matches, because there had always been a football team in Kisjenő, but after a while even these outings had come to an end. Violetta didn't like Vida drinking beer after the match with his colleagues and old acquaintances, not to mention that he had a kid in tow. Every so often, we join in the 1 May and 23 August Parades, but in such a small town, where one is a stranger to none, it's not really possible to organize a proper parade. After the speeches delivered on the football pitch, the crowd carrying flags marches along the high street, and then the men head to the pub for a few beers, the women straight home. All this is far too flippant, it's impossible to scan or even sing properly, and besides, there tend to be more people at an average funeral, for that is actually taken seriously by everyone.

This is a farm, my mother would say in anger, exasperation or desperation, because we live at the very end of the street, as always, everywhere. The last but one house is ours, beyond which it's only reeds, fields, railways and the areas *beyond the tracks*, places that are considered akin to the world's end, a landscape dominated by marshes, thickets, the backwaters of the river Körös with a strip of forest on edge of the horizon. Nobody has the slightest idea what's beyond all this, and I'll make it my business to discover one day. From the end of the street, one can see the giant railway bridge that dominates the horizon, it is this bridge through which every half hour or so a train rattles through, which makes our house tremble a little together with the glassware in the kitchen cabinet. Even the Hungarians calls this place a *Cartier*, a quarter beyond the cemetery, along the railway tracks and twenty minutes on foot from the town centre modernised in the seventies. This is extremely far. The synagogue and all the bourgeois-looking houses are demolished, blocks of flats are being built along the high street, the latter is all I can remember, the old Kisjenő doesn't exist for me. When I realize that it did actually exist, I don't live there anymore, I don't have the strength to research the past of my birth town, but I'm always pleased whenever I stumble about information on this topic. I don't want to go back to the unhappy scenes of my childhood, all I see is that grown-ups can't be merry about anything, or even remotely satiated with what there is and with what they have achieved. All this looks as if they have already decided that it can't possibly be good here, ever. Our house only happened to be seen as any good when my parents sold it, and when my father realized that it was his life's work, despite the fact he was unable to finish it properly, but this wasn't really his fault.

X

Itchy Feet

You always get itchy feet, my mother bursts out reproachfully, and all I can say, as I have said it a million times before, yes I do. My defining experience is that being at home isn't great, and it takes me a long time to figure out why that is. At first, I was really curious. I'm at Ágya, aged five or so, and I see a tree on the field, neither too close nor too far away, the dirt road takes me right there, it feels great to walk in that warm dust, although I'm not allowed to go barefoot, the dust nevertheless seeps through the leather straps of my sandals. I have no idea what I'm doing on the street or how I managed to get out of the house. I'm on my own a lot as there are no other children of my age in the neighbourhood, Tarsanyi is much older, he's already at school, his packed lunch of bread and dripping is my favourite, the one my grandmother is actually making and taking over to theirs, as I'm only prepared to eat it in this way. Évike isn't at Ágya, the girl whose little brother died of meningitis, Zólti Patkány lives very far away at the other end of the garden, so I'm on my own. Grandpa must be having a nap and Grandma is out somewhere in the village, a tranquil summer's day. I want to go up to that tree, there's a stubblefield on the left side, the scary geese are grazing somewhere around Éralja, on the right-hand side it's the Kenderes garden, with a field-guard's shelter at its bottom, housing several barrels of mash, so there are plenty of wasps, and I'm not allowed anywhere near there. I'm not afraid to go as far as the tree, but beyond that is another matter, or at least that's what I think. We are talking about three hundred metres or so. Effortlessly, I make it to the old pear tree, it's not quite by the roadside but a little further into the field, surrounded by thickets, nettles and thistles. I know I should turn around, because I'm scared to go any further, but I simply have to touch the tree, despite grappling with the stinging and scratching vegetation around it. Giant ants are crawling up and down the cracked tree bark, and when I blow at them they stop for a moment, then they start fleeing like mad in all directions. I can only touch the tree for a moment, the ants don't really sting but crawl all over me, which I find terrible. I carefully walk around the tree, only to spot a roe on the other side. It fixes me with a curious gaze, it will run away any minute, perhaps it's trying to frighten me, I think I'll be scared but the roe doesn't jump off, instead it keeps staring at me, then takes a few steps and looks at me again, after all it's just another youngster, more or less like me. Then I see another tree, also tall, old and pinny, also by the roadside, at about the same distance as the first tree is from our house, I must exam- ine it from a close up, as it turns out I'm not afraid to come this far or go even further. As I start off on the dusty road in the summer afternoon, no longer afraid yet curious, the roe decides to join me and follows me at a short distance, if I stop it also stops, and if I make a move it also carries on, grazing on the grass here and there, listening on, and ambling in my wake. I make it to the tree, an old willow, beyond which there's a deep dent, with water gleaming among the reeds. The *büntős* snake and reed wolf suddenly come to my mind, my grandfather would talk about them every so often, now, fearful, I start running back home. The roe will keep gazing in my direction for a long time, unable to understand what could have possibly happened. My grandmother is also unable to understand and can only scream at me, so I can't tell her what happened, I can't even get a word in, which makes my grandfather burst out, stop screaming, the child is back, what else do you want? I start crying, like somebody who has been lost, suddenly realizing what a terrible thing that actually is.

As a rule of thumb, no one is phased by my wandering all over the place, I'm not being guarded or locked in, they know exactly that the garden is no less dangerous than the fields, and it's up to me to look after myself, or else I'll be told off. My grandparents at Ágya don't feel that I need constant supervision, they don't educate, teach or pester me. They don't really want anything from me, they have no educational principles, I'm a little bit superfluous, often a nuisance, but only insofar as any other living being that doesn't require much care or impose a new world view. In addition, my mother also pays for me, though my grandparents will later lend us that money to help towards our house-building costs, it's really hard to decide whether my grandmother was wicked, penny-pinching or just someone with foresight when she demanded money to look after me. They don't really care about my stammer, I can't recall them ever telling me off, correcting or stopping me in my tracks, he'll grow out of it, they say. We cast molten lead, make coal water, in case I'm ill, we visit the midwife as there's no doctor in the village, when I do something wrong my grandmother screams, and when this gets really serious, she hits me, my grand-father does none of these. I don't have to change or transform for them to love me, and I don't have to ask for forgiveness in case I break or refuse something. They never say they love me, according to my grandfather, one doesn't need to say such things. They are rather cold-hearted people, with no emotional side to their lives.

At Barót, on the other hand, things are otherwise. We head there during the summer holidays with my mother, Father lugs a large yellow suitcase on his bike to the station, we also have a carrier bag and my mother's handbag. We are very excited about this journey, can we get on the train, will we have seats, what sort of people will we travel with, in Arad we have to change trains and my mother will have to manage it all alone, with me as the fourth piece of luggage. Mother has been cooking all night, so Father has food for a few days while he's at home alone. She has packed all sorts of goodies for us too, and we are taking tons of things to my grandparents, mainly food items, they keep saying that they have everything but we don't go for that, and anyway it's bad manners to show up empty-handed. We have to make a point of us living a good life, cherries, tomatoes and peppers are already in season where we come from, even if not in our own garden, the train can easily carry all his luggage, the only snag is getting on and off, but someone is bound to help anyway. I don't understand why my mother is this agitated days before we travel, and when we are about to leave, the tension in the house is more palpable than if we were going to school or we were late, which we never are, that only happens to my deskmate, Albi, because he comes from that kind of a family, my mother observes.

Now she feels all jittery, going on about how she has to do everything all by herself. She has to take me home to Barót, for her that is home, and she has to take me there on her own, yet again. The neighbours in Barót are convinced that my father has left us, they have only seen the Kisjenő crowd together a single time, an occasion I can't remember. On the train a well-minded man even asks, after he tries to help but underestimates the weight of our suitcase: don't you have a husband, madam? I can't remember whether my mother replied to this, but she does tell everyone that my father is a very busy man, he can't go on annual leave during the summer because that's peak season at the cannery. My mother also works in agriculture but she can get a few days off to take me home despite the summer, and in winter we don't travel anyway. She has to take me home to Barót for the whole summer because there's nobody to look after me, she tends to explain apologetically. I don't know who's looking after the other kids in the neighbourhood, we usually hang out together playing football, jumping on and off trains as they are about to slow down, going fishing, burning reed, stealing fruit, hunting rats and engaging in many other useful and hardly dangerous pastimes.

I enjoy travelling and I like it at Barót, so I'm not particularly bothered by the fate of children left without supervision, and even my mother relaxes after the excitement of changing trains at Arad. By the time we get to Déva, everything's just fine, she produces a thermos flask and some snacks, I can tell the names of all the stations by heart, there are plenty, as the slow train makes its way towards Brassó. There's always something to see, mountains, hills, factories, rivers, Saxon fortified churches and Gipsy shanty towns that we find rather amusing. There are people from all walks of life on the train, they take a seat, exchange a few words with my mother, get off, then other people join us, sometimes the train gets really crowded, other times it's nearly empty, and this is when my mother gets anxious, one can't even go to the toilet as we can't leave our luggage unattended, let alone me. Ágostonfalva is approaching at breakneck speed, this is where we have to get off, and my mother keeps praying that there is someone to help us. On one occasion in the past, the door wouldn't open, and someone's heel got stuck in a gap between the steps, or the train stopped in an area where one had to walk through nettles and puddles, not to mention that there's also the kid and the luggage to worry about. We've always managed just fine, never had any issues, there was never any danger despite me hoping that one day something would finally happen, but it didn't. My mother kept worrying and being frightened for no reason, and it was also for no reason that I took over some of her anxieties, because at the end of the day, I was rather curious about potential dangers. I had no idea back then that these very long train journeys kept reminding her of the agony of her life, she ran away and ended up regretting it. She's in bitter suffering for her youthful disobedience, but all in vain, things can't be changed, and this is the rightful punishment of those who don't listen to their parents. I don't realize back then that this is a holiday only for me, for her it's a walk to Canossa, though she doesn't know that either. In the autumn, I'm usually taken back home by a relative from Barót, in this way almost everyone in the family has made it to Kisjenő, and could see it for themselves how we've progressed with the house, how warm it is there, so the grapes are almost ripe. We take pictures of everyone and put them in the family album, the entire family all together, the very family that can't ever be together but we have a camera at hand to help. It takes me a very long time to come to terms with the fact that my mother isn't always trying to place me with someone because she wants to get rid of me or she doesn't love me, but because she herself is longing for being taken care of. What she'd like, is a sense of security and to place herself under some sort of tutelage or supervision, because my father lacks any kind of authoritarian trait, which is a sign of weakness. It's great that he doesn't drink and doesn't beat us up, but the rest is no good, because there is no rest, although he brings his paycheck home, mind you.

I don't have to worry about this back then, because in Barót one can see the Hargita mountains from the end of the street, there's a stream splashing past our fence, Uncle Will and his three sons live within running distance, they will let me join their American Indian troop inspired by *The Last of the Mohicans* and *Winnetou*. From now on, the Székely hunting grounds will await me too, together with the woods, the dam on the stream and a raft, we could carry on endlessly, taking in all the other bits and pieces that a boy needs for a carefree summer holiday. Whereas in Kisjenő there was nobody available to look after me, I can reveal hand on heart that in Barót this Native American lifestyle often led us into danger, and it's a miracle that no one got hurt, but it is precisely this miracle we were experiencing that it was all about, lasting until our college days. In this sense there was boundless freedom in Barót, we went where we wanted, we didn't even have to ask for permission, only let them know. I have never seen young boys play the same game for so long, with such focus and discipline anywhere else, except for the novel *A Pál utcai fiúk* [The Paul Street boys], in relation to which many people have questioned the ability of children to organize themselves to this extent. I, for one, know full well that they are perfectly capable to do just that, but they need to be let live.

In Barót, the Apache accepted me as the last of the Mohicans without any further ado. I don't know why I ended up as Uncas, perhaps because I was the weakest, literally the last one, I needed some time to adjust, I was also a scaredy-cat, after all, this new environment was rather alien to me, especially at first. It was mesmerizing to hide behind a plum tree on a hill, wearing a badly stitched feather head-dress, holding a barely functional arrow and kitted out with a knife with a bone handle. Seeing that I was the one tasked to keep watch, I was also thinking about how I should let the others know if the shepherd dogs came any closer. They did tell me but I couldn't remember whether I should let out two long cries, or three short ones, I was far too excited and happy. The dogs were huge and totally wild, I was also afraid of the vipers though we had never seen any, and we ended up looking for the knife with the bone handle for hours on the first day, as we did many times later on. I was pretty bad at both shooting with the arrow and throwing the tomahawk, and reached exhaustion, to the point that I could barely gasp for air. I had to stop several times on my way up the hill and my heart was about to jump out of my chest, yet they waited for me and didn't laugh, so we carried on regardless. We'd always build a fortress in the morning, because we were fortress-dwelling Native Americans after all, I later tried to call ourselves Pueblo, but this didn't go down well. We gathered branches to build a hut, to be precise we set aside an area in the thickets where we could find shelter from the rain. For lunch, we usually grilled some bacon, then we practiced handling weapons and explored the woods, trying to make it to some unknown corner. We didn't spot any actual bears back then, apart from their footprints and excrements, but of course I will get the opportunity to see bears from a close up, on my own, later on, by which time I'm nearly a grown-up. The forest was large and scary, but as we were growing up it seemed to shrink. By now, this game of pretending to be American Indians seems like the same old endless story, it's always summer, always holidays, always the bluish South Hargita peaks: Nagy-Piliske, Kapus-Mountain, Mitács-Meadow, Kakukk-Mountain, Lucs. Our weapons have become much more dangerous, we've moved on to shooting our arrows from a distance of a hundred metres, our knives and axes flying in the air with more and more precision. We'd practice this day in, day out each and every summer, so we were able to protect ourselves in case an invisible enemy happened to hit upon us. There was no enemy though, at times we even regretted this, but learned to accept it. We were also missing the horses, but there wasn't much to do about that either, we did get the chance to mount some horses as they were cooling themselves in the woods, but as there were no reins to hand, the whole exercise didn't amount to much. We had a dog though, called Manix, a genius mongrel that loved climbing trees, it would simply run up and down the thicker branches, getting hold of countless cats in this way. As we grew up, pretending to be American Indians turned into longer and longer excursions in the forest. We have all retained a passion for the woods, one of us even made it to the Mont Blanc, and I managed to climb the Kaçkar in Turkey, that's also almost four thousand metres, a few times we have almost bit the dust in the Fogaras Mountains in winter, but this story belongs to our adulthood already. Uncle Will would regularly take us on his night-time raids, spotting bears and deer, he was up to date with our American Indian games too, despite not having read the books on which they were based. We didn't have to explain to him why it was important to cultivate such an imaginary world and be dead serious about it, because one is only able to accept reality to the extent one is prepared to accept the dreamworld. Will didn't have pedagogical principles, but he liked the forest, and in exchange, the forest took him seriously, and so did we. In all other respects, he was an aggressive, unreliable and hysterical beast, at work it was either him wanting to strike someone to death or others trying to beat him up, all this isn't a big deal in a coalmine, but we felt really comfortable in his company.

It's no big deal to be a guest or a grandchild, as long as one doesn't have much to do with the problems and conflicts of grownups, the latter are really pleased if kids are out of the way, and one simply accepts that some matters are out of bounds, and neither related interest nor personal opinion is welcome. I wouldn't have had any issues with these summer holidays if I didn't have to attend church every Sunday morning and afternoon in Barót. If I didn't have to listen to all this religious nonsense, albeit accompanied by a brass band in the afternoon and with the occasional guitar playing. If I didn't have to show respect to all these devout people as they go about their prayers, adding the odd twist stolen from here and there, whilst others burst out crying, and assist with a straight face at the performance of this hypocritical congregation rehearsing in front of God. If only I could confront the fact I didn't believe in any of this, and therefore God would punish me, but even if I did believe in this stuff, I'd be still bored to death, hate all this and find it shallow. If only I could confide in someone that I was unable to do this in this way, like my father had already done so. Unfortunately, my American Indians would throw themselves into the practice of religion, orchestra rehearsals, the reading of the Holy Script and other delights of congregational life with the same childish enthusiasm they displayed when being American Indians or while rafting. At first, I envied them, because I could sense that they were part of a community that I didn't belong to. Then I felt sorry for them because religious life denied them experiences such as going to the cinema or watching TV, and in general they lived in a poorer and more isolated and repressed world, despite Barót being a more urban place than Kisjenő. Finally, I ended up laughing at them, but this only happened when I got to read my father's Bible annotations during these endless prayer meetings, first out of boredom, and then because I was able to encounter stuff no one had ever mentioned before. There's something funny in teenage kids confronting one another with Biblical parables when they argue, only to find that grown-ups can only understand the Scripture at this same level. To this day, I fail to understand how grown-ups could cope with all this, being up to date with each other's shenanigans. Sure enough, one day Will ends up calling the preacher a son of a bitch in front of the entire congregation, though he doesn't get anywhere with that, and Uncle Tom hangs himself though no one understands why, just like no one has a clue about Uriah the Hittite or Abishag.

We pray an awful lot, morning and night we all kneel down and go through our sins, asking for forgiveness and mercy, whilst the other kneeling members of the congregation say grace and seal it with an amen. Owing to my stammer, I didn't have to say my own stuff out loud, they were happy with a Paternoster in my case, which was a major concession, and in time I learned not to pay attention to all this drivel, my grandfather is talking to God, not to me. One evening I saw my grandmother fall asleep leaning onto a stool, and snoring really loud during the prayer, in her open mouth I spotted her only tooth, Grandfather cleared his throat when he finished, so we could all say amen together. We'd pray both before and after meals, five times a day, like in Muslim cultures. My grandfather would occasionally come up with extra prayers too, making us say grace to the one in Heavens by kneeling down in the field, stable or forest, even in the chicken shed, though this latter occasion wasn't orchestrated by him but by the preacher. We didn't have to kneel down but did sing at the end, which made the woman next door think that Grandmother must have died since she wasn't out there with us. Grandfather had the gift of the gab and was an intelligent and agile man, in possession of all the tricks of the trade needed for farming, woodcarving, barrelmaking and beekeeping. He had also been a woodcutter, after all every Székely is skilled at this, plus he had also been a miner, a soldier in Horthy's army, a border guard in the battle of the Úz Valley and a prisoner of war in the Krasnodar camp in Russia. He'd talk about all this really clearly and concisely, it was most enjoyable to listen to him, and we could ask questions and talk to him. If I didn't understand something, he'd draw it or map it out using pebbles or woodchips, he was familiar with the forest, mushrooms and plants, like a proper fairy-tale Székely grandfather, an entire universe in his own right. Yet he was afraid of electricity because he didn't understand it, despite not having any issues with lightning or thunder. When he and a neighbour made a grenade washed out by the floods explode in the garden, the pair of them burst out laughing like some naughty boys, and then kept searching for more for days on end, but to no avail. Whenever there was talk of God, Jesus or the Scripture, and this was a common occurrence, his face would stiffen, restless blue eyes turning cloudy, gazing into the nothingness and then over my head, his voice and articulation changing, reminding me that everything was exactly the way the Scripture said. Some people wouldn't take notice, this was the cause of all the troubles in the world because everyone wanted the fleshpots of Egypt, having abandoned God's path. I'd always stand there in awe of this, he was very fond of the exile in the wilderness, and I could barely comment on this. For me, the wilderness was in Ágya, although Moses had never made it there, whilst the Sinai was a desert, although Grandfather wasn't familiar with this word, it's not mentioned in the Scripture so it can't be important. There were no further questions, so we finished with a prayer, he wiped the tears off his face and we carried on, continuing with our activities as before. For me, his preaching or testifying wasn't about transfiguration, but about him being absent and being somewhere else, even if the ceiling had collapsed, the forest sloped or the buffaloes trampled on us, I was left to my own devices and not even allowed to make a move. I was afraid of these situations because I was unable to follow what he was saying, and had he checked, he'd have figured out that I wasn't paying attention. He'd usually check on me following the Sunday prayer at church, though I only had to remember the sermon, the lesson, and learn the wisecrack of the day, he never asked about his own words, who knows, perhaps he didn't quite remember what he said either. Later on, I was able tell in advance if he was about to start preaching, so I cleared out of his way. He'd let me, as he didn't really need anyone's assistance for this, he'd come to a halt, look into the nothingness and mutter something, hat in hand, then kneel down if it wasn't muddy, or just lean his knee against a wall or a tree, and pray. He had never hurt me, not even shouted at me, but I saw him hit a buffalo in anger because it joined the herd from a nearby village. By then, he was the only person in Barót to own a buffalo, but it would always run away whenever it was in heat, so one had no choice but bring it back. The buffalo collapsed in pain, and Grandfather kept flogging it until one end of the long and hard rosewood stick was frayed, I was watching all this standing by the stable door, but when Grandfather saw me, he threw the stick away. This is the punishment for disobedience, his eyes conveyed, but since I was their grandchild, they refrained from giving me orders.

XI

The Order of Things

Everything had to be deployed according to the strictest order, and if I didn't do something the right way, then I had to do that again until it was right. If I didn't say the right thing the right way, then I was corrected, in a kind voice that wouldn't take no for an answer, as many times as necessary, and despite me asking for clarifications, all I was told was that this is the right way, and that's that. As far as everyday activities or farming was concerned, this was a no brainer, it didn't even occur to me that I could know the answer, or I could do the work in any other way. I had to take part in everything they did, but all this was at least as exciting as pretending to be American Indians, and I experienced the same feeling of spatiality. In the cooperage, there are ten different planes, each has a name of its own, stave clamps, drills, gimlets and a whole bunch of chisels, all kinds of wood, oak, beech, hornbeam, acacia, ash, elm, cornel, fir (spruce, pine, cembra, silver), at least ten kinds of willow, maple, poplar and birch. All can be used for different purposes, and making a barrel or a tub, or even just exchanging a stave is an incredibly exciting challenge. Only making hay compares to this. My grandfather tells me, as we take a break between building haystacks, that in the past they'd move up the mountains for weeks in order to deal with the mowing and hay drying, or with cutting wood in the winter. They'd only come home once a week, because one can carry about a week's food supplies on one's back: potatoes, cornflower, bacon, cheese, onions. Making hay is exciting because I thought, felt and understood that this process extends from the leaf of grass to the milk itself, and both I and my rake are part of this broader picture. I once watched a buffalo give birth, as its calf comes into the world, the *cub*, we waited until it was able to stand on its feet, though by then I had already seen such a thing, as lambs are also born this way, and people too.

My view on the order of things is that I might have a role in that, and in case I know something better, for instance that it's not five but six o'clock, then I should be able to say that, after all we are aiming for truth and for being right. But my grandfather didn't appreciate the fact that I was more aware of time than him, because if the position of the sun on the sky shows him that it's five o'clock, then the watch shouldn't show six, the switch to Summer Time must have just happened around that point, or he simply got lost in his own rhythm. So I go in the house to check the exact time on the cuckoo clock, on which I learned to tell the time and read Roman numbers the previous year, as it happens from Grandfather himself. It's actually rather pointless to check the time, I have just come out to the garden a few minutes earlier, perhaps Grand-mother sent me to call him. By the time I get back, it's quarter past six, as the garden is quite large. That's impossible, Grandfather says again, carrying on with the weeding, while I stand there clue-less. I happen to mention over lunch one day around this time that Ceaușescu isn't a king but a president, the general secretary of the Communist Party, this is what we've been taught at school and it's important. I also said something clever about space research, as we learned about that too, but then I decided to keep quiet as I could sense trouble. I didn't yet know that it is a mortal sin to cor-rect or berate Grandfather, and it's simply not acceptable to say that he didn't get it right, or he made a mistake. First, he clicks his tongue to signal that this is enough, and whoever doesn't get it or doesn't know their place can soon follow the buffalo's lead. It's irrelevant what the time really is, whether the boards we put under the barrel are mouldy, and what they say in the papers. It's irrelevant what I see or know, what matters and what happens is down to Grandfather's will, this is the order of things. If he says it's five o'clock, then it's five o'clock, the boards aren't mouldy, Ceaușescu is the king of Romania and no man had ever walked on the Moon. We are late to service, the board breaks, who cares about space research or Ceaușescu, but children should just keep schtum, once and for all, they could never be right or in the know. We leave with a delay, Grandfather growls at me that I should hurry up, it's a sin to be late, he doesn't even shave or change, only kicks his muddy wellies off and puts some boots on. It's my fault that the board breaks under the barrel, Grandfather looks at me in anger, then sends me to play, dismissing me with a wave of the hand, then removes the board, the one that's mouldy, but he wasn't prepared to look at it or acknowledge what I was saying. Yet it was even more awful when Grandmother educated me concerning my place and that I have to be obedient, otherwise God will punish me. In other words, if I say that we should hurry up because it's already six o'clock, and not five, and we'll be late, we will indeed be late, and it will be me who's punished by God, despite being right yet contradicting Grandfather. In this case, it is preferable to be late for service, although back then I didn't think this through quite in the same way, I was very scared though, and whenever they explained to me the order of things a world collapsed in me and I was on the verge of crying.

The universe has three pillars in Barót: my grandfather, God and reality. Everything has to happen the way grandfather says, because that is God's will, and reality should simply take note of that. The rest of us are only hanging around, and we have no choice but to tremble like a buffalo if we can't find the order of things or don't know our place. I never got a good hiding, they simply told me that I didn't really exist. This was terrifying and unacceptable because they did this systematically, I was in a hermetically sealed world, my mother, my godmother and even my uncles believed in this, and it didn't occur to any of them that this may not be quite right or quite God's will. In case I say something that doesn't fit with the order of things, that issue simply doesn't exist, it is as if I never said it, and if I insist, they snap at me and everything goes on as before. In the end, my mother will hit me, enough is enough, it's much better if she's the one that hits me than life at a later date. I understand soon enough that if they ask me about something, I shouldn't respond but say what they expect to hear. Nobody can cope with a world collapsing in on them, every day, after a while I can't take my grandparents seriously, we live in alternative universes, without overlap, although they do love me a lot. They are average Székely people, my grandfather dominates everyone, and Grandmother articulates the ideology: everything has to be exactly as Grandfather wants it to be. One can imagine the role of reality in all this in the course of the fifties, and one can ponder on the place of Jesus Christ in this world, after all, we made much more regular references to him than the average Székely family. As an eight- or ten-year old, I'm not thinking of such things, but my uncles Will and Tom are much more likeable than Grandfather, for him even the American Indians are non-existent, but for me, it was sufficient to get out of the house and head in the direction of Water street to forget about the order of things. Grandmother would continuously warn me about stuff, don't do anything stupid, don't light a fire in the forest, don't stay out till late, an entire litany that ended with make sure that news about you doesn't reach home earlier than yourself, but by then she was the only one left to hear it. The American Indians were already waiting for me in full armour, the Hargita was looming from afar, and when we took a break to have some grilled bacon for lunch, we often forgot to say our prayers, though we did remember at a later point. God forgave us, Grandfather didn't know about it and this was reality, the one and only.

The scariest thing was the flood that affected the whole of Transylvania in 1975. As a rule, the Barót stream was flowing on the other side of the street, but following abundant rain it would often take over the street itself. So everyone knew that whenever the Southern peak of the Hargita was covered in dark rain clouds in the afternoon, the stream would burst its banks before dark, or, as people would put it, *high water would be on its way*. By the next morning, it would be back in its usual bed, and by the third day, it would be almost clear again, though still a bit murky and cold despite the hot summer. I can't recall whether I was aware of the Biblical Flood back then, or I only connected that to the '75 flood later, but it makes no difference. It was raining day in, day out, the water in the riverbed was muddy, carrying branches and twigs and we knew that this was a sure sign of flash floods, for days on end the water levels would be rising to a disquieting proximity. Every so often neighbours would bring news of massive rainfalls in nearby villages, such as Magyarhermány or Nagybacon, and I'd keep wondering what could possibly make those so massive since it was raining here too, without a break. One night, a neighbour knocked on our door to say that we should wake up, the *high water* is now here and indeed by the next morning it had already reached the footway. I haven't seen anything like this before, such a colossal amount of water in front of our house, the water sounded and smelt different from usual, I could smell the scent of wet forest, as if that was also pouring down together with the rain. Soon after Uncle Tom came round and got the water pump, the *hidrofor* from the cellar and brought it into the house, we took everything we could out of the cellar, filled all tubs with drinking water, I was involved with this work all day too, and was seriously worn out by the end. The rain kept pouring down and the stream just grew and grew, I stuck a branch into the wet soil, but when the waves got to it, they didn't withdraw any longer, the water just streamed along the footway into our yard. Looking out to the street, I could see the rippling water claim the field on the other side, the whole street a fast river harbouring the dark-red vortex of imminent deluge. Water levels were growing steadily and I found myself locked into the house, inspecting the horrific picture of the street from the window, there were giant tree-trunks floating, the dreadful water roaring along, shaking not only the trunk of the old lime tree by the window but also our whole house. Water levels are indeed rising visibly, one can see this on the tree trunks, fences and flower gardens, the cellar is already filled with water and this water didn't get there taking the stairs but came up from beneath the ground, like a spring, and it even started spraying out of concrete walls. The well is full and the backyard is also underwater, yet the water levels keep rising and the rain falling, we make several journeys to the attic and bring up bread, bacon, flour, everything we might need in case the water takes over the house. We place bricks under the feet of the beds and wardrobes, remove all carpets, the water is rising higher and higher and it's about to enter the house, it's a matter of only four inches. The water is already waist-high in the garden, Grandfather can barely make his way out of the shed and the stable, the buffalo, the only animal they keep at that time, is wailing in the water, Grandfather throws it some straw, for the last time, the pigs are squealing, there's nothing we can do, so let them swim. The water is flowing in the direction of the back garden, and I can see from the kitchen window that Grandfather has to hold on to the garden fence in order to be able to move forward. We can't see this, but he will later tell us that the water lifted the gate out of its hinges, and it also knocked a neighbour's house down, the water might even flush our gate away, there's no way we could fix it, the current is too strong, and besides, there's a drop in the ground level too. Eventually, the rain stopped by the afternoon, so we went up to the attic and took a tile out of the roof to be able to look around. Everything's under water, all the way to the nearby mountain, tree trunks are flushed down at breakneck speed in what is supposedly the riverbed, at times there are animals too, we can't make out whether they are sheep or goats, there are also haystacks and bits of roof among the debris caused and collected by the flood. Then it starts to drizzle again, and this makes this sight even more depressing and horrific. It won't take our house away, will it, I ask for the hundredth time, and they reassure me that it won't, this is quite a newly built stone house, but I can tell from Grandfather's voice that nothing is entirely certain. Later, he starts muttering again, singing softly, then we all take a seat at the table, pray and share a meal as if this was our last supper, he takes the Bible and starts reading the story of the Flood. We are God's chosen people, this goes without saying for me at the time, so we can't get into harm's way. At some point in the afternoon, we notice that the water levels have gone down an inch, and I can't help thinking that my mother should really turn up and get me, I had enough of this summer holiday. Needless to say, my mother doesn't come, the whole of Transylvania is under water, and for many years from then on, every time it thunders or starts raining, I can hear the roar of the stream in my inner ear. Next thing, the water begins to withdraw just as fast as it rose, and by midnight it's out of our garden, Grandfather tries to push the mud out with a snow plough, but it keeps pouring back. There's an entire sea of mud in the wake of the flood, and even years later, one can tell the unique sediment of the 1975 vintage apart, this will be followed by others, but those are darker, this is bright yellow soft sand. I hear for the first time the news that this catastrophic flood was caused by excessive deforestation, *forest-tainting*, because in this way the rainwater could run down the hillsides swiftly and without obstacles. Back in the day, there was such a thing as an ecological conscience in Székely Land, but nobody saw the point, after all how much can another metre of water possibly cost God? Not to mention that people have been sparing no effort at cutting down the forests ever since.

Returning that autumn to Kisjenő was like descending into a vale of tears on earth. As we say our goodbyes, Grandmother is crying, Grandfather is crying and I will burst out crying soon, it's cold, and there's fog at dawn in Székely Land as we get into the car that will drive us to Ágostonfalva station. We cross the river Olt on a ramshackle wooden bridge, underneath the river is ink black, murky and menacing, it's quite misty, we have to wait for a long time at the level crossing, one train follows another, so we almost end up missing ours. Despite my hopes, we never actually miss it though, as grown-ups often feel the need to leave home hours earlier, like village people usually tend to do, not entirely trusting the time displayed by clocks and watches. Being on time means that we aren't late, and we do everything to ensure this outcome. The fact that my father always gets to the station the last minute and he's the last person to buy a ticket, stepping onto the train as it whistles to pull out of the station is an eternal scandal in my mother's eyes and causes her unbearable anxiety, like the journey itself for that matter. It's a pointless, senseless activity that only gives way to doubt and disrupts that closed organic world in which we live. Those who are familiar with Székely Land know exactly that this inwardness is precisely what makes this hostile natural climate and brutal social context somewhat liveable, and this world actually tends to experience its various states in a predominantly carefree fashion. Travelling and breaking out constitute the end of this carelessness, the oft-discussed homesickness is basically not a moral category but a feeling, a longing for the intimacy of child-hood, a craving for the warmth of the sheepfold, that clads brutal fathers and apathetic mothers into kindness and transforms fight-ing families into idyllic communities. This is the topic Áron Tamási writes about in a beautifully ornate style, and Gáspár Tamási in a precise and matter-of-fact fashion. Home can't be translated into anything else. Those who left, have left forever, there's no way back to oblivion. I experienced the drama of being torn away every single autumn and this lasted for a good hour and a half, until we reached Segesvár to be precise, that's where Székely Land ends on a mental map, as far as I'm concerned in any case. Westwards from there, the dark green of the vegetation fades lighter, the sky, the clouds, the sunlight and the water look different, possibly because early morning gives way to midday.

When I was a child, I used to travel through Transylvania by train twice a year, from Arad to Brassó and back, and for a long time I was unaware that this was precisely the subject of all those books. Somehow, there wasn't any talk of this, we discussed it neither at home nor on the train, for some reason Transylvania wasn't fashionable at the time. And then, all of a sudden, I understood. Our train was being stationed at Alkenyér (Şibot) for quite a while, it was a hot day at the end of the summer, with an awful lot of waiting, flies and boredom. I did manage to catch a glimpse of Pál Kinizsi's statue many times before as we were travelling through, he'd be staring at the train through his iron mask, but this time we were positioned in such a way that I could actually read the Romanian text carved into the stone plinth. I'd prefer to get off the train to see it from a close up, especially the weapons in front of the statue, but of course this isn't allowed. The name on the plinth reads Paul Chinezu, but I already know from my mother that this is in fact Pál Kinizsi, and this place was the scene of the battle of Kenyérmező. I remember it well, as there's a comic about King Matthias in which the artist Ferenc Deák depicted Kinizsi as he's lifting three Turks at a time in his victory dance. I manage to connect these things, perhaps not straightaway as the different bits of information that I possess have obviously come from various sources, but nevertheless it becomes crystal clear to me there and then: this is it. A shiver runs down my spine, a sensation I haven't experienced before, a realization that this is no story, picture book or TV film but reality, of which I'm also part of, this is happening to me right here, right now. History can be just as intimate as a family, and the process of becoming aware of things leads from an idyllic state straight to chaos. I didn't know what to make of this experience at Kenyérmező for ages, all I did was look forward to spotting the statue on our journeys, and I was always sad if another train happened to obstruct the view, this wasn't a frequent occurrence though, it was usually right outside our carriage window. I'll experience something similar in Kolozsvár when I first take a look at the statue of King Matthias, but this will happen much later and last a lot longer.

In Kisjenő, there's nothing, this was the defining experience of all my arrivals back there, and I've always found my mother's childish excitement bizarre, what can possibly make her so carried away? She doesn't understand that for me, being there is good, and being here is bad, or at least of no importance, and now I can start my year-long countdown until she takes me there again. I used to await the annual journey to Barót as if only that world would have had any meaning, anything else being grey, boring, monotonous and characterless. The next summer was so out of reach and so far away as returning home was to my mother, the home she had to renounce for good, despite her always talking about going *home* whenever we went there. For her that was the only place she considered home, nothing else could take its place, everything was measured up against it, and perceived as good or acceptable but mainly bad, the idea of difference being a worrying source of anxiety for her. My mother also cultivated the order of things, and the expectation that things should be deployed in the exact order she dictates, that's the only correct way, this is what she learned from her father. She may not succeed in fulfilling this aim with the same drastic means as my grandfather, but she's having a stubborn and steady go at it. Whoever resists this attempt or dares to doubt the very sense of this order, is seen to be committing an offence or a criminal attempt against the entire family from Barót, which in a sense is identical with challenging God the Father, seeing that Uncle Gyurika's worldview is hovering above my mother like the Superego in the wildest Freudian theories.

XII

Home

There was a sort of monotonous and wistful peace in Kisjenő, where tedious waiting would carry on for so long that it was pointless to even mention it. I corresponded regularly with the American Indians, but there wasn't much to write about as they carried on pretending to be Native Americans whereas I didn't, we lived in two different worlds, plus the summer came to an end soon. My Székely's accent stayed with me for weeks, and my mother would always smile with the enthusiasm of those who suddenly come across a bit of vernacular. My father would dismiss it with a wave of the hand, he'll grow out of it, while the other kids would just grin and laugh, and it was hard to tell whether this was because of my stammer or my accent. This didn't really matter anyway, because unless they wanted to tell me off, they didn't actually take note of my stammer, and I'd return from a much richer linguistic universe. You know many more words than I do, a friend pointed out to me, and he was quite right about this because one tends to perceive the world as a vaster space if one is at home in several dialects at once.

In the autumn of 1975, a few days before that start of the school year, I put down the last fairy-tale book of my life and read the novel *The Last of the Mohicans*, to finally find out who I was meant to be in the American Indian gang at Barót. This moment basically marked the beginning of literature for me, I started to devour books and since there were barely any other books about Native Americans at the time, I was forced to try alternatives. I knew the story of Uncas inside out, I could cite entire passages and I'd always burst out crying by the end, though I tried to keep this to myself. I was saddened for a long time by the fact that there were hardly any kids in Kisjenő who could fall under the spell of the American Indians, we'd watch Gojko Mitić and Pierre Brice in the cinema or on TV and carry on as before. It was particularly painful for me that in those hundreds of Westerns shown on Romanian Television in the late seventies, First Nations would usually appear as stupid, laughable or even evil. They're just like Gipsies, my father observed, which I found really insulting as it turned out that he hadn't read the story of Winnetou and Old Shatterhand. He was unaware that Lajos Kossuth would read the novels of J. F. Cooper in prison, and in this way, Uncas was indeed connected to the Hungarian Revolution, in my mind we had ended up with the exact same fate as the Redskins. *Native American words on the radio*, I should say, but this is a later phase by which point my father was totally uninterested in literature. One couldn't play American Indian games in Kisjenő, but since the *Cartier* was surrounded by the remains of a colourful marshland, our childish imagination had populated it with imaginary creatures. There were leeches, grass snakes, plenty of mosquitos, frogs, we went fishing and, in case we slipped knee-deep into the mud, we knew that Babao could grab our ankles and not let go. I have no idea who this Babao was, but it had a fiery and watery version, Albi's one-armed grandfather told us about this, though I couldn't take this seriously, as they couldn't take the Native Americans seriously, either.

Albi was my best friend, they lived in the house next door, we'd go to school together in the morning, sit together in class for years and spend many years in harmony despite agreeing to differ in many respects. I was interested in the wilderness, he in football, I liked humanities, he liked maths, he was short and sturdy, and I tall and skinny. He was better than me at most things, but all this talk about the American Indians and Székely Land really touched him, I have never had a better audience than him. We took each other seriously, as young boys tended to do, argued only very rarely, though I did throw the pliers at him once because we couldn't decide whether a particular nail was a cog or not. I envied him because he had siblings, his oldest sister was better at football than me, a great striker. Her technique was excellent and precise, she kicked the ball with maximum force and ended up the only pro-fessional footballer among us, nearly making it on the national team. She'd always hang out with us, we'd go fishing, hiking as well as to school together, and we couldn't grasp how Tamara could catch bigger fish than us, this drove us to desperation. Albi also had two younger sisters, their mother was a stay-at-home wife and their father was braving it on some farm, sometimes he'd come home on horseback, other times on a motorbike, but mainly drunk. Unimaginable scenes were taking place in our neighbour-hood, worthy of Italian films, once even a pressure cooker exploded and we could hear everything despite the fence my mother had built out of Eternit boards, and despite us closing all the windows whenever Aunt Zsú was screaming and shouting. They were a family unlike us too, sometimes they had a car, other times they didn't, they'd go to restaurants or dancing, they even made it to the seaside, they'd often swim in debt but then manage to pay it back, no one would know how and wherefrom. They were our perfect opposite, though I didn't understand this back then, they lived a much more colourful life than we did, were always a great mess, a complete mayhem, but I liked being there whilst my mother didn't, she preferred it if their children came round to ours.

Every so often, Uncle Fjodor packs all of us kids onto a horse-drawn cart and drives us to the fields, to Dohányos, an old farm that used to belong to the Earls of Csernovics. Other times, we are squeezed into a motorbike sidecar, holding on to dear life at bumps, there's too many of us and all this is against the law, Albi and I have a go at driving a tractor and then a lorry, and at shooting with airguns, using our home-made bullets. The best bit is when Uncle Fjodor plays football with us, he throws his bag on the ground, kicks his shoes off and starts dribbling, wearing only his trousers and white shirt, while his wife screams: *feriyour-sooooooooocks!* He's the one who takes me for the first and last time to a restaurant in Kisjenő, Nylon is still a decent place back then, there's even a band and one of our neighbours plays the accordion, they also serve lunch, but later only Intim will do lunch, though not for long. I can't finish the first steak of my life, it would last me a whole week, and after lunch Albi and I share a beer, we don't like it but are proud to have tried it, don't mention this at home, his father warns us, and we do indeed keep this a secret, as ten-year-olds tend to do. Albi's father is really cool, mine is only a gentleman, I tend to think at the time. Uncle Fjodor is basically the first Romanianized Hungarian person I get to know. He went to Romanian school, always lived and worked in a Romanian environment, only his wife was Hungarian, with whom he battles at knifepoint over many issues, especially over that it's pointless to send the kids to Hungarian school, but the wife wouldn't give in. She's another Transylvanian fugitive who got stuck on the Plain, like my mother, except that she's not religious but of a fiery and hysterical disposition. Perhaps not even my grandfather can curse in quite such a colourful way as she scolds her children or cats, in this respect the potential of the Romanian–Hungarian language combination is astonishing—*büdös kurva bulandra* and a *futǎ-te Stalin, basszon meg Sztálin, rakja belétek a Dumnezeu a faszát, egy nagy mocskos scroafa vagy*, azaz *koca*—filthy Gipsy whore; may Stalin fuck you; may God stick his cock in you; you are a ginormous filthy sow. At first this scares me but I get used to it, I realize that this is only fireworks, a sort of soundtrack, and she's much scarier when she's quiet. Uncle Fjodor considered himself Hungarian but his Romanian was better, he spoke a very interesting mix that later reminded me of the csángós, his Hungarian intonation is typical for the Plain but his Romanian accent isn't, it's the one spoken in Oltenia, in the South, so there's a bizarre contrast between Romanian melodiosity and Hungarian roughness. He'd always apologise to us for not speaking good enough Hungarian. I found this annoying, as I thought that his language skills were quite good, but he didn't try hard enough. He identified whole-heartedly with the system, showing no opposition whatsoever. According to my father, all he knew about the world was what was said at the Party committee meeting, he was a typical party apparatchik who'd diligently listen to Ceaușescu's speeches and elegantly outdo everyone on the football pitch. Then, all of a sudden, in the eighties, his colleagues start calling him Hungarian and he gets a year suspended sentence for some petty crime. He feels that this can only happen to him because he's Hungarian. He doesn't know that the Romanian state and party leadership is carrying out a process of ethnic cleansing, whereby Hungarians in key positions are removed from office, mainly on the grounds of professional misdemeanour or error, these are petty affairs yet are not investigated at the relevant workplace but by the secret police and handled by the state prosecution service. We cheer together during the '82 World Cup, watch every single match and are ecstatic whenever there's a Hungarian goal, at other times there's indignation all round. Albi and I will go to a Hungarian secondary school and even share a room in our last year. Following the regime change, Uncle Fjodor will become a presbyter in the Calvinist church at Kisjenő. My father lectures him on theological matters on their way to church, but on the way back, they discuss politics and complain about bishop Tőkés. My mother is angry with them about this, as they spoil her religious mood. And anyway, since when is it acceptable for devout Christians to admonish a bishop, asks Aunt Zsú who's Catholic.

Except for Albi's family, the Toldis are the only other Hungarian family on our street. Our neighbours include Romanians, Gipsies and Germans, one can always play football as a few people are bound to be out there kicking a ball, I can't do anything else with them and we have very few points of contact. Despite this being a predominantly village environment, people's mentalities are reminiscent of housing estates. Families have nothing to do with one another, people aren't related, everybody's only concerned with beautifying their own house to the exclusion of all other concerns, they keep silent about their world back home, yet they have no other handles on reality and know about nothing else. All houses look alike and people lead similar lives, it takes time for personal traits to show themselves on the walls or fences. Nobody feels any motivation to let others into their personal universe, because they either think that it's unimportant, ridiculous and everybody would look down on them, or, on the contrary, theirs is the only one that makes sense, so either way, people feel a little awkward. When it comes to hierarchies, our *Cartier* is at the bottom, we are the riff-raff and the upstarts, who don't belong to the original texture of the town, and I find that pointing out whose son I am means nothing to the indigenous population. They might just about have an idea of Ágya, that's the poorest and most run-down Hungarian village around here, but nobody has heard of Barót and I find it particularly hard to convince people that Székelys are Hungarian, which always makes me really upset. We are often visited by relatives from afar, and this is quite a big deal, especially if they arrive by car, our first visitor couldn't even make it all the way to our house because of the mud. Unlike my mother, most neighbours don't long for their homeland, only the Puşcariu family will move back to the Danube Delta, where they had originally come from. They are Gipsies, my father tends to say, but according to Mother they are quite all right, she finds most Romanians and Gipsies nicer people than our Hungarian neighbours.

The Toldis are proper peasants, they move to our street soon after us, from a neighbouring village, bringing all their village customs with them, they always behave as if they were at home, in the garden or the stables. They are sturdy, loud and aggressive, and they also believe that the only world that makes sense is the one they left behind. They end up in conflict with everyone soon, be it on account of the footway, a bike or some puppy, it doesn't really matter, they simply have a tendency for domination and they barely speak Romanian. They typify Hungarian incompatibility and searching for conflict, as they are always trying to demonstrate their excellence and therefore look down on everyone. Their previous home was ten times the size of the current one, yet they didn't fit in with anyone there either, a neighbour observes maliciously. We are lucky as we don't have mutual spheres of interest, they live five houses down on the opposite side of the street, and we are far above them in this imaginary hierarchy. Mr Toldi— the only man my father honours with this title—seems to respect us for some reason, he senses that my father is an educated man, the kind of person he would have also liked to become, he has a camera and some binoculars made in Japan, the sort of thing I've also been dreaming about for years. Later on, he'll buy a sidecar motorcycle and will take me camping to the banks of the river Körös. He will also try to make wooden sculptures. Decades later, he'll send me his monograph about his home village, an interesting example of popular literacy, and I conclude that he should have really been given the chance to study, after all it was socialism that offered the most favourable climate for the emancipation of the poor from their spiritual and intellectual misery.

The Toldis are into nature, they know about plants, fish, the marshland, the forest, they know all sorts of details despite not reading books, they live close to nature and are curious and observant, but their tendency for looting keeps coming to the fore at all times. It's hard to get anywhere with the two boys, though it's even harder for them to get on, they are much stronger and larger than me, always looking for trouble, constantly fighting with everyone, as they can't really play football, either. Compared to them, I'm weak, frail and a scaredy-cat, they don't see me as a rival but I take them seriously. I'm good at school, read a lot, so am well informed, which they aren't, but they are brave and strong. There's some sort of a naively honest camaraderie among us, they'll become my mates and together we'll discover our surroundings and even venture to the nearby woods. We'll discover the reeds, the thickets, the backwaters of the Körös, the fens in Ágya, saliferous rocks and the irrigation canals of the old rice field, our relationship as comrades is unbroken. They prefer being outdoors to staying at home, their mother also sends them out to the fresh air and as soon as we are out of the built-up areas, we stop engaging in rough-and-tumble play. As a rule, they get hungry and thirsty before I do, but they are interested in everything, so are ideal companions for marching up and down the wet plows, sinking swamps and arid stubblefields. We aren't bothered by the cold, wind or rain, even enjoying these ordeals as this makes us men, their father tends to observe, and he's happy to join us whenever he can. I really hate the fact though that they always want to take everything they see on the field or in the forest home, bits of wire, screws, horse bones, pheasant feathers, anything that can be moved even if it's completely worthless. They always try to remove whatever they can from agricultural machinery, they open tyre caps, force tractor doors open, as they always carry screwdrivers, sharp knives and pliers. Once they lay hands on some piece of metal, they take turns in carrying it or hide it, so they can take it home on the way back or on some other occasion. For a while, I try to persuade them not to do this, but then I give up, this is clearly what they need to do, so I get out of the way and carry on walking, and when they've finished, they catch up. Even years later, I come across useless acquisitions being tossed about their home, and they no longer know where they got it from. My parents have strictly forbidden me to take home anything, we don't touch anything that isn't ours, whereas the Toldis touch everything they possibly can. The good thing is that the woods and fields tame people in time, and this disturbing tendency for looting gives way to poaching, practiced by many others, but there and then, this is a manly virtue and is unbelievably exciting. There are plenty of nooses and all sorts of primitive traps that need checking, and to this day I'm not sure who dealt with them, though I suspect it was mainly their father, Mr Toldi, who'd put them out at dark and his sons, and I would check whether anything got caught in them. We'd often find pheasants caught up in copper wires and it would always be their turn to take them home as their rightful dues. We kept roaming around with Joe and James for years, during which time it became obvious that the fauna of the Great Hungarian Plain was extremely varied, deserving to be discovered, there was no doubt that this was also a place of lights and colours, and the claim that this amounted to nothing couldn't be further from the truth.

Yet this process of discovery isn't entirely devoid of danger, because at dusk on a winter day an Aro off-road vehicle pulls up on the Körös dam, with a gun barrel sticking out. We are hiding under nearby blackthorn bushes and have been crawling for at least an hour towards a herd of fallow deer, there are about twenty beasts, including two with giant antlers. Initially it was my obsession that we should get as close as possible to every single beast, but soon my mates get the hang of this and start enjoying it too, we are prepared to forget about everything during deerstalking. One makes less noise alone, but it's much more fun in the company of others. The fallow deer can't see properly at dusk, so as long as we don't move to the side and they don't get a scent, they are easy to approach. At this point, Brehm's *Animal Life* is one of my favourite readings and I know that fallow deer were settled to the area around Gyula from Germany. I was able to tell many such details to the boys, but now we are crawling in an inch of snow behind the blackthorn bushes, we have developed quite a routine over years of practice. We could crawl an awful lot before being noticed, it's very cold, my gloves are completely wet and our shoes are filled with snow, but we are tough. The deer don't react to the car, but following the gunshot, a young hind collapses, the others run towards us but then come to a halt and dash away on the frozen wheat fields, just about missing our hiding place so we can actually see them jump over the ditch in which we are lying low. We are so afraid that we barely dare to catch our breath, and even our hearts stop beating. A few people get out of the car, head towards us talking in a loud voice, they light a cigarette then get hold of the deer, drag it away and drive off into the sunset. Fuck them, Joe says several times, and I burst out crying for the hind that got shot down. I can't even imagine what would have happened if these secret police workers got interested in what the deer were trying to avoid, they only cared about the meat. I have never seen a gun like the one they were holding up, certainly not as part of hunters' or forest wardens' kit, it will take until I join the army to come across another one. We have encountered poachers before, though never at such close up, and we've always tried to avoid them from afar. This occasion was the scariest, and to this day, I fail to understand how come they didn't spot us with their telescopic guns, but I guess they must have felt absolutely safe.

There are plenty of wild animals in the area, Prince Joseph and the Tisza government introduced a thorough game management, and in the wake of Trianon, their forests were handed over to the Romanian king and then to Ceaușescu. At the station in Kisjenő, one can still see the concrete platform, surrounded by chestnut trees and fir trees, where the king would disembark his train when arriving for the hunt. Grandma Zsüli had even spotted him once, though she couldn't recall whether this was Ferdinand, Charles II or Michael. The Romanian state classed these forests under special regime and put them under full governmental protection, so nobody was allowed to hunt there except for foresters and secret service personnel. Road signs would make it clear that it was strictly forbidden to enter the forest, despite the fact that nobody would have even considered going on day trips or excursions in the area, and wood theft wasn't yet the done thing. When it came to plough fields, on the other hand, there would always be plenty of serious damage, in fact, there would often be next to nothing to harvest as the roes and fallow deer would weigh down the wheat and the wild boars would bear down the corn or the watermelon. The reproduction of pheasants was artificially enhanced, seeing that the cold winters and icy springs didn't foster adequate growth, to say nothing of foxes and wild cats that would also decimate the number of eggs or chicks unable as yet to fly. My grandmother would regularly contribute brood to the pheasantry, and it was she who told us that there was a castle hidden in the thick woods. This image had stayed with me ever since, like a deer-patterned wall hanging, and when I first visited the site, I was shocked to find that it looked exactly the way my grandmother had described it.

We didn't pretend to be Native Americans, but I found a second, alternative reality in Kisjenő too, met with suspicion and animosity by my parents. They simply couldn't make heads or tails of this business of wandering about or hanging out in thickets. With the exception of poultry, my mother is repulsed by or afraid of any other animal, while my father claims that fields are meant to be worked upon or stolen from, seeing that regular village folk are fed up with nature as a rule of thumb. I'm convinced that this isn't true, as I have met plenty of village people who did enjoy the woods, the fields and the wilderness, and found that it was mainly those who had issues with their own selves that had reservations about nature. These people would hardly spare any thought on their surroundings, but seek refuge in their daily routines instead. The ultimate lesson one learns in the woods is that safety either lies within oneself or doesn't exist at all. To my chagrin, I'm not allowed to keep a dog except for a few days, following which my mother has it taken away because it growls at her if she has a go at me, not to mention that we have nothing to feed it, we haven't got enough leftovers for a dog. We don't have cats either, but why should we have a cat anyway? We'll end up having one when we get overwhelmed by farm fever though, and the wheat stored in the attic attracts a nest of mice and rats. In my view, my father must have read that cats are the best antidote for mice in some article, but perhaps he heard it on Hungarian TV, after all, we learn all matters of import from that source. For a long time, Hungary appears as some extension of reality, as a more genuine world situated geographically close yet in fact disappointingly removed from the constantly deteriorating and impoverished Romania. In this parallel world, everything is better and more human than here and, most importantly, is Hungarian. Everybody in my immediate surrounding had access to such a duplicate world that they perceived as more genuine than the existing everyday one, for me this was the forest, for my father his vineyard and Radio Free Europe, for my grandfather his alcohol, and for those in Barót, God. My mother had never had such an alternative, and she was always suspicious of other people finding theirs more important than day-to-day duties. My mother is a true materialist, even though she doesn't realize this—she always wants to go to church but it happens to be rather far and she doesn't have the time, she attends funerals instead, for one can break into a satisfying song there too.

XIII

School

There are very few Hungarian children in Kisjenő, barely twenty in all the primary years put together. I can only remember those in year four, because my attention is entirely focused on what they are learning, seeing that it's a lot more interesting than what we are meant to do. I'm generally lagging behind with writing and other stuff as I keep daydreaming and doodling, and whenever the older ones don't know something, I just blurt it out or prompt them to the right answer. During break time, we fight with the Romanian kids, Pityu Kovács in year four is a proper giant, so much so that even the Gipsy kids think twice before rubbing him up the wrong way. Pityu simply dispels the bevy of shrieking kids swarming around him, laughing all along like a contented and chubby baby, and this is the way I picture Miklós Toldi too. Throwing snowballs usually turns into throwing stones, and Romanian–Hungarian football matches end up in tussles, which can only be brought to a close by the vigorous intervention of our teacher. Every so often, the Romanian kids in year four charge into our classroom as the bell rings, and pushing our teacher, Aunt Babi out of the way, they throw themselves at us and knock our books and pens off the desks. On one occasion, they even managed to whack a vase off the teacher's desk, so in response we chase them along the corridor, at the very end of which they form a compact group and, since they are in a majority, force us back into our classroom. To this day, I marvel at the fact that this major ethnic conflict was only deployed at school where it was part and parcel of our daily routine. I can't recall any direct confrontation on our way home, and after school, we'd be kicking up a row based on other priorities and groupings, even though in primary school I learned the insulting words *bozgor împuțit* and *szőrös talpú oláh*—stinky bozgors and Wallachians with hairy foot soles.

I can barely recall anything else about my first two years at school, except for the first dead body I've ever seen, that of the deaf-and-dumb boy who lived right next to the school. He wandered off one day and got run over by a train. We went to pay our respects at his bier after school, can't remember whose idea it was, but we even picked some flowers and it was my task to place them on a chair by the coffin, on which occasion I could also take a good look at the coins placed on the boy's eyelids. A very old woman offered us some sweetbread and praised us for being so well-mannered, but at some point, all the women broke out in hysterical wailing that scared us away. Soon afterwards, the railway claimed another victim, a man from a neighbouring village, under the train, his blood-stained head ended up stuck between the tracks, people came over to see what was going on when they became aware of the creaking sound. We were playing football nearby and went up to the railway embankment to see the blood trickle down the gravel. A woman in the neighbourhood tried to keep the children away, but in vain, the corpse was so interesting that she had no chance of holding us in check. According to my mother, there was nothing wrong with seeing such things and no need to be afraid of the dead, only the living. Despite this, we were rather scared when walking along the embankment, but this was our main route when going swimming or fishing. We introduced the rule of looking back at every telephone post, whether we could hear a train coming or not, and in case we could catch as much as a glimpse of a train, we'd immediately get off the tracks, even if this meant jumping into thickets, brambles or reeds. In fact, we continued to make our way along the embankment for years. I can still walk on the railway tracks for miles, it's like a meditation of sorts, and whenever I fail to manage it, I know there's something wrong with me as I can't focus and involuntarily keep looking back every other second.

Every morning, a huge flock of kids would make their way to school from the *Cartier*, there was no pavement yet, only a narrow strip of concrete here and there. We'd routinely push one another off this strip until we were all lathered in mud, so at times parents would transport their brood in wheelbarrows to help them cross the giant puddles that took over most streets. At school, we'd slide across the classroom floors treated with oil as if we were on ice, we'd even wet it during breaks to keep it moist. What a heroic age! At this point, our parents are still quite young, and tackle the multitude of irresolvable tasks awaiting them with faith and hope. They are in the fervour of territorial conquest, there's a tiny opening in this darkest of dictatorships, one has a chance to settle somewhere and start something new, there's work, food and as much free time as one can fill with oneself, during which one can also finish the work that can't be completed at other times. The children are at large, nobody has time to look after them, they roam free, always out and about, the boys, and often the girls too, playing football. This is the period when it hardly occurs to anyone that there could be something wrong with socialism and the regime in place, those who had opposed it were removed already, and those who might challenge it are still too young. Most people dream of a social system they can identify with in some way or other, even if not entirely, and we have no reason to doubt that our problems can be solved in the fullness of time, and the ones that can't, aren't really our concern.

I was in year three when, to the desperation of my mother and all other mothers, our Hungarian tutor group was transferred from the Romanian primary school in Kisjenő to the Hungarian school in Erdőhegy. This three-kilometre distance represented an insurmountable obstacle for them, as they knew that soon enough their offspring would be able to wander about town without supervision. This is exactly what happened. My mother would lead the troops in the morning, walking past the cemetery and the clinic, but then she'd stay behind once we got to the office where she worked. From there, we'd head across town on our own, all along the high street, there were only a handful of cars back then, so we'd mainly come across farm carts, especially on a Tuesday as that was market day. As soon as my mother made it to the office, taking all her worries and concerns with her, we came to life, removed our hats, scarves and gloves, and started a running contest all the way to the corner, turning from model children into proper kids, usually arriving at school completely out of breath. Albi would usually fight his sister, Joe'd tackle James, whilst I'd carry on walking by myself, as I learned soon enough that if I tried to separate these siblings, they'd all turn against me. When we got to the watchmaker's, we verified the correct time; in front of the bakery, we took a deep breath and checked whether Manó, the German shepherd was lying by the fence, as it was trained not to let anyone in when its owner wasn't there. In the hardware shop, there was a red Jawa motorbike for years, even though it couldn't be seen properly through the shop window; then it was the turn of the forest office, the former princely castle with giant cherry trees where we were never allowed into the garden; and from there the bridge was just a short running distance away. The latter was my mother's main worry, she was afraid that we'd fall into the river. I have no idea why she thought that, perhaps because she had always suffered from agoraphobia. I have no recollection of anyone falling into the river from the bridge, except for the bag of a classmate, and this only happened because he kept balancing it on his head and the wind blew it away.

The reason why I mention my mother so often is that I'm just like her in many respects, and because I have no recollection of my father at this stage in my life, it feels as if he had disappeared for years, even though he wasn't even ill at that time. Yet I remember that he brought back the best chewing gum in the whole wide world from Budapest, they were green and white menthol balls, and the fruit-flavoured varieties that were brought out later came nowhere near. We kept chewing it for days and weeks on end, we'd store it in a glass of water to make sure it didn't get dusty or flies didn't get to it, then we'd sprinkle icing sugar or pour spirits of salt on it, it could cope with just about anything, including being shared between a few of us. One evening Father got home really late, as he had to attend a mandatory crow shooting session with the comrades. His shoulders were black-and-blue, because nobody had told him to hold the gun close to his body, or in case they had, he didn't follow this advice. I was very excited by all this at the time, because I thought of my father as a proper hunter, although I felt left out seeing that neither did he take me with him, like Uncle Will, nor did he bring the gun home. I wanted to find out how many crows he shot, but he just dismissed all this with a wave of the hand, he couldn't see any because he took his glasses off, and what's more, he even closed his eyes following the bang. He was annoyed about wasting the whole afternoon with the hunt, and to top it all, he also had to go for a drink with the comrades, which made my mother irate: Feri, how could you possibly go for a drink! What else could he have done when they were shooting crows with the comrades, and the comrades might have been also shooting at other stuff, though my father didn't comment on the latter seeing that it wasn't really relevant anyway. He was a little tipsy but in very good spirits, and before he went to bed he gave me a used 12-gauge shotgun shell, the fresh gunpowder smell of which I kept breathing in for days, but only when no one was looking as my mother had warned me that it was poisonous.

I may not have been the kind of child my father was interested in spending time with, but it's also quite likely that my mother did everything she could to keep me to herself and Father agreed that this was the way of the world, after all kids are women's business. I can't really tell whether I missed him at the time, or it only occurred to me later that I should have missed him. I'm keeping a tally on the back of a notebook, to count the number of times my father spends his afternoons at home, it's obviously my mother who's made me do such a thing. I can't remember missing my father, but I did enjoy whenever Uncle Fjodor played football with us, or Mr Toldi took us fishing, mayflies and giant fish fluttering about the surface of the water, despite us never managing to catch anything. I can vividly recall as I'm crying over the first unsolvable maths problem, my mother screams at me and then cries with me because she doesn't know what to do either, and then we decide that I won't be good at maths, seeing that she wasn't either. Another afternoon we keep practising somersaults and we decide that I won't be good at gymnastics either, then we cry for a while, and PE classes will be at the centre of my anxieties at school, as this used to be the case for my mother too, together with music. At school in Arad Uncle Ernő will teach us everything we need to know in gymnastics, after all, there are people who don't just know this, and I'll almost receive a top Baccalaureate score in maths, but all this is far ahead in the future, as for music and dance, I have yet to fulfil these pledges. My mother can't dance either, though she can sing, whereas my father is good at dancing but pretty bad at singing.

I have a single serious competitor at school in Erdőhegy against whom I have to measure up on a daily basis, I'm usually the one to lose and this is because of my stammer. At times, I'm unable to say anything, can't recite a poem, answer a question, report back or tell the most banal story or joke, I can't solmizate at all, tap out a rhythm or sing a song. It soon becomes obvious that this isn't because I haven't prepared for the class, and it's only the music teacher who thinks that I'm an idiot and I should attend a special needs school. To be fair, everybody thinks she's an idiot, on account of her clothes and behaviour, she's simply too beautiful a woman for this sort of school and town. Most teachers usually allow me to write down what I'm unable to say out loud, though I always have a go at the latter first. I can't really hear my own stammer, but I can feel that I'm not getting where I should, I change the order of words and sentences, and of lines and stanzas, I keep searching for an easier way of saying things, and sometimes I can find this, other times I can't. Occasionally I have to rephrase my sentences as I go along, having to add or remove something depending on whether I come across words I can't pronounce. I don't recall ever getting a bad mark for this, but others would laugh at me as I'd struggle, and when I couldn't come up with a solution, I'd resort to paper or the blackboard. My classmates would usually accept that this was the way I was, four or five of us were far ahead of the rest in most subjects, the Gipsy kids were unable to read even in year eight and they made up half of the class. Without them, there wouldn't have been enough children to form Hungarian classes in Kisjenő, as this had been the case in many other schools all over Romania.

I only have to take revenge once for all the grievances I had to suffer on account of my stammer. Dezső, a sturdy and cantankerous boy, two years older than me, keeps driving me up the wall all day; he draws attention to my wobbly voice and calls me a goat, and even has a go at twisting my nose and ears. Everybody guffaws, which emboldens him to hit me on the chin, not very hard but I still end up biting my lip and can feel the taste of blood spurting out, so I turn away, ready to withdraw. I'm on my way home, but on the corridor Dezső grabs my collar and, holding on to my backpack, tries to push me to the floor. I pull the bag out of his hands and, turning around, strike him as hard as I can. I'm utterly furious and throw myself into this battle with all my weight, at which point he steps forward and my fist strikes him on the forehead, he loses his balance and falls under the fire-escape ladder, unable to move for several seconds. He somehow gets stuck under the ladder and can't get out for a while, then he simply won't dare, so I just stand there victorious, making it clear that I'd hit him again in case he did get up. For a few minutes, I feel like Old Shatterhand until I start worrying about being torn to pieces by the Gipsy lot. Yet nothing happens although several kids from the estate are there to witness this affair.

I have no problem with Romanian, despite it being the horror subject of Transylvanian Hungarians, I don't stammer in Romanian, however, my teacher and form tutor is none other than the woman who should have been, or in fact had been for a while, my father's fiancée. She's pestering us with composition all the time, no matter what I write, it isn't good enough, although I'm the best at writing in Romanian. She and my mother can't see eye to eye, and the latter often returns home from parents' evenings crying, I have no idea what could they possibly argue about, there have hardly ever been issues with my learning or behaviour at school. The problem is that my mother wants to teach me Romanian, but she isn't good enough at it, she translates everything literally and speaks with a strong Székely accent. She doesn't understand or care about the word order or grammatical accords in Romanian, plus there are a few other nuances that one simply can't pick up at a grown-up age, even native speakers fail to use them systematically. In effect, these two women are engaged in a symbolic battle over my father, by way of my Romanian compositions. The teacher is rather mean, and registers me as a student using the Romanian variant of my name, Gavril Vida, this is the version on my gradebook too. In vain does my mother approach the head teacher, this can't be amended, even though my birth certificate lists me as Gabor, with a swallowed accent on the 'a'.

My mother doesn't give up easily, so we keep trailing through the book entitled *Correct Romanian* over and over again, and as a result, she learns grammar and I'm able to speak. I also learn to write pretty decent compositions, I no longer have to translate what I want to say from Hungarian, but my tutor is still unhappy as I tend to write under-length. In year eight, I win the Romanian subject competition at local level, despite not wanting to even show up there, but my mother and teacher make me do it. Mine is the best submission, and yet they decide against sending me to the county-level competition, and although I had no initial plans to attend, I feel deeply offended. This is the first time I sense the unbearable weight of the Transylvanian minority fate, even though I haven't yet heard of this term and we don't actually live in Transylvania proper. A Hungarian child, imagine that, the head-master muses, and when I'd like to hand in my passport applica-tion at the police, he doesn't sign it off. I'm most afraid of the Romanian school, the high school, the big school as my mother puts it. We hardly ever go there, except to visit the school dentist, attend some events or sort out the odd organizational matter. Hundreds of children keep shouting in Romanian, and even though I speak the language, I find the crowd frightening as it feels different from our kind of rampages. The rumour that we shall also go to this school crops up several times, and this makes me overcome with the darkest fear. Our school has about a hundred pupils and five permanent teachers, it's a small and intimate Hungarian village school, whereas the High School stands for the town, and people there are Romanians.

I enjoyed going to school in Erdőhegy, I was really interested in maths, though I was only good at geometry, I was fascinated by triangles and trigonometry and our teacher gave her heart and soul to us. She'd catch the bus from a nearby village at dawn, and we'd often start with some extra lessons as early as 7.00 a.m. We enjoyed roaming the dark streets and even darker dam in winter, and would often steal coal or wood for the school by sticking our hands through the loose slats of the odd woodshed. We'd also nip over to the garden of the Romanian church next door and grab bits and pieces from the rotten fence to make fire with, seeing that it was so cold in our classroom that we had to keep our coats on at all times. We'd always play football during break time, and we had a really cool history and geography teacher who enjoyed kicking a ball with us. Our biology teacher could have even been a relative from Barót, being the cousin of my godfather, she had a huge library, and when I visited her every now and then, I was allowed to pick whatever book I liked and take it home. She also taught chemistry, and for a while physics, and was able to explain cells, atoms, Galileo's motion experiments, acids and salts like any old-school teacher, and as a result I have been interested in all this ever since. We saw her as a warm-hearted aunt, she was a spinster, lived on her own, the boys often mocked her and I was deeply ashamed of their behaviour, even told her once how awful I felt about this. Come on, she smiled at me, I can only see roses in the places of your heads, they remind me of the roses in the botanical gardens in Cluj.

The first lesson was usually taken up with the arrival at half past eight of the classmates travelling to school from Ágya, as the bus was often late. I can't possibly understand how could a bus clock up a delay of over an hour on a distance of only seven kilometres, but we welcomed this hoo-ha, not to mention that there was always a whiff of cows and the odd story to tell. Some people still managed to miss the bus, and this also came with a story, so by the time everybody calmed down it was time for a break. Village schools can be really cosy. In case water levels were high at the river dams, mostly in springtime, we'd go to take measurements during our breaks, and as an expert in floods, I was able to assess whether water levels were rising or ebbing. I almost fell into the river once and got covered in mud head to toe, so had to have my back cleaned up at the water fountain. I haven't missed a single day of school, and I've never been ill except for the days when my mother took me to Arad to have my speech defect *checked out*. Yet it wasn't school as such that I liked, but reading, everything and anything. I have vivid memories of French lessons where an irate lady would hit us on the head with a large ruby ring if we didn't know how to conjugate verbs, and I generally didn't. I didn't really spare a thought on Hungarian, and hated grammar, I was meant to read tons of classics such as Jókai, but despite the seventy volumes we had at home we didn't have any of the mandatory texts, someone must have taken their pick of the best, my father fumed. It only emerged later that we had a real treasure trove of Jókai books, all the works ignored by literary history. There was a phase when our music teacher was taken away by the devil—as someone had put it—and an old man would make sure we kept quiet in class. He knew not a thing about music, couldn't even sing, but was able to locate the record player, so we'd always listen, and all this felt a bit like the radio programme I used to tune into with my grandfather, there was even the odd piece I recognized.

Whenever we didn't attend school or wander about, we'd play football. I'm not a good midfielder but great in goal, Albi, on the other hand, is the best striker in the *Cartier*, and we almost always win if we manage to be on the same team. This soon becomes obvious to the others and we are put on separate teams, defending the goal against him is a serious task, he knows all the tricks one can possibly learn on the pitch. Goalkeepers must be able to cope with conceding a goal, with being defeated and floored, they must also accept the fact that the tiniest mistake can cost their team the match, and that every saved ball is only a partial success because the next ball is already on its way. A good goalie is a lone warrior, and his key weapon is intuition, in slow motion replays one can see that they often sense where the ball is coming from even before it had the chance of being set on its way. Hard to get into detail, but this is something I've experienced many times. I've often fantasized about becoming a famous goalkeeper in a major team, but when I first got the chance to stand in a proper goal, I realized that I'd never be able to jump high enough. This happened when I attended a trial session in Arad, where they told me that I was doing the right moves but was too short. I may have been aware of this already, but still went for the try-out on the off chance. None of this really matters today though.

Needless to say, my parents won't even hear of sports, my mother that is, because my father's opinion was irrelevant, even though he adored football and was actually pleased in his own way about me taking up basketball at school. There were hardly any sports programmes on TV that he wouldn't watch, it looked like he wasn't interested in anything else, seeing that Radio Free Europe had no TV version. It often occurred to me that my father would watch football matches with the devotion other people dedicated to religious processions, and I didn't need to consult sports encyclopaedias as I could just ask him whatever I wanted to find out. After all, sport was the mid-twentieth century's religion with genuine mass appeal, and was consequently utilised by both the Nazis and communists to this end, owing to television it basically reached everyone and all people had to do was to marvel at the mythical confrontation between angels and devils, available to anyone for free. Watching TV in those days was quite an innocent endeavour, there weren't enough programmes to fill the day, we'd often sit around waiting for programmes to start, just watching the monitor test image as it was shaking, rippling, or, as we put it, snowing, or fleas were jumping about, all depending on the position of the aerial or the weather. The roof tended to leak precisely where the aerial slipped out from under the tiles, we were constantly trying to fix this but was never perfect, one time a storm managed to position the aerial at a perfect angle, sadly the next one came along only to wipe out the whole arrangement.

We normally play football on the meadow by the railway tracks, that's where Aunt Nancsi's geese and Aunt Kati's cows or pigs are grazing. There's plenty of gravel on the pitch, we have to remove them all but we can't do this with the poo, that's usually wiped up by myself as I throw myself at the ball, or Albi, as he's taking a slide just about to strike. My reflexes are good, I'm quite flexible and bold, and learned quickly not to worry about the state of my face, I have no qualms about standing in as a striker if need be, and I'm often kicked in the face, stomach and balls, never deliberately though. Having said that, I never suffered a serious injury, though I fainted on two occasions. The first was like a short power cut, and when I came round from the second, I realized that a whole group had gathered around me and someone said softly in Romanian: *Trăieşte*—he's alive. When I'm about nine or ten years old, my ball is still quite new, and the older ones are merciless at striking. I enjoy this rough game and on a good day, nobody has a chance at scoring against me, but every now and then I get confused and do something stupid, I drop the ball or just happen to look away for a moment, so I provoke everyone's ire. The worst thing is that the goalposts nailed and fixed together with so much care are usually removed in-between games, so every match begins with marking off the pitch and getting rid of the gravel. All kids are told in no uncertain terms not to throw stones onto the pitch, be it at cows, dogs or one another, but nobody cares.

As my father tends to say, one is meant to watch the programme not the TV, so we just switch off in case the programme
is uninteresting. Despite us living in Romania, we watch
Hungarian television almost exclusively, these are two independent
aspects of the universe, and I find myself genuinely taken by surprise when I realize at Albi's place next door that there is such a
thing as Romanian television. The latter broadcasts the Muppet
Show on Saturday afternoons, and Westerns in the evening, and
on Sundays there are some cartoons at noon and sports in the afternoon, which we skip in order to watch or listen to Hungarian stuff
instead. My mother naturally hates all this, as she's carrying on
with her work in the kitchen, and authoritarian traits come to the
fore in my father whenever there's a match, no matter what TV
series might be showing on the Romanian channel (*Dallas*, *The
Onedin Line* or *Poldark*). He's the first to tell me about the
Hungarian Golden Team, and I receive a leather ball when I'm in
year three, it will lay claims on being the one and only proper ball
in the *Cartier* for years. Many a times I take it with me to school
and we kick it about during break times, in PE if we are allowed,
and on the way home across town. In the absence of balls, we make
do with cans, bottles, chestnuts and ice balls the size of a child's
head, and kicking these along the way home makes my shoes fall
apart. As a rule, PE is a torture because we don't have a regular
teacher, there's no gym hall, sometimes we put some mats down
in our classroom or on the corridor to practice bucking, but mainly
we just focus on athletics and football. We usually go to the river
dam to run, 600, 800, then 1000 metres, and this causes serious
agony to most of us since we tackle this without any training and
at breakneck speed. After the first 200 metres we feel a burning
sensation in our lungs, we can barely breathe and are feeling dizzy,
our teacher shouts from his bike that he'll fail all those who stop,

but then shows some mercy and says that people can have another go next time. Who can possibly improve within the span of a week? No to mention, that it's only the dentist that I fear as much as long-distance running. All of a sudden, we find ourselves having wandered off along the dam, and our teacher freaks out that they'll close the school, and everyone will have left for home, so he heads back on his bike to catch at least the cleaning lady there. Anikó, the best runner, decides to follow in his wake. For some reason, I head off too, and make it to the school without any major effort and feeling rather jolly, I don't even feel tired despite the two-kilometre distance, if not more. All you wanted was to check her butt out, Janika, my deskmate observes mischievously, and I have no idea what he's talking about. For me, what matters is that this is my first ever long-distance running experience.

It's around this time that owing to the large number of Hungarian children in Kisjenő, it would be possible to start a Hungarian year group at secondary school level. This is in accordance with the law, and several determined parents and teachers get involved in hatching a plan. Needless to say, the head teacher in Kisjenő hasn't heard of any of this, he hasn't even read the relevant legal article, and soon enough the whole attempt will peter out, even though the initial plan was to go as far as Ceaușescu if need be. As it happens, even these brave parents and teachers fail to sign the application. A Hungarian inspector in Arad asks my mother what harm would it do to her child if he attended Romanian school? Following the 1989 somersault, this comrade will occupy an important role in Hungarian education matters. My father isn't present to give them a smack, and the whole cause is left dormant, but my mother decides that I should attend Hungarian school, come what may. In my view, she's the bravest and boldest parent at this point.

XIV

Illness

I'm the first to notice that my father is unable to close his right eye, though it may well be that everyone has already been aware of this long before me. We are at my grandparents' place in Ágya, it's a summer afternoon in 1979, we have most probably been to church and had lunch, Father is taking a nap in the summer kitchen. My mother is somewhere outdoors, and for some reason I happen to be in the house and that's when I realize that my father's right eye is wide open. I assume he must be awake and is only pretending to be asleep, so I start talking and laughing, and he seems to be playing along, although he keeps snoring at the same time. In vain do I insist that I can see through him, I can see full well that he's not asleep, he has his eye open, and I even call Grandma Zsüli to show her that Father isn't asleep. I want every-one to know that he's just fooling me, he's only pretending, but I can see through his tricks. Father is in a really deep sleep, unaware of all this, while everyone else is unprepared to take me seriously. So what if he has his eye half open? I don't know at what point Father has realized that half of his face got paralysed, perhaps that very autumn, in any case by then it was too late for anything to be done, or this was the sort of paralysis for which there was simply no viable treatment even if he sought immediate medical assis-tance. The following winter, he'll spend weeks at the University Clinic in Temesvár with a brain tumour. Relatives start collecting money for an operation, but all he wants is to die. He'll give up smoking overnight and adopt all sorts of lifestyle changes, be it on the recommendation of doctors or on his own initiative, most of which are interesting, useful and worth considering, but since they return no immediate success, are discontinued, though we pass them on by way of advice to others. Next, we find out that there's actually no tumour, yet from then on he remains a sick man, he's always being treated with something or other, at times for months, and he recovers from all illnesses except for his facial paralysis.

I can't get away from the idea that he must have been given the wrong treatment, and many of his later problems stem from those six weeks of agony in Temesvár, during which he collapsed emotionally. In my view, my father's medical history would be a more interesting read than his secret police files, from this point onwards illness is his main preoccupation, he reads both our Hungarian and Romanian medical books from cover to cover, and from these he finds out how to lead a healthy life. Of course, everything carries on as before, but the rhetoric gets stronger, after all, one should look after one's health. The fact of the matter is that any activity is potentially damaging to health, and as Grandpa Joszip Vida would note, it is life itself that's most damaging. His paralysis was caused by draught, so from then on, no two windows could be opened at the same time in the house, for my father this will become the most wounding factor, on a par with alcohol and spices that my mother blames for everything. Looking back, I can see that my father was struggling with serious mental health issues, he couldn't sleep, was suffering from high blood pressure, lower back pain and heart arrhythmia. He'd go from one doctor and one test to the other, try out alternative therapies, baths, treatments, masks, herbs and kefir fungi, and after years of experimentation would end up vouching for just two miracle cures: garlic and wine. He'd order a wide selection of medication from Hungary or Germany, there are some that make him unwell, yet he continues to take them religiously, as he's an orderly and reliable man. One day I spot a strange West German box containing a selection of colourful capsules, and before I could think about the consequences, I have already swallowed one in secret. I'm worried for days about what could happen, but nothing will. However, as the stocks start running low, it becomes obvious that one pill is missing. There's major panic and we keep searching everywhere, goodness gracious, the West German medication runs out ahead of time, and although I feel remorse, I keep silent. It's impossible to obtain more of this medicine, and as it runs out, my father realizes that he's actually feeling a little better, he can no longer feel that queasiness he used to. When the replacement finally arrives, he only takes one capsule and puts the rest aside, so later we end up keeping nails and screws in its box, to at least get some benefit out of this deal.

He takes so much medication that it's basically irrelevant whether he forgets the odd one, and at times his sweat smells like a pharmaceutical waste bin. It doesn't occur to anyone that my father is suffering from psychiatric disorders, he can't talk about this either, and thinks, like most village people, that those who have mental problems are automatically mad. My mother surmises that he might be suffering from medical illness, meaning that whenever he sees a doctor, he's in a worse condition than when he doesn't. She's fed up with all this too, she doesn't quite suggest that my father is a hypochondriac, she wouldn't go that far, so we make use of the *fear of white scrubs* instead. I can't remember how we ended up with this, as I didn't coin this phrase myself. The fact of the matter is that this sense of duty towards the medical profession suits my mother, as she can exercise total control over my father, she can persuade him to give up just about anything, and in exchange he's entitled to sit around, lie down, listen to the radio and watch TV as much as he likes. Above all, he can rest. And indeed, he's often tired and sleepy, he sweats a lot, has little patience, and most of the time isn't interested in anything. Every so often, he comes alive and starts working on something, but gives up at the sight of the first crooked nail, and takes revenge on the hammer or the plywood if they don't obey him. On such an occasion, I notice that he's able to hit the nail perfectly with his left hand, even in really awkward places where my right hand simply wouldn't fit through. I often see him use his left hand when hitting the calculator keys, but if he notices that I'm watching, he switches hands at once.

By the eighties, the Ceaușescu regime has practically liquidated psychology, both as science and praxis, so those who might want to turn to a psychologist do need to know exactly what they want and who to look for. In my father's case, such an option didn't even come up. Who could he possibly talk to about his unhappiness or his problems with the secret police? So he just turns to himself and succumbs to despair, he can't find a viable way out. He comes up with new things at times, starts gardening, samples grape varieties and unusual fruit trees, his main area of interest is chemical plant defences, and later organic farming. In actual fact, however, he's waiting for the collapse of communism, and for a better world, that will never come, hence he doesn't really believe in it. All these are attempts at escaping the reality in which my mother has taken over total control. She's the one who carries me along, as well as my father, she'd cope with a family of ten, she'd dish out their responsibilities to everyone, with which no one would manage to cope on time. It's impossible to do something just right, in a way that doesn't warrant her to adjust it a little or to comment on it, highlighting a sense of deficiency, doubt or disapproval. This is an awful time because my father directs all his anxiety and tension at me. He's all alone with his doubts, we are practically living in the shadow of death and it comes to light that we are terribly afraid. We shall never get over this fear, in which everyone is basically on their own. Those six weeks will always feel like an exam we have all failed, both in our own right and as a group, and even though the discipline itself is scrapped for our sake, that's no good to any-one. From this point onwards, we do know that we don't believe in God or in providence. We know exactly that there is nothing to look forward to after death, and that no one will be there to help us when we get to that point, as everybody is on their own then. That cold winter we end up learning this together, my father, the theologian, my mother, the believer, and I, the little boy, but despite knowing all this, we refrain from saying it out loud.

We are at home alone with my mother while Father is in hos-pital, and we barely notice his absence. I particularly like Sundays because then my mother travels to Temesvár on the early morning train and only comes back at night, so I'm home alone and this is strange and exciting in equal measure. I can do whatever I like, so I check out the whole house, poke my nose into everything, find a few West German sex magazines and large quantities of Yugoslav condoms which contribute to my enlightenment. I make a major effort to put all this back as they were, I know that my mother checks everything and am surprised to this day that she didn't notice these explorations. I think she must have been too tired and distraught, as for me, I only looked at these things once, I didn't damage anything, besides, there weren't many interesting items to start with, seeing that we were rather poor after all. Back then it was much more important for me to get started as early as possible, it was a tough snowy winter and we were able to trace all sorts of animal footprints in the reeds for hours. The ice broke several times under our weight, but the water wasn't very deep, we just ran home with frozen feet. We soon learned that the reeds can be quite dangerous because water doesn't freeze properly around the reed stalks, and it melts or turns slushy there first, so one has to come out lying on the belly to avoid the ice breaking up further. This was the sort of thing Mr Toldi would teach us, together with the lesson that we should remove our wellies when our feet were very cold, scrub them with snow because that would warm them up. No need to worry about wolves, though we would have liked to see some. According to records, the last wolf was killed in the Ágya forest in the fifties, but having said that, we should beware of tame foxes because they could have rabies, so we should avoid falling asleep in case we take a rest somewhere. Indeed, we almost fell asleep in the hay with James, this was in a stable out in the open fields, where the thermometer showed minus 25 degrees. When have you left the house, my mother tends to ask as she gets back, and I reply half an hour ago. I can even see the train cross the bridge while standing on the ramparts, and usually make it back in time for the half-past-three service. One day my mother didn't make it home with this train, she had to take a later one because she fell over at the railway station in Temesvár. She bumped into a pile of stones or bricks, and her leg started to bleed through her stocking boots, then swelled up and turned blue. She was wearing the exact same boots as her colleague who was run over by the train because her heel got stuck in the rails and she couldn't free her leg in time. This incident comes to my mind whenever I see such footwear, and they have just come back into fashion!

I have really no idea why my mother never took me with her to the hospital. Perhaps she wanted to protect me from the hassle of this whole situation and from the sorry state of my father, being as he was in a dark place. He had no other obvious problems, wasn't bleeding or dying, plenty of African students could practice on him and thus pass their exams, and whenever possible, he helped them along so they could become doctors in their home countries. I don't remember when my father went in and out of hospital, all I remember is those Sundays when I had the opportunity to wander around, even though my idea of freedom was actually quite different. We learn about suspected cancer, facial paralysis and being given the wrong treatment only later, narrated in my mother's words and the odd detail corrected at times by my father in his trademark fragmented style. Then he suddenly comes home from hospital, everything carries on as before, and he'll live for another thirty years. I can barely recall how he was before the hospital, he doesn't drink or smoke, does his job and brings the money home. Sometimes he's extremely anxious but controls himself, other times he's lethargic and hence there's no need to. It's indeed my mother who has to be in charge of everything, from bringing firewood in to carrying water, from queueing for goods to cooking, and from my maths homework to helping Father with the paperwork he has brought home from the office. I've suffered from depression myself, and know what it feels like when one just slows down, even forgets to pedal and falls off a bike, like my father, can't sleep at night and then falls asleep in the middle of the day while writing or talking. On the plus side, in case my father has ever regretted not being able to drive, he can now be glad about it.

In the environment we inhabited at the time, emotional problems have no relevance whatsoever, nineteenth-century mercantile materialism has just about matured, the soul, a fantasy, doesn't count, dreams are nonsense, the only reality is matter and money. We tend to watch a programme called *Családi kör* [Family circle] on TV, it's usually right before some other important programme, or tucked between the news and a film, which we wouldn't want to miss for anything. It doesn't occur to anyone that such programmes could be about us too. These Budapest people are really stupid, my father observes every now and then. We're so lucky not to have such problems, my mother adds, we aren't that kind of a family. Péter Popper and Jenő Ranschburg keep nodding, yes, very good. It's not fair to expect psychological affinities from my parents, or to assume that the culture of the late twentieth century has made it to our doorstep in the guise of Hungarian journals and radio and TV programmes. We live in the darkest Ceaușescu era, and such a world has no relevance to us. We read and watch all sorts, but these things have no impact on us because they don't deal with the real. The only reality is the way we live. Yet how is it possible to love in the absence of the soul? After all, we live in love.

Two important events are connected to my father's illness, of which I have very limited awareness seeing that in those days I'm not yet told anything. This is understandable, but I won't get involved in coherent conversations later either, and things will only crop up following some argument or quarrel, when my mother is no longer capable of controlling herself. At some point in the eighties, my parents went on a shopping trip to Gyula, and once there they made a detour to the bookshop even though it was common knowledge that Romanian customs officers would confiscate Hungarian books. There was no relevant legislation in this sense, but they'd just rip the wrapping paper off regardless, to check what was in the package. I had no more ardent desire than to read the works of J. F. Cooper, so my mother bought me *The Pathfinder*, *Leatherstocking* and *The Prairie* on such a trip. At the border, the Romanian officer did indeed check the books, and my mother told him that they were adventure stories for children about Native Americans. They didn't confiscate them, despite the fact that they could have done so, they were able to just take whatever they wanted or liked. Soon thereafter, however, my mother was summoned to the police station, and an agent questioned her in detail about everything, including the books, and the sort of things she'd read and the items brought back from Hungary. It was an amicable conversation so to speak, at the end of which he warned her not to talk about this to anyone, not even to family if she didn't want to get into trouble. Naturally, my mother told all this to my father at the earliest opportunity. He was summoned in too, but he didn't say a word since he was told not to say anything, even though this was really difficult in these conditions. My mother did indeed ask him whether he was called in, and when he was summoned in again he was asked what she said at home. He was called in a few more times but he never told anyone what happened next. My mother wasn't summoned in again, they could tell that she was useless, but my father looked entirely reliable. I have no idea whether they wanted to make use of him or just had their way with him. I don't think that he took part in any organized resistance, he barely kept in touch with anyone, except for the TV reporter Sándor Csép who visited us every now and then. He was the only Transylvanian person who could have possibly had knowledge of anything of interest to the secret services, but it may well be that they just asked questions about what was going on at his workplace. Industry was basically under the jurisdiction of the secret services, and if he was chosen as an informer and forced to report on others, he was subject to controls, in vain did he object and claim that he knew nothing. In addition, he might have also been put under pressure for his studies in theology, but he'd keep silent on this subject. In 1985, he reproached me for wanting to bring trouble to the house, as he knew full well that as a student of Hungarian Studies, I was likely to join the list of those under surveillance.

The second incident is much more muddled, and I know a lot less about it. My father was the payroll officer at the cannery in Kisjenő, and one day a seasonal worker reported him for not having received his salary. In a normal society, something like this is handled at company level, but in this case, the prosecution service got involved and it took ages for my father to prove that the comrade in question was rightfully paid for every single hour he had worked. Did the aggrieved party turn to the prosecution services out of their own volition, or they were advised to do so? Could this event be part of the broader wave of ethnic cleansing whereby Hungarian company directors or managers were removed from their jobs for various reasons, and every little unfounded complaint triggered serious investigation? No idea. It seems to me that Uncle Fjodor also suffered a heart attack around this time, but he'd drink a lot, according to my mother. After the regime change, I asked my father whether we should ask to see our secret police file, and he said I better not, which I now think was the right thing to do. Illness and secret police matters blur together in my memory, and it would be a cop-out to suggest that it was persecution that made my father ill, as it did many other people. I don't want to link these elements together into a firm cause and effect system, far from it. When around the age of forty I start having health problems, my father reacts by observing that troubles do start around that age, even though I'm still unsure whether these are caused by draught, an alcoholic seasonal worker, an evil secret service officer or they just happen anyway. I have never had the sort of problems he had, yet was still unhappy, and to ease my sorrow and helplessness, ended up drinking.

In my view, this secret-police business could have ruined any marriage, yet my parents' marriage wasn't ruined by this, seeing that they must have already been in the midst of a serious crisis if they didn't even acknowledge or confront it. All the fuss around the books about Native Americans made it clear to my father that my mother can't be trusted with any confidential information, she is far too unstable and will slip off a word here and there, not to mention that, as far as he knows, honest and loyal people like him simply can't get in harms' way. My mother is fully aware that my father doesn't share all information with her, she can sense the lack of trust and exclusion, and this deeply hurts her self-esteem. As far as she's concerned, family members should know everything about one another, or at least she should know all things. She doesn't understand that in case she gets summoned to the Securitate and is asked whether my father told her that he had been interrogated, they are already able to second guess the answer prior to her opening her mouth as she is unable to put on an act and turns crimson at once, thus instantly busting my father. Consequently, my father will get a good hiding, either because of having told her about the interrogation despite the interdiction, or because of lying, in the event of denial. My mother is never summoned again, and my father doesn't get beaten up, but we end up with yet another failure and the loss of mutual trust. To make things worse, next time my mother brings me the popular historical novel *Eclipse of the Crescent Moon* in her handbag. This isn't even unavailable or censored in

Romania, but she buys it regardless, she quite likes the book cover featuring a scene from the film version, or at least she says so in hindsight. My father goes haywire at this, having learned from the previous incident, he didn't even visit the bookshop and had no idea of Mother's purchase, after all she promised that she'd only take a look and not touch anything. My father is questioned again about what they were looking for in that bookshop in Gyula, and he tells them things he hasn't even seen himself, just heard from my mother, whereas to Mother, he tells what he knows from the secret police officer, namely that they are aware of everything and are simply checking whether he is telling the truth. My mother keeps claiming to this day that somebody she doesn't know must have been observing her, even though it was actually my father who observed her, as he was tasked with this. From then on, the novel's Jumurdzsák lives on our bookshelf, together with the spying epitomised by this character.

For a while, my parents worry about house searches, so my mother moves the Hungarian flag that came with her dowry to a safer place. My father would like to burn it, together with his books on theology, but my mother objects. You're such a coward, my mother tells him. And you are such a silly goose, he replies. My mother is playing against my father, and wins, she's one of those people who are prepared to risk everything for the sake of power, and despite being raised to be a servant, she could have become a top manager on account of that single gesture of hers rooted in a Nietzschean will to power. My father doesn't want to fight, he doesn't need anyone to share his fears, he's unable to communicate, so just turns to himself, in fear. From then on, he listens to Radio Free Europe a little less loud, but the beeps can be heard from the street anyway, everybody is listening to this station, even the police. Except for my mother, for unlike my father, she's loyal to the system, to say nothing of the fact that she's busy and doesn't have time to listen to all this crap talk. The sheer voice of Kató Bányász can make her get the shivers, a journalist who incites from Rome and is on the top of my mother's hate list, possibly because she's a woman. My mother often reminds us of her prayers asking for some important programme or sports match to take place on the day of her funeral. I have no idea what my father thought of all this, but I was seriously scared of any attempts at forecasting my mother's death seeing that I had deep memories of her gall-bladder attacks when she'd throw up all over the kitchen floor or in the backyard. On such occasions my job was to make her some camomile tea, this would disinfect her stomach, following which she'd throw up yet again and then lie down looking deathly pale, or stagger from one place to another. I was so scared that I'd even call the next-door neighbour to help. In hindsight, she'd always know exactly which dish had caused the problem, even though it was usually the last one she'd remember, so after a while there would be no safe food item that had never triggered a crisis. Having said that, she'd always be back on her feet the next day but carry on eating caraway soup with toast or polenta for days. As for me, I'd be scared to death of these crises for years. What would happen to me if my mother were to die for real, and I was alone at home with her? After a while I'm able to sense the arrival of such attacks in advance, as there's always some tension in the air. I'd quite like to vanish in good time, but this is far from easy, considering that her attention is always focused on me, and if I were to run away, I'd also have to find a way to come back somehow. We aren't having an argument, she keeps repeating this, and then falls ill, and I know that this is all my fault. There are many things more disgusting than shit and vomit, although she falls short of specifying what those are. There must be some sort of clinical explanation for my mother's attacks, even though none of the tests had led to any findings. Most of her attacks would follow a very precise and clear scenario, and despite the fact that only medical staff would be privy to the somatic components, everyone would be driven up the wall by the underlying psychic aspects. My mother is the only person who refuses to acknowledge this, though she concedes in hindsight that it all might be rooted in her *nervous disposition*.

Where am I during all this time? If not at school, then mainly on the fields, or in the woods and reeds. It's not exactly fun being at home, there's too much tension, my father wouldn't say a word for days, even weeks, and whilst my mother is trying to keep up with him, she can't stay silent, mumbling to herself, like Grandpa-Uncle Gyurika to God. She's having a conversation with the radio and addresses what she'd tell Father to the presenter, she adds all sort of commentaries to what is being debated on air, especially if Radio Free Europe is on, a station she hates because they keep lying at all times. My mother is on the side of the regime in power, unlike my father who can easily be distracted from following the programme that is of a pretty poor technical quality anyway, not to mention that he can't hear very well with one ear because of his facial paralysis. We live in a one-bedroom house, so there's nowhere to hide, and no personal space. The bathroom isn't ready yet either, but even when it is, my mother will barge in without reservations, just to say something or check whether everything's all right. She'll never understand that everybody, even animals, are in need of private space, and in case this isn't possible, then one has to pretend and act this out. For example, the whole family turns away when Grandfather is washing his genitals, and older children aren't listening on as their younger siblings are being made, or in case they are, they are held back by fear and keep quiet.

So I'm left with the outdoors. After school, when there's nobody home, I quickly have lunch and do my lessons, and then head out into the open fields, either by myself or with whoever might want to join me. I often leave the door or gate open, as I don't really want to go far, only to the railway tracks, but then I forget about everything, as if the curtains had been drawn behind me. Every so often, it occurs to me that the gipsies may have looted our home, and I hotfoot it back at once. My first glance is at the alarm clock ticking away on the kitchen cupboard, if that's in place, it means that all is well, I consider it the most precious object in the house, fully convinced that the looting gipsies wouldn't hesitate to take it. In my childhood, I have no recollection of any break-ins in our neighbourhood, though in the eighties there will be cases of people stealing food, fruit and vegetables from gardens, and poultry and rabbits from backyards. Thieves equipped with axes and knives have even taken pigs, and on one occasion it was the larder belonging to the mayor in Kisjenő that got looted. The entire town was amused at the fact that, using a long stick, thieves managed to unhook all the sausages and salamis, and remove them through the airing hole. Our world was much more worrying than this, however, because by then everybody was aware that looting had been taking place on a national scale in Romania, and whatever wasn't protected at gunpoint would vanish sooner or later. People weren't simply stealing because they needed something specific, but just for the fun of it, as a matter of habit, and because the regime was about to collapse anyway.

At first, I used to be afraid of being on my own. I knew that grass snakes wouldn't hurt me, but since all the other kids would

scream and run away at their sight, and most grown-ups had reservations, preferring to swat these reptiles wherever possible, I
ended up being afraid too. Having said that, it was rather difficult
to walk about the swampy thickets without coming across some,
they could even be spotted in gardens too. All of a sudden, I
stopped being afraid though, no idea how that happened. One
afternoon, my father and I swatted two fully-grown grass snakes
in our shed, and I got hold of their tail and dragged their dead
bodies to the potato patch at the end of the road, I must have been
around twelve then. Everybody was horrified at my bravery, and
for a second I was overwhelmed with white fright but carried on
regardless, feeling like Indiana Jones, hero of the day. Their skin is
actually rather soft and dry, not mucous, but my mother wasn't
interested in any of this and made me wash my hands. I didn't
object this time, after all I have yet again jumped over my shadow
and was immensely proud of myself.

I first got the hang of rambling after I waited in vain for my
friend James who didn't turn up, so I went round to their place,
but they weren't at home. I waited for a while at the end of their
street, holding on to my penknife in my pocket, then I walked
over to the railway embankment, the last place that still belonged
to civilization so to speak, where I could still hear my mother's
voice without her being able to see me. There was a ditch under
the embankment, the Májer stream, that channelled an entire system of backwaters into the Körös river, surrounded by willow trees,
elderflower and sloe bushes, as well as reeds and widespread jungles
of Japanese wild buckwheat. Over time, people would start throwing all sorts of rubbish into the riverbed, but in the early days
there's hardly any garbage, and in case somebody does throw a random object away, another person is likely to take it home with

them, after all paper and foil can be burned, rubble is swallowed up by the mud on the streets, whilst manure is brilliant for the garden. The railway embankment, or rather its section up to the iron bridge over the Körös, the Májer-stream and the river's flood protection dam form a marshy triangle, where the castle park of Archduke Joseph used to be in the olden days. The presence of giant platan, oak, cedar and lime trees indicate that there was a time when the place wasn't overgrown by thickets, but it was an English garden for the delectation of the aristocracy, one can clearly see its outlines on military maps dating from the First World War. This section is known as Háda, also featuring an orchard, some of the weathered old trees were chopped down around the time we moved to the area, only a few patches were left in place, a handful of giant stumps, together with a few Methuselahs by the house of Lajos Olosz along the river Körös. The railway bridge was built in 1922 when parts of the section connecting Arad with Szalonta ended up on Hungarian territory, thus defying the view that the new border was traced along the North-South railway tracks, after all, this forty-kilometre hiatus is living proof of that. They had to dig out enormous quantities of soil in order to build the embankment along the dam, and there were water-filled mine holes on either side of the railway tracks. In my childhood, this triangle was a sort of no man's land, every so often used to grow wheat or maize but as a rule, it didn't yield good crops due to the inland water or, later, the draught. So it became a place where people came to steal, to illegally depasture animals, to poach, to cut reed or acacia pickets, this is where we picked elderflower or lime amid the all-encompassing and ever-growing thickets. There were a few paths leading left and right into the thickets, and we could indulge in fishing, even bathing in the lakes, witnessing the hatching of wild ducks and coots, and spotting the odd musk rat or runaway French beaver, because this was a time when everyone was breeding nutrias in the hope of getting rich overnight. There was also a fox nest by the embankment, and one winter we saw swans landing on the surface of the largest lake. This two-or-three-square-kilometre wilderness was an ideal playground for me, this is where my childhood took place in fact, and where I went on my own for the very first time, feeling like a fugitive that is neither being chased nor called back by anyone. At first, I got scared by a blackbird, then a quickly vanishing lizard, even though I already knew that it wasn't a snake. Then I decided to just sit down on an enormous tree stump, the size of a room, I can't even picture the magnitude of the tree it had once been, seeing that it must date back to the Ottoman times.

The snag is that meanwhile my friend James went to look for me at home, but since I said that I'd go hiking with him, I got caught out straightaway. My mother kept screaming, father nowhere to be seen, and I had to promise that I'd never ever roam around on my own again. This was one of those promises of course that no sane person could expect me to observe. All I had to do was make it to the railways, and I was free! At first, my mother would follow me but she wouldn't dare to enter the thickets on her own, so she'd soon stop looking for me. This is exactly what happened on my tenth birthday too, when, in my absence, the children invited to the party polished off the birthday cake and drank the rare treat that was Aracola juice, whilst I was out and about observing muskrats all afternoon, picturing them as beavers. I only made it home in the evening, completely shattered and covered in mud. The thing is that I'm a proper trapper, uninterested in cake and children's parties, even though I was quite annoyed at the fact that not as much as single crumb was set aside for me.

My mother is arguing with me all the time, and as far as I remember, she tends to slap me for pretty much anything whenever she can reach me or I let her. I'm always covered in mud, scratches or grazes, once Albi and I even take a pheasant caught in a trap home. This is a proper heroic act and the soup made out of it will be delicious, but before that we argue for ages whether this was theft or not, and whom exactly we robbed. According to my mother, the state, because game belongs to the state, but in my view, whoever laid out the trap. In the fullness of time, my mother will get used to me always being out and about somewhere, after all it's much better than loitering around in town all day. She says this to one of our neighbours as if we didn't make it to the town centre twice a day, on our way to and from school. We bum around the empty streets and allotments, climb trees, hang from carts and trailers, beg for chewing gum from foreign tourists, in winter we venture onto the ice of the Körös river and fabricate all sorts of home-made fireworks, aiming for a *blast*. This is the time when most other boys my age start experimenting with alcohol, Voichiţa next door falls pregnant aged thirteen, and Bandika is taken to the house of correction in Codlea (Feketehalom) for repeated acts of theft at the age of twelve. It was his father who reported him to the police, back then he was the only person I was remotely afraid of. The gipsies from Erdőhegy beat the short policeman with a moustache to a frazzle, an old hag even whitewashes the fainted man, and hardly any of my female classmates from the Gipsy slum finish the eighth grade, seeing that they are usually married off long before that.

Being in the town centre can be dangerous because dozens of Hungarian Gipsy kids are loitering around the cinema, they take our money and empty our bags, there are always flocks of them, and we are seriously scared. My mother allows me to watch every single film that is being shown in town, because she also used to watch every film during the freest period of her life, at Udvarhely, but at times I'm so afraid that I can't sit through an entire film. There's no age rating, anybody who can reach the counter is allowed in. Romanian gipsies don't steal or rob, they just break out in fights for no reason, there are serious gang wars, for instance for ruling over the Jewish cemetery or the garden of the medical practice where one can play football for a little while, but then those in charge are likely to chase people away so that thistles can carry on growing unobstructed. Albi, Joe, James, Marius and I are neither attached to any gangs nor do we form a proper gang in our own right, we are just a bunch of little boys who are rightly afraid of those older and stronger than us. I sew a secret pocket under my collar where to keep larger coins or paper money, in case I'm stopped, I hand over my small change and they won't find anything even if they turn my pockets inside out. This method has worked really well for many years, earning me quite a few friends along the way for as little as fifteen bani. When Limping Lúcsi invited the whole class to her birthday party, only a few of us had the courage to venture out to the notorious Gipsy slum by the cemetery, where apparently people inhabit abandoned crypts. We are terrified but far too curious, so Lúcsi and her father come to meet us on the way as there is no such thing as house numbers or streets around here. We want to see where exactly they white-washed that policeman whom we find rather likeable owing to his moustache and motorbike, even though he's actually a cantankerous bully. Lúcsi's family lives in a pit-house, it's tidy enough despite the penetrating putrid smell, and we eat some cake and drink Pepsi, which in those days is a rare treat even if we have to share three bottles between the eight of us. We don't stay very long as everybody's rather ill at ease, Lúcsi's father is smoking and offers us some cigarettes too, but we refuse. The grandma is grinning as she shows us the whitewasher, I whitewashed him in a shot, I'm not afraid of jail, she says, and sure enough, she doesn't get arrested. This outing is at least as memorable a field trip as the visit to Vilma's where I had the chance to observe poverty from a close up. I will be able to conjure up its smell whenever I remember it. After Lúcsi's birthday, the Gipsy kids from Erdőhegy will stop bothering us, we'll keep a fair yet respectful distance for many years to come, and when I strike Dezső down for mocking me, nobody comes to his aid or to take revenge. Many years later, we meet at the cannery where I'm a mechanic and he's a seasonal worker, you've made it, man, he greets me.

Wandering the fields is much preferable to heading to the pub for young lads, my mother observes, especially since many boys my age drink themselves blind, they can't yet hold their drink. Yet adults keep pointing out that one has to get used to it, men simply must be able to have a high tolerance of alcohol. Uncle Bandi, who teaches me fascinating swear words and who was born in the vicinity of modernist poet Endre Ady's village, owns up to having started smoking and drinking at the age of thirteen. His father offered him the first cigarette, so he could get used to it and wouldn't have to beg from others. Older boys would often hide behind the toilets as early as the upper years of primary school, at times pooling their money together for half a litre of the cheapest brandy, then turn up in class rather tipsy, stinking of alcohol. As my mother reminds me a million times, I'm not allowed to smoke or drink because I'm on medication. The others think I'm mental because I tell them the reasons why I'm not allowed to do any of this. I don't want them to think I'm a total coward, although stammering is not a sign of cowardice but of weakness when it comes to men. I very rarely get involved in fights, and whenever possible, just step out of the way. I'm not exactly lacking courage, but this is hard to demonstrate to others at school, they are not roaming the fields and the furthest they might venture is fishing in the river or in the backwaters, should they be allowed. Our dealings with Joe and James are entirely alien to them, in vain do they read books about Native Americans, it wouldn't even cross their mind to stalk or observe wild animals. The forests are far away and they aren't driven by any desire for discovery, in case I mention that on Sunday I went to the woods, all they can ask is whether it was in order to chop some wood.

Very few of these village kids will attend secondary school, out of fifty only four of us will go to university and none of us will get a place first time round, but even so, this is a great achievement. Ours is the bumper generation following the Second World War, and in Kisjenő it is really rare to be offered a place at university. Having said that, many people would remind me that having a degree can't buy food, this was a view held not only by Hungarians but Romanians too. As a rule of thumb, only those villagers tend to study whose parents have already done so, or who consider this important for some reason, like my father's teacher. In this sense, the forest was a godsend, as it sheltered my dreams from an environment in which nothing apart from moneymaking had any significance, and in which people would not only live by and aggressively promote these rules but display hostility towards any attempt that neglected any useful or useless characteristic in order to seek or at least presume inner values. It was enough for me to walk up to the railway embankment and look towards the east, to the Somosi forest, where on a clear day one could make out the fortress of Világos, and I already left behind the pressures I couldn't quite pin down but experienced on a daily basis. Known as anxiety, this feeling doesn't allow you to breathe, talk or think, I don't know where it's coming from, what or who it's caused by, but it's embedded in the foundations of my being, in my everydays and in my feast days, in my every relationship. It messes everything up and turns things upside down, I try to escape it and even manage to leave it behind for a while, but then I find it waiting for me at the railway tracks, like a faithful dog, knowing full well that I'd be coming back. His nerves are weak, my mother explains to people in case they mention my stammer or its accompanying symptoms and gestures. My father's nerves are weak too, but he doesn't stammer, he doesn't say a word, and we are both at the bottom of any social hierarchy as solitary father and son that we are. I ask him once as we are walking on the embankment what's beyond the forest. He doesn't know, and when I suggest he check it out, he just shrugs, and we go straight home. I don't know what we are doing there together, perhaps I was out and about, and my mother sent him to find me, or we went to gather some acacia poles, who knows, in any case this outing certainly wasn't a frequent occurrence.

The Somosi forest is three kilometres away in a bee line, but it's hard to get there because of the backwaters and channels. There was a constant heavy rainfall in the seventies and eighties, with much of the forest also underwater at times, turning everything into rush-beds, marshes and reeds. One can suddenly find oneself sinking into the ground, and there's no guarantee that it's possible to retrace one's steps. Most of the forest is planted, but there are several ancient oak trees, with impenetrable thickets taking over the deforested areas. The forest plots are separated by strikingly even, kilometre-long fences, and the glades are planted with maize to attract wild animals, so there's a generous scattering of high-stands. All this is proper forest management after all. In my child-hood, it was Ceaușescu and his entourage that came on shooting trips to these parts, and like in the Barót area, there are rusty signs everywhere pointing out that *Accesul interzis în pădure*—no entry. We didn't worry too much about such interdictions, have already been there on our bikes, and met the forester who didn't say any-thing. Actually, he said hello, which is a rare treat around there because foresters were at most times involved with something dodgy and hated intruders, but on this occasion, we weren't seen as a source of much danger. Our first hiking trip is a flop because we aren't yet aware that the forest is entirely surrounded by the backwaters of the Körös river, we can't find a crossing anywhere, there's far too much water. Beyond the reeds, there's the green for-est but not even a single tree on our side, the sun is shining bright, it's hot, we are thirsty and tired but chuffed at having almost made it to the forest. It will take years until we systematically explore the area, so whenever we can we head to the forest. It's like a magnet, and we are already planning our next trip on our way home, seeing that we have yet another corner to examine as we haven't been there at all, or just in case we have, it was a very long time ago.

One of the major discoveries of my life are the red deer living in the Somosi forest, we find some footprints and then actually spot the deer themselves, alongside wild boars, wild cats, martens, black storks and foxes, everything will become rather normal over the years and impossible to get bored of. I'm not yet fourteen when we first go fishing at night, by the forest, we don't catch anything and get bitten by mosquitoes, but we are let loose unsupervised under the night sky, around the campfire, and everything seems just wonderful. We don't have a boat or an Uncle Matula of sorts as in *Thorn Castle*, but our favourite film on Hungarian TV is based on István Fekete's young-adult novel of the same name, and I'm reading the original Hungarian edition of Brehm's *The Life of Animals*, I'm interested in all of it, even unicellulars, though I can't take home all seventeen volumes at once. This marks the start of the next stage of enmity with my mother, as she wants me to stop reading and focus on studying, or to read only after I finished with studying. So I try to hide my books in the most unexpected places in the house, not with much success, not to mention that this is plain impossible when it comes to the large-format Brehm volumes. The fact of the matter is that there isn't all that much for me to learn, I'm easily the second or third best student in class, only struggling in maths, not because I don't understand it but I find it boring, especially algebra. I quite like geometry and am interested in everything, even physics and chemistry. Besides, my love of reading gives me an insight into most fields, alongside TV, which in those days transmits a serious dose of knowledge to those who can be bothered to pay attention. I'm also just getting interested in palaeontology and mineralogy, and this fuels my rhetorical question as to why didn't Noah take some dinosaurs into his arc? This can only mean that there weren't either any dinos, or arcs. We have several stashes of the magazine *Élet és tudomány* [Life and science], perhaps we used to have a subscription at some point, and a massive Soviet history book, in Romanian translation, on the Middle Ages, it contains plenty of colour plates mainly on Eastern cultures. It's a masterpiece of Russian encyclopaedic knowledge, disguised by the Bolsheviks to make it look like it was about class struggle. Do your homework, my mother keeps nagging, and I make every effort to finish it at school so I can immediately produce it at home when she gets back. See, it's finished, and I'm ready to get going. In case I'm not out and about, I'm reading at all times, I don't care that I'm on my own, I don't even play football, if I have a good book to read I just lend my ball to the boys and keep reading. Strikers would never do such a thing, but goalkeepers aren't proper footballers anyway.

XV

Summer Holiday

We've only been on summer holiday once, in 1980, when my father was seriously ill, no medication would help with his face and he was also troubled by sciatica. We are going on a trade union-funded three-week recreation to Felix Spa, one of the best-known thermal spas in the world. Soon it becomes obvious though that we didn't come on holiday, my parents are about to receive treatment, including massages, gymnastics, paraffin masks, pretty much everything that balneology can line up in order to reinvigorate and entertain hard-working people. There's a strict daily routine, treatments are taking place at exact times, and so are baths, lunches and dinners. My father thrives on this lifestyle, he has never experienced it before, something interesting and enjoyable happens every day, Mother, on the other hand, hates this and is restless all day. We sleep in a tight hotel room, eat at the canteen, she's really weary of the treatments as she has no health problems. At times, she has a stabbing pain in her lower back, but mainly because of carrying heavy stuff and of too much dishwashing, and anyway, the food is rubbish, she doesn't want anyone to touch her, massage her, or make her do any exercises.

It's really awful when my mother is bored and doesn't know how to channel her energies. She does quite a bit of handiwork, especially at night before falling asleep, but she doesn't really manage to get absorbed in macramé or crochet, and with her attitude, there's absolutely nothing she could do in Felix, except for swimming, one can't even watch Hungarian TV at the hotel. I end up learning to swim pretty well as I keep practising all day, and when my parents are receiving their treatments, I visit a game room where I entertain myself with one-armed bandits. Under fourteens shouldn't even be allowed in, but no one asks any questions. On the first day, I win thirty lei, this is a lot of money back then, but then I slowly lose it all together with the ice cream money I receive on a daily basis. On one of the last days of the summer, I win another twenty lei with a coin found in the grass, and decide not to play again, a promise I have kept to this day.

Time passes slowly, and my mother hates this uneventful world. We inspect the water lilies and the redfish on a daily basis, take a look at all the foreign cars, I come across the first black person in my life, we go swimming, and then there is time again for treatment, masks, massages, physiotherapy and utter boredom. Then my mother comes up with the idea that we should go home because the strawberries must be ripe, and we have to pick them at once in order to make jam. So we go on vacation from our holiday, we literally run away for a long weekend, but, to be on the safe side, we buy a kilo of strawberries at the market, just in case, the harvest is pretty good at home too, and we finish picking just in time, right before the massive rainfall that would have knocked everything to the ground. The jam is ready in no time, and we bring a jar for Father too, so he doesn't starve in his solitude at Felix and, above all, can take pride in our skills and diligence. We didn't abandon our home and garden, even though the weed had grown so high that Mother would have rather started weeding straight away. She couldn't care less about vacations, which is why we'll never go away again, not to mention that holidaying is most expensive, the food is rubbish, the whole thing is beyond boring, and plenty of work fails to get done as a result. Since my father missed his portable radio so much, we brought it in for him, he absolutely hated being left out of world politics.

We go out for a meal on our last night at Felix. Hotel Belvedere is the fanciest place in the entire resort that we can gain access to, so we make a major effort, Father is wearing a suit and arranges his tie at length in front of the mirror. He keeps checking whether his face shows any signs of improvement after the treatment, both my mother and I think it does, but he just dismisses this with a wave of the hand. The restaurant is packed, and since we haven't booked, we have to wait a little. There's music, illustrious company, and some people are throwing shapes on the dance floor. Finally, a table becomes available at the far end of the room, by one of the pillars from where I can no longer see the band or the dancers. At long last, a waiter puts in an appearance, and it takes even longer until he brings our Wiener schnitzel with chips and coleslaw. I don't know what else is on the menu, we've made our choice without consulting it, my father has a glass of white wine and I get a Pepsi, I relish it and ask for a second helping, which will make me unable to sleep at night as it apparently contains caffeine. This is the first and last time that we have a meal out as a family, Father shows me how to use cutlery properly, seeing that neither Mother nor I can manage this. He cuts up the meat for me, he does this for himself too, slices it all up saying that this is how they've always used to eat. I have difficulty holding the fork in my left hand to this day, have to pay a great deal of attention and am prone to forgetting the rules. That dinner cost a fortune by our standards, it wasn't even good, so we stopped eating out. We chose Wiener schnitzel not because we couldn't have prepared it at home, but because everybody knows that it's best to eat breaded meat in a restaurant, it's cooked properly and one can actually identify what's what on the plate.

This is the time when Romania ceases to exist from a gastronomical point of view. Provisions are becoming an ever more serious problem, this is a shortage economy, there are quotas and rationing, even though these operate at variable levels in the different counties due to impenetrable local conditions. The black market is firmly established and gaining in importance, and pretty much anything can be obtained at extra charge. Offering bribes, brandy or coffee can solve practically any problems, but without them, not much can be achieved. We hand over some brandy at the hotel too, I didn't even realize we had some on us, which is why our suitcase must have been so heavy. We have a reservation for a triple room but they don't have any of those apparently, it doesn't matter that we paid for it, so we resort to a bottle of brandy that can solve the matter, and indeed, they produce a spare bed and not just a cot, and exchange my meal vouchers from child to adult portions. Romania has been struggling ever since to move on from the custom that obtaining anything illegal at a cost isn't considered corruption, except for situations when one has to pay extra for one's fair share. That's an outrage, no less. The psychology of corruption is more complex, of course, but we generally tend to get worried if doctors or officials don't accept bribes, we think that there must be some major problem that they choose not to disclose. My parents have an argument over this, travelling and carrying luggage is a nuisance, we have never stayed at a hotel before, my mother is concerned about the balcony on the eighth floor, she's worried that I might fall out. There are all sorts of other issues too, we have to bribe the doctor, as well as the blind masseurs and the women who apply the paraffin masks. Once we've solved everything, there's boredom again, what shall we do here for three weeks? So we run off to pick strawberries, and let out a sigh of relief. We'll never go on holiday again. From now on, my father travels to Felix alone, in winter, usually over the holidays when the resort has fewer visitors and it's cheaper. He doesn't even come home for Christmas, only for New Year's Eve, he's undergoing treatment as he is ill. Mother learns facial massage, and will keep massaging Father's face for many years. He likes the attention, but since there's no improvement, they stop after a while. He'll never be able to close his right eye, it keeps watering, is prone to inflammation and really sensitive to draught.

The eighties have brought us to the verge of a totally eroding world, where socialism had lost momentum. We don't yet live much worse than before, in fact, it's relatively better compared to the post-war period and the fifties, but this is already the beginning of that amorphous greyness and erosion that will make people's lives sour for decades, the world will be a dead end, and day-to-day hassles can no longer be invested with meaning. My first disturbing image hails from this period when people are forming long queues for sugar at the back entrance of grocery stores, where goods are normally unloaded and rubbish is collected. I cannot believe that there is no sugar, and everybody can only receive one kilo, and in case people join the queue the second time, they will not be served. Typically, the queue is at the back door and in the inner courtyard, but as more people join in, the end of the queue snakes out onto the street. People are squashed together, pushing each another, shouting and screaming, until the police turn up and everyone falls silent. Let's buy some sugar, my mother suggests, so we join the queue. This is my very first time in such a situation, I feel weird, as if I was at school, and all these grown-ups are behaving really weirdly. I don't yet know that the age of plenty is giving way to an age of necessity, when we have to queue for everything, mill about, drag others out of the way and guard our place in the queue at all costs, making sure we aren't pushed out or brushed away and hoping that the shop doesn't run out of sugar, flour, milk, bread or meat in the meantime. At times, we join the queue even when we don't actually need the items on sale, but we might need them later. We are rushing to lay hands on soap, shaving blades, medicine, cotton wool, bus and train tickets, elbowing our way to the cinema or the swimming pool, and in order to get in or out. Stampedes will form the foundation of collective behaviour, and, as a result, I hate crowds to this day. It's hair-raising that people are still capable of jostling one another in queues, on buses, trains or the post office even today, as if they were missing a habit they formed in their youth. Queues become the stage set for a complex social life, people would have exchanged only a fraction of this information otherwise, this way there is time to talk about the ways of the world, gossip about this and that, get to know one another and experience mutual disappointment in case goods run out. Often people had no idea what they were queuing for, and it wasn't at all unusual that lunch ended up consisting of marine fish rather than meatballs, because the former was the only thing left on offer.

Everybody used to loathe this fish hailing from faraway oceans, with a dreadful dislike beyond comprehension. Once my father insisted that we try it and found it rather tasty, but we generally valued fattened carp over mackerel or herring. There was a time when one could only buy meat if one also purchased a kilo of frozen sardines or herrings, everyone would give the latter to their pigs, it was so smelly that, according to a neighbour, even cats wouldn't touch it. The most memorable queues were for gas tanks, called *butélia*, because there were such shortages that ours was empty for weeks on end, even though we used it as sparingly as we could. Mother would cook on an electric cooker at night, we used a cunning trick to steal electricity despite it being cheap, we were a bit concerned of getting caught but nothing happened, after all one of our neighbours worked at the electric plant and did the same. In the seventies, a Molotov truck was driving from village to village to bring gas tanks to those needing to exchange their used ones, the whole thing was fairly cheap, but after a while the truck stopped coming and one had to go to the company selling them, called Competrol. Every family was entitled to a gas tank every two months, a register was kept to this effect because nobody was allowed to have two tanks at a time, although many actually managed. Gas shortages continued, by which point people would simply leave their empty tanks, chained together and with their names scribbled on, at the gates of the gas plant, as there was always someone on duty there. There happened to be an empty plot at the end of the road where people would regularly build campfires, roast bacon, and warm themselves up in winter or shudder under umbrellas and raincoats in the rain, loudly cursing the system. Every so often, the phone would ping in the office to announce that the trucks transporting the gas tanks have left Temesvár. Everybody went on alert at once, people dashed off to find their tanks left in the queue, but at times the truck simply wouldn't make it to the plant and people would have to wait in vain for weeks. Old ladies slumbering on stools in front of shops selling milk, bread or meat from as early as three am to be the first in the queue have become a regular sight in eighties Romania, together with women clutching babies in order to squeeze in front, or young children available 'for loan' in order to facilitate this trick.

Books have been written on the sociology and psychology of queuing, and I, for one, still feel dirty after each shopping spree to this day, as if I'd been forced to participate in some nefarious act. Back then, I didn't even have to queue very often as shopping wasn't one of my tasks, my mother did her best to protect me from this torture, but I witnessed a few hand-to-hand fights for bread, and especially train tickets, when I emerged in a torn coat, down-trodden shoes or lost some of my buttons. We have decided to keep a toilet roll on which my mother marked the year, 1985, and it now acts a souvenir of sorts. An acquaintance had an entire car-load of them, and let us have about a hundred rolls. I can't recall suffering any major shortages myself, because there weren't serious food shortages in the Arad area, as one could obtain pretty much anything from the black market, people could go shopping to Hungary for stuff one couldn't find at home, to say nothing of the fact that my mother was as resourceful as ever. In those days, people developed serious skills in food preservation that led to a sort of home-made food industry that combined traditional and modern techniques, it was far more than a mere hobby, as it was stemming from dire necessity. After years of hardship, seventies Romania starts feeding itself and accumulating stocks, knowing full well that hard times are on the horizon again. It's simply a must to have a sackful of sugar, salt, flour at home, five kilos of beans, three kilos of rice, a sack of potatoes, cooking fats, oil and honey. We always use the longest held supplies, and replace stocks as we go along. The first large deep freezers appear around this time, one can freeze an entire pig in these and keep it for up to a year, but other food items can be stored too, such as bread or vegetables. Electricity is still fairly cheap, and despite the regular power cuts, green beans or peas can be kept for ages, there is no frozen produce in the shops, and barely any products at all. One has to prepare everything at home, there are hardly any processed goods but one finds that cookery books and recipes start circulating from one end of the country to the other, there is an entire cookery folklore comprising a multitude of simplified or misinterpreted recipes. Next, there's the era of replacement ingredients whereby, due to poverty, regular ingredients have to be substituted with something else. One has to come up with replacements in the case of cakes and confectionary in particular, as the absence of butter, cocoa, chocolate, cream, coconut, vanilla and such-like represents a challenge even to the most resourceful housewives.

This is the time when whole-wheat flour disappears in Romania because they close down all of the Ganz mills still in operation, rumour has it that they even mix in fodder feed and barley. From now on then, it's never clear how the dough will look like and how the flour will turn out in the baking process, seeing that quality does matter for scones but it's absolutely essential for doughnuts, strudel or sponge cakes. I ordered some quality flour from Hungary, my mother tells us, as she's often led to utter desperation over the state of the dough that either wouldn't rise or bake properly as a result of unsuitable flour. She's not really into cooking or baking, but is doing it regardless, stubbornly and systematically, she doesn't mind the time it takes. One absolutely has to have something to eat, this is her point of view, even though it's hard to get it right for my father, both as far as his taste and mood is concerned. My mother thinks her cooking suits Father's taste, she learned this from Grandma Zsüli, but Father doesn't actually like that stuff beyond a sort of nostalgia for the taste of his distant childhood. He's never pleased with anything, even though his skills don't even extend to making a decent omelette. His favourite pastime is roasting bacon in the garden on Sunday mornings, this is as important for him as it is for American Hungarians according to Imre Oravecz in the *Kaliforniai fürj* [Californian quail]. The problem with skewers and fires is that this business takes up the whole morning, and we are both full by the time we have to eat lunch. Mother hates roast bacon and bread and dripping with onions, not to mention that due to us barbecuing for so long the whole day's agenda is overturned. My father would never agree to barbecuing somewhere in the open, he insists on doing this at home, so there are always arguments or at least sulking whenever there is nice weather on Sunday mornings. Mother is unable to let us get on with this ceremony, she always interferes with observations on the fire, the skewers, the chair, the tray, the bacon, the wasps, you name it, even though she'd actually prefer to get on with the cleaning and tidying, she'd like to shake out the carpets or air the bedding in the sun. Due to the smoke, she can't, and, worse still, even has to shut the windows.

I quite like grilling meat, but that's out of the question as it is a total waste. Something like this is only possible when we slaughter pigs at Ágya, this usually turns into a minor family kerfuffle, and I'm looking forward to it just as much as to the annual journey to Barót. My grandparents didn't keep pigs in the past as there was no point, but then they started to keep one for us, which we'd always pay for at market rates, and another for themselves, as pigs tend not to eat properly on their own, in this respect they are just like people. At times, we slaughter the two pigs at the same time, but this involves a lot of work and it's better to slaughter them separately, as it always goes much faster the second time round. When we are dealing with the first one we always have to recall how we did this or that the year before, according to ancient customs, and make plans for doing things differently. Uncle Joszip Joszipovics secretly instructs me to put slightly more of every spice except for salt into the sausage mix when no one is looking, because then everybody will be pleased and Father can praise the merits of sticking to the original recipe. At this point my uncle winks at me, sure, we've stuck to every single detail in the ancient recipe, just as it was printed in a small handbook published by Ceres, Bucharest.

We haven't yet made it to this event though, as it is really problematic to get to Ágya. These seven kilometres represent an almost insurmountable distance, and it is just as challenging for us as it is for my classmates. There's only one bus a day and plenty of passengers, the bus station isn't even far from us, it's right next to my school, but due to the crowds one is unable to get on the bus at any other stop. The journey amounts to two hours if not more, including the walks to the bus stop, especially at Ágya where one has to walk for about a kilometre, but the bus isn't much faster as it is only trudging along the stony road covered in potholes. The journey would only take an hour door to door if we travelled as the crow flies, and I even know the way across the fields, but I only managed to persuade my parents once, they'd rather suffer on the bus even though my mother always falls ill and my father gets irate. It would be faster on bikes too, but we don't ride bikes in cold weather, we always walked when I was young, my mother decrees at a time when I'm twelve and she's not yet forty. The point she's trying to make is that walking is embarrassing, a pointless activity that is best to avoid. Only those people walk who can spare the time or who have no money for the bus. Nobody knows back then that walking is actually good for the health. By the time we make it to Ágya, it's usually evening, and pitch dark as they only connect the village with electricity in 1980. My parents are struggling with the oil lamps as their eyes are not used to them, my grandmother usually makes some pasta filled with jam, or produces some sausages set aside from last year's pig slaughtering. We tend to have lunch and dinner in the summer kitchen, Grandfather gets mildly drunk and will soon start an argument with my mother, the most they can hold out is until the next day. I really like the wine my grandfather makes, it's just a home-made plonk that everybody has around here, it contains Noah grapes in smaller or larger quantities, so it's rightly known as a headache-inducing wine. I am allowed a glass after lunch too, which I especially deserve if I eat well, meaning a lot. My mother immediately starts to sulk because of the wine, she scolds me not to even think about having some more, and instructs Grandpa not to give me any. It wouldn't be difficult to avoid this argument, but my mother gets aggressive in the presence of someone tipsy, she must make a point and keeps repeating it until Grandma tells her to stop. I know already that as Grandpa is pouring and drinking his wine, Mother is getting edgier and edgier, until an argument unavoidably breaks out.

Our evening is spent rummaging among tools, equipment, bits of plywood and dishes. Uncle Joszip Joszipovics also turns up, he's the slaughterman who will direct the entire team. He likes a drink, so they pour him a glass, funny and jovial, a man who knows plenty of anecdotes, he plays a lot with me when I'm a child, teaches me all sorts of things and I'm his permanent assistant. After a while, I could probably do everything by myself, though I'm not prepared to kill animals. Joszip Joszipovics is a resourceful man with exceptional dexterity, he is a Jack-of-all-trades who can make lathes, electric hoes, blasters and pumps, he knows all about horses as well as about accounting, he used to be a free-lance wrestler in his youth, in addition to being a ladies' man. He's in a good mood after the first glass of wine itself, and my father would happily join him but my mother stops him: Ferike, don't drink! This gets on Grandpa's nerves, what the fuck, I'm the one in charge around here. At the end, there's a huge argument, and I sneak out to the stable where I can still hear the loud voices as I'm staring at the greenish glimmer of sheep's eyes. Grandpa also comes out, he stinks of alcohol but isn't yet wobbling, we take some hay to the manger or cut up some sugar beet, then go to fetch some firewood and coal to heat in the main house, where it's extremely cold and won't really get much warmer but we sleep under thick duvets. The coal smoke is billowing above the backyard, Grandpa and I are heading over to the house as I hold the lamp and he carries the basket, limping along ever since he has broken his heel bone that is unlikely to ever heal again.

By the time the pig is slaughtered at dawn, Mother is usually unwell and Grandpa already drunk from the first two shots of brandy, even though there's a lot more to come till evening. Basically, everybody is drinking all day long, except for Mother. Everybody knows what to do, or at least pretends to know, except for Father. My task is to pour water as they are cleaning intestines out for sausage casing, it's a pretty disgusting job but according to Mother there are many things more disgusting than shit, she refrains from telling us which are those though. There's an ongoing disagreement between the group of men and that of women, they keep messaging each other to hurry up and finish this or the other faster. They are always drinking, Mother complains, and she's absolutely right. At Ágya everybody is drinking, even women, this is the norm there. Those who don't drink must have some problems or are ill, perhaps afraid or are *believers*, like Mother, who flies off the handle upon hearing this because she does indeed believe but her religion is Catholic, that is to say Protestant due to her marriage to my father. Who can possibly follow this? In the course of the morning, my uncle's wife also joins us in the disgusting precision work that is cleaning intestines, she's the expert at this. She knocks back a few glasses of wine too, especially after she's finished blowing into the small intestines, to check whether they have holes as the sausage meat wouldn't be able to stay in otherwise. Large intestines are clean if they stick to the wall after *poking*. Everybody's in a good mood until there's an accident, or something breaks, tips over, spills or burns, or somebody cuts themselves on the hand, usually my father or I. We have roast meat for lunch, that's the best, I'm allowed to roast the meat on a spit and I take in the atmosphere, the fire, the tasting in the afternoon, but I'm dreading the argument likely to break out in the evening when Grandpa, drunk off his ass, will fall out with Mother in the usual and unavoidable way. This time the argument will involve everyone, everybody shouts and screams, and will end up crying. On Sunday, Mother will have a gallbladder attack, she's already unwell when we are melting the lard, but she holds out until we get on the bus, she manages to cope somehow and only lets herself go once we are at home . . .

I can't recall the reasons for these arguments when I was a child, but it would seem that they always followed the same scenario. The match would always take place between Grandpa and Mother, as a battle between two radically opposed personalities. I would find myself in the middle, but Father would never interfere and Grandma only very rarely, usually demanding to stop it once and for all! As a rule, it was a typical match among alcoholics, and

I can't understand where Mother could have possibly learnt her part so well, though I have an inkling. Grandpa is lying down or sitting on a chair in the corner, smoking and pouring himself some wine, talking about the war yet again, which bores everyone to death apart from me, everybody is working following the motto less talk, more work! Mother keeps interfering all along, for instance when Grandpa says that the Russian soldiers ended up burning to death in the tobacco factory at Temesvár, my mother slips in that they had asked for it, or when the Germans went blind from drinking wood-spirit, she snaps that they had it coming. Mother comes up with all sorts of quips, she pulls Grandpa's leg until he retorts after the umpteenth glass that enough is enough, Iboly, you have no idea what we're talking about. He was just talking about his horse that, as a hussar's horse, was trained to refrain from taking over the captain's horse, and when he would have needed to ride to the front in an emergency, the horse simply went on its hind legs and threw him off. Rightly so, Mother quips, it serves them right, drunkards deserve their fate, and it's irrelevant whether the outcome is a lost horseshoe, a crashed plane, a faulty safety-bolt, everything happens for one reason—Grandpa's drinking—this is why food gets burned, soup boils over and oil lamps go sooty. After a while, Grandpa can take this no longer, stands up with all his might, he's almost two metres tall, and signals that we should go as we have work to do. Mother shouts that I should stay inside, it's cold out there, but I'm already on my way, so Mother runs after us and carries on shouting, to which Grandpa responds with such epic swear words that I find myself shivering with fear.

I have no idea why Mother is so concerned about alcohol, why this insurmountable irascibility that always makes her battle with

253 | SUMMER HOLIDAY

drunkards and keep on preaching as if she was an activist of the Salvation Army. Having said that, she's actually one of them, sort of. I don't yet know that the first husband of my grandmother from Barót had a serious alcohol problem, I don't realize that Uncle Tom has a serious alcohol problem too, I'm only aware of Grandpa Joszip Vida's drinking, who drives Mother up the wall, and to be fair, me too, but whom I love dearly because he is present in my life as if he was my father, seeing that my actual father isn't. Akin to seriously abused children, Mother regularly displays such aggressive behaviour, and her personality is shaped by her traumas. Grandpa-Uncle Gyurika doesn't drink, but his children are just as afraid of him, he regularly beats the older ones in full view of the young, while the youngest is tormented by everyone without anyone realizing, what's more, Grandma even provides an ideological motivation stating that it's all for the best. It's this simple, but I don't get it back then. Later, my hunch is that mother would have liked to rule the roost, but that was impossible seeing that Grandpa was a tough, rude, honest and determined man, who wouldn't recognize any earthly authority above himself. He liked my mother as she was hardworking, but he didn't take her seriously beyond the norms of his culture. As for my mother, she wanted precisely such a man, except for the drinking.

Pig slaughtering is always a serious expedition because we have to make it home with heaps of luggage in mid-winter, and this is extremely complicated. There is no pavement along the side of the road in Ágya, only a very narrow concrete strip that is cracked in most places, so we have to use a wheelbarrow to transport our stuff to the bus, likely to be overcrowded on a Sunday afternoon. I'm sitting on this digger's wheelbarrow too, as Grandpa pushes it tottering along. We have no wheelbarrow in Kisjenő, so we have to lug our stuff across town ourselves, Mother and Father complain of back pain, and I'm just a child, seen as yet another piece of luggage, not to mention that the house has cooled down in our absence and the first thing we have to do is light the fire. We have to go back and forth a few times to bring this or that, and it's always the same fuss. It will take many years until we slaughter a pig at our own place. After the death of my grandparents, we are obliged to become more independent and handle pig slaughtering on our own, as a result of which it will never be a family feast but another job that needs doing. We can manage it, faster and easier, but we enjoy it a lot less, at most, we experience a sense of relief upon completion. It is customary in those days to offer acquaintances a taste of the various home-made produce, the people we value or we owe a favour receive some meat, the others mainly sausages and liverwurst. Every time it's our turn to receive some, we note that ours is better, we make the best produce far and wide. Most of our neighbours have no clue and don't even observe basic hygiene, there was an occasion when the station master sprinkled their sausage meat with washing powder instead of salt, they even mixed it in before they noticed and had to throw everything out to the amusement of the entire street. As it happens, they got the washing powder from us, somebody helped us to obtain it, and we were really afraid that this could get us into trouble, but it didn't.

We are surrounded by primitive people, some well-meaning and others less so. Mother is very amicable with our next-door neighbours, yet she keeps her place and resents them for any offences and envies those who seem to be better off. A smarter item of clothing, some fresh plasterwork or a car always remind Mother of our poverty, but having to put up with these of all people . . .

Father looks down on everyone, irrespective of their ilk, but even he is annoyed by the fact that some people with next to no education have a higher standard of living than us, and have no idea that the world is in such deep shit. Those we look up to live far away and we have no contact with them, yet they do exist. The woman next door, the mother of my deskmate and best friend is rivalizing with everyone at all times, she wants everything my mother happens to have, be it a hat, a shoe, a coat, some folk-weave items, embroidered cushion covers or macramé. Mother hates this copy-cat approach, but helps her regardless. Albi and I wear the same hat and shoes, and carry the same school satchel for years, we can't get rid of the neighbour, to say nothing of the fact that there isn't much on offer in the shops, we usually go shopping to Arad or Várad and buy the shoes or clothes we happen to stumble upon. For a long time, it looks like Aunt Zsú and Mother were playing best friends, but then they break out in a fatal argument because they miscalculate the price of the pig that we buy from them. My father insists that we should use other methods of weighing in addition to scales, but alas, the result is a few kilos extra, that leads to screaming and shouting and they want us to now pay for the difference, as well. We aren't talking a lot of money, but prestige is invaluable. Instead of jumping at each other's throats, the two women make scenes in front of their respective husbands, giving rise to an avalanche of hitherto repressed tensions. This marks the end of a friendship, even though we remain on good neighbourly terms, but when their pressure cooker explodes and the soup hits the ceiling, Mother notes after the initial fight that this serves them right, why didn't they pay more attention. So much for rivalry, that we also buy a washing machine just because they already have one, and it's useful, but Mother is scared of any electric devices and, like her father, can't make sense of electricity.

There's only one other event comparable to pig slaughtering—New Year's Eve, when relatives from Barót visit us, usually my godmother Heléna and godfather Guzman who claims that the reason for all the shortages is that the Germans lost the war and the Jews acquired everything. Never mind, the Hungarian flag will once more fly high in Kolozsvár one day. It took me forever to take this seriously, but we are experiencing a revival of this idea, so I have to accept that these things do exist. My uncle belonged to a circle of people who connected the decay of Hungarians to the Jews, that of Transylvanian Hungarians to Romanians, and no reasoning could persuade him otherwise. He spent the best summer of his life at a military camp run by SS officers, somewhere around Szászrégen in 1944, from where he simply pedalled home to Barót when the Romanians switched sides. His worldview fits, without any stylization, a more or less standard Albert Wass novel, as if he had been a minor earl and not the son of a Transylvanian schoolteacher who also went into teacher training but was thrown out by the popular democracy, that is the Jews. He has no other issues, he's a full-blooded chubby man who loves good food, drink, partying and singing, in short, he's a jovial and musically gifted man. Legend has it that at Aunt Anette's wedding party, he got bored of listening to the masterpieces of Romanian folklore, produced his accordion and played till morning for the Romanian guests who 'kicked off their shoes' and ended up dancing on tables. They enjoyed his tunes so much that they forgot their own music once they got the chance to sample the sweet essence of Hungarian musical superiority . . .

This sums up Godfather Guzman, his final act was playing the *Székely Anthem* on a church organ, that's where the ambulance found him, and when he died his last words were: doctor, this oxygen would have been enough for an awful lot of welding . . . He's really one of a kind, a firm and strong man, with a worldview and profession of his own, he builds his own house, raises two children and gives up his ghost in the service to God and Country. Our house comes to life as soon as they arrive, we have to buy ten litres of wine and ask our odious neighbours for more in case we run out, then they come round to ours too, uncle only speaks a bit of Romanian but the wine helps, we are on good terms with everybody, midnight in Romania, midnight in Hungary, Székely Anthem, fucking Romanians, especially if Uncle Joszip Joszipovics and family also join us from Ágya and Aunt Anette from old Romania, whoopee! Truth to be told, such a family party only took place once. When Grandpa-Uncle Gyurika found out that our guests polished off thirty litres of wine, he asked everybody to keep it quiet, and scolded Mother to no end. Meanwhile, Father worked out that it was eight adults over four days . . .

My memories of these New Year's Eve parties are about antici-pation, as we are peeking out into the dark to check whether the train has arrived, until Uncle Guzman shouts from the open car-riage door: Ibike, we are coming! Needless to say, Heléna and Guzman are mainly interested in Hungarian television, they are staring at the screen all day with the doggedness of children who are forbidden to watch TV at home, and then indulge in anything that happens to be on air when they are at Grandma's, so much so that they even forget to change channels. As far as I'm concerned, they always brought the world from Barót with them, its language, accent and words, to such an extent that the odd classmate would ask whether I spent my holidays in Székely Land again. To be honest, I had no other desire those days than to see the snowy peaks of the Hargita, but I have to grow up first for that. There is something childish in their obsession with television and mine with Székely Land, Mother's with family and Father's with nothing much, seeing that he is bored of this all. He can't stand Guzman's Hitler Youth talk for long, a Protestant Hungarian shouldn't berate the Jews, he tells me later, without Jewish culture there wouldn't be Christianity. According to Guzman, it's the fault of the Jews that there is no proper Christianity. He also finds Grandpa-Uncle Gyurika mad, and the religious fervour of Barót-based Baptists rather ridiculous and hypocritical, and since he lives there, he can see through both their theology and their misrepresentations. They may well achieve salvation but that's a long way away, so what's going to happen until then?

They both radically oppose socialism and the Ceaușescu-regime, but Guzman is not prepared to listen to the Romanian programme on Radio Free Europe, for him they are the same stinky Romanians. My father argues that we live in Romania, and Guzman retorts, so what. So we drink, as only Godfather can sing, fortunately he doesn't bring his accordion which is just as well as Father would run away, but he can still manage to hum a selection of operetta hits. The other issue with Guzman, in my father's view, is that he doesn't know anything about wine, he just gulps it down regardless of grape varieties, whether it's red or white, and when he drinks, he is really categorical, hungover and argumentative who lectures, puts down and ridicules everyone. Sooner or later, he'll start criticizing me too, in his view my parents are too liberal with my education, I'm not respectful enough, children should lay low, how do I dare not eat fatty meat cuts, apple cores and hard bread crusts when these contain so much vitamin? Mother is driven up the wall by his tipsiness, so she argues back, they will fall out sooner or later, but she carries on whispering in the kitchen with Heléna whenever there's no preparing or eating of meals, or they are bored of too much TV. If only there were no feasts or Sundays, Mother whispers many a times. I navigate between the group of men and women, sometimes I wish I was my childless godparents' son because they are much more jovial and relaxed than my own parents, other times, I'm glad I'm not, because I dislike Guzman's violence.

The case of Aunt Anette is somewhat more complicated because her husband Michelin is *Romanian through and through*, he doesn't understand a word of Hungarian and it doesn't even occur to him that he could learn the language. Somebody is always trying to interpret for him, but Géza Hofi's eighties political cabaret is almost impossible to translate, and so is most of this Székely–Hungarian universe. I am tasked with conversing with him so he doesn't get bored, my godparents speak next to no Romanian and he can't really make sense of my father's political and religious ideas. Aunt Anette is totally devoted to socialist Romania, her husband can cope with people speaking evil of the regime, but she can't, she is the Romanian nationalist in the family, she is both censor and head of the family at once, a *homo rumäniensis* who will discover Catholicism after the regime change and will do her best to catch up with a forty-year hiatus. Uncle Michelin is the most patient man in the world, truly meek, who doesn't understand much of what Hungarians and Székelys are about, and has no radar for detecting ethnic conflicts. He likes Hungarian cuisine, because Aunt Anette follows the recipes of Mrs Zathureczky aka Manci Zelch, and this is the case for all women in the Székely branch of our family except for my mother. In honour of Uncle Michelin, at New Year's Eve we all have to listen to the Romanian Anthem while standing, this isn't his idea, we are volunteering it upon Aunt Anette's request, but only the two of them are actually singing along. They find our Romanian neighbours rather suspicious on account of their dialect, and Uncle Michelin will fail to understand that there is a Romanian continent called Transylvania even when he relocates to Kolozsvár. I will always find it hard to get used to his Bucharest accent, and I usually have to ask him to speak a little slower. I look at this man, an excellent mechanic, who sits through these rowdy, or at times pious, family sessions smiling, without the slightest complaint, like a true autist. I often felt awkward seeing him left to his own devices, and never translated Godfather Guzman's comments. How could I possibly say 'bloody Romanians'? After the third day, I'm desperate for this whole thing to come to an end, I'm not allowed to go anywhere as we have guests. But they leave before everybody could totally fall out with one another, and we bemoan their departure. Life goes on, our relatives live far away and we, here, are foreign.

XVI

Arad

When in September 1982 Mother left me, with a small yellow
suitcase, in the courtyard of the student hall on Tchaikovsky street,
we had already gotten to know a few second-year students and
they offered to keep an eye out for me. The administrator also
reassured us that everything will be just fine. Marius, the janitor,
will soon arrive and he'll take me up to the dorm and introduce
me to the house rules. We were loitering about the courtyard of
the one-storey U-shaped building with an outside gallery, our luggage lined up under the thuja shrubs. The boys who already knew
each other started playing football, kicking the ball at a single goal,
the rest of us standing around, some accompanied by their
mothers, others alone, I can't remember any girls though there
must have been some. Early on, we managed to take a look at the
dorm through the window, there were two bunkbeds, a table and
some chairs, but nobody mentioned that I'd be allocated to the
larger dorm, without any tables or chairs, alongside twenty others.
Before she left, Mother reminded me yet again that Father also
lived here, so I'd be just fine, not in the least because one of the
cooks was from Grandma's village. Aunt Maruca confirmed that
the food was good indeed, and that she used to know Great-
Grandpa Rhédei, whom I didn't. What a small world! The janitor,
nicknamed Majmuca [Monkey], arrived late afternoon, I have no
idea whether he was drunk or not, but he certainly appeared rather

edgy. He was a skinny, chicken-breasted young man with wild hair, hence his nickname, who had a go at lining us up which led to no result. He was smoking most of the time, which wasn't yet forbidden or considered a sin.

Somehow, we managed to squeeze into the dorm, choose a bed and wardrobe, even though there weren't enough of the latter, and first year students had to share. Our wardrobe still had both of its shelves in place and could be locked, which made me one of the lucky few, I had to share it with a Romanian boy from Világos, so I immediately handed over the second key to the huge Chinese lock that I brought along, after all my father was born at Világos. Opposite the wardrobes, there were a number of sinks, equipped with cold water taps only, while the toilets were at the end of the corridor, the walls decorated with oil paint displaying decades of urine stain and an impressive collection of graffiti. In the dorm there was an old tiled stove, a score of beds lied up in two rows with a corridor in the middle, as if we were in a military barrack, blue curtains on the windows, beyond which there was the street, with rattling trams and the area known as Rácfertály. The older boys help me put on the bedsheets and sort out my stuff, just in time before the janitor starts shouting that it's forbidden to sit on the beds, let alone to step on them with shoes. When he leaves the room, we sit down, the older boys even lie down, two minutes later the janitor screams again, get up at once, everybody out, but for some reason we don't go anywhere, feeling rather perplexed. First year students don't understand this approach, but the older ones just keep grinning, *pizda mătii*, Matei Filipescu says half-aloud, he is in year three and a featherweight boxer. The janitor can hear him as he says fuck you, stops for a second but doesn't turn around and then walks away.

At this point I should quote Géza Ottlik's seminal novel *School at the Frontier*, or at least paraphrase it with minor adjustments, even though our school wasn't a military academy only a secondary school specializing in the petrol industry, and the walls didn't feature *The Anatomy Lesson of Dr Tulp* but one of Romanian artist Nicolae Grigorescu's oil paintings with oxen. All conversation takes place in Romanian, as the only Hungarians are the Merényi siblings and I. Lacimarciferi were an inseparable trio, they'd never beat me too hard as I wasn't a serious opponent, but my stammer was a major handicap and there were hardly any nights when I didn't go to bed crying. There are hardly any humiliating situations that I didn't experience, and I had more than my fair share of being exposed to teenage cruelty. I was naive, gawky, in addition to which I stammered and was weak, they took away all my stuff, and if I tried to show resistance, they hit me and no one came to my defence. Laci ruled the roost, riding his high horse, and he was an absolute authority in the group, a true gang leader in the vein Ottlik also describes. He had a dogsbody, a stupid Székely kid called Marci, who played judo and was tasked to be the hitman. Feri was in year four and was moved to the halls in punishment, I would have been able to deal with him on my own, and even had a go at this once because he grabbed my cock, no one stuck up for this back then, it wasn't the done thing, even though it was the worst form of humiliation. They were usually hanging out as a group of three, or at least two, and if I riposted, I was the one to come off badly. Unless one of them went straight for pummelling, kicking, or hitting me in the stomach, it would all begin with a sort of game, whereby they'd ask me something, I'd respond, and if I didn't stammer then they'd start quibbling until they found an excuse, interrupted me, and laughed at me as soon as I started to stammer. Don't lie, one of them would caution me, I'm not lying, I'd say, by which point they would have already hit me, you're lying, I'm not, bang!

There was room for everything in this scenario and I was unable to break out of it, most of the time they only aimed at laughing at my expense, but they'd mercilessly take away my money, food and clothes, and torment me at will, seeing that this was pretty much their only entertainment during long winter nights. The Romanians were unable to follow what was going on, but they kept giggling, they could sense how down and out I was. I was terribly ashamed of my vulnerability, so didn't talk about this to anyone, not even to my parents or the teachers, needless to say, they warned me not to say a word. I wasn't complaining back in the day when I was at kindergarten, and I won't do that now that I'm living in halls. I knew that, sooner or later, all this would come to an end. To save the day, however, I must stress that later in the army I will show such attitude to the corporal trying to pick a quarrel that he gets it straightaway that I know the deal. I won't rub the floor with a toothbrush, won't measure the dorm with a matchstick, won't wash anybody's dirty socks, won't volunteer for anything, won't get involved in slap-in-the-face competitions, won't dash for second helpings, and in case somebody hits me, I hit back at once, be this a game or in earnest, it's all the same. Having said this, we never got to such a point in the army, as all was rather short and sweet. Not so at Arad, this is why I still have to save the day because something has broken in me for good. It took me thirty years to be able to engage with *School at the Frontier* as just a novel, and the jury's still out whether I'm actually a proper civilian, because my time at the student hall and in the army blur together. I have seen plenty of people tumbling, staggering and having fun, but the wicked and the guilty have never got their due punishment, they didn't even flunk. Ottlik, on the other hand, is a genius.

So my mother enrolled me in the school considered to be the worst in Arad, since we knew that some of the best teachers worked there, seven of whom had also taught my father. By this point they were fed up with the world, teaching and the regime, they were barely interested in the curriculum and the political nonsense they had to force down our throats. At times, it looks as if everybody would have preferred to spend these four years until the baccalaureate in a sort of tranquil truancy: our teachers looking forward to retirement, us to the summer holiday or at least workshop practice and my mother to me coming home on Saturdays so she could cook for me, wash my clothes and sign my gradebook in which one low mark followed the other. I learn absolutely nothing, I read this or the other during the afternoon quiet hour, Jack London is my favourite author, at night we paint the town red, and in spring I start writing *my memoirs* in a check notebook. In short, nobody cares how exactly I spend my time. I'm not good at maths but manage to pass, the other subjects are going well without any major effort, we are studying technical subjects in Romanian, I find that hard at first, but we have excellent teachers who are also engineers, and the world's prettiest woman is our geology teacher, all the boys are in love with her. I've already shown interest in geology and the world of minerals, have been to a coal mine and thought that geologists have beards, their job is hiking in the mountains to gather rocks and minerals. As opposed to this, the first living geologist that I meet is an ethereal woman with green eyes.

One of the topics we debated one break time was whether dinosaur fat could be classed as petrol. When our beautiful teacher told us that we don't know for sure how petrol came about, there are two theories, one arguing for organic, and the other for inorganic origin, I got really sad because this meant in fact that we didn't know anything. Public belief back then was that we'd run out of petrol in no time, the last ice age wasn't fully over and the next was on its way, winters were already really cold after all. To this day, I'm convinced that the Earth will start to cool down, nobody will know why, seeing that it has already cooled down and warmed up so many times irrespective of any human endeavour. Everything is a matter of scale. Palaeontology has a unique melancholy, after all, through it, mankind can study the transience of the world. I wasn't actually taken by the thought of millions of years or the muddled theories of evolution that even secondary school students could easily question, but the magnificence of our transience and minuteness, and the fact that we were able to know all this, perhaps this was why this existed in the first place, so that we could imagine it. I was fascinated by the giant drill-cores that were lying about in our classroom, and on it, we were able to work out the geological layers and ages, though we were unsure which pattern originated where. *Rudapitecus hungaricus*, I said once to our teacher when we spoke about human evolution in passing, and we discussed that it wasn't possible to originate humans from apes, not even from a common ancestor. She asked us not to tell anyone that she held this view because she would be kicked out of education, and she wouldn't like to go back to work at an oil well. Next, we covered the Neander-valley and Crô-magnon findings, and the remains of the *Australophitecus*, we were very interested in these and didn't want to settle the argument between the supporters of creation and those of evolution. As I was sitting in the front row, she was explaining all this to my deskmate and me, the rest of the class making the usual racket at the back. Every so often, I tell myself that it was Sophie Marceau's lookalike who taught me geology, except that it was really hard to understand her strong Moldavian accent.

Yet life was much harder and more prosaic than this would suggest, because students living in halls had to fulfil regular kitchen duties. Aunt Zsula and Maruca seemed jolly enough in their chubbiness, but they didn't do much apart from stirring the odd dish and giving orders, and there was work aplenty. The only reason I didn't throw up the first time I had to do the dishes was that I got up at five o'clock in the morning and forgot to have breakfast. At lunchtime, I was still retching from a margarine called Marga that I was unable to wash off my hands, its disgusting stench hovering about my hands all day. I must have peeled at least twenty kilos of onions that made me weep no end, and my female colleague—back then there were girls, as well, in our hall—pushed me as I was bending down to scrub the bottom of a hundred-litre pot, and I fell into the swill. We grappled a bit with one another, but Aunt Zsula started to squeal and we never got as far as making out.

All in all, this beginning had its ups and downs, but I got used to it because the kitchen also offered me protection insofar that I didn't have to attend school or quiet hour that day. Afternoons were fairly calm as the supervisors tried to prepare dinner at the same as lunch, so we only had to warm it up and do the dishes in the evening, and by the time I made it back to the dorm, the nasty older students were already asleep. Aunt Maruca would usually prepare something tasty for me on account of knowing my great-granddad, she could be really nice, but in case she wasn't pleased with our standards of dishwashing, we had to start it all again from scratch. There was no hot water, so one had to heat the water up on a giant cooker and then transport it to the dishwasher by the bucketload. There were no proper dishwashing detergents except for a powder called Tix, and some really smelly baking soda, but since one cooked with very little fat, it was possible to wash the leftovers away with just a little hot water. The only snag was that there was no way out in case an older student decided that I had to be on kitchen duty in his place. At first, I got beaten up for my defiance, but later I tried to play it in such a way that at least I got out of the most excruciating maths lessons. On the plus side, I acquired some basic cooking skills, even though I didn't realize that at the time.

There was another rota for cleaning duties, we had to take the ash out and light the fire in winter, bring in twenty buckets or so of coal and light all the tiled stoves while our colleagues were at the afternoon quiet hour. This was a harder job than kitchen duty because firewood was often moist, the coal contained slate, so I had to make use of all my fire-making skills, running from one dorm to the other and making sure the fire doesn't die out, or at least the stove is still lukewarm, by the time my classmates were back. The fact of the matter is that it was never warm enough, we were shivering with cold that winter at school, in the hall, in the workshop, just as the whole country did. Once I got beaten up because I didn't manage to light the fire in our own room, I spent the entire time saving a piece of fossilised wood which I took to my teacher, we even managed to categorise it, but its name escapes me at the moment. In punishment, my roommates kicked me in the stomach, everybody in the dorm was meant to hit me once—this was the custom—after all the fire was barely flickering, and

we were all was cold. Despite my natural sense of defiance, I could-
n't even lay the blame on the stove or show them the fossil. It was
February 1983 when my father visited me as I was just about to
remove the ash from the dorms and take it down to the bins. I was
wearing tracksuit bottoms, dressed as if I was going to PE class, it
was frightfully cold both inside and outside, but I worked as hard
as I could despite being really skinny and depressed. At first, there
was a flicker of enthusiasm in my father's eyes, he spent eight years
in this building too, but he got seriously upset when he saw the
plaster falling off, the rusty balustrades and the ice on the bathroom floor, seeing that we didn't heat the bathrooms at all. He
must have smelt the stale scent of all these people confined
together, needless to say, there was no hot water and hence no
opportunity for bathing or showering. He wanted to take me out
for a walk in the town, but my bizarre conscientiousness made me
say no, and I carried on with my duties. He told me that he hadn't
seen such war-like conditions ever since the war itself, but I
reassured him that this wasn't so bad, and I'd carry on living in
halls for another year, until my rebellion properly started. My
worst memory is that I had to burn the belongings of a classmate
taken to hospital with some contagious disease. The nurse said that
all of his stuff had to be burned, books, notebooks, clothes, the
lot. So I asked whether I could get infected while handling them,
but she said no, but then why do we have to incinerate everything,
to be on the safe side, she said.

Initially my biggest problem was that regulations only permitted us to travel home once a month, on the final weekend.
Why on earth, I have no idea, but the janitor tried to take this very
seriously, so I already started proceedings on a Thursday to obtain
a written permit, signed by the head teacher or the assistant head,

by Saturday. This was no mean feat because the stamped pro forma was only available from the janitor, and he tried to come up with all sorts of obstacles even though he had no right to do this. We also had to have a meeting with the head teacher or one of the assistant heads, which in a school with over a thousand students was fairly complicated, not to mention that there was an ill-meaning assistant head teacher who never signed my form and I didn't dare to forge her signature. In addition, there we many compulsory activities scheduled for Sundays, such as the so-called patriotic work and military training, but I always played truant because I realized early on that the worst punishment was to be locked up in the student hall. There was nothing to fear, as no one was ever kicked out.

One Saturday afternoon, when the janitor had the gates locked to prevent anyone leaving—if I'm not mistaken, we were meant to collect scrap metal—I jumped out of the first-floor window onto a truckload of sand. The boys threw my bag after me, I stuck my middle finger up to the janitor and sprinted off in the direction of the church in Rácfertály to catch my tram. This took place in the spring of 1983, by which point I was already quite resolute, but I don't know what would have happened had the pile of sand not been there or had I miscalculated my jump from such a high window. There was no other way of escaping from the hall during daytime, somebody even painted the name Doftana in large black print on the wall, this was the notorious Romanian prison where communists and Iron Guard members were incarcerated in the thirties, and our building was reminiscent of its inhospitable greyness and gloom. People in neighbouring houses hated the kids that kicked the ball over, as nobody knew who'd be responsible for building a fence high enough, the school or the neighbourhood.

Meanwhile, students carried on stealing from neighbouring gardens, cherries and leeks in the spring, and apples in the autumn, but in case they tried to escape that way, they didn't get very far. As a rule of thumb, neighbours bore a grudge to us and told the janitor if they noticed anything untoward, they were reliable citizens in this sense. It's not a good idea to live too close to schools, prisons, barracks or hospitals, as people are likely to assimilate into their environment. Luckily, it was relatively easy to mislead the old porter as he wasn't mean, but one needed time and at Saturday lunchtime I was always in a rush. If I couldn't take my bag with me to school because Majmuca wouldn't let me, he'd often make me unpack the stuff I prepared for home, I was unable to go, because then it would have become obvious that I was about to escape, and my mother was always on the side of the system, whereas my father refused to take sides. To compensate for my escape, I'd always be on kitchen duty the next Tuesday or Wednesday, this looked like an authorised absence my parents knew nothing about, and by Wednesday I'd already had a new plan for travelling home. To this day, I'm convinced that the weekend begins on a Wednesday.

In hindsight, everything looks easy enough, however, we didn't live in a free world where such escapes would be classed as pranks but in the increasingly dark Ceaușescu-regime where any offence could be interpreted as an act against the system. Police would carry out identity checks at all times, they wanted to see our grade-books, IDs, school tag numbers and if one couldn't explain where one was going and why, the police could do whatever they felt like. Clear explanations were particularly needed in the morning and in the evening, and they either believed these or they didn't. Truanting, smoking, being a little loud or going for a beer could easily turn into police investigations, everybody feared the police in those days and had good reasons to do that, though teenagers tend to see fear as a challenge. As the old saying has it, do the thing you fear most, and the death of fear is certain. So we are standing at the railway station in Arad in our blue uniforms, and behind a briefcase placed on the floor there is half a litre of cherry liqueur, every so often we bend down, take a sip, and put it back. By the time we notice the policeman coming towards us, it's too late to run away or do anything. He comes to a halt, greets us and introduces himself, this was the rule back then too, though very few would observe it, asks for our IDs, checks them and asks about our school and whether we are going home, yes, great, goodbye, turns around and off he goes. For a while, the liqueur in the bottle is still shaking out of fear, but then we quickly quaff it down.

On another occasion, two policemen were rounding up at least ten pupils my age on the railway platform, no idea for what reason as I was waiting for my train, standing by a pillar, but suddenly one of the policemen grabbed my arm and pushed me into the queue, *hai și tu*, he said, come along!, and I didn't even have time to ask where we were going. He was a sturdy, pot-bellied man, so I didn't dare to put up any resistance, but when they were marshalling us through a dimly lit corridor, I quickly stepped into a dark door frame and stayed behind. I saw this trick in a Polish partisan film, and though it worked for me, my legs were shaking as I followed the long and winding road to my train. In those days it was common practice for the police to inspect the satchels and pockets of pupils, to take their cigarettes and penknives away, or to send them for haircuts and shaves, this happened to me too, many times. My worst memory is connected to a morning when several hundred teenagers were queuing for tickets for *The Empire Strikes*

Back, jammed into the narrow alley in front of the Studio Cinema. All of a sudden, a police car appeared at the end of the alley, and somebody announced over loudspeaker that everybody should go back to school at once. The crowd was prepared to disperse, but there were policemen at the other end of the alley too, and they started to hit out at the fleeing kids. At that time, I was attending school, or to be precise, workshop practice, in the afternoons, but was unable to offer any proof of this, I'd usually go to the cinema in the morning, and travel up and down on the tram because we weren't allowed to stay in the dorms during the day. These were the house rules that basically made us loiter on the streets. Truancy has taken seriously worrying proportions by this stage, the police is taking action and at least twenty kids are brought in to the station where they get their ears clipped, and a few days later both the local Romanian and Hungarian press condemn this student attitude and list the names of all caught truanting, half of whom are from our school. Despite this, I continue with my daily morning cinema habit and I find at least two hundred kids there at all times, I often panic that the police might raid the place again, but nothing happens. For the police it was important to demonstrate that they were able to show their might if need be, and that more than enough.

This was the context for my daily struggle for survival as a student in year nine at Arad, not so much in a physical but in an emotional sense. It was very demanding and essentially made me blind to most sights of the city except for my school, the halls of residence, the station and as much of the high street as could be seen from the tram. The latter was only relevant in case I managed to squeeze into it, if not, I walked or ran to the station to catch my train, and on Monday mornings I went straight to school, it was usually dark in the autumn and winter, seeing that classes started at 7.00 a.m. with double maths. I often thought of Damjanich's sword, but haven't made it back to the museum since. We were routinely woken up at six by the porter screaming like a sergeant, the janitor tried to make us do a bit of a morning workout at first, but soon gave up because it was muddy outside and he was unable to manage us, all he did was scream and shout, as he was essentially afraid of the older students. Next, there was breakfast and at quarter to seven we had to line up and march to school which was only a few minutes away. One had to be back by half past two in order to get some lunch, so there was no time for anything, perhaps for going to the market, but I had no money. All I did was look around at the pawnshop where I spotted a Zenit camera, and it would take me ten years until I started taking pictures with one of those. In the afternoons, we had a three-hour-long quiet time at school, where we were marched back in rows of two, then dinner in the evening followed by the usual ruckus.

One of the best things was basketball, and PE in general, I had a huge need to exercise that I was unable to satisfy in such circumstances. We had two training sessions a week and I was a fairly good player, being the tallest in the team, but these sessions often finished late and I missed dinner, so, like most teenagers, I was always hungry. What's more, there was never enough food, let alone for people doing sports. So I stopped growing, whether for this reason or another, and whilst I was the tallest in the first year, soon everybody took over. It's really hard to play against people who are twenty or thirty centimetres taller, even if one is agile and can jump pretty high. I liked playing basketball but wasn't a particularly good player, for me it was a relaxation of sorts from the hell I was experiencing on all other fronts. I never made it on the main team, but I didn't really expect that either, the older ones went regularly to the national championship, and I was very proud when they won. Uncle Ernő taught us everything we needed to know as early as the first few PE lessons and training sessions, so I found out that I can leap-frog, rope climb, throw weights and the discus. All I needed was someone to show me the technique, as these were average tasks for average people, and I managed to overcome the fear planted in me by my mother. Every so often, I managed to throw a left hook, or we passed the ball at a particularly great pace, and this coordinated movement, rhythm and focus gave us such joy that it made us believe that we could one day become excellent basketball players.

I never managed to do a proper headstand or handstand, luckily I wasn't the only one, and in case PE was the first lesson of the day we tried to get there early, even before 7.00 a.m., so we could warm up and have a little practice before the teacher and the other students arrived. We were soaking wet in the ice-cold gym while the others warmed up, so Uncle Ernő sent us out to play football. He tried to make me refrain from throwing myself on the concrete floor, but in vain. When they totally forbade us to play football in the school yard, after a mud-soaked ball accidentally landed in the teachers' room breaking a double window, and a ball kicked the odious assistant head in the back, this time on purpose, we moved on to basketball, and had to agree with Uncle Ernő that this was a truly elegant game. There was a healthy sporting life in those days in Arad, and I would have liked to have a go at rowing or parachuting, but parental consent was needed for these sports and they refused point-blank. You are there to study, my mother insisted, I'm not paying for you to play sports, so I had to accept this and never became a proper sportsman. It was around this time that I lost interest in my grades, I researched, read and learned everything about the subjects that preoccupied me, but was happy with just about scraping through in the ones I hated. Top grades won't buy you anything in the shops, my deskmate Sanyi pointed out, he was a head taller than me and boasted having only read a single book in his life, Robin Hood, not even that till the very end, but he knew plenty of jokes. We were in a mixed Hungarian–Romanian class then, where the twenty-four Hungarian students were joined by eleven Romanians, we studied geography, history, biology, maths, physics, chemistry, biology and of course Hungarian in our mother tongue, the rest in Romanian. It's pointless to even mention standards, with my roughly 60 per cent performance I was among the best students, basically nobody was learning anything, and we wouldn't learn much more when we later passed an exam to be in a purely Hungarian class. Very few people from our school tended to go to university, as most of them had no ambitions in this sense. There were five schools in Arad that offered education in the Hungarian language, and a single theoretical high school in which about half a class was studying maths and physics at full blast, most of whom would secure a place at university.

As a year-nine student, I find workshop practice the most exciting subject after PE. A whimsical teacher shows us the basics of locksmith craft, so we spend our time welding, filing, whetting and repairing bits and pieces. He's the kind of man who can immediately sense if someone is interested, and those who have the affinity can learn to repair bikes, engines, coffee grinders, hair driers and umbrellas, or just hand the teacher the tools and deal with the various minor tasks. It's also possible to join the teacher when he's moonlighting as a car mechanic or is fixing doors, windows, roofs, you name it, anything that brings in a bit of extra cash. Meanwhile, the girls are learning to knit and crochet. Still, there was one girl, Carmen, who was excellent at welding, you have the hands of a surgeon, the teacher told her. Soon, I'm promoted to locksmith's apprentice, whose job is to heat the workshop in the morning, seeing that I'm the first to arrive, and I also stay on longer at lunchtime in case we are tinkering with this or the other. Starting from year ten, we spend several weeks in a factory where they make railway telecommunication devices, and over a three-year period we cover the various departments, starting from the foundry to the carpentry, there are always a few workers who are happy to teach us the tricks of the trade, and I'm interested in everything, so are a few mates. My hunch is that I could have turned into a decent apprentice if this kind of education had been taken seriously, but it wasn't, we had a go at this, that and the other, and then moved on to yet another thing, never getting to the bottom of anything. Romanian industry was crumbling by this point, seriously creaking at its joints, there was covert unemployment at factory level, production was chaotic, partly due to outdated technology but mainly to the tremendous waste, theft and general corruption all round.

In one of the workshops, we were tasked with smuggling in the daily portion of alcohol for the workers, and also provided alibis as they were drinking and playing cards, often enough it was us doing their work, which wasn't all that bad because it's much harder to spend eight hours loitering about and doing nothing than actually working. In these situations, I felt that something was finally happening, but I freaked out whenever I pictured myself spending my entire life operating machinery in such a factory. It wasn't the monotonous work that scared me but human behaviour, the internal relations among the working class, the hate, betrayal and denunciations, as well as the ongoing pettiness that I came across all the time. I still don't know what makes a bad turner better than a good blacksmith, or an illiterate electrician better than a good tinker, but there were strict hierarchies among these professions. I simply couldn't understand why everybody thought I was barking mad when I was more excited by the smithy or the foundry than by moulding plastic. I absolutely hated sweeping the floor under the drawing tables, I much preferred carrying coal in a wheelbarrow or shovelling sand into moulds. I didn't yet know that the working class was actually trying to get away with work, because it didn't make us free or more noble, or at least not in the manner things were being done back then.

I realized that there were hardly any people who liked their job. It wasn't simply a matter of them having had enough of day-to-day routines, but most of them lost interest in their profession altogether, and didn't really understand why they were meant to do certain things. They were also unaware of basic principles, such as what is electricity, what solidifies iron, what is air pressure, tension, distortion, thermal expansion or friction. It's not that I expected ordinary Romanian workers to be interested in natural sciences, but those who had no clue about these phenomena were actually in danger on an industrial site, even if they happened to be there just to look around. Accidents were frequent, as nobody paid attention to health and safety, or to discussions at party committee meetings. Basically, people were only interested in lunch breaks when they could take a piece of glowing iron out of the forge and roast bacon over it, or heat up the soup brought from home, and secretly gulp down some vodka or beer, despite it being strictly forbidden, but life wasn't worth living without this, and lunch even less so. Then they could concentrate on holding out until the end of the shift, in order to go home. I was appalled by this prospect, and thought that it wasn't advisable to blend in with the workers when they poured out of the factory in their thousands, even if some would take us out for a beer, as a sign of regarding us as proper men, after all we were working together. Despite having the opportunity to encounter so many interesting and valuable things, I concluded that all this didn't have much of a point. We keep filing, hammering, handling machinery, then get paid, spend it on food and drink, only to start again with the hammering and filing: what the hell, this can't possibly be all that life has in store!

The influence of my father and grandfather spared me from any illusions about the construction of socialism, and when Soviet president Brezhnev died, I knew that socialism would come to an end. If this doddering old fart can die, then anything is possible, I said to myself while sitting on a bench in the courtyard of my hall. I didn't initially understand what was going on. The janitor was supposed to hold a political meeting, the assistant head was perhaps also in attendance and addressed the meeting about something or other, and then I stopped paying attention. All I could think about was that when Stalin died people were crying, according to Mother, yet I wasn't feeling anything and neither were the others. The weather was quite mild, the meeting would be over soon, we'd have lunch and carry on as before, someone even produced a ball and started playing football. Oddly enough, the janitor didn't tell them off as he would have normally done, somehow, he was also unsure what to do.

The one thing I missed the most during my first year at Arad was the forest. I had never lived in such confinement until then, and during the three unperturbed hours of the afternoon quiet time I couldn't think of much else than the unreachably distant woods of Kisjenő or Barót, seeing that even the banks of the river Maros or the Csála forest in Arad were out of my reach. In hindsight, it's difficult to decide whether I was dreaming of hiking in these forests or just of solitude, because in this new world I didn't have a modicum of personal space or time, not even the wardrobe or the bed was solely mine, not even my clothes, so the notion of private sphere withdrew to the realm of memories or dreams. When I started writing my *memoirs*, the exact same thing happened to me that would always happen every time I started writing: I entered the world I was talking about and forgot everything else, I identified entirely with what I was narrating, dreamt about it at night and imagined it during the day, all this yielding great fluency in writing, until the flow suddenly stopped. Then I had to re-read the text and start thinking about what it was really about.

Back then, I noted down in great detail what happened in the vicinity of every single tree, bush and puddle, but in time I realized that the same thing happened everywhere, rabbits, deer, foxes, pheasants, snakes . . . and that this narrative only meant something to me, conjuring up a world into which I could temporarily immerse myself. All this had a topography and chronology, but then shifted towards generalizations. Likewise, our wanderings had a routine of their own, which found their parallel in my narrative, so if one had already seen a pheasant, the other thousand were no longer interesting, or if the ice had broken under us five times, it was enough to talk about it once, as that was able to sum it all up. I got tired of very detailed narration and gave it up, somewhat disappointed as I had said everything yet there were still some blank pages left in the notebook. To be fair, I wrote in tiny letters, but still. The last few pages had the most abbreviations and words crossed out, as an indication that by then I'd got tired and fed up. I haven't yet shown this text to anyone, but still consider it a serious training practice in the art of writing.

This sense of deprivation led to the habit that, as soon as I got back to Kisjenő on a Saturday afternoon, I quickly had lunch and headed to the open fields or at least to the railway tracks at once, so even if I couldn't get very far in the autumn or winter dusk, I could at least catch a glimpse of the reeds or the dark strip of the Somosi forest. I could barely sit through Sunday lunch, dying to leave for the forest and immerse myself into freedom. This is the first autumn when I stay out in the dark on my own, it's mating season for the fallow deer and I end up watching them for hours in the moonlight, it's mid-October, and on my way home I stumble upon a herd of wild boars. The situation is frightening enough as the forest comes to life around me, the herd rushes past, so I can't really see them properly, only sense them behind me, but then they overtake me and are suddenly snorting and grunting in front of me, it feels as if the entire forest was clattering by, before it all goes back to silence. The scariest thing is the sound of a barn owl on a branch above my head, I freeze for a second, and to this day get more scared of pheasants than of brown bears. The autumn forest is magnificent and when the evening falls, I'm still out and about, so I start running home along the river dam, I realize that I can easily run these five kilometres, which shortens the hour-long walk to twenty minutes, but sadly this doesn't solve the problem. I can see from the embankment that the lights are on and my mother is waiting for me at the gate, she looks desperate, and always makes a scene when I'm not back before dark. Mother is busy cooking, doing the laundry, ironing, packing my bag, while

Father is watching TV and I'm out and about whenever I can. I feel remorse about being so useless, and instead of staying at home and talking to my mother, perhaps helping her with the dishes, the odd job or at least with the packing, I'm wandering about the forest like my demented Uncle Will, only to write interminable letters about my adventures to the American Indians at Barót. The next day, I'm already up at four as I must absolutely have breakfast, the train leaves at five, needless to say my homework is done and everything is just fine, except for the nausea caused by sleeplessness and the early morning tea with bread and drippings. The train is extremely crowded, but my nausea eases off, and I crash into maths class without seeing or hearing anything, I can still feel the scent and silence of the forest around me, but there's no one I could share this with.

The best thing about school is that my form tutor is Géza Kovách, the legendary Uncle Gazsi, excellent local historian, teacher and alcoholic. There are thousands of anecdotes about him, he taught many generations and was a really charismatic man whose wisecracks could amount to books, he had a kind word for anyone and kept count of everybody. Yet I didn't enjoy his lessons because, back then, there wasn't much good to be said about the teaching of history, and my interests and readings went far beyond the school curriculum. By then, I had already developed a habit of reading all the schoolbooks at the beginning of the year, to see what to expect, and in case something set sail to my imagination, I tried to find out more about it. We were keeping an eagle eye out for Uncle Gazsi's wisecracks, such as 'son, you'll get such a slap in the face that you'll turn into a wall painting, and your father will go mad because he won't recognize its artistic style.' These made the entire class burst out in hearty laughter, but he also knew countless jokes and anecdotes about Napoleon, Hitler, Kossuth and the fourteen Arad martyrs, on which topic he lectured annually and even wrote a book. The first time he gave me credit for my comments was in a lesson on politics where we had to commemorate the unification of the three Romanian principalities. He started by serving up some standard fodder that nobody paid attention to, it must have been 1 December or we were learning about the seventeenth century Romanian ruler Michael the Brave, all I remember is that he suddenly asked what the problem was with these three principalities, his shrill voice sounding as if he had just snapped upon hearing some stupid student reaction. Everyone fell silent at once, who knows, he asked looking at us from behind his spectacles. There were only two principalities, I said in a barely audible voice, not even standing up as if I was trying to remain invisible, perhaps it was forbidden to say such a thing although I had heard this from my father. Top marks, Uncle Gazsi replied, and carried on highlighting the importance of the unification and its impact on world history, the class didn't really notice anything, or at least pretended not to, and despite my fears, this didn't get me into trouble.

Uncle Gazsi came to visit us at home over the odd weekend, he used to teach my father too, and while we were having lunch over a few glasses of wine, he'd improvise on the most varied topics, from Trianon to the Katyn massacre, and from Auschwitz to 1956. He also knew, for instance, that at first even the renowned historian Constantin Daicoviciu had doubts about the theory of Daco-Romanian continuity, but then got used to the idea, and ended up being credited as one of its founders. Uncle Gazsi would deliver an entire arsenal of local history facts over such wine-fuelled afternoons, and he took as much pleasure in storytelling as my

grandfather. At times, he'd get so drunk that he couldn't go home
and slept at our place, which was excellent because then there was
another performance at breakfast and lunch the next day. In case
this happened on a Sunday, we travelled together on the early
morning train on Monday, he'd usually take me for a coffee at the
station café and then hail a taxi to school. It was Uncle Gazsi who
told me that the Vida name had already been mentioned in records
from the era of King Sigismund, it was among those few names
that survived the period of Ottoman rule. In the abandoned part
of the cemetery in Ágya, I had indeed found a cluster of Vida
graves, even that of a lieutenant in the 1848 revolution, so it wasn't
actually certain that all of us had always been peasants, there were
names such as K. Vida, S. Vida, F. Vida, Nagy Vida, before this
branch of the family died out. I was occasionally tempted to
become a historian or at least conduct some historical research,
but in those circumstances, this wasn't viable. Historiography was
treated as a strategic sector by the Romanian state, and I didn't feel
enough strength to gnaw through the Daco-Romanian problem,
seeing that even the founder of the theory knew that it was all
bluff.

It was absolutely fascinating to see that Uncle Gazsi wasn't
afraid to talk about such things, he wouldn't shut up even if a
neighbour came round, he'd quickly check whether they could be
trusted and carried on with the show. One winter Godfather
Guzman was also present, whom he quickly reprimanded on the
topic of the Nazis, the Second World War and the Székely leg-
endry. Uncle Gazsi was originally from Udvarhely, so Guzman's
Hitler Youth pedantry simply couldn't face up to his erudition and
broad awareness of facts. My godfather acknowledged this, and
always referred to him thereafter as a man of great learning. The

highpoint of all this was that they carried on singing the umpteenth Horthy-song at the top of their voice, my father walking
up and down in despair, and Mother dismissing it with a wave of
the hand, they are drunk, not much can happen. After they both
lost their voice, they had a go at marching but it didn't work out,
as the pavement was too short. At this point, Guzman's wife
ordered him to stop showing off, after all he had just had a heart
attack, and Uncle Gazsi told us how they swam across the river
Elba, so they could end up American prisoners of war, rather than
Russian. Those in the battalion who were not up for this, never
made it home.

It would seem that Uncle Gazsi was the man who consolidated
my belief that the world in which we lived was corrupt through
and through, seeing that it was founded on such historical and
ideological lies that were not only discussed by inflammatory
Western radio stations but also by my teacher. He was firmly convinced that socialism would soon collapse, but the chaos that
would take its place couldn't deliver much good because nobody
was able to handle or transform the Balkans and Byzantium, only
adopt the mentality that built its politics on the habits of barbar-
ians living at the edge of civilization. When shepherds are allowed
into Baroque palaces together with their flock, one shouldn't talk
about the shepherd being driven by class hate, but about the fact
that he needs stables, sheep-pens and campfires. This is the
Balkans, the joy of unaccountable devastation and the annihilation
of culture with the rationale that it's no longer needed, so let's enjoy
destruction. The Balkans are contagious.

Go to the library and read, Uncle Gazsi told me many times.
He didn't actually have to insist, but this was a welcome endorse-
ment in front of my mother, letting her know that she shouldn't

worry about my progress, I was a quiet and diligent kid, not cut out to be teacher, but more than capable of sitting in libraries or museums as I had the brains for it. Yet my impression was that there was something wrong with my brain, because even though I enjoyed books about Native Americans, Jack London and various travelogues such as the works of Gábor Molnár, Thor Heyerdahl and Marco Polo, I soon got bored of them. I only read a few Rejtő books, I found them funny but not quite the real thing, as for Agatha Christie or Simenon, their texts were so dreary that I'd been unable to touch them ever since. At the age of fifteen, I'm encountering the first literary crisis of my life, I simply don't know where to begin or to continue a book, I'm either bored or don't understand a word. Needless to say, I read all mandatory readings from cover to cover, but none of this means much to me, I'm struggling with classics such as Jókai and Mikszáth, hating them with all my heart. *Be Faithful unto Death*, by Zsigmond Móricz, goodness gracious! I've suddenly stopped finding Petőfi a serious poet, perhaps Vörösmarty can live up to this, and Romanian literature is even more disappointing, if I can even put it this way. I don't recall how long this phase lasts, I'm feeling quite low, even guilty, and am unable to move on or to do something constructive. Even scribbling is getting harder, so I'm left with a sense of lethargy and the daily fights in the evenings, with some technical drawing thrown in for good measure as I'm quite good at it. So I offer to complete the projects of the older students in exchange for being left in peace, but the teacher realizes that this isn't their work and gives them a low mark because they refuse to reveal the actual author. As for me, I get a good hiding for not having paid enough attention to such details, and have to live with the threat that in case they fail at drawing at the end of the term, they'll smash my face. Eventually, they don't, and soon we make it to the end of this interminable school year. After all, everything comes to an end, it's just a matter of holding out.

It is the last week of term and only a few of us are still loitering around the halls of residence. We play football in the afternoon and are basically bored shitless, teaching is over as we are attending workshop practice, my nemesis Lacimarci have already finished because they are transferring to another school, so nobody is fucking with me. In the evenings, Matei Filipescu is looking for boxing partners and soon it will be my turn. He's a slim, dark and lively boy, I haven't had many dealings with him so far, but I find him calm and well-meaning. He tells me that I have a reputation of being a bruiser, so let's give it a go, he puts on his gloves while we bandage my fingers, he won't hit very hard as this is just a game, come on, let's keep on moving and stick to the rules. He doesn't hit hard indeed, and I've learned as a goalkeeper not to worry about the state of my face, but when he shows me a few tricks it actually hurts quite a lot. I'm reasonably good at this, so he decides to teach me, we stop, then repeat, bend down, step back, keep going, elbow, pacing, springing, keep hitting, he insists and encourages me. Suddenly my fist slips through his gloves and my right hook hits him on the forehead, he loses his balance and falls back on the bathroom floor. As if in slow motion, I can still hear his head crash onto the floor, his nose starting to bleed at once. He comes round very slowly, as the rest of us are standing around utterly clueless. Everything is covered in blood, even though he is lying on his back, soon blood gets into his throat, which makes him cough, and when he sits up blood begins to pour out from everywhere. Somebody runs down to the kitchen and Aunt Maruca calls the ambulance, they turn up fairly swiftly, followed by the assistant head and then the janitor. Matei doesn't end up in hospital but it emerges that he had an earlier nose injury that was quite serious, so he won't be able to box for several weeks. My punishment is to clean up all blood in the bathroom. *Măi băieţi, măi*—boys, boys!—the assistant head keeps repeating, shaking his head, after Matei confirms that this wasn't an actual fight and we had no arguments to settle.

My vacation begins with working as a day labourer at the so-called Dohányos, the one-time domain of the earls of Csernovics, which is now a totally run-down state farm. Uncle Fjodor is one of the bosses, he got us involved because at school they required a certificate confirming that we had worked for two weeks during the summer holiday. Our parents held the view that work was a good experience, so just get on with it, especially if it's compulsory. Our job was to build stacks and bales of hay, straw, alfalfa or suchlike, from seven in the morning to seven at night. We realized soon enough that this work exceeded our physical abilities, and got totally exhausted after the first few days. But there was no way out, and after the first week we were puzzled to find that we could actually manage this, our muscles adjusted to the situation. I can recall the very afternoon when I discovered the hitherto unnoticed veins on my lower arms, and learned that this was the source of strength itself. The tractor was slowly pulling the two trailers while we kept loading the bales until we were finished with the regulation load of 96. Alfalfa was heavier, two of us had to lift a single bale, and we were feeling fairly wobbly when we had to handle bales that were pressed while still a little moist. Other times we were stacking hay under the direction of old peasants, we had to build stacks the height of several floors, this was based on serious science, and we also had the chance to hear about the heyday of the farm, the abundance of fish in the river, and how awful this world had turned out in the meantime. We learned not to drink water until lunchtime because otherwise we'd be thirsty all day, not to drink alcohol until evening because otherwise we'd get a stroke in the sun, and to fasten our belts before lifting heavy weights, as also illustrated by the thick belts worn by peasants in Máramaros. It was a joy to listen to these old Romanian men bringing to life the world of my grandfather, though in Romanian, it was the same world yet totally different, one of the men also made it to the Russian front but couldn't remember where or why. I have always found this bizarre, seeing that most old Romanian men just settled for summing this up with *acolo, la ruşi*—there, by the Russians.

This work was a chore far above our abilities, its best part was riding our bikes home in the early evening and stopping for a quick dunk in the river to wash out the dust from our pores. At night, I'd invariably sleep like a log, the duvet staying in the exact spot I placed it, as if the night had only lasted for a moment, before I knew it, the alarm clock rang again and I conscientiously jumped out of bed, as I wouldn't have wanted to stay away for anything in the world, and this carried on year in, year out. By the end of these two weeks, we felt pain in every single nook and cranny, had sore muscles and even got ill for a couple of days, feeling dizzy and restless. The reaction of Albi's grandfather was that every day would look like this in old age. We couldn't care less about this back then, of course, and I figured out that there would be no signs of sore muscles if I started the day with a good swim. The best thing about Kisjenő was that one could swim upstream in the riverbed of the Fehér-Körös, surrounded by willows, this was great training and a test of strength, following which we could just float or play ballgames at a leisurely pace for miles. Once I got caught in a fishing line, with the head of a catfish still attached. We worked out that the rest must have been eaten by otters, their footprints were all over the mudbank but we were unable to spot any despite looking out for them for weeks. For a while thereafter, my nickname was Vidra (the Hungarian for Otter), but I hated it, no nickname had ever stuck with me. It will take thirty years for Albi to mention that he has finally spotted another otter . . .

When I returned to my hall of residence on the first day of year ten, my heart sank. What if Lacimarci hadn't actually transferred to another school, what if they were going to live here again, but as it soon turned out, I'd managed to get rid of them forever. The nightmare was over, and what's more, I was already in my second year at high school. So I ended up with three protégées straightaway, they were from a nearby Hungarian village and knew next to no Romanian. This year there were no girls anymore, and fewer of us overall, a new janitor was appointed, I got my own wardrobe, which I didn't even bother to lock as I knew that those curious to see what's inside would open it anyway. All in all, I didn't find the start of another school year so bad, and I was certain that no matter what, I'd attend the laying of wreaths at the scene of the execution of the Arad martyrs on 6 October. This was strictly forbidden, and as soon as the Hungarian state delegation left, police would immediately carry out identity checks and take several people into custody.

There was one thing I didn't anticipate, namely that those Romanian roommates who didn't even bat an eyelid or just grinned while I was being tormented, would now imagine that their time had finally come. At first, I didn't make much of the fact that one of the boys from the Mócvidék (Ţara Moţilor) region came up to me and told me that this was Romania. After a short argument, it turned out that he was annoyed by the fact that I'd speak to the three boys in Hungarian, his impression was that we'd talk about them in a demeaning or offensive way. I explained to him that I spoke good Romanian but the boys from these remote villages didn't, they'd learn in due course, not to mention that we were having a private conversation, like the ones with him, the latter always in Romanian. Crişan was a tall, sturdy boy who must have thought he was a lot stronger than me, so he suddenly grabbed my shirt, trying to lift me, but he overestimated himself, or my shirt, because when a button snapped, he suddenly let go, upon which I got hold of his hand and pushed him away. He didn't object, understood that I was stronger and didn't touch me again, but from then on, he'd lead the offensive against us. As a rule, their strategy was for several of them to attack us at once, but they weren't organized enough and didn't really want to fight either, they enjoyed being spectators at large-scale kerfuffles though, and in the case of Romanians versus Hungarians they were supporting the Romanian side, actively if need be. Many of them were present at the Matei Filipescu incident and witnessed my earlier outbursts, they clearly didn't want anything from me other than us to stop speaking Hungarian, Crişan summed up. I was prepared to negotiate pretty much anything, except for this.

The four of us sleep in the same corner, and with the addition of a new bunkbed, there are twenty-two of us in the dorm. It's great to sleep in the corner, I tell the boys, let's not provoke the others and not shout out loud in Hungarian, it's best to sit in a corner if we want to talk to each other, keep quiet and ideally make sure that at least two of us are staying in at any one time. For a long time, the Romanians are satisfied with the odd comment,

Crişan always has some ironic observation about the Hungarians, calling them with the derogatory term 'bozgor'. He must understand some Hungarian because he senses my stammer but doesn't know what to make of it, he tries to imitate my strange words but I ignore this as I don't want to pick up the ball and run with it. Next, they come up with all sorts of pranks, they mess up my wardrobe, scribble on my books, put a drawing pin under my bedsheets, and one night even put some macaroni in my boots. Most of the time, I'm chosen to be on the receiving end of their provocations, the other three only very seldom. To be fair, these pranks are pretty average for a student hall, even summer camps are hard to imagine without them, and one can conduct these playfully or brutally, but somehow we always end up being called names. I don't normally display an emotional reaction to this, I know that *bozgor* is derogatory term for Hungarians, it apparently means homeless and it's generally used in that sense. This term wasn't of common occurrence in the Romanian world I experienced till then, and in case it did come up, people went for the kill straightaway. I'm not yet familiar with Sándor Szilágyi N.'s humorous explanation that this word came about as a result of merging *bazmeg* (fuck) and *ungur* (Hungarian), and needless to say, it's not featured in any dictionaries. Once I asked Crişan what the word *bozgor* meant in his opinion, as I didn't understand it, and since he seemed very surprised and didn't know, I turned to the entire dorm, well boys, what does the word *bozgor* actually mean? This went beyond the boundaries of safe expression for me because all of a sudden a muscular and burly bloke showed up, who didn't live in our dorm but often came there. *Te bag în pizda mătii, asta-nseamnă*—go fuck yourself, that's what it means—he said in a menacing voice and the entire dorm broke out in uproarious laughter.

This scene ends right here, as something else comes up and the bloke has to leave, although he'll grab my throat in the canteen later, as if he wanted to strangle me. We stand in that position for a few seconds, I tell him to remove his hands, he lets me go and walks away, he isn't a natural bully which strikes me the most and makes me fearful. The conflict carries on, in the shape of arguments, slaps in the face, flapping, pushing and swearing, but we are striving to leave as few opportunities to this as possible, we make every effort to stick together and even join one another when going to the toilet, as if we were girls. They resort to a new strategy, involving three very skinny small Romanian boys who have just started at our school. They come from a village high up in the mountains and are still children really, don't even have pubic hair and behave in a really childish fashion even though they are fourteen, they are the clowns of the dorm in every sense. These new boys ask me to help them with their maths homework or with French, they are basically illiterate and it's pretty clear that they are after picking a fight, so they find some excuse, they start pushing, tear up one of my notebooks, break my pencil, and then the old ones can intervene to retaliate for the grievances of the young ones. I have no chance against four or five people against me, armed with towels, brooms or pokers, I end up in a corner after the first clash and try to hit back from there, but everybody knows that I'm not given to brawls. The decisive battle is yet to come, they are only waiting for the right moment to finish me off. I decide not to wait for that. I grab the small ones one by one when there's no one present, take them to a dark corner such as the female toilet, and promise them that I'll swat them if they ever pick a quarrel with me. I slap them just in case, I have no intention to spare either them or my palm. After this, they don't dare to pick on me, so the strategy of terror worked, I can let out a sigh of relief, but it's not over yet. One night they try to tie my feet to the bed, but they don't manage because I sleep in a sleeping bag. I'm woken up by a loud scream followed by laughter, as the slip of paper tucked between the toes of a Hungarian boy goes up in flames, they are trying to hold me down, but I free myself and score a header into somebody standing next to me in the dark, and as I jump up everybody flees. By the time I open the zip on my sleeping bag, everybody's gone.

From then on, there's some kind of attack every night, in every imaginable way, involving fire, water, pillows toothpaste, somebody is always on duty, so it's really hard for us to sleep in these conditions. Luckily, two classmates are doing karate and I learn a few simple but efficient moves and kicks from them, which I practice when no one is watching. I train every day, and if I can't find a suitable place anywhere else, I often withdraw to the toilets for this purpose, tiredness, exhaustion and stress makes me determined and aggressive, I'm looking forward to the big fight even though I'm also very scared. I practice in front of an empty cupboard in the bathroom, I'm standing there in such a way to see the reflection of my hand as it just about touches the surface of the chipboard, it doesn't even make a sound but it definitely makes contact. I can manage long sequences by then, and my breathing technique is fairly good, we have seen a few Chuck Norris films, everybody is dreaming of such skills and thinks that this is what makes them brave. Suddenly somebody enters the bathroom behind me, I don't want them to see me so I try to step away, this makes me misjudge the last move and my hand hits the chipboard, leaving behind a fist-shaped hole, the echo of a crack, Crişan's shocked face and a jet of blood spurting from my knuckles.

The news of the hole spreads fast, people come round to check it out, they talk about it, and I happen to know that somebody had hit that surface earlier with a hammer or a metal pipe, but then they pushed the missing piece back into place. Luckily, they didn't glue it back, there is no kung-fu fighter who could smash such an intact surface. This event puts an end to overt provocation, but the conflict isn't over because one night they lift my mattress and I roll off in my sleep, my arms are in the sleeping bag so I can't place them on the floor as I'm falling, so I land on my face. My head lets out a thumping sound, as if the ceiling had fallen. Blood is pouring out of my nose, as in Matei's case, but that was an open combat, half play, half accident, and this a hateful attempt. Everybody pretends to sleep whenever I go to the bathroom. My bedding, my pillow, as well as the dorm and bathroom floor is covered in blood by morning, a huge blood stain showing on the sleeping bag to this day. Strangely enough, this doesn't even hurt much, as if it was just a mild flu, but my nose swells to the size of a potato turned green and purple by the sun. The janitor wants to find the culprit but I couldn't identify anyone as it was night time, so everybody keeps silent, and I don't really want any procedure or investigation. The next day, I remove the rosette from the water tap in the bathroom, hold it up in the dorm to make sure people can see it. Finally, I look at Crișan, and put the knuckle-duster under my pillow. And this marks the end of the first and last ethnic conflict of my life. For months to come, I get a nosebleed from pretty much anything, and still can't decide whether I won that day or simply wasn't the loser. From their point of view, I obviously got what I deserved, and I know that I stood up for myself. Perhaps we recognized that we could carry on like this for all eternity, but there was no point and we lost our impulse anyway. Our relationship stayed frosty, but we had refrained from picking any fights thereafter.

The Hungarian boys have gradually learned Romanian, and the Romanian stopped picking fights. Relatively quieter terms ensued, involving kitchen duty, carrying coal, workshop practice, basketball and a few afternoons when I went strolling around Arad for my own delectation. I wasn't interested in lunch or the janitor, I earned my right to be there and asked everybody to leave me alone. I was writing my novel in which these battles appeared in detail, far from the world of adults who wouldn't have been able to be part of this even if they wanted to. Every so often, when I was really fed up with this confinement, I walked along the banks of the Maros to the railway bridge at Mikelak, from where on a clear day one could see the hills and fortress of Világos. Most of the time I thought that far away, at the bottom of the Hargita mountains I had relatives, while these people here were foreign.

That winter my grandfather died. My parents didn't tell me about this or ask me to come to the funeral, they only told me after I got back home on a Saturday that he died and was buried. Old age, my mother said, he wasn't actually ill, but I know that he drank himself to death, even though my grandmother was wrong when she claimed that there was a blue flame in his throat and mouth, that came from the popular imagination, and was seen as the punishment of drunkards, whereby the flames of hell in their throat eventually burn them. By then, he had been lying in bed for weeks, and suddenly he got up and went to the larder where he found a bottle of medicinal spirit with which Aunt Vilma would wash his back. He drank it all, lied back and died. He was entirely cold by the time Grandmother got home from the village. There was hardly anyone present, and they didn't even bother to tell me about the funeral. My mother explained that it was very cold, the trains and buses were running late, they could barely dig his grave, I was far away, to say nothing of the travel and school, but then she got into all the minute details, as she normally would . . .

I understand that they wanted to spare me, but what they did was to spare me, the only grandson, from the funeral of my grandfather. This sparing was so successful that not a single personal object had survived, they tidied up the house so swiftly as if they wanted to make his very memory vanish. It doesn't come as a surprise that I write my first short story about him, even though it won't be the first to get published, and I'll rewrite it many times until it reaches its final form. It's entitled *Grandfather Had a Horse*, even though he didn't, but he could have easily had one.

I didn't get the chance to say goodbye to him, the man whose gestures lived on in me, his toughness, stubbornness, incomprehension, determination and that endless solitude that he carried with him for eighty years. I often think that I was the only person he loved and trusted. He even told me about the gun, the barrel of which he hid under the eaves, it was a Mannlicher-Schönauer that made it into several of my writings, but then in 1967 it was his Jack-of-all-trades younger brother Alexander who was repairing this illegally owned gun, and when somebody denounced him, he brought the barrel over and asked Grandpa Joszip to hide it under the eaves, among wires and sticks where nobody would look for it. They searched the house of Alexander, who was known for dealing in all sorts of forbidden stuff, but couldn't find anything, however, one of Grandpa's drinking mates spotted the barrel and reported him too. So they searched our house too, but couldn't find anything else apart from Father's theology books which didn't interest anyone. My parents will be afraid of house searches from then on. My grandfather is arrested and interrogated for days, then beaten, he'll throw up blood for ages but keeps saying that he found the barrel in the garden and had no idea what it was. Needless to say, they didn't believe his story because he was a gendarme in the army, how could he not realize that this was a military gun, where are the other parts, but Grandpa kept silent despite all the beatings, he simply refused to grass on his brother. He got away without prison because the owner of the gun must have been in a really important position and took measures, but the man who denounced him would vanish from the pub whenever my grandfather and I showed up. I don't want to swat you in front of the kid, he said to the man years later, but I couldn't make sense of this comment at the time.

I really enjoyed my grandfather ringing the bells in the church at Ágya, and I accompanied him whenever I could. He'd let me climb to the belfry, which wasn't entirely devoid of danger seeing that it involved an old ladder covered in pigeon poo, but he trusted me. As I was climbing up the tower on such an occasion, I spotted the old eighteenth century painted ceiling boards that used to be in the church and were relocated here after restauration. There wasn't the slightest attempt at observing symmetry or order, but for me, this random arrangement got to symbolize the sky itself. I often dream about wandering the reeds with my grandfather, and then the sky above us is just like this, reminiscent of a photo showing a distant galaxy. Most of the time I dream about mandalas, the symbol of perfection as Jung would put it, where else could I have seen such a thing other than on our bell-ringing adventures when I climbed the belfry tower, and stood right next to the cracked bell that carried on resounding until it finally fell silent.

XVII

Transylvania

This particular phase of my literary attempts came to end at the same time as my extended reading crisis, both as a result of a brief encounter. I happened to be rummaging around the antiquarian bookshop in Arad, where they had piles of beautifully bound illustrated books in German, seeing that the Transylvanian Saxons, Schwabians and Germans were emigrating in large numbers, selling off their books and other belongings for peanuts. I was interested in an original edition of Brehm, since I was studying German, but I found it expensive. We don't have this kind of money, I thought in addition to finding the Gothic print a serious cause for concern. It was February, perhaps March, and I was loitering in the streets for ages despite the dreadful cold, aiming to arrive back at the dorm as late as possible. School usually finished at three o'clock, so we had to ask the kitchen staff to save our lunches for us, which by then would have gone entirely cold, and I was debating whether I should bother with this at all, considering that it was probably some more pigwash as everything had started to taste exactly the same for some time. There wasn't much of an interest among the books, I had already leafed through and put back most of the titles I wanted to take a look at, when I came across a very strange little grey book, suddenly popping up from under the shelf or perhaps the torn jacket of another volume.

'—gasping gloomily, on heavy stairs, under the weight of heavy memories, up, up, sometimes with ease and other times in tears, unstoppable. For how many levels?'

It is generally possible to read through a volume of poetry in half an hour, but I was already on my third go when the bookseller told me that it was closing time and I could take the book with me and bring the money in later. It was obvious that I didn't have cash on me, and the book was really cheap anyway. Holding this book in my hand, having come across the poet I had been always looking for, transformed this cold and starved afternoon into the opening of a secret door whereby one suddenly enters, inevitably and with perfect timing, the world of wonders. For weeks on end, I'd keep reading the book day in, day out, and had almost learned it by heart even though I was struggling with poems and didn't remember the exact words. To my great dismay, I could understand this, it was readable, relatable and crystal clear, it was about me, talking to me and for me. All of a sudden, I was sitting face to face with Domokos Szilágyi and the texts and poems in front of me had revealed themselves, making me able to see, hear and feel them. This is how literature offered me a chance for a second start, I found what I had to read: everything that was poetry. I'd quite like to know more about what happened to me on that afternoon in the bookshop, seeing that my worldview, readings and studies to date didn't exactly pave the way for an immersion into contemporary Hungarian poetry. Perhaps the only way for such things to happen is to pick up a book and refuse to leave the bookshop until the volume is read from cover to cover or one is sent home with it. I was completely alone with this experience, I didn't know anybody interested in such matters, there was no information or help from the Hungarian teacher who merely churned lessons out. We found her classes boring and often laughed at her, even though I got top marks easily since I knew my stuff, was good at literature and had acquired the habit of reading. From then on, I'd carry this little book of poems with me for weeks on end, and consult it whenever I got stuck with the text, my feet barely touching the ground while walking.

This phase lasted until I won the county-level competition in Hungarian literature, and made it to the national competition that took place in Suceava under the generic title *Eminesciana*, together with the Romanian and German contests. The Hungarian term was literary Olympics, or the *Olympiad*. My success caused a major stir, my Hungarian teacher being particularly taken by surprise and even said that she disliked my paper, but I dismissed that with a wave of the hand. After all, I made it to a national competition just like that, even though national only meant seventeen counties, the number of counties offering Hungarian-language education at secondary-school level at the time. In a manner of speaking, I did catch up with the basketball team and was invited to accept my award from the head teacher at the end of the year. Our school was considered the weakest in Arad, and I wasn't even among the top students. Extracts from my paper were published in the local daily, *Vörös zászló*, and I was given three days off to prepare for the competition. Of course, I didn't do any of that, opting instead for all day hikes in the woods as it was a windy spring and hence easy to get up close to the fallow deer. In the end, my paper turned out to be the weakest, it was on the topic of *Seeds under Snow* and I didn't know that Ady had written such a poem, my books failed to mention that.

The week before the competition, I tried my luck with my very first article, knocking at the door of the *Vörös zászló*'s editorial office. It was about an amateur production at Kisjenő—living proof that other people had also got fed up with nothing ever taking place in this town. There were plenty of factual errors in the text, yet they published the article with only a few minor grammatical corrections. This made me feel like a major star and I immediately joined the society of *Young Reporters*, where young Turks like me were sharpening their claws under the guidance of Árpád Hudy. He was the one to lend me the works of Antal Szerb, and make me aware of names such as Pilinszky, Nietzsche, Plato, Max Weber . . . From then on, I'd spend my Wednesday afternoons at the editorial office of the *Vörös zászló*, talking about any random topic that happened to cross our minds and unpicking each other's writings, genuinely astonished at how short afternoons could be. I was able to see for myself how a daily is being put together, we visited the printers and were more or less up to speed with censorship, though not self-censorship just yet. It was disappointing that we weren't allowed to write about stuff we would have liked to address, and the topics available were of no real interest to us. I spent months on a report on our workshop practice but it failed to come together, so eventually, I gave up. Even though I wasn't yet able to understand the situation of the Hungarian press in Romania, I was sensing the uncertainty regarding the regime and was pretty clear about the fact that I had accumulated an ever-increasing vocabulary that under no circumstances could get into print. Together with my friend Kohn, we made a list of forbidden words, and I even tried to come up with a piece of writing using them, but to no avail. I realized with horror that any word could be forbidden and banned, consequently, the Hungarian language itself could be potentially banned in Romania. This was the tendency in those days, despite the fact that all I could see or wanted to see was that the editor of a provincial daily was almost as free a person as a geologist wandering the hills and mountains.

'[A]nd oh how loose gets the tether, when bright-lit skies bring good weather!' It was at Suceava that I first got confronted with Hungarian high-school students from Transylvania. It was in this town in Bukovina that I realized that there was a continent called Transylvania, with its own culture, literature and world of its own about which I knew next to nothing. This place wasn't just populated with woods, religious fanatics, evil policemen and troubled poor but also with writers and poets, in short with civilised folk. This was never mentioned on Hungarian Television and even on Radio Free Europe only sporadically, it wasn't a topic debated in *Nők Lapja* or *Interpress Magazin*, seeing that I was an ardent reader of the latter. Few people in Arad had any idea of Transylvania whatsoever, and the only person I knew to hail from there was Uncle Gazsi. Despite my annual summer visits at Barót, I was only familiar with a very enclosed world, a tiny segment of the whole that I would have yet to discover. Together with a few students of my ilk, we spent the days marvelling at the Moldavian monasteries, streets and pubs, discovering not only a new universe but conversation as such. I had suddenly found and recognized the world I wanted to belong to, and which I had needed for so long. Years later, I'd meet some of these students at the entrance exam and at university, but the virtual community I wanted to belong to had existed already, I'd just spotted it but it was still disappointingly far away. I'm standing by the tomb of Moldavian ruler Stephen the Great at Putna Monastery, and can only think of the fact that I know nothing about Transylvania, not even where to begin learning about it. This whole thing is like the monument at Alkenyér station, I can see it but I'm not aware what exactly I'm looking at.

I can't recall exact details, but I'm guessing that we were travelling to Barót when we made a stopover at Kolozsvár with my mother, we had a few hours to kill because of some timetable change, we had no other business there and this extra time clearly made our journey a lot longer. I had no expectations from Kolozsvár, not even presuppositions, I knew that King Matthias was born there, saw some postcards in my mother's collection. We were travelling with our usual yellow suitcase, by this point carried by me, the train, the rush, the landscape that I'd keep marvelling at for years, I wouldn't get bored of it despite knowing every single tree and cliff in the Vadu Crişului Gorge at Rév. We leave our suitcase and travel bag at the left-luggage office, since we have a good few hours, perhaps four, and neither of us has been here before. My mother has a natural curiosity too, so we head towards Horea street (today named after King Ferdinand) and come to a halt in front of a grey building named Department of Philology. This is rather uncanny, seeing that one of my mates with whom we played Native American games had expressed an interest in studying Hungarian, whilst I'm not yet ready to even dream about coming here. I find myself puzzled that there is such a building in the first place, that this is for real, the university is none other than an immense, gloomy grey building and not an imaginary place where ideas and poems can wander freely. We hang around for a little while in this fascinating town, but village people that we are, we tire of all this sightseeing rather quickly and flee from the noise and crowds into the various churches on the way. With my mother, it's basically compulsory to enter every single church and I don't even object, in fact, I have continued with this practice wherever I go. Even though I had visited many churches in Arad and Szeben, the Black Church in Brassó included, I haven't seen any in

Transylvania to be a match for St Michael's Church. To this day, I rarely go past it without sitting down for a few minutes, this is the centre of the universe for me, and yet I'm not even Catholic, not to mention that I share my father's opinion on religion. It certainly can't be the way it is said or described, but the unutterable does manifest itself every now and then, and sacred spaces are a case in point, God is omnipresent but we can sense this presence much more in certain locations. Having said that, this isn't even about God, it is us who are weak and in need of the heady air of his house alongside a series of additional circumstances. For me, Transylvania is above all an awesome religious experience, beyond the speakable and the describable, slipping away from me no matter how hard I try to cast my net to put it into words. I'm a believer without a congregation, as Mircea Eliade contended and I'd find out much later. On this occasion, I didn't meet King Matthias, he was there of course and we might have even looked at one another, I nodded at him and imagined him getting off his pedestal on a quiet night, seeing that nights were still pretty quiet in Cluj those days. I have no idea whether we made it to the botanical gardens, or we went there some other time, it makes no difference, the point is that I was touched by the spirit of the place and this was for real, or in case it wasn't, then there's definitely no such thing as the real.

When I was in year ten, I explained to my parents that if they wanted me to go to university, I couldn't stay in a dorm anymore because it was impossible to study there, to say nothing of the fact that I had enough of that lifestyle anyway. My father doesn't object though he's humming and hawing, questioning how come I don't like it when he was fine with it, but my mother understands my point. So we find a suitable accommodation *in-town*. It's in the home of a family like ours, Tibiszeg is a boy my age, also an only child and also with a rakish uncle, it feels as if I were a member of the family already. I have no idea where do such daredevil uncles suddenly crop up from, who could have never been our fathers and we'd never end up like them either, and in case we tried, this would certainly lead to family tragedies or at least major scandals. My mother can get Father to do whatever she wants, and us too. This strategy works perfectly whenever she knows exactly what she wants, but when she doesn't, the whole system, and even the world, seems to collapse. As my mother puts it, the problem is that it's not Ceaușescu who's in charge, but his wife. Like most dominant women, my mother hates women's rule, she hates women in leadership positions because she doesn't use the word 'woman' and she wouldn't take on any leading roles. She either has a manager whom she can boss around, or time's up for the next gallbladder attack.

Zoliszeg is a renitent uncle who teaches us to play table tennis. He puts his coffee mug on the table, even his burning cigarette or his beer glass, and our task is to hit them or at least scrape them, which is a very hard job. Up to this point, I'd thought I was okay at playing table tennis, but it soon turned out that it was all wrong, I wasn't even holding the racket the right way and my footwork was also bad. One can learn anything from Zoliszeg, he's flippant, arrogant and malicious, but also patient like a proper coach and he's prepared to play with us night after night, letting us practice, demonstrating, exhorting, you idiots, once again, one more time. Neither he, nor I understand how come I'm able to return serves I shouldn't be able to, there are skills I simply can't yet have as a beginner, but then I ruin some really easy serves, you're an idiot, Zoliszeg says, and that's that. It takes me a very long time to get used to this annoying fluctuation which makes me feel like a genius one moment and a clumsy idiot the next, it's really hard work to come to terms with my own fickleness. We play proper matches and the winner can carry on playing, so we are often up half the night at the light of a 500-watt bulb, sweating and shivering, fighting incredible battles, we'd even stay up till dawn but the landlady eventually commands us to call it a day. There is something in these manly power games that urges me to want to win, but of course I fail, no matter how hard I try. If I give up or lose interest, on the other hand, I find it much easier, and there are moments when even Zoliszeg can't catch up with my ten-point lead he negligently granted earlier.

In hindsight, all I did that year was sports and reading, I felt safe and got along with people, attended maths lessons because I wanted to be a geologist but the teacher got rid of me when he realized that I had no real interest in his subject. As it happens, I was pleased with this because the afternoon conversations at the editorial office of the *Vörös zászló* slowly made me realize that I'd end up working in some branch of the humanities anyway. I don't really know what could have made anybody think that I should become an engineer or an accountant. My mother kept pointing out the advantages of a warm, or even unheated, office, over hammering in an inspection pit with mud sliding down my neck and oil dripping on my head, not to mention the shivering cold when crawling under cars or tractors. In her experience, people either worked with bits of paper or with metal, back then agriculture was a scene of total abandonment, so it wasn't even to be thought of. At this point, geology was gradually disappearing from my horizon, I could hardly get past the romantic phase, but if managed, I could see the filth of petrol wells and the endless night of coal mines. Another job I'd have loved to do was forestry, but one needed maths for that too, to say nothing of the fact that I had seen the foresters in Kisjenő and Barót, who the fuck wanted to hunt or get involved with wildlife preservation alongside Ceaușescu and his dogbodies?

I often wondered what would become of me, and channelling Domokos Szilágyi's iconic protagonist, I pictured myself as a sort of no-name, but I would have never dared to dream about becoming the actual No-name himself. A great deal of time had passed in this relative comfort and well-being, seeking refuge in poetry, but despite reading protestant dogma and books on predestination, such as the one by Balázs Sándor, I was only interested in football, athletics and table tennis. In a more exciting dimension, I was also involved in typical teenage conversations with my friend Kohn, walking along the banks of the Maros, reflecting on the state of the world and asking rhetorical questions. Wondering whether anarchy was better than police states, he argued that it wasn't because in a police state one could at least be certain about whom to shoot. What would happen when socialism collapsed, as that was to be the next stage, it looked pretty close already and, indeed, wasn't far off in the future. The best, however, was this unlimited flow of texts that surrounded me, I realized that it was much easier for me to talk if people helped me rather than if they aimed to silence, correct or judge me, and if they allowed me to say what I wanted, adding their own comments. Hard as it was to talk, it felt great, but writing was even harder.

We also played a lot of tennis that autumn, but my wrists had soon given up, swelling from all the effort and my bad technique, so I'd just stick with football, table tennis and weekend hikes in the woods. I'd often go as far as the Székudvar woods, right next to the Hungarian border, from there, at night, I could see the lights of Gyula while watching the deer fight, all this felt like a film set, and since there would be nobody in the vicinity of the border, game would move about freely during the daytime too. One day, a rude forester threatened that he'd shoot me if I came his way again, but displaying the arrogance of Uncle Will, I told him there you go, do it now, you wouldn't have to see me again. The sight of my binoculars led him to believe that I was the son of some big cheese, even though my point was that I could easily avoid him in the future if that was needed. Basically, this was a very unpleasant encounter, I didn't think he would have shot me but I did realize that it wouldn't have been easy to explain under duress what exactly I was doing, at night and with binoculars around my neck, only miles from the Hungarian border. The forester failed to understand why I wanted to watch deer battling each other from a close up, what was in it for me, so I explained in great detail what was going on, why they were rutting, which did impress him and his anger subsided. You know far too much, he said, and let me go. I felt as if I wanted to take on the entire the world, wanting to conquer fear itself, which was the easiest to do in the woods. When feeling well, I wasn't afraid of anybody or anything, but that wasn't always the case. Essentially, I was a lonely teenager spending too much time on his own.

Nothing of particular note takes place around this time, except for *The Tragedy of Man*, a seminal Hungarian play by Imre Madách that I keep reading over and over again, and which makes me conclude that human existence is pointless. People keep lying about this, so something must be seriously wrong here, but I don't know what. I have to travel to Temesvár to find out. There's another *Olympiad*, yet again the seventeen counties, I'm one among the familiar faces, I'll be one of those whom people will remember and who decides to study Hungarian literature at university, even if things will turn out differently. It's impossible to sum up the hustle and bustle of teenagers if they are allowed to spend time together without much supervision. By this point, we can definitely sense the oppression, we are often stopped on the street by plain clothes 'teachers' who want to know which school we are from and who our chaperons are. We don't know. So they make a note of our names and ask what we were singing. It's not easy to explain in Romanian that it was a song by Hungarian rock band LGT called 'This Space is Ours'. The whole thing is like a dream, I go to the theatre for the second time in my life to see *Flowers for Algernon*, I see a live ballet performance featuring Jean-Michel Jarre's *Oxygen*, alongside being exposed to a myriad of other impulses that let hell break loose in me. All these people understand what I'm on about despite my stammer, it's obvious that Romania wants to oppress and annihilate everything that is a matter of life and death to us, it's the darkest of dictatorships and life is unbearably hard, despite the odd experience of freedom such as someone reciting Ginsberg's *Howl*. It's decided, there and then, that I want to be a student of Hungarian literature, no alternative is imaginable, I want to be like the Transylvanians, I want to be one of them and with them. After all, haven't I been preparing for this all my life, from the beginning of time?! At this competition, my paper is no longer the weakest, but only within an inch.

I obtained what was most important and I needed the most, the certainty that what I'd want and what I'd like actually exists, it is real and not a figment of my imagination. There are other people out there who, like me, keep mulling over poems and ideas, and who can continue my sentences or correct my potential inaccuracies, which is far from rare. They know plenty of things I haven't even heard about, so I must get to speed with all of that, and of course there are things they haven't, either, and the same goes for these. For days on end, I keep staring at a girl from Marosvásárhely. I'm suddenly less interested in the world and the vortex that surrounds me, I keep seeing her eyes and her blue jumper everywhere, and keep hearing her voice whenever there's some singing or guitar playing. We must have had many conversations on topics ranging from the mundane to major concerns in the world, I can barely recall any of this except for the emotional overflow that, at the time, prevented me from coming up with further thoughts or sentences. There's of course the sadness that I'll have to return to Arad and life will carry on pretty much as before. I'm still rather shy and reserved, I think I'm small, stupid and clumsy, I'm not at ease in company where I'd have the opportunity to meet people, despite dying to have a say and to be noticed, but then the days and nights come to an end and nothing happens. Back then, I blame all this on my stammer, and it will take a long time until I realize that, in fact, the stammer is rooted in the same emotional state as my anxiety and inhibition. By the time I formulate a chat-up line, someone else has already chatted the girl up or the opportunity has gone by. I know that nothing would happen, nobody would laugh at me or mock me, this isn't that kind of crowd, and still. I'm concentrating so hard that I can barely hear anything, I'm in a trance of sorts and there's a party in the study room of our dorm.

As soon as I get home, I write a long love letter to her, this is the first and last attempt of mine in this genre, I'm about to explode as a fake yet fairly rhythmic text pours out of me, what an incredible task to associate sentences to such emotional outbursts! I know very little about the fact that literature is an emotional journey, and that the interaction between thought and emotion is a manifestation of the soul. It's very unlikely for us to meet again, I didn't even expect her to reply to me as I was an insignificant bloke and knew that such beautiful women wouldn't have time for me. Poets and unrequited love belong together, and although I know that I won't be a poet, I'm in love, despite not wanting to be or not in this way, this is precisely the feeling that poets have been going on about for so long and, to be fair, it's a rather heroic pose. As it happens, I receive a reply fairly soon, saying that she wouldn't have expected to generate such deep feelings in me. She doesn't try to get rid of me or laugh at me, but I don't know how to continue this or how to court her, so I write about random stuff that crosses my mind. We'll end up corresponding for years, in a sort of senti-mental friendship that, according to some, is impossible between men and women and, according to others, is fine if that's all that can be mustered. Back then, I was propelled by my feelings because I'd met the most amazing woman, and to this day I think that she emerged from my unconscious, like an archetype, or she was my anima, despite not having yet read Jung at that stage. All I know is that there's an insurmountable craving in me, I must write to her or call her, and then of course will only say silly things, we'll meet in a year or so at the entrance exam or perhaps earlier at a preparatory session, she'll get a place and I have to join the army. This is the point when we really conduct a soul-searching corre-spondence, as I get sent various tasks I have to carry out because otherwise I forget everything at an alarming rate. I don't know how to handle this outpouring of love at the time, so I lock it up some-where, hoping that it would peter out on its own or at least fade away, but I can't help shaking whenever I see her, and by now I know that remains of this very first encounter will stay with me forever. Meanwhile, a quarter of a century has lapsed, more than enough time for people to change or for time to cozen us out of ourselves, but if everything changes then there must be something that stays unchanged too. I haven't ended up a writer solely because of her, but without her, I wouldn't have become one, and without her, I wouldn't have even known how to get started. With the very beginning, seeing that I knew nothing.

At this point, Romanian secondary school education is characterised by utter corruption, the system is trying to dismantle everything that has survived from earlier traditions. Almost everybody is studying at an industrial school, the notion we call humanities is redundant and it can only play an ideological or propaganda role. There is an unimaginable leap of quality between the baccalaureate and the entrance exam, everybody is tutored in the exam subjects, even if they attend schools with high standards where they still take teaching seriously. One has to start preparations for the exam in good time, it involves considerable extra work and financial sacrifice. Besides, after several years of study it's very difficult to switch to something else if need be. Studying is not only an activity of the mind but a family investment, the child is the racehorse that must produce the required result. There is neither a shortage of teachers famous far and wide for their skills in helping students to prepare for the exams, nor of charlatans. After a few attempts, some of the candidates do get a place, but I know many people who have never managed, boys end up drafted into the army and girls get married off, but despite the significant drop-out rate, the really stubborn ones, the *veterans*, keep going year after year. The Hungarian Department only has six or seven places per year and there are at least ten times as many candidates, in some other humanities fields there are even fewer places. Expectations and Transylvanian competitiveness require candidates to be already familiar with, and in fact know by heart, most of the material that would be studied at university. The baseline is the history of Hungarian literature published by the Academy, known as *Spinach*, and it is advisable to be familiar with as many other sources as possible. Candidates practice writing papers for years, learn them by heart so they wouldn't have to think at the exam, only write, write and write. This whole business is essentially the competition of Hungarian teachers with one another, conducted by way of their students. The situation is absurd, because they are asking candidates to already know what they'd be learning at university, and this isn't even the worst situation, because there are specialisms where they literally have to learn the entire textbook by heart, or one of Ceaușescu's speeches, and the teachers marking the papers only check punctuation and word order.

Knowing that I didn't have a chance in hell didn't make me lose my calm, so in May 1985 I started learning French, but realized soon enough that I wouldn't get anywhere if I was only memorizing random words on my own. I threw myself into the Arad public library, fortunately they had all six volumes of the *Spinach*, and quickly read through the first three. As I was doddering home on those quiet afternoons, I couldn't resist the thought that Antal Szerb should have written this work, as then it would have ended up so much better and definitely more interesting. I was of this opinion despite hearing the Hungarian teachers debate at the Temesvár *Olympiad* whether Szerb's idea of literature was still up-to-date or entirely dated. Whenever I think back to this debate, I get the shivers, because, mentioning no names, the woman so vehemently opposing Szerb, and hence arguing against what she called *conservative reactionary perspectives on literature*, went on to have a prominent career after the regime change. It's impossible for me to evoke the full extent of the information explosion brought about by this spring, there was a huge chaos in my head, mainly because I was still equally interested in everything and hadn't yet understood that this was far too much, and also because I was unable to organize stuff, so everything interlinked and tangled up with everything else.

My restlessness came from the fact that the most important ideas of modernity contradicted the religiosity I was mostly comfortable with, take or add the odd conflict. The modernity I encountered at the age of seventeen was rooted in the axiom that there was no God, there was no transcendental reality, and since this was posited by the entire modern world, something would go wrong, or had already gone wrong, with me. I simply couldn't understand how the entirety of religious culture could rest on an error or a fraud, even if we were on the best possible path to discover the truth. What would become of us if God really was against human progress and was an opponent of freedom? In hindsight, I had spent months seeking an answer to the question whether there was a God, perhaps it wasn't even an answer I was after but the certainty that there was indeed a God, I was after a guiding sign, but this wouldn't appear and I was getting impatient. Needless to say, my preferred option would have been to find this confirmation in the work of a favourite author. So I was in a very strange state of mind, reading all afternoon and absorbing everything that came my way. Basically, I was like a mushroom sprouting after the summer rain, but behind all this there was also a sense of doubt, I was unsure whether all this made any sense, after all existence or human life didn't make any sense either, and mushrooms did vanish without a trace only after a few days. My interpretation of Madách, same as Ady, ultimately meant that there was no answer to my question: life exists because it wants to be alive, give me a break! Attila József or Domokos Szilágyi offered even more disappointing answers: you know there's no forgiveness, or crash landing. It was in the midst such struggles that my theory on deferral came into being, in short this meant that even though human existence was pointless, and therefore we should put an end to it, we nevertheless would introduce a deferral in case something came to light, and then another one, as we did before. It wasn't down to mankind to take a final decision in this matter. Then to whom? It would appear that I hadn't yet come across this notion of deferral anywhere, but it could have of course been a reminiscence of some sort, a fragment of a conversation. So many people had thought about this prior to me but, nevertheless, it feels good to reinvent the wheel every now and then.

There was hardly anyone with whom I could have had long conversations on these philosophical concerns, as if I had sensed that these awkward metaphysical problems, propped up by the odd citation from poetry, were mainly about my loneliness, doubts, anxieties and uncertainties. Since solving actual matters took a very slow pace, brooding on philosophical matters such as the pointlessness of life and existence was a perfect alibi. We don't have time for such stuff, my mother tends to say whenever I try to articulate an idea in order to clarify my reasons for wanting to study Hungarian and French, hoping to make her understand the metaphysical problems that I'd end up researching at university. She is absolutely convinced that nothing will become of my plans, even though one of my cousins with whom I played Native American games will get to study Hungarian, but he's a hardworking person and a regular at church. He has faith, my mother adds, because by then I have started to exhibit serious doubts regarding the religious behaviour expected in the family. Following our rare attendances at church, my father and I tend to unpick the sermon to bits, which my mother finds indecent, even blasphemous. Our reverend has a habit of examining the theory of predestination, despite the failure of more accomplished philosophers to get to grips with this topic, and often arrives at the paradox between divine omnipotence and goodness. But where does evil come from, I tend to ask, is it a creation or a fellow traveller. My mother gets this, knowing that the pastor is about to divorce and has a drinking problem, but I'm preoccupied with predestination, free will and determinism together with the theory or the denial of the trinity. All this is dismissed by my father with a wave of the hand, Karl Barth has produced extensive dogmatics on this topic yet nobody reads it anymore.

Early summer that year, I went with my classmates to the Csála forest to pick some green twigs. The aim was to decorate the classroom of the graduating Hungarian class, but all this wasn't so simple because there happened to be a restaurant and beer garden in the forest, where we managed to spend most of the afternoon, nursing beers. Meanwhile, the girls gathered the raw materials and by the time we returned, everything had been prepared. On our way to the pub, I entered into an argument with someone, they insisted that I sat on the luggage rack of their bike, seeing that we were going rather far, but I insisted that I could easily jog there and back if need be. We placed a quick bet, and I wouldn't be able to recall how many beers I would have owed in case I was unable to run without taking a break, but in any case, I was blissfully unaware of the fifteen-kilometre distance. It seemed to me that the beers made the others forget about our bet, but it stayed with me like a bad conscience. I realized that I had overshot the target and started to worry about running such a long course. The deadline looming, one afternoon I decided be what may, and began training. There was a paved road up to the airport and then to the forest, and I was as surprised to find how easy it was to get to Hármas island. There, I waded into the muddy Maros river, and after a short rest, started to head home. Parachutes were soaring above the airport, so I slowed down to watch the mushroom-like umbrellas and see a sturdy An-2 touchdown. Back then, there was very little traffic at the edge of town, there was a quiet, almost village-like calm, cows staring back at me from beyond the ditches and, despite the setbacks, the whole endeavour seemed pretty quick. I'd earn my crate of beer, after all, I only stopped to take a good look around and not to rest.

I had never had such a strong muscle strain in my life than over the next two or three days, and it showed no signs of wanting to ease off. I had no choice but take a hair of the dog that bit me, my landlord's son came with me and, although my leg was hurting, it soon stopped. From then on, we went running almost on a daily basis, there were some really difficult moments and the shoes available those days in Romanian shops put a massive strain on our feet, they even fell apart, but we were impossible to wear out. Long-distance runners are familiar with the sensation of stepping out of the body when one can't feel anything any longer, it's really easy to move and to live, and one's feet no longer touch the ground. Pure ecstasy. Back then, we hadn't yet come across physiological explanations for this, but could see that it was like a drug, kicking in around the eight-kilometre mark. We'd even throw in incredible flourishes, such as adding in extra distance because at times it was easier to carry on running than to stop, despite the suffering. We wouldn't bother with timing ourselves for ages, but then it emerged that we were ten minutes off the women's world record at ten kilometres, so it wouldn't be impossible to catch up if we trained regularly. Can't believe you could beat the women's word record, Zoliszeg teased us maliciously, so we stopped timing ourselves, just kept running in order to feel good and not to get tired. I had never run longer than twenty-five kilometres, though I contemplated running a marathon at one point. I knew one had to prepare for that, but there was always something else to do, and when I tried, I realized that my lifestyle and self-discipline would no longer accommodate the necessary level of training and gradualness. The next autumn my result on the thousand-metre course was nearly a minute better than the year before, our teacher couldn't quite believe it, so I had another go and then another, each time with a better result, I couldn't stop bragging. To this day, whenever I get overwhelmed with problems or sadness, I know I have to run, hike or cycle, it's as if I wanted to slough my skin, once I'd almost managed even though I didn't set out to do so. God is present in the panting and beyond, there's no need to run an entire marathon for that. At that stage, however, I hadn't yet contemplated that he might also be present in language.

Needless to say, life is hard. The next autumn we find a French teacher through some newspaper ads, she doesn't really want to prepare students for exams, but we end up making friends. She can see that I mean it, so we keep pushing on at a heightened pace with all that's required, stuff that I should have learned already, but French and German were taught only as seriously as all the other subjects, and I didn't take them any more seriously either. I must come to terms then with the fact that I'm a slow learner, I tend to read everything once, and the stuff I'm interested in stays with me and finds its place, I only have to read twice the things I don't understand, but how could I learn stuff I don't understand? Mrs Vulpescu, whom I call doamna Vulpescu, is entirely immune to such reasoning, not to mention that I have to translate all my complicated constructions into French, no good to say that I didn't actually mean it that way. Write it the way you think it, she tells me in a kind yet malicious voice. Anybody who has learned a foreign language at an accelerated pace knows that there are moments of amazing progress and moments of trudging along, and it can feel as if one didn't even know the stuff they were able to use correctly the previous time. One has to learn to study and muster the discipline required for studying, in fact, everything has to be started from scratch. Despite this, my French will never be solid enough and my education will remain quite patchy, no matter how often I take a pledge to systematically read this, that or the other. The fact of the matter is that I have many unfulfilled hopes, just like my unsuccessful attempt at training for a marathon.

I'm already aware by this point that I won't be successful at my first university entrance exam. I should have started serious study two years earlier, but I wasn't yet mature enough for this then. So what, doamna Vulpescu observes, who gets to like me fairly quickly and accepts me in her strangely exotic world only known to me from my readings. Her grandfather came to Romania from America, he was working for a local branch of some trade organization after the First World War. He married an Armenian woman from Bucharest and had a large family, they had relatives in at least five or six Western countries in addition to New York and Jerusalem. Her grandfather initially spoke English, the grandmother French, the extended family mainly Romanian, despite the notion of multiculturalism or Europeanism not being in use back then, this was something very similar, American,

Armenian, Jewish, Romanian, born in Temesvár, married to a half-Hungarian man . . . This is the first time I meet Romanians who haven't been elevated from their village environment by socialism, and who do not communicate with me in terms of overt or concealed anti-Hungarianness. In those days, many people aim to represent the Romanian state, the nation or the homeland in the face of foreigners like myself. My teacher introduces me to everybody who turns up at her place, there's incredible coming and going, people are relaxed and considerate, I don't always understand what they are talking about but I pay attention, and everybody addresses me as Monsieur Gabor.

I don't stammer in French but have difficulty speaking. We mainly speak Romanian, my French is less good than her Hungarian, so whenever I fail to understand or overlook something or I'm not thorough enough, she mocks me in Hungarian, her accent is rubbish but she tries to be grammatically correct, all this is very funny and we laugh a lot. Your language is just as difficult as Armenian. She opens up entire worlds to me, makes coffee before lessons, always a different kind, when we get to Proust she bakes some proper Madeleines, I try roast chestnuts for the first time and get in the habit of drinking tea, green, black, Indian, Ceylon, Chinese, Russian, each from a different cup and following a different ritual, accompanied by mandatory cultural history. Her flat is like a small museum, featuring mainly the decorative or carved bits of old bourgeois furniture, they dismantled them when moving house or being evicted, and nobody was able to reassemble them, to say nothing of the fact that there isn't enough space as homes have got smaller and smaller. Wardrobe frames, glass doors and carvings are built into other surfaces where possible, or simply lean against the wall or the shelf, like a strange sculpture. Ebony, mahogany, yew, ash, I have to touch them all, seeing that wood has a unique feel, eradiation and soul. She shows me some jewellery, crystal glasses, a broken Chinese vase together with the missing shards in a paper bag, everything has a story, everything's a fragment, a detail, ten different silver spoons are remains of twelve separate sets that have been scattered around the world. Books everywhere, tiny statues, paintings, a genuine gramophone, cigarette ash, dust, painterly disorder, decadence, postcards from all over the globe, a stamp collection, a pipe set, Cuban cigars piled up in a flat that looks like an antique shop. When we get really tired of French grammar, she plays Chopin for me, like the women in my short stories. The architect imagined trapeze-shaped rooms in this block of flats, so no furniture can be fitted in except for the piano. It was brought in through the window by a crane, they even had to break through walls, as a result of which the neighbours denounced them for breach of peace. They are all peasants, she says with a grimace, and I don't quite realize then that in her, I have met the first urban Romanian. She's deeply outraged by the falsification of history and culture that's taking place at the time, she considers the Romanian myth of Miorița a fake, I don't yet get this, but she's had enough of the archetype of the Romanian peasant and the Balcanic shepherd, of *naţionalism de prost gust*—garish nationalism—she has nothing to do with the Dacians and the only reason she cares about Romans is that she studied Romance languages, Romanian, Latin, French and Italian. I leaf through Mircea Eliade's history of religions in her library, published back in 1985 in Romanian but unavailable in bookshops, I read Cioran in French for the first time, though I don't understand it, she tells me about the resistance of Romanian intellectuals, she knows Doina Cornea and is aware of Éva Cs. Gyimesi's letter. She has two major problems, that she can't have children and isn't allowed to visit France. Just emigrate, a high-ranking officer once advises her, but she doesn't want to. *Vreau să-l văd mort pe Ceauşescu,* she says— I want to see Ceauşescu dead. Even my father doesn't hate the regime as much as doamna Vulpescu, or at least not as loud. They are listening to us, she says one afternoon, and points at the listening bug installed under the tabletop, I bend down but can't see anything. She's a short, dark Armenian woman, I'll grow old from one minute to the next, like Oriental or Gipsy women, she tells me despondently. There is something sad and bitter in her being, she tells me after each class that I should get away from this country, nothing good will become of us here. I haven't yet heard such a damning opinion on Romania till then, and this is hard for me to get to grips with, seeing that she could be American, Armenian or Jewish but is Romanian, whereas I'm only Hungarian and that's that. What the hell have we lost here, she asks every now and then, and her tone is more despondent than ever.

The next spring the national *Olympiad* was taking place at Kolozsvár, but I didn't qualify because that year Arad county was only entitled to send three students, and I didn't get a high enough score. It was a humiliating situation, the other three went to the same school and were taught by the same teacher who'd become a school inspector after the change of regime. I wasn't represented by anyone, even though it was a well-known fact that I wanted to study Hungarian at university, a rare thing in those days at Arad. Doamna Vulpescu tried to console me with the fact that Emilia Eberle didn't get a place to study PE in Bucharest, despite her Olympic silver medal and being a world champion gymnast. I had seen her out and about a few times, she was a major star, like goalkeeper Helmuth Duckadam. This was the way this country worked, I should have learned to deal with it. I didn't pull a long face though, because around that time something important happened that helped me escape my bad mood and represented an unexpected turning point. One of our teachers, who taught all sorts of subjects with an ideological focus, and originally must have trained as a psychologist, drew me aside in a break after a relatively long attempt of mine at answering a question, and told me to observe Ceaușescu as he gesticulated with his hands while talking. Why did he have to do this, she asked, seeing that the entire country was laughing at him, and, just to be clear, she showed me how he usually did it. Well, he's beating the rhythm because, like you, he lives with a stammer. You have to find your own rhythm, practice and internalize it, you don't have to gesticulate with your hands or stamp your feet, it's more than enough to have a metronome in motion in your head. The teacher then took a good look round, because it wouldn't have been great if we got overheard, but since we were among ourselves, she added that Ceaușescu's problem was that, as he got older, he was less and less able to follow the pace of his hand movements. He hadn't internalised them, and as a result, one day his words would simply get stuck during a speech. Until then, I hadn't even noticed that the Golden Calf stammered, but would do without a fail thereafter. I was warned that the king was naked, and I saw that myself.

Back then, I'm unable to deal with my stammer properly, and feel weighed down by all the things I have to drag along as a result. The problem isn't the stammer itself but the fact that, over time, one finds it a deficiency and tries to avoid situations where this could matter or people who are likely to mock or are hurtful. One reformulates one's words and learns to swap problematic terms with utterable ones, and is later annoyed about not having said what one really wanted. The odd stammer slips in anyway, so the cat's out of the bag, and there's always a sense of doubt about actually making it to the intended point. Next, one starts again, by explaining things or just keeping quiet. One's nearest and dearest see this vain effort the most often, and this intimate sphere is the one that gets most affected. It's incredibly hard in this way to establish relationships, say anything, join groups, make phone calls or introduce oneself, seeing that any well-meaning comment can cause confusion, turmoil or misunderstanding. You're mocking me, suddenly someone tells me on the train and grabs my neck because he's also stammering, he thinks I'm copying him, he's a beefy lad from a nearby village and I can barely explain that I'm not, far from it, but the others are laughing, enjoying the situation where the large stammerer is beating up the small one. Girls have more patience, they turn away when they feel like giggling, they don't look me in the eye but once I've made it to the category of amusing objects and people, there's no need for me to say anything, it's enough for them to just lock eyes. This is the age when girls laugh at anything, and I don't even get the chance to put in a word because their giggling evokes a situation where I'm ridiculed anyway. This makes me realize that I have a much easier time if people address me, I always have a few words lined up that I can say without stammering, no matter how inconvenient the sounds I have to utter, I can take a deep breath, look the person in the eye, get hold of their attention, please don't let me go, because I can talk coherently and intelligently. It is rare in our culture to find people who are prepared to pay close attention to others, as a rule of thumb, people carry on with their own business, interrupt one another and are only waiting for the moment they can take to the floor. It's pointless to say that silence is golden, we know exactly that this is rarely true, and those who don't talk, look as if they didn't even exist. Once I tried to explain to someone that the roe (*Capricornus capricornus*), roebuck, doe, fawn, isn't the female of the deer (*Cervus elaphus*), also known as hart, hind, fawn, but two separate species. At first, they were interested in what I had to say, but then they started to smirk, asking whether I really meant ha-ha-heart? When I tried to tell this to someone else, hoping that they'd comfort me or at least see my point, they asked what did I want to say with these deer and roes, and why did I want to explain this to such people in the first place? I generate laughter whenever I open my mouth, in case there's no other fun, I'm right at hand, how did you put it last time, someone asks, faces instantly starting to jerk and people guffawing. On another occasion, a girl with whom I had danced half the night suddenly told me, loud enough for everyone to hear, to learn to stammer fluently. This is proper scalding, especially given that she knew this and we haven't just met each other then. I immediately flee from that party and don't want to be with people anymore, I don't want to say another word. She writes me a letter the next day, asking for forgiveness, she didn't want to hurt my feelings, and this is even worse. I stop hanging out with people after a while, instead I read and play sports, the whole twenty-four hours in the day wouldn't be enough for me to catch up with everything I have to do, not to mention that being tired, rushed around and unslept doesn't help with overcoming my stammer. You have weak nerves, my mother points out, but I dismiss this, come on, I run forty-five kilometres a week if not more, how could I possibly have weak nerves?

Around this time, I also realize the sad fact that what we call Hungarian literature from Transylvania isn't a collection of masterpieces, but rather something that seems to deliberately omit the stuff I really like. I'm totally fed up with everybody working on the elevation of the worker–peasant power, even though this isn't visible in the poetry of Áprily or Dsida, or the prose of Benő Karácsony. By then I know that the construction of socialism is a rhetorical aspect that has to be referenced everywhere, but isn't it enough for writers and poets to fight oppression in their own way? Anti-fascism, the friendship of people living next to one another, socialism. Is this the essence of literature? Really? If I become a writer, I'd have to do this too? But who's the oppressor? The one who's lying. Suddenly, I figure out the meaning of things: fighting against oppression. After the regime change, it has come to light that most contemporary authors opposed the dictatorship, as for me, my sheer age meant that I was on the right side, in opposition.

My other thoughts were about imagining how Antal Szerb would have handled writing the *Spinach*. It's this simple: it should be seriously revised or rewritten. Alongside weeding out proletcultist or ideological bullshit from the various studies, I started to master a reading technique whereby I was able to jump over passages I disliked or found boring, and at times, I even noticed that the author wasn't too convinced either. Most books would have had a foreword or afterword in those days, be it a classic, contemporary or foreign author, and at times these were really significant essays and studies from which I learned an awful lot, though there were a few idiots too, compared to whom even I didn't think of myself too low. There were authors about whose work I barely read anything, for instance I couldn't find anything remotely intelligent on Berzsenyi's poetry or even locate his collected poems, he seemed to resist me big time, which I resented and feared that I'd have to write about him at the exam, but I didn't. There were of course plenty of topics I hadn't even heard about, neither then nor to this day, I thought I'd get away with it. But there's no such thing as getting away, every ruse comes back to haunt you. Being self-taught is a double-edged sword, on the one hand, one can read or learn whatever one wants, on the other, one has no idea what others know and what's being left out. The easiest route for me would have been to find a good Hungarian teacher in Arad, but I didn't think it necessary, I thought I'd manage literature on my own, akin to Martin Eden who becomes a writer without any help, upon landing in Oakland. At this stage, Jack London was still pounding in my head, and I was embarrassed by the ridiculous amount of money my parents would spend on me without any visible result, especially seeing that this money could have been needed elsewhere too. An additional disquieting factor was that the most interesting readings didn't quite fit around the framework of the school curriculum, and anybody who has lived in a diaspora or in the countryside is familiar with the absence of books and with the ultimate obstacle of not having anything. I didn't yet realize that entire generations of Hungarians in Romania were left out of contemporary Hungarian culture, this wasn't an evolutionary aim at pulling apart, no special route or relational system, but simple degradation, because everything that should have been public property in terms of knowledge was none other than the privilege of a gradually shrinking group.

The letters of my unrequited love reinforced my belief that I was on the right track, and saddened me because they made me realize that I was heading nowhere. Doamna Vulpescu encouraged and tormented me in equal measure, so I got through *The Little Prince* in French and some Saint-Exupéry I managed to lay hands on, in Hungarian or Romanian, next I took on Camus and Proust, then Kafka and Faulkner. I was desperately searching for authors and works on a par with these among their Transylvanian contemporaries, especially since the label 'on a par with standards of world literature' often appeared in my critical readings. So I thought this must be like the women's world record, even if it can't be measured exactly it can be seen that András Sütő isn't in this league, but how about *Abel Alone*? Sándor Kányádi, Domokos Szilágyi, Gizella Hervay, László Király, Ádám Bodor, Attila Mózes, János Székely . . . No need to be ashamed, but still. Then I read Éva Cs. Gyimesi's book, *Teremtett világ* [Created world], and suddenly obtained the clarity I needed: literature is freedom! But what is freedom? And what is beauty?

Next, it's August 1986 and I'm standing on the corridors of the university looking at the exam results, I'm the thirteenth under the cut-off line. I'm surprised at how well I've done, I'm basically the twentieth in the field, so it's actually possible to get a place, I say to myself. I recognize a girl who sat next to me at the Hungarian literature exam, I hadn't yet written anything and she had already requested some extra sheets, she handed in a sixteen-page paper while mine barely stretched to four. In the end, her grade was significantly lower than mine, and she was seriously struggling to understand the reasons behind this injustice. I told her that we'd meet in two years, in 1988, seeing that I'd be in the army until then. In any case, the decisive feat of arms was the oral exam, and when Éva Cs. Gyimesi nodded, I got started in a slightly trembling voice and managed to say everything, to be precise, I didn't because she interrupted me saying that it was enough. In vain did I feel that for me this was a victory of sorts, because as my mother put it, life was hard. After I graduated from high school, I was sent to work at a petroleum spring but when I turned up, the human resources guy told me that a hundred and fifty people received placements there, they had no available jobs, and I should find work elsewhere. I had no desire to work in the petroleum industry, but it was important to go to the army from a workplace of some sort because then one could return there and the time spent in the army counted as employment, even though I wasn't too bothered about this aspect back then. Unemployment had become an increasingly major concern in eighties Romania, though in hindsight it would appear that everybody had a job. Those who had no money or contacts could only find work in construction, mines or agriculture, but once one was in post and was well-behaved, it was rather difficult to get fired. Having said that, anybody could find themselves transferred to a building site in Bucharest or to the Danube-Black Sea Canal, if in no other way than by being called up in the army, so it did matter what and where one worked, to say nothing of the fact that new starters were badly paid even then.

It was this summer that after a lot of planning and daydreaming, my friend Kohn and I headed to the Hargita mountains on our very first excursion without adults, not only did we have to carry our often twenty-five kilo rucksacks but also overcome endless dangers caused by inaccurate maps, inflamed teeth, wandering cold fronts and many other minor factors. We almost ended up sleeping in palm-deep water as early as the first night, but we couldn't actually fall asleep due to the thunderstorm. At dawn Kohn, showed me his swollen face, and standing in the pouring rain we realized that all the other campers fled the scene in the course of the evening, everybody vanished from the Bucsin-peak and we were the only brave people camping in the plashy grass. When we got to the chalet, the Székely man in charge seemed really surprised to see us, what the hell are you doing here, this isn't the Hargita. Soon we made it there all right, but first had to find a dentist, and then waited for good weather for days on end in Csíkszereda, a place that at the time felt like a proper Hungarian town. I hadn't been anywhere until then where everybody would speak Hungarian around the blocks, Kohn had already been to Budapest but that was different. We crossed the South Hargita all the way down to Barót, by which point the weather got milder and it only rained every other day. We took in all the sights, as I showed Kohn everything of any importance, such as the iron blast furnace in Bodvaj, the house of Father Elek Benedek in Kisbacon, the Hatod, the Almási cave, and the Barót forest where one could still make out the traces of our Native American life. My grandfather was struggling to come to terms with the fact that Kohn was Jewish, yet he refrained from discussing the Old Testament with him claiming that he wasn't really interested in that topic. He'd eat pork regardless though. Back then, even Kohn was unaware that he'd soon live in the Holy Land, despite me thinking that he'd been preparing mentally for this all his life, and in a good twenty-five years, he'd run a marathon on my behalf too. Apparently, I taught him to run, though I couldn't recall us running together in Arad, only that his portable radio wouldn't work on top of the Hargita.

XVIII

The Army

When in the early Autumn of 1986, an officer on the recruiting committee asked me what combat arms I'd like to choose and I replied that I'd like to be a parachutist or a mountain infantryman, he replied with a slight smirk on his face: *serios mă*—is that so, huh? I'm sent to Buzău, and for a short while I'm rather hopeful seeing that one of the largest military airports is in the area and there are plenty of parachutists around. We are about to find out on our train journey that we'll be cartographers though, and I immediately think that this is an opportunity to acquire the skills of Colonel Percy Harrison Fawcett. *The Secret of the Mato Grosso* has been one of my all-time favourite reads, and I'm yet again sensing the spirit of adventure as I've already carried some theodolite on my back and, though forbidden, I also leafed through an Austro-Hungarian map. That's all there is to it.

Hundreds of people get on the train at Arad, carrying wooden suitcases, this enlisting is like a folk fiesta, people are drinking and singing, proud dads, sobbing mums, everybody hammered. At Lippa, a drunken lad falls out of the train, he won't be a soldier anymore, the train is delayed, site examination, police, ambulance. This is starting out well. At Ploieşti, we miss our connection, so we only make it to Buzău in the course of the night, we find a hotel near thestation, five of us sleeping in a double room, we don't really sleep but drink and play cards till morning and watch the stars through a crack caused by the last earthquake. It's very hot but there's no water, instead we have plenty of beer purchased at the station bistro in five-litre bottles, this is our last night of freedom, tomorrow is 15 September, the first day of school.

There's a scream and suddenly a pair of boots are flying my way, then there are some bits of rag I have to sew together in order to make myself a jacket and some trousers. I can fix a button, but the sleeves of the jacket are twice torn off by the corporal, I can't allow him to get away with this for the third time, I'm a locksmith not a tailor, I snap, so he just moves on, as there are many others he can call to order. I undo the sewing and carry on trying until I manage, we don't have to wear the uniform that day, I'm driven up the wall by this situation, there's no mirror but I can see the others in all these shabby and patchy clothes, we look like prisoners of war in some American film. The parchment-dry boots are covered in dust and cobwebs, and as we clean them, we breathe in the smell of rancid stinky feet lingering in the barrack. After getting changed and shaven, one can barely recognize those with whom one had spent a few hours beforehand, the officers are screaming at all times, nobody understands what, one should react somehow, they are screaming again, every so often they get us out in the yard, make us lie on the ground or run around, we don't know how to keep in line, don't understand these commands, so they make us run again, down-up, keep in line! What's up? They are screaming and swearing, it's hot and dusty, our jackets and trousers get wet, there's no running water to have a wash, and by the end of the first night many suffer from blisters seeing that the ill-fitting boots have hurt their feet. We have to clean our boots in the dark, first the right and then the left one, or the other way round, but somehow, somebody always manages to hang the wrong one on the pole by the wall, so there's more screaming, running, lying on the ground, jumping up, the freshly creamed boots attract dust like there's no tomorrow, so we start again from scratch. It isn't muddy yet but it will be soon, Ottlik summed all this up perfectly, one could even argue that *School at the Frontier* is about to start again, though this is a lot worse and we are no longer children.

On our third morning at the barracks, we have to take our suitcases with us when we are called out to the yard, we get some vaccine, not sure what for, perhaps typhoid and cholera, then everybody is given pair of wellies as well as quilted jackets and trousers, we are going to the Bărăgan Plain for some agricultural work. They hand out dried food to last us about three days, some cheese, a piece of bacon, some liver pate, brown bread and a packet of toast. At this point, many of us have some leftover food brought from home, and there's a small shop at the barracks too, so one can buy the odd thing. Nobody is prepared for what's in store for us, the barracks are an unbearably oppressive place, really crowded, there's constant screaming and shouting, but nothing happens in fact except for a helicopter taking off in our vicinity, we don't see this either, so let's get a move on . . .

Murgeanca is a small place on the Romanian Plain, on the shore of lake Strachina not far from the Danube, a guy from Galac warns us when we first smell the sewer-like odour of the swamp: *miroase a Dunăre* (smells like the Danube). It's an agricultural site in a deplorable state, a few stables, broken-down combine harvesters, tractors, an office building, a canteen and barracks. We have to pull out dry sweetcorn stalks with our bare hands and create some sort of an assembly area by stamping our feet on the dirt floor, we dig out a whole for our toilet, running up and down and being made to lie on the ground and jump up on command until dusk. We get our drinking water from a forty-metre-deep well, we're using a bucket and our palms, since hardly anybody has cups or crockery. We can use a tin trough for washing, there's a warning that this isn't drinking water, it stinks, it's sulphurous and can cause stomach ache, and when the pump breaks down, we have to make do without water for days. There used to be a barbed wire fence around the barracks in the past, but by now many pillars have gone missing, someone points out that this makes the place look like a concentration camp.

Wake up is at five in the morning, then some exercise, a quick wash, loads of military bullshit without which one can't start the day, one can shave in the dark and without water, the officers supervise this with great care, seeing that hygiene is paramount. Breakfast is at six, I have never had cheesy paste or mushy beans for breakfast, nor some sort of ratatouille or green bean pottage, from now on, this menu is either for breakfast or for lunch or dinner on a rotational basis, the only exception is Sunday night when we get a piece of bacon and some cheese. It will only take a few days and the previously scorned toast will be in great demand, it's impossible to chew it unless one soaks it, but if one doesn't pay attention it can instantly soak up all the tea and end up looking like kitchen swill. We are already out on the field by daybreak, our job is to peel sweetcorn, there are mountains of it, we'll never get to the bottom of this. They make us run every now and then, lie on the ground—jump up, keep going, faster and harder. It's a hot autumn spell, we'd quite like to take our jackets off but aren't allowed, we have to keep them buttoned, the plastic collar scratches my neck, and we aren't even allowed to roll up our sleeves, keep running, crawling, down-up, and in case we have to

move from one place to another, we get there running or marching. Needless to say, we can't actually carry this out on the
ploughed fields or in the swamps, so we stick with lying on the
ground and jumping up and just carry on working. Water is
delivered in a cistern once a day, in the afternoon, and it's often
wasted, finally we end up drinking out of our caps until an officer
knocks mine out of my hands, how dare I not salute him. At night,
there are at least two alerts, get dressed, dash out, headcount, back,
another alert, and so on, this goes on for days because we aren't
working hard enough. They'll reduce our food rations if we don't
get our act together, nobody can receive or write any letters, and
we'll end up punished in front of a military tribunal. The amount
of peeled sweetcorn will double in a few days, we work from dawn
till dusk, the officers select the best workers in a group and we all
have to adjust to their pace. The group that has finished the
required amount can take a rest, for a few days this method works,
but then those who have already finished their share are sent back
to help the others, so the whole thing stalls, lie on the ground—
jump up, run here, run there, flat crawling. Our hands are
chapped, and our thumbs are bleeding, with cuts down to the
bone, we're out of plasters so people try to bend their thumbs but
this way it's much harder to peel, there's no progress, so we're back
to lying on the ground—jumping up, running and flat crawling.
Our nails crack and blood is spurting out of the back of our hands,
we have no change of clothes, our trousers and jackets show salty
sweat marks, we stink and are itching all over, we can still wash in
the evening but only have the same rags to put back on, so after
the first week it itches, after the second it stings, after the third,
who knows . . .

No idea how long this *sweetcorn front* lasts, perhaps for three weeks or so, we are newbies and they can do whatever they like to us. We are a hundred and fifty high-school leavers from Romania who can't yet grasp that physical and mental strength is a limited resource, just like air and water, even though we have no intention to put up resistance, pretend to be ill or to escape. We still believe that those who carry out their duties will be left alone, but it soon emerges that this isn't the case. One day, at dawn, as I'm dizzily shaving by the tin trough and can only barely see my face, having to feel my lips and the two blemishes, unlikely to heal anytime soon under the fold of my chin, I have a feeling that this is no longer me and that no part of my body is quite where it used to be. I have no time to deal with this, I have to make a new hole in my belt almost daily, it's hard work to drill a hole in this thick shiny leather and I'm caught up in a strange daze, slowing down, sensing voices travelling from afar where everything is blurry and muted. As soon as I get the chance to sit down, I fall asleep, I'm not even hungry and I can fall asleep on the field even while eating, dropping my plate and the bread held in my hand. This happens to others too, though I'm not really paying attention, we carry on peeling sweetcorn and my arms repeating that movement at night, someone's arm keeps wobbling over from the bed opposite, people are moaning and groaning, above and all around me. There's eighty of us in the barrack, it's hot, dusty and it stinks of urine, but this sense of slowness is so intriguing, so understated, not good, the officer shouts, and everybody starts yelling, don't give a damn, we get on a trailer, jump off, lie on the ground, jump up, run, crawl, somebody falls asleep while lying on the ground, they kick him, sweetcorn again, an entire mountain of it, peel, throw, grab a new one, peel, throw and so on.

It was the sandstorm that put an end to this state of affairs. As soon as the hot red cloud swept through the field, we were unable to see a thing and our mouths, eyes and hair, as much as we still had, got filled up with sand. Sweetcorn stalks, peel, cobs and tumbleweeds were carried about by the wind, the storm rumbling, screaming and whistling, and even the most wicked officer couldn't come up with anything beyond ordering us to lie on the ground, this time joining in to execute his own command. In case we lifted our heads, all we could see was everyone covered in this fine soil, surrounding us as if we were condemned to death like in those films about the desert. The wind racing on, tousling the dry stalks, whistling, but this sound is actually much deeper, coming from afar and heading even further, connecting heaven and earth. Enormous warm drops are drumming on our backs, perhaps mingled with hail, then there's a short pause, followed by an endless and steady scattering of short sharp drops akin to needle pricks. In half an hour, the hot sand of the desert turns into a sea of sticky brown mud, and as we emerge from it, the wind keeps blowing at a steady pace, ushering in a grey rain and we are clueless as to where we should go and where we actually are other than standing in this ankle-deep slush. It's noon on a normal workday, but we can't argue with the weather, despite the wind calming down, we are so scared that we march straight back to the barracks and a period of rest is declared. We are shaking under our blankets, all wet and covered in mud, we try to light the fire in the utility stove but the wind blows the smoke back, we keep trying all afternoon but in vain. All of a sudden, our barrack reminds me of a mountain chalet, everyone's getting chatty, with stories to tell and memories of A-levels, school, maths, university entrance exams for many of us, family, mothers and love. For a second, we can see ourselves as we really are, this whole thing is like a fucked-up school trip that should come to an end as soon as possible. The next morning, it's raining again, we are called out only to stand ankle-deep in the slush, but after breakfast we are waiting for the tractor to take us to the field and it doesn't come, it never does in such weather, a local explains. Still, we run a few laps until our work clothes get soaking wet, then they dish out some quilted jackets, trousers and wellies, they make us lie in the mud and then, just to top this, march us up and down in the rain, which almost makes the mud wash off a little.

This period of rest, lasting for a day and a half, is incredible, we are just sitting around, sleeping, in the evening the tractorist hands us a bucket of red wine through the window, we ladle it into plastic bags, tear the corners off and drink like animals. We managed to light the fire, although it's far too hot right next to it and still too cold further away, still, we dry ourselves and the wind calms down, while the rain is steadily pouring down, gushing along the roof, the puddles form one huge pool of water in front of the barrack, and going to the toilet is a high-risk operation seeing that most wellies have holes in them. There is nothing more desolate than a soggy steppe. The tractor is slowly easing on, at times sinking axis-deep into the mud, getting stuck in the odd bump, then we jump off the trailer and give it a push, as often as it takes, but in case it's the engine that breaks down, we have to wait for a replacement tractor as the kind of push this would need isn't possible in this mud. After the storm, we'd never work as hard as we did before, the officers tried every trick in the book but the mud and our tiredness and apathy put up a strong resistance. Next thing, an insidious epidemic swept through our contingent, everybody throwing up and having a runny poo for two days, this really knocked us out. In vain did we report being ill, the commander claimed this was due to us drinking all the time, even though we only managed to bag the odd bucket of wine here and there. It was a cold morning, and when we were about to move from one pile of peeled sweetcorn to another, the officer gave the command 'double march'. I would have welcomed a bit of running, hoping I'd warm up, but I could feel that there was no way I could lift my wellies out of the mud, I was just standing there, unable to move my legs stuck in the mudberg. The others were in the same situation, just staring ahead and the one standing first in line shrugging, we simply can't, there's no double march today. The officer kept yelling for a while making us lie on the ground, but we failed to stand up, he yelled in vain, then kicked a few people, somebody stood up then the rest of us too, but there was no lining up. We were sauntering along the field like a bunch of quilted jackets held together by some wire, and the officer had to acknowledge that this didn't even qualify as a case of non-compliance.

One day at dawn someone faints when lining up, they keep shaking and slapping him for a while to ensure he isn't faking it but he isn't, so the next day he's taken to hospital. After this, there's someone needing to be taken to hospital almost every day. The nearest doctor is in Țăndărei, so after a while an astonishingly fat nurse snaps at the commander: *criminalilor*—criminals! Those who end up in hospital tend to stay there irrespective of their condition, so they soon send an army medic to us, and he only takes people to hospital if that's greenlighted by the commander. We are dizzy all day, tottering about and barely able to work. I haven't been able to eat for three days, I weigh fifty-five kilos and instead of my usual sixty-three, they weighed us when I joined the army, that's how I know. This is the kind of diarrhoea people can easily catch on holiday, and it goes away after a bit of fasting, but we can't afford to do this at our pace of work, if I don't eat I can barely walk, and if I eat I'm sick and everything just runs through me. We have no access to doctors or medication, some of the boys start snivelling and coughing, then boils and anthraces appear, under the armpits, in the groin area and even on someone's cock. Yet we have to keep on working, the engineer has already complained that our productivity decreased. So the commander comes up with the idea that we should be up earlier and have a longer morning exercise routine.

I have read so many stories on concentration camps that I shouldn't even mention all this, but the thing is that we aren't prisoners of war, captives or deportees but soldiers in the army of socialist Romania. To be fair, we haven't yet sworn an oath, but this doesn't really make a difference from a legal point of view, contrary to what some people might think. A few soldiers occasionally try to escape, but they are promptly brought back from Fetești station by a jovial policeman, in his private vehicle no less. It's a Sunday evening and the boys are waiting for the train from Bucharest to arrive, it's delayed, and they all look like prisoners, after all not all prisoners get to wear the regulation stripy clothes, they often wear shabby uniforms like us. Our officers are all drunk, so nothing will become of this, the policeman takes a quick look around and observes that it's just like in a prison, *ca la pârnaie*, and confirms that they used to house prisoners here in the past. No need to overdramatize this as nobody has given up their ghost, only one of us had lost a finger due to bone infection, but it's anyone's guess what would have become of us in such circumstances until Spring. Our morale is at rock bottom, and we are getting to a point where absurd gestures can no longer be over-ruled with humour. We've become deeply embittered and speechless, sporting the same hunched-up shoulders which, due to the cold, can simply stay that way for good. I won't open the letter received from home for days and I don't have an appetite, but in case someone receives a packet, we stuff ourselves yet still stay hungry, and some of us throw up at once. All I really crave is a sip of vodka or cognac, I don't need much to feel numb but at times we get properly wasted. The tractorists bring us wine and brandy, and it will only emerge later that half of the squad no longer has any boots or belts because we sold our belongings for booze. Every so often, we get aggressive, we nearly lynch an otherwise quite humane officer when he finds a bottle of cognac among our stuff and pours it out. He has a point, but doing this to our face is a provocation, we wouldn't have issues if he had just drunk it. The officer will get seriously scared too, and such conditions bring out the animal in all of us. Interestingly, his is the only name I still remember, and we'll get on quite well in the times to come.

If we weren't aware that all this sweetcorn we peeled was left out on the fields and exposed to the elements, rain then snow, if we didn't see thousands of tons of turnip gathered from the fields being left to rot in piles, if we didn't occasionally have to load dead cows on trucks and if we didn't feel that all this work was in fact in vain and utterly pointless . . . One Sunday afternoon, we are watching TV, seeing that we even have one of those, and there's a programme about I. A. S. Ograda, our agricultural farm, showing our engineer and commander together with a regiment of smiling soldiers in freshly ironed clothes and with badges on their caps, picking sweetcorn and loading it in brand new wicker baskets onto a trailer. This is another record crop, as usual. *Ca la televizor* (as on TV), someone points out, and this will be our go-to phrase whenever something doesn't work out, but even if it does.

As time went by, it got gradually colder and the mud deeper, and the unsurmountable problems of organizing our work granted us more and more frequent respites. The officers were just as bored of this as we were, they also had to live in mud and filth, even though nobody relied on their solidarity. One time our tractor broke down in a vineyard where crops were left to rot over an area over hundreds of acres, we stuffed our faces all morning which of course led to further diarrhoea, but nobody cared. Some other time, we were passing by a tomato and then a cabbage plantation, and the tractorists brought us some halva, Turkish delight and biscuits. In case the shop by our barrack was open, we bought vodka and plenty of Silvania champagne, we even used it for shaving when there was no water supply for days. We'd often grill unripe sweetcorn on the embers of field fires, and eat it with the milk and bread brought to us by old peasant women, who looked just as sad and shrivelled as the women portrayed in Russian films. We just kept repeating Arad, Szatmár, Kolozsvár, struggling to explain where these places actually were, they only had a faint knowledge of Bucharest and Galac. We'd pick sweetcorn all day and wouldn't even make it to the end of the row. At night, we'd hear strange barking sounds, and the tractorists told us these were jackals. We ended up working alongside common criminals, nits and scabies were not uncommon, and one morning the snow arrived. We were standing on this endless plain, hands in pockets because we had no gloves, and anyway, one can't pick sweetcorn in gloves, there's no glove that could stand the test of tear and wear as much as the human hand. The snow held out for a few days, it wasn't very cold but the wind kept sweeping through the plain and we didn't only stuff our wellies with newspaper but also rolled some around our waist under our coat. The lining of our quilted jackets shrank to pieces, the collars got really shiny or tore off, buttons fell off so we had to use wire instead, we wouldn't shave for days because in this biting cold even the most pedantic officer failed to make us comply. At night, we'd gather around the utility stove, knocking back red wine, and in order to avoid having to go out for a wee, we drilled a hole in the wall and stuck a pipe through. There was no more morning exercise routine, nobody bothered with cleaning the barracks, and our squad was just as abandoned as Romania itself, seeing that it didn't take much for order and discipline to vanish, and this wasn't even such a great loss at times.

By the time we finally made it to the army base in early December, frozen through and completely mangy, I found myself overwhelmed with child-like excitement at the sheer sight of bare acacia trees, leaking grey blocks of flats and ordinary civilians wearing plain clothes: yet another human being, a tree, a park, a lamp, a playground, a statue! As we were sitting on the truck we kept staring at a middle-aged woman, she also looked at us with a sad and cautious gaze and asked one of the lads: how many years? We didn't understand her question, so she repeated it: how many years of prison? The truck moved on, turned into the courtyard and we got off, taking our belongings, somebody tried to give us orders but we just sat on our suitcases. The commander told us to stay put, I could tell that he couldn't believe his eyes, so he just circled our group and made a face. He ordered two days' rest to the entire squad, in the showers we could finally check out how ridiculously slim we had become. Finally, there was water and light, it was warm, but a hundred people showering at once could only make me think of one thing, namely that the door opened inward, and as they switched the cold water on, it turned out that this was indeed the case.

Compared to the Bărăgan, this feels like a sanatorium despite lasting until Spring and being an infantry training unchanged since the First World War. We keep running up and down the lawn splattered with cowpats, holding bayonets attached to AK-47s, we soak up all the puddles and then carry on sliding on the snow and ice. We are often about to choke in our gas masks, they steam up a lot, and we spend most of our time with the maintenance of our clothing and equipment, our outfits are soaking wet, the guns are rusting, the boots are rotting and falling apart as they can't ever get properly dry before Spring. Only one smell compares to that of a hundred army boots put out on the corridor, that of a hundred unwashed people who have no change of clothes or clean bedding. Life at the army base is boring, everything takes place in a very tight, enclosed and crowded space, it feels like a prison or a hospital, people are no masters of their own selves, daily routine is ruling the roost, seeing that the ultimate goal is to undermine individuality. I have no idea who might expect responsible behaviour from us or why, though this is only an issue when we happen to have fully loaded rifles in our hands. Despite the primitive conditions in Romania at the time, certain things can't be achieved with a group of secondary-school graduates in 1986, the system and its ideology have completely discredited themselves, nothing works and keeping up appearances is no longer tenable. There's forty of us, and the four corporals who initially have unlimited power over us, lose it soon enough seeing that, to their misfortune, they are less educated than us. Working together on the fields helped with moulding us into a relatively homogenous group, and there's a sort of student-style solidarity that didn't actually operate back at my own school. Group behaviour is the best way of bringing out the difference between those who went to secondary school, vocational schools or are illiterate, the major opponent of dictatorship is education, which is why it has to be liquidated and transformed into a barrack or a stable. I keep marvelling to this day what a difference this slight and recent tradition of secondary education has made in this country.

Any activity is taken on by at least twenty people, so in case someone starts hiccupping or coughing, this is picked up by at least twenty people; everybody eats a clove of garlic, so in case it stinks, it should stink a hell of a lot more, we even smear the dorm's wainscoting with it because the lieutenant has made the mistake of telling us how much he hates it; in case someone's hair is shaved off in punishment, at least half of the squad has their hair shaved off, then we start growing moustaches because that's allowed, but only every second of us, and then every third, before we all suddenly shave them off. The point of all this is that nobody should be left on their own, not even when being mistaken or defiant, we don't leave anyone out in the cold ever, not even when going mad or just not giving a damn. Everybody deserves protection, help and cover. It doesn't always work to perfection, but usually there isn't enough time to be put into smaller groups when we are defiant, the method tends to be to distribute renitents within a larger squad, and we are also being threatened with this, but for some reason nothing happens, perhaps we weren't dangerous enough and didn't quite represent a menace to the overall operation of the squad.

I remember it well when one evening we decide, in the toilet—where else?—that we should learn all the regulations by heart, things like everyone should have freshly polished boots, buttons shouldn't be fixed with wire or the fucking guns shouldn't ever get dusty. We must ensure that these *nenorociții ăștia*—fuckers—can't do with us as they please, by this point it's clear to us that for any tiny mistake they'd punish the entire squad, and all this according to the teachings of Makarenko who also learnt this in the army. So let's show who we are and what we are worth. All this feels as if we were a football team in a locker room, there isn't an opinion leader among us but we share a moral ground, we unanimously despise our superiors, it's not difficult for us to distance ourselves from them on a linguistic level and to keep asking back if we don't understand something and carry on playing the clever clogs. No idea why, but we don't seem to manage singing at all, yet *go ahead and sing* is part of our training. There's a jazz trumpeter and a Gipsy musician amid us but we aren't prepared to march and sing at the same time, and we haven't even had an agreement on this. I've never belonged to a group where thirty-five out of forty people are prepared to co-operate without any fiddling about, let's show that all this is a mere trifle, and in case we don't manage, seeing that it's a serious mental and physical torture, at least we shouldn't hurt one another. Word spreads of an eager beaver squad, and our officer is even priding himself with us dealing with everything so well and so shrewdly, *am băgat spaima-n ei*, he boasts to a colleague—I made them shit-scared. Soon after this, when he's making us lie on the soaking wet ground just to make a point, the entire squad disperses in the dark and the officer is left behind with three corporals. We scatter about the army base and keep hiding for hours, the ruckus goes on all night, and even though gas masks are brought out the next day, the victory is ours, despite the corporal on our side being incarcerated for a few days as if the responsibility were all his. The officers try to find out who organized this action but they fail, this is in fact bordering on mutiny. In response, they torture us as much as they can but at the first sharp-shooting exercise, thirty-eight out of forty people give an outstanding performance, way ahead of even the student squadron. All this is taking place on 25 December 1986, and I manage to forget completely that it's Christmas.

Our commander promises, like all his predecessors for a hundred years, that the best shooters will be allowed home for a few days. None of us are, and at the second shooting only the odd bullet hits the target, I close my eyes and pull the trigger. Scandal. The next shooting goes remarkably well and a group of lads from Bucharest is allowed home for 48 hours, but many of them complain that they won't go for such a short while, scandal breaks out again, going on leave also takes place on command, everything does, the commander screams. Yeah, we know, the rain too, somebody mumbles behind me and we burst out laughing like a bunch of girls, we are standing to attention, our officer is fuming but we are guffawing. Any dictatorship is powerless in the face of this, as it's possible to stand to attention during a barrage of fire but not of laughter. The bloke behind me has a saying from seminal Romanian dramatist Ion Luca Caragiale up his sleeve for everything, he wants to be an actor and he's driving me insane. An ice-cold drop of water is dripping down in the middle of my back, I try to make myself as small as possible, we're trembling and shivering, the officer is giving a speech, but Sebastian keeps whispering one of Don Leonidas' lines which wouldn't make much sense on its own but seems to perfectly fit the officer's screaming. I whisper to the soldier standing in front of me, I can see him tense his entire body, goodness, he'll pass this on. The only thing that's worse than this is when some Székely brother, of whom there are a few, tries to make a report or explain something in their broken Romanian and pitiful accent. It's heart breaking and even the officers are struggling not to break out in laughter, but for those who speak both Romanian and Hungarian, this is unbearable.

These are dark times, the pointless drills, the cold, the pressure of constantly being on alert, aside from all the nagging and monotony that suck people down and turn them totally blank and impassive. Days and weeks blur together, it makes no sense to count the days that have passed or are left to go. No wonder that those who don't mind talking about their experiences in the army were usually cooks, stokers or drivers. There are hardly any anecdotes about crossing the surging Ialomița river, twenty-four hour forced marches, frozen toes or how it feels not to be able to open one's fly with numb fingers. As for the wind, the essential information that needs sharing is that it blows twice a year: from left to right between October and March, and then from right to left, seeing that this was a very hard winter. There must have been some corps in the Romanian army that were highly trained for the military profession, but I, for one, know next to nothing about this. Those who followed on TV the shooting in December 1989, probably have serious doubts about the ability of this army to come up with anything in a war situation, but then again, according to later analysts, we could have ended up with a much more severe bloodbath, so perhaps this army wasn't all that infamous after all.

Exceptional people can be found everywhere, but on an army base one can get an insight into the scum of the country, be they ordinary soldiers or colonels, rank makes no difference whatsoever in this respect. I have suddenly encountered people of completely different complexions and habits, this is a space that accommodates the mountain shepherd and the winner of the classical guitar contest, the Hungarian Jewish colonel from Nagyvárad and the fisherman from the Danube Delta, there's even a soldier of colour alongside Székelys and Tartars, Csángós and Catholic Bulgarians, Turks and Hutzuls. I've had no idea there are so many ethnic minorities in Romania, there's an amazing range of dialects, many of which I can't grasp at first, but I can see that Romanians come in many guises, far from the way Transylvanian–Hungarian hatred or flippant superiority would have pictured it, such Romanians don't actually exist. I can also sense that everybody's faking it, nobody takes a single command, regulation or instruction seriously, this happens with some sort of common agreement, and may god protect us from those idiots who don't or don't want to participate in this. It's increasingly obvious that, in private, everybody is aware that the system has failed but nobody acknowledges this in public, we carry on watching television, babbling and clapping at political events, god's nincompoop is stammering but nobody's laughing, not even me.

It comes to my mind that I once witnessed a group of officers drinking some incredibly stinky brandy, its dreadful stench even managed to cut through the odour of shoe polish and the smell of our leather equipment. It's a really pleasant autumn but we're bored to death, some of our squad are on a field trip carrying out some measurements elsewhere in the country, there are only about a hundred of us loitering about the base, in charge of the kitchen, the abattoir, the glass factory, mending fences. Time is passing very slowly, the officers are bored too, we aren't allowed to play football or sports, so they just keep drinking whenever possible and we have to join them. I hate drunken officers, the army is all about controlled violence, after all one is taught to kill and Russian writers have said pretty much all there is to say about bored garrisons, sooner or later they'll start shooting at one another. We were within an inch of such acts ourselves, we've had suicides, fugitives, psychos, a myriad of horror stories are doing the rounds and unfortunately most of them are true. One of the officers tells us that carrying arms while on duty is a reward for getting through the training. The best bit is being left to stand alone at night guarding the ammunition depot, able to think about anything that happens to cross my mind, I even wrap the gun in my mantel so it doesn't get covered in dew. Sparse acacia forests and being on night-time duty are not everyone's cup of tea, whereas loaded guns are good company but bad counsel. I have an obligation to shoot at anyone who might attack me, this is solely my decision and we are at peace as long as I don't pull the trigger. How can they possibly claim that this sort of service is a reward? Any service is servitude. Still, walking in an acacia forest, hands in pockets, and not being afraid of one's own gun is the closest thing to freedom in the circumstances.

One afternoon, the sergeant in charge of the depot stops me in my tracks. He had once hit me and I promised that I'd kill him if this happened again, it was a really ugly scene but we patched it up and managed to avoid one another wherever possible. He drags me into the depot as if I was some booty, only to find all the officers unbuttoned and red on the cheeks from drink. Without any further ado, the commander asks me what's going on in Hungary. I don't know, nothing. There are several Hungarians in senior roles at our unit and the political propaganda is constantly going on about Horthy's revisionism, yet I have to explain that Horthy was an actual historical figure, by then Romanian public opinion knew next to nothing about him (and they still don't) but they understood the term revisionism all too well. Up to this point, it seemed as if our aim was to overtly protect socialist Romania from NATO, and, covertly, from the Soviet Union, our favourite neighbour being the Black Sea. Right now, however, it seems that

Hungary is becoming a menace, and I'm obviously a member of the Fifth Column, together with all other Hungarians. Many people keep asking why aren't we serving in the Hungarian army and they are genuinely surprised to learn that there are ethnic Hungarians living in Romania, but then the smarter ones get pre-occupied with whose side we'd take in a potential Hungarian–Romanian war. In such situations, I usually draw attention to Liviu Rebreanu's *Forest of the Hanged* and those who read this novel, about a Romanian officer in the Austro-Hungarian Army hanged for espionage and desertion, end up shocked by the enormity of matter.

Trying to sum up twentieth century Hungarian history in Romanian is beyond challenging but, despite my reservations, the fact is that I sat an exam to study Hungarian at university and if I can't handle this and explain the situation then who can? They call my bluff, pour me a glass of brandy and then another, of course I haven't yet read the recently published *History of Transylvania*, though I'd quite like to, I keep coming up with woolly answers such as that I haven't been home for a long time, Arad is in this country, what could I possibly know that they don't, seeing that I'm an ordinary soldier and they are officers. What happened in 1956, the company commander asks and expects a straight answer, from man to man. They aren't into the otherwise interesting ancient history or Finno-Ugric relations but the here and now, and I can't gauge whether they are testing or provoking me. I tell them everything I know, though it's hard to recall what I must have pieced together from information gleaned from Radio Free Europe and my father's comments. For a short while, I'm the embodiment of Hungarian freedom fighting, *bine profesore*—well done, profes-sor—the sergeant says with flushed cheeks, we have come round and continue drinking together, and when they finally let me go, he warns me not to tell anyone about his. From then on, they invite me for regular chats, one of the lieutenants with an alcohol problem is particularly preoccupied with Hungarian culture and has read every single Jókai and Mikszáth novel available in Romanian. I'm asked to discuss *A kőszívűember fiai* [The heartless man's sons], the 1848 Revolution, the Reformation, he's interested in all sorts of things including Camus, his favourite author whom he read in French, he's incredibly cultured, judging by his library that I can see when we take him home after he passes out while drinking.

Next, they send me on a five-day leave to find out what's going on in Hungary, and they beg me not to tell anyone, not even at home, it's a proper secret mission but I should bring back some brandy anyway. Around this time, a few of my friends decide not to return from Hungary and this takes place with the tacit agreement of the Hungarian authorities, some people have run as far as Vienna or Munich. Having said that, I've had no idea that those classmates of mine from Arad have already moved abroad. Why have you come back, the company commander asks without any negativity, he's simply curious, what I don't understand is how come he doesn't grasp that I simply want to live in Transylvania and don't find Romania the worst place to live in the world. The same thing will happen here, he said thoughtfully while drinking my father's brandy, by then I was certain that in 1956 there was a revolution in Hungary. We were unsure whether we should fear or rejoice at the idea of a potential revolution here, I, for one, was afraid that nothing would happen at all.

On 15 November 1987, I'm just finishing my shift at the watchpost at dawn when we are taken to vote, I have no clue what's going on and couldn't care less, we are always on duty, I only manage to sleep longer than five hours once a week, and this makes people really stroppy and edgy before turning them into total zombies. I'd like to have some rest before breakfast, this hour before my next shift would be worth its weight in gold, but there's a call from the office about a red alert and everybody must be woken up. We are old hands now, they should really leave us alone, it's probably our last time on sentry duty and the world should really manage without us for these two days, but goddamit, it doesn't! We are told to double the watchmen on the morning shift, the watchtower can barely accommodate one person let alone two, then they dish out all sixty cartridges, I've never laid hands on this many, the two nearly full magazines pull my belt down, it's raining and it's cold, and the most we can muster is swear at yet another idiot who had come up with all this. The whole town is quiet, the watchtower is overlooking the shunting yard, beyond the rail tracks there is a military cemetery with more than ten thousand First World War victims in a mausoleum, we once peeked through the tiny iron window and saw a large pile of bones in a giant pit, clearly an exhumed mass grave. There's an Orthodox church in the cemetery where they hold services lasting all morning, old women lighting candles. We tend to leave our plain clothes there so we can go to town incognito, needless to say, such acts are strictly forbidden.

Officers arrive shortly, one after the other, we have to get the emergency vehicle ready, its battery is flat, so we give it a good push but after ten minutes it runs out of fuel, luckily the captain of the watch, a major, is a smart and hardened guy and doesn't make a fuss but takes action. He tells us that something has gone terribly wrong, and his face looks more careworn than ever, he doesn't know exactly what's happening but takes a seat on his bed in his room, asks for a cigarette and says in a quiet voice: nobody loads their gun, absolutely no one. We are on total alert but there's no wailing siren sound or trumpeting, this often happens at night, but now the squads are called out one after the other. There's silence, the usual shouting, clattering of arms and trampling seem rather muffled, people are standing for hours in the yard fully kitted out for a long march, and this waiting and uncertainty is by far the worst.

By the next afternoon, everybody knows that there was an anti-regime demonstration in Brassó. It's strictly forbidden to bring radios to the base, but of course some people still do and despite the jamming, Radio Free Europe can reach us, as it does the entire world. What will happen if they order us to shoot at the crowd, somebody asks and there's no response, because anyone who had participated at sharp shooting practice knows that after the command 'fire', there's a short silence but then somebody is bound to pull the trigger. This time, there are no crowds and nothing happens. It seems to me now that on the night when we were watching the express train from Kiev from the watchtower, I knew exactly that this army had no other point than repress any movement that could overthrow the regime. I had no other desire than to get rid of this gun for good, I felt dreadfully tired and bored of all this, not to say afraid, because in all honesty everybody was afraid. We had two months left, nothing of any note happened, or rather the same nonsensical events took place all the time, which could be developed into anecdotes despite being run of the mill army stories and were only special because they happened to me. I spent my second Christmas and New Year's Eve at the army base, life goes on without me, who needs festivities, I mused as all I wanted was to be left alone. I was twenty, felt very old, my mind laden with the taste and memory of completely pointless experiences. To this day, more than twenty years on, I picture myself as a soldier every time I have a bad dream, a gun is hanging down my neck and I'm taking part in some nebulous action, with the odd shooting thrown in, which usually means that I'm in a really poor mental health.

It's getting harder and harder to pin down what I actually did during these sixteen months of my life, but it's crystal clear that there's no way I could continue where I had left it when I was drafted in. Whenever I'm reading Ottlik, I think that I saw all this from a close-up of myself, and I envy those literati who manage to read the *School at the Frontier* as civilians. Yet we know that there's no such thing as civilians, there are only people who pretend to be civilians when they don't understand what they don't want to understand. Modern Europe has developed according to the logic of armies, without armies none of these would exist: plum dumplings, self-governing Székely village, Napoleonic Code, sailing and air traffic, Suez and Panama, Teflon and Zepter dishes, emergency medical intervention. There would be no nation, pentathlon and gymnastics, logistics, internet, civil service, football, pacifism and political compromise advocated by the Peace Party since civilians cannot be civil because what would then be their point of reference? Back then, we don't yet realize that there is something worse than regular armies, which is the war of irregular armies, and this will constitute the next era in world history.

XIX

And What Else?

You're looking good, my mother told me when she took me to the railway station for the last time and I already had my civilian clothes in a rucksack. Yes, I am, I thought, I had a brand-new winter outfit and new boots, which I'd quickly exchange for a worn-out pair. As a rule of thumb, women aren't into soldiers but they quite like uniforms, and they have a point—what can one expect from someone who doesn't even own a decent outfit? When I returned home in January 1988, I had nothing and felt like nobody. I sent my rather time-worn suitcase in the post and I got off the train clutching a French grammar book, which I had with me all along, thinking that in case I had the time and energy, I'd leaf through it in order to prevent forgetting everything. But I did forget regardless.

Before we boarded our train, we had dinner at the same station hotel where we spent a night in the autumn of 1986, hoping to sleep but failed. Something wasn't quite right this time either, we ate all eight chicken escalopes that we ordered but this wasn't enough, so we wanted some marine fish as that was the only thing they had, and by the time that was ready, they ran out of bread, so somebody ordered champagne! We got totally hammered, missed every possible train and since the restaurant also closed, we headed to the cemetery to serenade the heroes and our mates who'd continue in the service. I can barely recall anything except that we had to change trains several times because we'd always miss our connection, it was night, then day, and despite usually having an idea where I happened to be, this seemed like a totally pointless journey without any sense of freedom on the horizon. We'd keep finding further bottles of Silvania champagne, I'd keep hanging on to my French grammar book in its green plastic cover, taking great care of it and occasionally getting the creeps that I had lost it. Gradually, there were fewer and fewer of us, the silences getting longer and longer, and by the time we got off the train, we were no longer friends and wouldn't even write to one another, let alone meet again. I was sitting at the railway station in Arad on my own, with a hangover and, while waiting for my connection, I started leafing through the grammar book. Back then, I still had the letters of my sometime love, but this time I wasn't reading those, as opposed to so many times when I craved an intelligent word or some warmth. Instead, I was looking at the sequence of tenses, the so-called *concordance*, and realized in no time that I had forgotten the French declination and what's more, I couldn't even read, neither in French nor in Hungarian, after about ten lines I'd lose concentration, I wasn't even following the lines, my mind was entirely elsewhere, only god knows where.

This was a frightening and shameful state because it didn't go away once I recovered from my hangover. My father managed to arrange for a few months of unpaid leave from the cannery where I had worked before being drafted into the army, I had almost six months until the university entrance exam, but in vain did I leaf through my books and notes, week after week and month after month all I could think was that I'd forgotten everything in a complete brainwash. Doamna Vulpescu had indeed aged as she had said, or I hadn't seen her without makeup before. Her face, neck and hands were covered in fine lines, but she was really pleased to see me and said that I hadn't forgotten anything, people wouldn't forget but at times it was difficult for them to conjure things up. She said that I should rest and go hiking and just read what I enjoyed. I wasn't really interested in anything then, I was tired and felt let down because I didn't get the impression of being released from the barracks but rather that the entire world was a barrack, and that out here, we'd repeat, out of our own will, the same absurd things that we had executed on command in there. Doamna Vulpescu was also quite bitter, there was no heating in her home that winter, she'd have to wear all her clothes at once and even move into the Astoria Hotel because some mice had set up camp in her larder. I'm old and hysterical, she'd say, and her husband who was a doctor and vet failed to catch the mice and after a few days, doamna Vulpescu was sent packing from the hotel. After that, we'd have our lessons in cafeterias, once on the banks of the river Maros walking for at least ten kilometres, she was so edgy she'd even cry at times. She and her husband either divorced that year or the next, I couldn't recall.

I often had nightmares and in case I spotted some officers on the street, I made a big detour, despite knowing that I was wearing plain clothes, my arm would swing forward in readiness to salute and I often had to hold myself back. I carried an umbrella with me the whole spring, this hadn't happened to me before or after, but I was so affected by rain in the army that for a while I genuinely feared it and was repulsed by it. Now I realize that one doesn't need war to grind people down, I for one, can always be treated as a soldier. These days, when there are more and more men whose only experience of the army is mediated by films, I feel the same difference I used to notice between those who passed their

Baccalaureate and who stopped studying after year eight or ten: the lack of a shared experience, this is neither good nor bad, it's simply a factor of social division and it's best for everyone if this stays in place and if one's army knowledge is never needed to be used for real.

My feeling is that it's not good to return as an adult to the scene of one's childhood. It now felt as if this was no longer me, in vain did I wander the thickets, the woods, the floodplains of the Körös, everything had become strange and distant as if I was watching it through a flow of water while blinking. I had to realize that I had left this place at the age of fourteen never to return except for weekends and holidays, later I found myself sent home, and although it didn't suit me when I was far away, I didn't know anyone here and this didn't even bother me. The hardest task was to get on with my parents because in their eyes I was still a fourteen-year-old child, in vain did I insist that all sorts of adventures had happened to me in the meantime, I failed to translate this into their language seeing that, for me, they also stayed put in the place I had left behindall this time ago.

By that time, around March or so, French grammar and Antal Szerb had started to come back to me, I noticed that there was nobody I could talk about stuff that had a defining importance to me, the young reporters had scattered in the world, some went to Germany, others to Israel, and nothing was like it used to be, least of all myself. Like any former soldier, I was a precocious adult, and I had a vague inkling that I should start standing on my own feet, but how? Things, sentences, poems, fragments of texts and speech started to emerge in my memory like smoke scattering about in the mountains, but as soon as everything got cleared up, I was no longer facing the same haze and confusion as two years earlier.

There were questions and problems without answers and solutions, it was still unclear whether this was only down to me, but I felt that I had to get to the bottom of this and ensure that no veil would conceal reality from me. I also knew by then how easy it was to die.

It's around April or early May when I sense that I'm finally in possession of my mental faculties again, I can read, take notes, I always carry a pile of books from Arad and then from Kolozsvár, where I send my papers to an old lady who says it's okay but I should write more succinctly. I feel like a sponge again and this is great, akin to the feeling when after running twenty kilometres it's easy to move and walk, and if I could articulate the thoughts that crop up in my mind in such situations, I'd be a proper writer, but I can't. I had no intention of becoming a writer then, I haven't even written any decent letters yet. My worst memory of this era is the return of my stammer that I have almost forgotten about, because we rarely spoke Hungarian in the army and hence nobody noticed, I thought I'd got over it as they had promised, after all I got over so many other things. I'm of course sensitive but not weak or neurotic or easily tired, my hand has never been shaky while holding a gun or a grenade, I'm capable of confronting anyone if need be, and I can get out of harm's way, I'm an adult, but still. I decide then that I won't bother with stuff that was meant to be, I won't look into it, won't try to solve it or work it off, fine, I won't be a teacher, actor, TV presenter or priest. It's this simple, I often think, though I do know that it isn't.

What's university like, I ask my one-time love interest who keeps moaning about the mandatory military service for girls, they hate it a lot more than I ever did. They are about to go on shooting practice, so I show off a little and advise them not to worry about much else apart from holding the gun against their shoulder, as a Kalasnyikov can easily break the collarbone. University sucks, she says, but I refuse to believe her and ignore the reasons she brings up, despite these being accurate, precise and to the point. Easy for you to talk like this, I muse. We go for a beer even though it tastes horrible, in those days it always does, but for some reason this time together is important and I can recall every single sentence and gesture of hers, to say nothing of her gaze. At first, she was just a girl with whom I exchanged a few clever letters or at least I tried to be a cleverclog, but over the years or rather over epoch-making changes, she has turned into an amazing woman, straightforward, direct, intelligent who's also quite strong and abrupt. I can feel that she sees straight through me yet is kind and considerate, she takes me seriously and there's something unsettling in her being, a sort of restlessness, an exciting vibration, she can listen to me like no one else and I take this as an ultimate accolade. It's great to be around her, though she's out of my league, just like any other woman I might fancy. I was twenty and knew absolutely nothing about women, this was at least as awful as my stammer, it was the darkest burn, and since I had no idea about women, I also knew next to nothing about myself. I was dying to be loved but didn't know how to communicate this desire, and this made me even lonelier.

Since I didn't get a place at university that year either, I had no choice but start work at the cannery in my hometown. I was a newbie, yet again at the very bottom of the scale, displaying the calm of seasoned beginners and the bitterness of eternal losers, I knew what to expect and, as a result, I saved myself any potential disappointment. In the industrial hierarchy of our town, this place was at the lowest level, only agriculture was even lower, yet compared to the Bărăgan or the abattoir in Buzău this was a posh place, despite the dreadful stench and the rats. I'll refrain from conjuring up images of *putrefactio mundi*, but the only major problem with the food industry is that it's an industry and not a kitchen or larder. Our factory was exporting most of its products to the Democratic Republic of Germany and Poland, so I could lay my claims at having contributed to the collapse of socialism and the fall of the Berlin Wall. Work itself or the motley crew I was part of wasn't the main issue, I was used to these, but I had issues with the hopelessness of the situation and with realizing that the factory could keep making tins until Judgement Day and there would still be hungry mouths for whom this was good enough, and that there was no such thing as bad food, only people who hadn't been starving long enough. Let's hope it won't get any worse, people would say, and we knew that it would actually get worse. The reverse of this was also true: the worse, the better, this whole thing would collapse anyway, so why not just get over it.

For me, a tin of Hungarian ratatouille is the best way of visualizing Romania at this point. I know how it was made and of what ingredients, so it should be thrown out as it's essentially hazardous waste or scrapings, but we warm it up and eat with some grilled bacon or polenta and even find it yummy. We would have eaten this in Russia, I hear my grandfather's voice and I'm convinced that we couldn't even come up with a concoction bad enough for us not to eat it. I've been living this life for six years and this is me, take it or leave it, the end result of the dorm, the barracks, the canteen, the industrial zone, I keep reading all sorts all along these years, but the two worlds are completely disjointed, I'm not cut out for this line of work and the school that has protected me so far has slowly melted in my mouth like a piece of menthol sweet. One has to live in the real world, my mother insists, though my father says nothing.

This real world is the ratatouille made for the domestic market, known as *ghiveci*, somehow it has turned out exceptionally good so we keep wolfing it down. Overripe tomatoes, peppers and onions form an incredibly tasty mix, it's an absolute orgy of flavours that just happened to come together that particular night for no reason, so the women working at the factory alert us that this batch is exceptional. We are all marvelling at this and keep eating as much as we can, first with some bread and then on its own, stuffing ourselves. Twenty tons have been made, which we soon put into jars, label and the whole lot vanishes in a railway carriage in no time. We know that such tasty ratatouille will never be made here again, it feels as if this was our last summer after the end of the world, there will be no more light, warmth or wasps as we know it, this overripe quality will not happen again and after the brilliance vanishes forever, all we are left with is the stench. In vain are we trying to stock up and hide the odd jar here and there in the factory, we'll soon open these as we find them, but this will lead to disappointment because the flavours of that summer cannot be preserved, and further down the line all we can recall is that once there was something, something good, but nobody knows what exactly.

An even more real aspect of the real is a Gipsy girl who falls in love with me, or at least throws herself at me. I'm working on the tar roof of the factory hall, trying to fix the closing mechanism of the airing vent. The sun is shining, I'm sweaty, I'm always asked to do such pointless jobs as I'm not needed in the workshop, the general opinion is that I'm no good at anything, but then somebody just bursts out screaming that I should help them at once, where the fuck have I been all this time? Suddenly, a skinny naked woman emerges from behind the gridiron traverse that I'm about to start hammering, she removes her sunglasses, blinking like a cobra. Fuck you in the mouth, she says angrily with the typical obscenity of Gipsy women when they are trying to cover up but realize mid-sentence that they overshot the target, essentially meaning that I could let out an offhand smile. It turns out I have no cigarettes or water, so I offer to bring some, I'd quite like to make tracks, as I've never seen a naked woman from such close-up, especially not in broad daylight and on the roof of the factory hall, this whole business is very awkward. I like being watched, she says and leans back on the corrugated cardboard, showing me the origin of the world. So I watch. You haven't fucked yet, have you, she says in a mockingly condescending voice. Holy shit, you have such lovely eyes. Yeah, well . . .

Love, sex, stammer. *Flowers for Algernon, One Flew Over the Cuckoo's Nest.* This Gipsy girl didn't teach me bodily love, only showed me that it was something that basically ran itself or it could do so anyway. Her body was smelly, stinking of tobacco, and she was skinny and wild like a cat, also aggressive, crass and often talking in Romani which I didn't understand, but she reassured me that this was a sign that she enjoyed it. At night, by the time the agitation in the factory had wound down a little, she knocked on the stainless steel pipe of the cooking tower and I tapped it back, she came up and threw herself at me like a vulture, without saying a word. The whole act didn't last long, within a few minutes she turned from uppity and arrogant bitch into somebody that should have been loved, her eyes were begging but I didn't get this, my body wasn't always on board, either, it had plenty of glitches and we usually had to rush. She asked me to flee to the Serbs or the

Hungarians with her, but I didn't want to because I was afraid of her, I wasn't yet familiar with this aspect of life while she was already past everything, at times she'd cry but couldn't explain why. When she stopped coming to work, I missed her a lot. She was a woman who got round my inhibitions really quickly and easily, and by the time I came to myself we have already gotten high, there was no courting or poetry, she did what she wanted with me and knew exactly what she needed, I didn't, but at least I should have let it happen. In novels, this is the initiation stage, after which the hero gains full knowledge of secrets, but this isn't a novel and I wasn't a hero despite wanting to be one, all that came out of this was that I carried on with all my inhibitions. My world was hopelessly in tatters, seeing that whatever I would have been able to talk about was declared non-existent on a daily basis, and what did exist, I was unable to discuss. Still, there is a reality beyond language, in which sex and stammering are sitting side by side within me and playing chess, a bit like Satan and God. The problem is that God always wins. This Gipsy girl didn't teach me bodily love, only showed me that it was something that basically ran itself or it could do so anyway. Her body was smelly, stinking of tobacco, and she was skinny and wild like a cat, also aggressive, crass and often talking in Romani which I didn't understand, but she reassured me that this was a sign that she enjoyed it.

I started attending church in the Spring of 1989, because the Communist Party secretary at work tried to make me join the party. I told her that I couldn't join because of my religious oath, I hated the idea that somebody would get me on Sundays because this or that wasn't working at the factory. We lived close to the factory and by this point, several people took the view that I could become a pretty good mechanic if only I tried a bit harder.

Following my refusal, the woman threatened me that if I didn't join the party I could be drafted into the army and taken to the Danube Canal, but I knew that they couldn't conscript me within the next two years. This was the law according to doamna Vulpescu, I was no longer taking lessons with her but she had lent me all six volumes of Lagard & Michard so I could read them in French, I was also translating all sorts of other texts from Romanian to French and the other way round. In the evenings, I'd read Mircea Eliade's major history of religions, as I managed to lay hands on it at last. Finally, someone has made the point that there was such thing as god, in at least four thousand guises, if not more. I also found a Heidegger volume, in Romanian, but I didn't get very far with this, I only remember a few passages where the translator pointed out in the footnotes that these sections were untranslatable into Romanian. So I told the Party secretary that I'm definitely not joining: *categoric nu*. This felt like scoring a penalty once the goalkeeper is already out of the picture, for a short while I thought I was actually opposing the system. The woman begged me saying that her job was on the line, this would make no actual difference to anything, and she was right, but I thought that it did. Joining the Communist Party in the Summer of 1989 would have been quite pathetic.

Most of the time there would be me and about ten elderly women at church. I get the shivers to this day whenever I hear *Lord Our Hope*, because the women had beautiful voices but when I joined in . . . This sentence cannot be continued, but I usually thought of my hysterical music teacher who was a good-looking woman, seeing that even the preacher in Barót mentioned that when we sing, we praise the Lord twice, firstly with the lyrics and secondly with the tunes, well I'm such a double act too. As a matter of fact, this church-going period turned out a bit of a joke and I gave up on it fairly quickly, I realized that I wasn't an opponent of the regime just making a moot point, and if God saw this, he'd dismiss it with a wave of the hand. By this stage, I had a lover with whom I had a tempestuous relationship in which sex, stammering, God, Satan and the Communist Party were all together. I sent one of my short stories to a paper called *Ifjúmunkás* [Young worker] because as a publication for young adult readers, it looked like the only avenue open for submissions. My aim wasn't to get necessarily published but to hear whether my writing was any good. Lazics, the editor, said it was good. In those days, I had a subscription to various Transylvanian publications but they all featured the Golden Calf, I barely managed to find the odd text that I could actually enjoy reading, so most ended up in the fire, even the literary weekly *Utunk* [Our journey], though I was always happy to find it in the post box because that meant that it hasn't been discontinued.

Every so often, I'd run off to Kolozsvár and, making use of a borrowed reader's card, sit in the open access area in the Library of the Academy's reading room. This experience can best be compared to the internet, and if I didn't understand something, I simply took a lexicon from the shelf and leafed through it until I got weary of it. Any book could be consulted, and, more often than not, I completely lost my sense of time, leafing through the pages of books for hours on end, this must be freedom, I mused usually in hindsight. Around this time, rumour had it that the cross on top of Saint Michael's Church had been exchanged one night, some people even seemed to remember the sound of the helicopter apparently necessary to reach the cross made of pure gold. This was a really scary perspective, and despite it being completely unrealistic from a technical point of view, it fuelled the imagination, yes, anything was possible around here and I could sense that we were all losing our minds. I had visions of King Matthias getting off his plinth and ambling along or walking or trotting away. As I was sitting in the main square one day, perhaps waiting for someone who didn't turn up and enjoying the peace and quiet in the twilight, I suddenly seemed to picture the outline of the statue moving slightly, so I walked over and said in a half-aloud voice, my king, but before I knew it, a policeman carded me and gave me a short shrift: *dispari de aici, mă*—get the hell out of here!

From a dramaturgical point of view, it would be fitting if this identity check—the last of the era, if I'm not mistaken—had preceded the night when a mate and I slipped over the green border to the free Hungary. Yet this could have only happened in Autumn 1988, after the Gipsy girl vanished and I thought I could find her in the village where we cycled to attend a ball, perhaps she only existed in my imagination, though she must have been real if I was looking for her. It would be great if I was able to claim that we could see the lights of Geszt, considering that Péter Esterházy documented that this establishment was at only 870 metres from the Hungarian–Romanian border (see *Harmonia Caelestis*), but we were actually somewhere further south, I was a cartographer in the army, and although this didn't mean much, I was actually rather good at orienteering. What really mattered though was that we were advancing on the estate of the 'old madman from Geszt' (Endre Ady), possibly heading towards freedom. I was fascinated by the Ellenzéki Kerekasztal (Opposition Roundtable, the meeting forum of politicians opposing the regime in Hungary from within the system), in my view they had earned the right to organize it, but in my father's, they were simply granted permission. It makes no real difference in fact, and I'm attracted to this like butterflies to the light as this is a rather alluring comparison seeing that there is no street lighting in Romania at that point, whereas the sky above Hungary is like the Milky Way shining over the mountains.

The fact of the matter was that we were sobering up, alcohol had cleared out of our system, it was raining, dogs were barking, there were no border guards on either the Romanian or the Hungarian side, perhaps we were on the actual borderland or even beyond it considering that the soil looked different, possibly because it had been ploughed and harrowed much more often. And then, all of a sudden, my mate said in a half-loud voice: fuck this mud! I should have replied, why, what else were we trotting in so far? I felt like strangling him to make him shut up. I would have of course wanted to be with the Gipsy girl who showed me the origin of the world when I bumped into her on the roof, or perhaps I should have remembered that the world had an origin, on the very roof of that factory, or perhaps that Kolozsvár itself is a cunt. So we went back to the paved area, our bikes were still there, and just pedalled home, hi-vis jackets were not compulsory back then, so nobody could see where we had been hanging out.

The week when my first short story appeared in *Ifjúmunkás*, I also found out that I was offered a place at university, I got in, as we'd put it. I'm no longer sure what I felt then, perhaps that anything that had happened to me until then would lose its importance, just as all the struggles of running a marathon would be secondary once one crossed the finish line. The workshop had suddenly come to life, everybody wanted to leave but there was nowhere to go. I was celebrated like a hero, I'd be the first to leave, at a time when I almost started to feel at home and was on my way to become a skilled worker. At times, I thought this ambition would satisfy me, seeing that a good mechanic would always be in demand, or perhaps I was just tired, and sooner or later, one was likely to get used to drifting about. But as my unrequited love put it, or perhaps she didn't only I thought that she did, I had just about reached the waterline. For reasons impossible to grasp, that year I applied for a distance learning course, perhaps because I thought that getting in would be easier there, but by then there were so many veterans on the scene that we had the highest grades and I was the last one to get in. This meant that I had to carry on holding down a day job, with the added twist of occasionally turning up for exams at Kolozsvár. This whole thing was a farce, since by then the East Germans had got fed up with Romanian tinned food and swamped Hungary, they had to be allowed out because this many Germans couldn't be contained in one place, and anyway, what would be the point of that?

Approximately where we once wanted to cross the border but turned back because of Kolozsvár or the call of the Gipsy girl's rosy flesh, being afraid and cold and abandoned by alcohol in the mud, the Romanian border guards shot a boy dead, at a place from where one could already see Hungary. He had come from Máramaros to seek work, just as people would have regularly done so for the last hundred years. They shouted at him but he failed to stop, heading instead towards the border because he had seen some stables in the distance, he then started to run thinking that the soldiers were drunk and the soldiers also ran for a while before they shot him, in broad daylight and in accordance with the shoot-to-kill policy. We heard about this incident from a border guard officer while fixing his car at our workshop, and he complained that his nerves could no longer cope with this state of war. The army was still a vivid memory for me back then, and although I had never had to shoot at a living target, I could understand the absurdity of the situation, to say nothing of the fact that this wasn't the only horror story in our lives.

I think this was the period when I started to be afraid, but not in the sense of fearing for my life. By then, more than enough situations had demonstrated that there was such a thing as providence and, that there was God too. Yet this was something different, dark, cold, wet and sour like the blade of the knife with a silver handle, which I knew was in fact only nickel, if it touched my lips it didn't cut it but under the mucous membrane, I could feel the pulsation of the blood about to spurt out. It was a collective fear that nobody could escape because fear feeds on what we cannot openly tell one another, such as that we are all well and truly afraid. I was afraid, but the moment I managed to admit this to myself, I was already less afraid than before. I knew that as far I was concerned, the Ceaușescu-regime was over, this is why I turned back from the borderland, because I knew it was over. One should do something, I often said to myself, but for a very long time, nothing came to my mind because I thought that the world had to be in a particular way, and it was hard for me to grasp that, in fact, the world had to be reinvented on a daily basis. Nothing exists as a matter of course, and those who are unable to come up with something liveable and tolerable on this side of the sea of mud, are wasting their time going to the other, because they'll come across the same issues, or at least there's no need for big dramas such as our night-time adventure, seeing that they don't even have enough substance for a short story.

Having said that, this episode, for instance, is rather good: 'One October evening, after a long day of working, suffering and screaming, I climbed on top of the cooking tower and leaned my back against the warm iron pipes, it was an unpleasant and cold evening and I just kept staring at the Western horizon where I could see the lights of Gyula, we had no street lighting, we had nothing, while there, under the multitude of arc lights tearing open the night sky, there lied a free country, Hungary. Now it seems to me that I thought of the writer Péter Esterházy whose work I hadn't yet read but who lived on the other side and used to appear on TV quite often, I also thought that if I made it across the green border, the Hungarians wouldn't send me back, seeing that they didn't do that with many of my friends, either. I also thought, and in hindsight this is crystal clear, that I wanted to live in Transylvania, which meant that I had to look towards the darkness, because darkness isn't worse than light, only different.'

It was this otherness that I wanted to write about in my novel which ended up as this work, but I had to realize that there was no otherness, or rather that this otherness wasn't some sort of substance but a series of eventualities edited by myself. We could only talk about otherness if I was able to invent it step by step, sentence by sentence, because the past didn't exist as a matter of course, despite having been fleshed out with the contribution of my grandfathers and parents, my role would have been to deal with the future, so that it wasn't just different but, naturally, also better. I owed myself an insight into urban Transylvania, because I was quite fed up with this wildness, imperfection and neglect, and despite loving them so much, I realized that they'd lead absolutely nowhere. My one-time unrequited love also advised me to get over this once and for all, grow up and give up faffing about, re-read *School at the Frontier*, but this time really carefully, make up with my father and mother because they'd never change, trim by beard rather than shave it all off, learn French and visit Paris, and talk about all those things we didn't want to talk about, because that was also part of the real. In fact, the real was always the very sentence I had just formulated, and by the time I'd written it down, this claim would no longer be valid, no matter how many times I'd rephrase the whole thing.

I arrived at Kolozsvár on 15 January 1990 as a full-time student, carrying my metal frame backpack and sporting wild hair and a freshly grown beard, I really looked like a geologist or a student of Hungarian. I have no idea whether I actually greeted King Matthias on this occasion, as a good subject should have done, but in case I did, he most probably nodded back as he had done many times thereafter when we exchanged glances. What would you like to research, Éva Cs. Gyimesi asked at our first meeting, she recognized me since she'd keep track of everyone in the field. I told her that I'd probably write a book. About what, she quizzed me, and I blurted out that it would naturally be about this whole thing. She must have seen plenty of arrogant students, so I wasn't particularly conspicuous. She urged me to get on with the writing, and we had many conversations over the years, though not quite enough. From this point onwards, a new world had opened up for me, an entirely new era as it were. I may even talk about it one day. Half of my life's work is already out on the shelves. And in case anybody wondered whether that was all, I could even say, yes. But.

TRANSLATOR'S NOTES

PAGE 1 | **'Arad'**—Place names are used in their Hungarian version throughout the book, unless there is an established English variant. Please consult the Index of Place Names for Romanian (and wherever relevant, German) equivalents.

PAGE 1 | The *Toldi* trilogy is an epic poem written by Hungarian Romantic poet János Arany. It was inspired by the legendary Miklós Toldi, who served in the Hungarian King Louis the Great's army in the fourteenth century. **János Arany** (1817–1882) was born in Szalonta (Romanian: *Salonta*), not far from Arad, and is considered one of the most important figures in Hungarian literary history.

PAGE 3 | **Nicolae Ceauşescu** (1918–1989) was a Communist official, leader of the Romanian Communist Party from 1965 and President of Romania from 1974, until he was overthrown and executed in an anti-government civil unrest in December 1989, known as the Romanian Revolution.

PAGE 5 | **Béla Markó** (b. 1951) is a Hungarian politician and writer from Romania, former leader of the Democratic Union of Hungarians in Romania (1993–2011), Deputy Prime Minister (2009–2012). After withdrawing from politics, Markó returned to an illustrious literary career.

PAGE 6 | **Székelys** (also known as *Szeklers*, Romanian: *secui*, German: *Szekler*) identify as a subgroup of Hungarian people living mostly in Székely Land (Hungarian: *Székelyföld*, Romanian: *Ţinutul Secuiesc*) in Romania.

PAGE 14 | **Collectivization** was a policy of forced consolidation of individual peasant households into collective farms, initially carried out by the Soviet government in the late 1920s and early 1930s, and rolled out in most countries of the Eastern Bloc after 1945.

PAGE 16 | **Péter Esterházy** (1950–2016) was a leading figure of contemporary Hungarian literature. His books, written in a uniquely postmodernist style, are an outstanding contribution to post-war European literature.

PAGE 17 | **György Dragomán** (b. 1973) is a Hungarian author and literary translator. His best-known novel, *A fehér király* [The white king] (2005) has been translated into several dozen languages and adapted for the screen. Vida mentions the novel *A máglya*, translated into English by Ottilie Mulzet as *The Bone Fire* (HarperVia, 2021).

PAGE 23 | **Hungarian (Magyar) Autonomous Region** (1952–1960) (Romanian: *Regiunea Autonomă Maghiară*, Hungarian: *Magyar Autonóm Tartomány*) and the **Mureş-Magyar Autonomous Region** (1960–1968) were autonomous regions in the People's Republic of Romania. They were created following a Soviet-style administrative and territorial division, and the region encompassed about a third of Romania's Hungarians. In practice, the region's status differed in no way from that of the other regions, it did not enjoy much autonomy and the State Council of the Autonomous Region was merely a façade.

PAGE 26 | **Schrammelmusik** is a style of Viennese folk music originating in the late 19th century.

PAGE 27 | **Attila József** (1905–1937) was a major Hungarian poet. Hailed during the communist era as Hungary's great 'proletarian poet', his life, personality and works are now being re-evaluated in the light of his experimentation with modernism and psychoanalysis.

PAGE 28 | **István Bocskai** (1557–1606) was Prince of Transylvania and Hungary from 1605 to 1606.

PAGE 28 | **'Székely himnusz'** or **'Székely Anthem'** is a 1921 poem adopted by the Székely National Council as the anthem of Székely Land. It symbolizes protest against tyranny and oppression, and was banned in communist Romania.

PAGE 29 | **Agricultural cooperative**, also known as state agricultural cooperative—*cooperativa agricola de stat* (Romanian), *termelőszövetkezet* (Hungarian)—was a form of organizing small, privately owned agricultural holdings into larger, state-controlled units, as part of the Soviet model of collectivization.

PAGE 34 | **Securitate** (Romanian for *Security*) was the popular term for the *Departamentul Securității Statului* (Department of State

Security), the secret police agency of the Socialist Republic of Romania. Under Ceaușescu, the Securitate was one of the most brutal secret police forces in the world, responsible for the arrests, torture and deaths of thousands of people.

PAGE 37 | **Domokos Szilágyi** (1938–1976) was a poet, translator and literary historian, considered as one of the most important voices in post-war Transylvanian–Hungarian poetry. His work has been particularly influential on Vida's generation, reaching adulthood just before the 1989 regime change.

PAGE 37 | **Ádám Bodor** (b.1936) is an award-winning Hungarian author of Transylvanian origin. Several of his works have been adapted to film and translated into English.

PAGE 37 | **Pál Bodor** (1930–2017) was a Hungarian poet, editor, TV personality. In 1970s Transylvania, he was best known as editor of the Romanian State Television's Hungarian broadcasts.

PAGE 37-38 | **András Sütő** (1927–2006) was a widely respected Hungarian writer from Romania, with a career spanning short fiction, satire and historical drama. *Egy lócsiszár virágvasárnapja* [**The Palm Sunday of a horse dealer**] was one of his best-known dramatic works, while *Anyám könnyű álmot igér* [**Mother assures me of gentle dreams**] was a succesful memoir. Due to his dissent against the Ceaușescu regime, Sütő's works were banned in the 1980s.

PAGE 37 | **Hanna Honthy** (1893–1978) was a Hungarian opera singer and actress, critically acclaimed for her voice and acting talent.

PAGE 37 | *Csárdáskirálynő* (German: *Die Csárdásfürstin*) [**The Csárdás princess**] a popular operetta by Emmerich Kálmán, libretto by Leo Stein and Bela Jenbach. It premiered in Vienna in 1915.

PAGE 38 | **Gyula Illyés** (1902–1983) was a Hungarian poet and novelist, and a key representative of the populist movement in literature. He spoke up for the oppressed peasant class, as visible in *Puszták népe* (*People of the Puszta* [George F. Cushing trans.] [Corvina, 1987]), 1936. In November 1956, he published his famous poem on the Hungarian Revolution, which was banned from re-publication in Hungary until 1986: 'One sentence on tyranny'.

PAGE 38 | **János Kádár** (1912–1989) was a Hungarian communist leader and the General Secretary of the Hungarian Socialist Workers' Party, presiding over the country from 1956 until 1988. **Kádár-era**—As a result of the relatively high standard of living, Hungary was generally considered as one of the better countries to live in Eastern Europe during the Cold War.

PAGE 39 | *The Citadel* by A. J. Cronin was one of the most popular works of literature circulating in Transylvania in the late 1970s and 1980s, brought out in paperback by the only Hungarian publisher at the time (Kriterion). Most families would have owned a copy.

PAGE 39 | **Sándor Reményik** (1890–1941) was a Hungarian poet from Transylvania, active in the interwar period.

PAGE 39 | **Péter Nádas** (born 1942) is a Hungarian writer, playwright, and essayist known for his detailed surrealist tales and prose poems that often braid points of view or moments in time.

PAGE 40 | **Éva Cs. Gyimesi** (1945-2011) was a Hungarian linguist, literary historian and head of the Hungarian department at the Babeş–Bolyai University, where Vida also studied. She mentored generations of students, writers, literary critics and cultural commentators. She was a well-known figure in the anticommunist opposition prior to 1989.

PAGE 40 | *Ellenpontok* [Counterpoints] (Romanian: *Contrapuncte*) was a Hungarian-language Samizdat publication that spoke out against the communist regime and the oppression of the Hungarian minority in Transylvania. It appeared in Nagyvárad in 1982, and the Securitate persecuted and arrested many of its contributors.

PAGE 46 | *Harmonia Caelestis* [Celestial harmonies] and *Egy családregény vége* [The end of a family story] are two of the most iconic Hungarian novels of the twentieth century, both dealing with the complex relationship between fathers and sons, and authored by the most influential voices in contemporary Hungarian fiction. Vida, being a generation younger, thus also situates his own novel-writing project in a lineage of sorts, rightly hinting at the 'anxiety of influence'. *Harmonia Caelestis* is a monumental novel by Péter Esterházy, published in 2000 and translated into English by Judith Sollosy as *Celestial Harmonies*. It chronicles the epic rise of

Esterhazy's forefathers during the Austro-Hungarian empire until their dispossession under communism. *Egy családregény vége* is a 1977 novel by Péter Nádas, the narrative of which follows a boy who grows up in Hungary in the 1950s, and whose grandfather tells him stories about their family's past. The novel was translated into English by Imre Goldstein and published in 1998 as *The End of a Family Story*.

PAGE 48 | **1977 Bucharest Earthquake**—On 4 March 1977, Bucharest was hit by an earthquake measuring 7.3 on the Richter scale, during which almost every building in the Romanian capital shook wildly and thousands of people were killed.

PAGE 52 | **'would rather break like a tree, than succumb with glee'**— Quote from the popular poem 'Nyergestető' by Transylvanian–Hungarian poet Sándor Kányádi (1929–2018). The poem addresses the topic of Székely identity, and its title references an iconic site of resistance to Ottoman and then Habsburg rule. Nyergestető (Romanian: *Piatra Niergeș*) is a pass in the Ciuc Mountains, Eastern Carpathians and was one of the last locations of the Hungarian revolution of 1848–49. Today it is a Memorial Park.

PAGE 63 | **Zsigmond Széchenyi** (1898–1967) was a Hungarian hunter, traveller and writer, a major figure in Hungarian hunting culture.

PAGE 64 | **Ion Gheorghe Iosif Maurer** (1902–2000) was a Romanian communist politician and lawyer, he served as Prime Minister of Romania between 1961–1974.

PAGE 66 | **Abel** (Hungarian: Ábel) is the protagonist of a trilogy by Transylvanian–Hungarian author Áron Tamási. The novel referenced here is *Ábel a rengetegben* [Abel in the vast forest] (1932), translated as *Abel Alone* by Mari Kuttna (Budapest: Corvina, 1966). Abel is a Székely youth, who lives in the geographical area mapped out by Vida, sent by his father to act as a forester of sorts in the Hargita Mountains and to guard the felled trees.

PAGE 67 | ***Emberek a havason*** [**People of the mountains**] is a 1942 Hungarian film directed by István Szőts, based on a series of short stories by József Nyírő. The film is set in the Székely woodcutting community.

PAGE 67 | 'édesanya'—An emphatic term to denote 'mother' in Hungarian, as opposed to the simpler and much more common version 'anya'. Vida plays on the connotational differences between the two variants in this paragraph, and also parallels birth (biological) mothers and stepmothers. The term 'édes', which also means sweet, is often used to refer to one's birth mother.

PAGE 71 | **Miklós Horthy** (1868–1957) was a Hungarian admiral and statesman, who served as Regent of Hungary between the First and Second World Wars and throughout most of the Second, until October 1944. Following the Vienna Award in August 1940, Hungary took a revisionist approach to the Treaty of Trianon, and the Hungarian army marched into Northern Transylvania between 5–13 September 1940.

PAGE 71 | **The Iron Guard** (Romanian: *Garda de fier*) was a far-right fascist movement and political party in Romania between 1927 and the early part of World War II. Founded by Corneliu Zelea Codreanu, it is also known as the Legion of the Archangel Michael (Romanian: *Legiunea Arhanghelului Mihail*) or the Legionnaire movement (Romanian: *Mişcarea Legionară*). Iuliu Maniu (1873–1953) was a Romanian politician, Prime Minister of Romania during 1928–1933, and co-founder of the National Peasants' Party. In 1937, Maniu signed an electoral pact with the Iron Guard, in the hope that this would block King Carol's authoritarian acts.

PAGE 77 | **The Diet of Torda**—The Edict of Torda was a decree that authorized local communities to elect their preachers in the Eastern Hungarian Kingdom of John Sigismund Zápolya. The delegates of the Three Nations of Transylvania—the Hungarian nobles, Transylvanian Saxons and Székelys—adopted it at the Diet of Torda (now Turda, in Romania) on 28 January 1568. Despite not acknowledging individual but only collective rights to religious freedom, the decree was an unprecedented act of religious tolerance.

PAGE 79 | *Játék és muzsika tíz percben* [**Ten minutes of play and music**] was a popular quiz programme on the Hungarian Radio Kossuth station, running between 1969 and 2007.

PAGE 79 | **Góbé** is an alternative term for 'Székely', often used condescendingly, although there are attempts at reclaiming the term.

PAGE 81 | **Sándor Petőfi** (1823–1849) is considered Hungary's national poet. He was one of the key figures of the Hungarian Revolution of 1848, and his poem *Nemzeti dal* [National song] is said to have inspired the revolution for independence from the Austrian Empire.

PAGE 82 | **'Hungarian children heal the wounded and blood-stained feet of storks'**—This line refers to a Hungarian children's rhyme, alluding to the time of the Turkish occupation of Hungary in the sixteenth and seventeenth centuries, according to which Hungarian children heal the feet of storks wounded by Turkish children.

PAGE 87 | **Lángos** is a Hungarian food speciality, a deep-fried dough looking like giant donuts, usually served with sour cream, garlic and cheese.

PAGE 88 | **Sándor Rózsa** (1813–1878) was a legendary outlaw (Hungarian: *betyár*) from the Great Hungarian Plain. He is the best-known Hungarian highwayman; his life inspired numerous writers, such as Zsigmond Móricz and Gyula Krúdy. He enjoyed similar esteem to the likes of Dick Turpin or Robin Hood.

PAGE 92 | **'Tót'** is a Hungarian exonym for Slovak.

PAGE 97 | **'*Naturam furca expellas*'**—Horace, 'You may drive out nature with a pitchfork, yet she'll come right back.'

PAGE 99 | The **Thirteen Martyrs of Arad** (Hungarian: *Aradi vértanúk*) were thirteen Hungarian rebel generals who were executed in the wake of the failed 1848–49 Hungarian Revolution on 6 October 1849 in Arad, then part of the Kingdom of Hungary (now in Romania).

PAGE 100 | **Hawkeye** is a character in German author Karl Friedrich May's (1842–1912) adventure novels set in the American Old West. These books, featuring the main protagonists Winnetou and Old Shatterhand, were extremely popular in the Soviet Bloc, and most children of Vida's generation would have been familiar with them.

PAGE 104 | **Zsigmond Móricz** (1879–1942) was a major Hungarian novelist, writing in a social-realist style. His novels focused on the lives of the Hungarian peasantry and dealt with issues of poverty and deprivation. Vida mentions the novel *Légy jó mindhalálig* (*Be Faithful onto Death* [Stephen Vizinczey trans.] [CEU Press, 1996]).

PAGE 126 | **Count István Széchenyi** (1791–1860) was a Hungarian politician, political theorist and writer. Widely considered one of the greatest statesmen in Hungarian history, he is still known as 'the Greatest Hungarian'.

PAGE 132 | **Mór Jókai** (1825–1904) was a Hungarian novelist and a leading figure in the Hungarian Liberal Revolution of 1848. Jókai's romantic novels have been widely popular, and he was often compared to Dickens. Vida mentions the novel *A kőszívű ember fiai* [The heartless man's sons], translated into English by Percy Favor Bicknell as *The Baron's Sons* (1900).

PAGE 136 | **László Tőkés** (b. 1952) is a controversial Hungarian pastor and politician. He is a member of the European Parliament for Hungary, former bishop of the Reformed Church in Romania. He came to prominence following efforts of the Romanian communist regime to evict him from his post as an assistant pastor in Timişoara. The protest against his forced relocation turned into a large-scale anti-regime movement and helped trigger the Romanian Revolution in 1989.

PAGE 144 | The **Hungarian conquest of the Carpathian Basin** (Hungarian: *honfoglalás*, 'conquest of the homeland') was a series of historical events ending with the settlement of the Hungarians in Central Europe at the turn of the ninth and tenth centuries AD.

PAGE 153 | **'öcsöd to öcsöd'**—Vida uses a literary reference here: the eminent poet Attila József spent a formative period of his childhood at Öcsöd, where he lived for two years with foster parents due to the serious economic hardship experienced by his family.

PAGE 156 | *Erdélyi Helikon* [**Transylvanian Helikon**] was a literary monthly published in Cluj between 1928 and 1944. It was edited by the renowned writer and architect Károly Kós, and its contributors included major figures in Transylvanian–Hungarian literature, such as the poets Lajos Áprily and Sándor Reményik. Lajos Olosz (1889–1977) was a poet in the interwar period and, importantly in this context, born in the village of Vida's grandparents, Ágya.

PAGE 157 | **'1 May and 23 August Parades'**—During the communist period, there were centrally organized parades throughout Romania to mark 1 May (International Workers' Day) and 23 August (Romania's National Day until 1990, the day of the coup d'état in 1944 that led to the installation of the communist regime).

PAGE 165 | **Winnetou** is a fictional Native American hero of several novels written by German author Karl Friedrich May (1842–1912) and narrated in the first-person by Old Shatterhand, also featuring Uncas among others. These works were very popular with teenage readers in Hungary and Romania in Vida's childhood, also relevant here as they symbolize a romantic desire for a simple life in close contact with nature.

PAGE 165 | *A Pál utcai fiúk* [**The Paul Street boys**] is a youth novel by Ferenc Molnár (1906), and an all-time Hungarian classic about two gangs of schoolboys in Budapest. The book has been translated into several languages, including English.

PAGE 180 | **Áron Tamási** (1897–1966) was a Hungarian writer, known for his picaresque stories written in his original Székely style. Tamási emigrated to the United States in 1923, soon after Transylvania became part of Romania. He returned to Transylvania between 1926 until 1944, following which he settled in Budapest.

PAGE 180 | **Gáspár Tamási** (1904–1982) was a Hungarian writer from Transylvania, brother of Áron Tamási, author of a very popular book on local village life.

PAGE 181 | **Pál Kinizsi** (1432–1494), also known as Paulus de Kenezy (in Latin) or Paul Cneazul or Pavel Chinezu (in Romanian), was a general in the Hungarian army under king Matthias Corvinus. He is famous for his victory over the Ottomans in the Battle of Kenyérmező (Breadfield) in October 1479.

PAGE 181 | **King Matthias—Matthias Corvinus**, also called **Matthias I** (Hungarian: *Hunyadi Mátyás*, Romanian: *Matei Corvin*, 1443–1490), was King of Hungary and Croatia. Matthias established a professional army (the Black Army of Hungary), reformed the administration of justice, reduced the power of the barons, and promoted the careers of talented individuals chosen for their abilities rather than their social status. He has remained a popular hero of Hungarian folk tales to this day.

PAGE 184 | **Gojko Mitić** (b. 1940) is a Serbian director, actor, stuntman known for numerous Westerns produced by the DEFA Studios in East Germany, featuring Native Americans as the heroes (rather than white settlers as in John Ford's Westerns). He contributed to shaping the popular image of Native Americans in German-speaking and East European countries.

PAGE 184 | **Pierre-Louis Le Bris** (1929–2015), known as **Pierre Brice**, was a French actor, best known for portraying fictional Apache-chief Winnetou in German films based on Karl May novels.

PAGE 184 | **Lajos Kossuth** (1802–1894) was a Hungarian nobleman, lawyer, journalist, politician, statesman and Governor-President of the Kingdom of Hungary during the revolution of 1848–49.

PAGE 187 | **Csángók** or **Csango people** (Hungarian: *Csángók*, Romanian: *Ceangăi*) are a Hungarian ethnographic group of Roman Catholic faith living mostly in the Romanian region of Moldova, especially in Bacău County.

PAGE 193 | **Kálmán Tisza** (1830–1902) was Hungarian prime minister between 1875 and 1890. He is credited with the formation of a consolidated government, the foundation of the new Liberal Party (1875) and major economic reforms.

PAGE 197 | '*bozgor împuţit*', '*szőrös talpú oláh*'—These are strong terms of abuse, used by one ethnic group to insult the other: *bozgor împuţit* (**stinky bozgors**) is used by Romanians to refer to Hungarians, and *szőrös talpú oláh* (**Wallachians with hairy foot soles**) by Hungarians to insult Romanians. The term 'bozgor' means homeless, foreigner.

PAGE 300 | '**gasping gloomily . . . For how many levels?**'—From Domokos Szilágyi, *Emeletek avagy a láz enciklopédiája* [Levels, or the encyclopaedia of fever] (Bucharest: Irodalmi Könyvkiadó, 1967).

PAGE 303 | '**[A]nd oh how loose gets the tether, when bright-lit skies bring good weather!**'—Domokos Szilágyi, 'Bartók in America' (Frank Veszely trans.), *Kalejdoszkóp* (July–August 2015): 30–1.

PAGE 308 | '**No-name himself**'—Domokos Szilágyi, 'Utóhang (Apró ének Nevenincsről)' [Epilogue (Short song about No-Name)] in *Emeletek avagy a láz enciklopédiája* [Levels, or the encyclopaedia of fever].

INDEX OF PLACE NAMES

Arad (Romanian: *Arad*) is a city in the Western part of Romania, close to the border with Hungary. Historically, Arad had not been considered part of Transylvania but of the Körösvidék (Romanian: *Crișana*) region.

Bánát (Romanian: *Banat*) is a geographical and historical region that is currently divided among Romania, Serbia and Hungary. The region has historically been populated by a rich ethnic mix, including Romanians, Serbs, Hungarians, Germans, Ukrainians, Slovaks, Bulgarians, Czechs, Croats, Romani.

Barót (Romanian: *Baraolt*) is a town and administrative district in Covasna County, in the Székely Land.

Brassó (Romanian: *Brașov*, German: *Kronstadt*) is a city in the central part of Romania, surrounded by the Southern Carpathians, an important centre of Transylvanian Saxons in the past.

Bucharest (Romanian: *București*) is the capital of Romania, as well as its cultural, industrial and financial centre. In the interwar period, many Transylvanian–Hungarian young men and women would have worked or learned a trade there, prior to settling down in their local community.

Budapest is the capital of Hungary, and the focal point of Hungarian culture.

Csala Tower (Hungarian: *Csala tornya*, Romanian: *Turnul Csala*) a mythical site for the Székely imagination that appears in several legends and fairy tales that hark back to the times of the Tatar (Mongol) Invasion in the thirteenth century.

Corvin köz (Corvin Close) is an area in Budapest's 8th district, noteworthy for being one of the most important strongholds of the insurgents against the invading Soviet tanks in the 1956 Hungarian Revolution.

Fogaras Mountains (Romanian: *Făgăraș* Mountains) are the highest mountains of the Southern Carpathians in Romania. The Moldoveanu Peak is 2544 m.

Galac (Romanian: *Galați*) is a port town on the Danube River and a major economic centre. In the interwar years, it had a significant multi-ethnic population.

Galicia (Ukrainian and Russian: Галичина, *Halyčyna*; Polish: *Galicja*; Hungarian: *Galícia*) is a historical and geographic region in Central Europe, once a small Kingdom of Galicia-Volhynia and later a crown land of Austria-Hungary that straddled the modern-day border between Poland and Ukraine.

Gyula is a town in Békés County, Hungary, located on the Great Hungarian Plain, 5 km from the border with Romania.

Hargita Mountains (Romanian: *Munții Harghita*) is a volcanic mountain range, part of the Inner Eastern Carpathians in Romania. Peaks: Nagy-Piliske (Romanian: Pilișca Mare) Mitács-mezeje (Romanian: Poiana Mitaci), Kakukk-hegy (Romanian: Muntele Cucului).

Háromszék (Romanian: *Comitatul Trei Scaune*) was one of initial administrative areas of Székely Land, in the Eastern and Southern most corner of Transylvania. Its modern-day successor is Covasna County.

Házsongárd cemetery (Romanian: *Cimitirul Central*, Hungarian: *Házsongárdi temető*, from the German: *Hasengarten*) is one of the oldest cemeteries in Cluj-Napoca founded in the 16th century. It is one of the most picturesque sights of the city, covering an area of about 14 hectares.

Kisjenő (Romanian: *Chișineu-Criș*) is a town in Arad County, Western Transylvania, Romania, in the vicinity of the border with Hungary.

Kolozsvár (Romanian: *Cluj-Napoca*, German: *Klausenburg*), commonly known as Cluj, is the fourth most populous city in Romania. The city is considered the unofficial capital to the historical province of Transylvania.

Lake Saint Anna (Romanian: *Lacul Sfânta Ana*, Hungarian: *Szent Anna-tó*) is located in a volcanic crater in the Eastern Carpathians, near

Tuşnad. Legends are attached to its unique character and geological formation that are well-known in the Székely–Hungarian imagination.

Máramaros (Romanian: *Maramureş*) is an administrative division within Romania, situated in the North-Western part of the country, bordering on Hungary and Ukraine.

Máramarossziget (Romanian: *Sighetu Marmaţiei*) is a city in Maramureş County near the Iza River, in North-Western Romania.

Marosvásárhely (Romanian: *Târgu Mureş*) is the seat of Mureş County in the North-Central part of Romania, on the Transylvanian Plateau.

Mócvidék (Romanian: *Ţara Moţilor*, German: *Motzenland*) is an ethno-geographical region of Romania in the Apuseni Mountains.

Nyárád (Romanian: *Niraj*) is a tributary of the river Mureş. It defines an ethnographically significant region in Central Transylvania.

Nyárádszereda (Romanian: *Miercurea Nirajului*) is a small town in Mureş County, in Székely Land.

Pannonia was a province of the Roman Empire located over the territory of the present-day western Hungary. The term is often used as a synonym for Hungary itself.

Segesvár (Romanian: *Sighişoara*, German: *Schäßburg*) is a city in central Transylvania, close to the Western outpost of Székely Land. It is a popular tourist destination for its well-preserved walled old town, listed by UNESCO as a World Heritage Site.

Szatmár (Romanian: *Satu Mare*) is an academic, cultural, industrial and business centre in North-Western Romania.

Szentháromság Castle (Romanian: *Troiţa*) is an 18th century mansion in Central Transylvania built by the Berecky family, currently in a state of disrepair.

Temesvár (Romanian: *Timişoara*, German: *Temeswar*) is the main social, economic and cultural centre in Western Romania. Timişoara is the informal capital of the historical region of Banat.

Transylvania (Hungarian: *Erdély*, Romanian: *Ardeal* or *Transilvania*) is a region in today's central Romania, bound on the east and south by the Carpathian Mountains. It is a multi-ethnic territory, with Hungarian and German spoken widely in several areas in addition to Romanian.

[Battle of the] Úz Valley (Hungarian: *Úz Völgye*, Romanian: *Valea Uzului*), landmark battles, with major casualties, taking place during both the First and Second World Wars in the vicinity of Barót, along the historical border of Székely Land.

Várad, short for **Nagyvárad** (Romanian: *Oradea*), the capital city of Bihor County and Crişana region, is one of the important centres of economic, social and cultural development in the Western part of Romania.

Világos Fortress (Romanian: *Cetatea Şiriei*) is a historical monument in Arad county dating back to medieval times, now in ruins. Világos is the site that marks the formal end of the 1848–49 anti-Habsburg Revolution; the Surrender at Világos took place on 13 August 1849, and symbolizes the loss of ideals in Hungarian history.

In addition, Vida lists a selection of place names to suggest a wide geographical span; **Konstanca** (Romanian: *Constanţa*) is on the Black Sea coast, **Toplica** (*Topliţa*) and **Gyergyóalfalu** (*Joseni*) in the Eastern Carpathians. Békéscsaba and Debrecen are towns in the Eastern part of Hungary, whereas **Novi Sad** is the capital of Voivodina, Serbia, a town with a significant Hungarian population.